A DAY THAT CHANGED EVERYTHING

BETH MORAN

Boldwood

First published in Great Britain in 2020 by Boldwood Books Ltd.

I

Copyright © Beth Moran, 2020

Cover Design by Charlotte Abrams-Simpson

Cover Photography: Shutterstock

The moral right of Beth Moran to be identified as the author of this work has been asserted in accordance with the Copyright, Designs and Patents Act 1988.

All rights reserved. No part of this book may be reproduced in any form or by any electronic or mechanical means, including information storage and retrieval systems, without written permission from the author, except for the use of brief quotations in a book review.

This book is a work of fiction and, except in the case of historical fact, any resemblance to actual persons, living or dead, is purely coincidental.

Every effort has been made to obtain the necessary permissions with reference to copyright material, both illustrative and quoted. We apologise for any omissions in this respect and will be pleased to make the appropriate acknowledgements in any future edition.

A CIP catalogue record for this book is available from the British Library.

Paperback ISBN: 978-1-80048-138-1

Ebook ISBN: 978-1-83889-339-2

Kindle ISBN: 978-1-83889-338-5

Audio CD ISBN: 978-1-83889-335-4

Digital audio download ISBN: 978-1-83889-336-1

Large Print ISBN: 978-1-83889-728-4

Boldwood Books Ltd.

23 Bowerdean Street, London, SW6 3TN

www.boldwoodbooks.com

For my mother, Judith Robbins, a woman of extraordinary courage and wisdom. And in loving memory of Alan Sutherland who showed me that I was only afraid of the fear

The lark at break of day arising
From sullen earth, sings hymns at heaven's gate

— Sonnet 29

1

STOP BEING A LOSER PLAN

DAY ONE

It wasn't intentional. I didn't get woken up by my phone alarm blaring, spring out of bed and decide today was the day. I didn't open up Facebook and one of those irritating quotes – embrace the rain if you want to dance under the rainbow – actually inspired someone for the first time ever to change something. After cajoling my son, Joey, out of bed, I didn't gaze at his beautiful face as he poured a second giant bowl of cereal, raving about the school football match coming up, and in a surge of love and regret suddenly experience the pivotal moment in a decade of non-moments.

In fact, apart from the invitation that arrived in the morning post, most of the day went precisely as expected. Which was, in summary, exactly the same as pretty much every other weekday. I waved Joey off to school, reminding him to hand in the form about the meeting that evening and cleared away the breakfast dishes. I worked at my desk in the kitchen, breaking the monotony of writing about corporate social responsibility policies by swanning off to eat lunch in the living room, because that's the type of wild and crazy woman I am.

I rescued Joey's football kit from festering on his bedroom floor and stuck it in the wash, because despite telling myself on a daily basis that it's time he learnt the hard way, circumstances dictate that I also live with an extra-large pile of parental guilt, so I make life easier for him where I can.

By the time Joey came home at four, I had spoken to no one since he left, unless you count talking to myself. Oh, and to the enormous spider who appeared out of nowhere and started edging across the kitchen while I debated whether to have another chocolate cookie or the bag of seeds I'd bought precisely to avoid eating a whole packet of cookies.

'I'd get out of here if I were you. While your impressive size might earn you respect in the spider world, my son doesn't take kindly to home invasions by anything with more legs than him, and he'll be home any minute. Go on, shoo. Or else I'll have to squish you.'

Too late. While the spider was weighing up whether to heed my advice, Joey burst through the front door, in his usual whirlwind of energy and enthusiasm.

'Hey, Mum. I'm starving, are there any of those cookies left?'

I clicked save and pushed my chair back to face him. 'Hi, Joey, and yes, I had an okay day, thanks. How was yours?'

'Oh. Sorry, yeah. It was good, actually.' He paused, mid-search of the snack cupboard, to offer an apologetic smile. 'We did this experiment in science where we had to heat up this white stuff, and— WHAAAAAAT!?'

In an instant, my strapping thirteen-year-old reverted to a frightened child, leaping up to sit on the worktop, cookie packet hugged protectively to his chest.

'How long's that been there?' he shrieked.

'Not long.'

'Why didn't you tell me the biggest spider in the universe was right behind me?'

It was a pointless question. We had been through this too many times before. Joey knew that the reason I hadn't told him was because of what would inevitably happen next.

And, in line with the rest of the day's predictability, it did. After a brief negotiation about Joey's phobia, the value of the spider's life and what I was willing and able to do about both these things, given that I didn't think it was quite worthy of calling either the police or pest control, I ended up scooping the monster arachnid in both hands and facing my own worst nightmare.

'Ready?' Joey looked at me with solemn eyes as he gripped the door handle. He tried to keep his voice steady, but the rise and fall of his chest betrayed his terror.

I nodded, aware that my own eyes, while the exact same light brown as my son's – caramel, his dad used to call them – were darting wildly like two wasps caught in a Coke bottle.

Before I had time to take another wheezing, shallow breath, Joey flung the door open and ducked behind it. I threw myself forwards, crashing against the door frame, eyes now firmly squeezed shut, and flicked my hand outside. A sudden gust of wind sent me reeling back in panic.

'CLOSE THE DOOR!' I gasped, clutching at my heart as it careened about my ribcage and stumbling back into the middle of the kitchen.

'Is it gone? Are you sure it's gone?' Joey garbled back.

'Yes! It's gone. CLOSE THE DOOR, JOEY, NOW!'

I heard the door slam, took another two calming breaths and forced my eyes to take a peek. 'Oh, please.'

The spider levelled me an ironic gaze from the welcome mat. It was so humungous I could see the lazy challenge in each of its eight eyes.

'What? What? What is it? Is it still here?' Joey spoke from where he'd scrambled behind me.

'It might be.'

'WHAT? Where-is-it-what's-it-doing-is-it-moving-is-it-near-me-how-is-it-still-inside? MUUUUUM!'

'It *may* have blown back in and now be sitting on the mat.'

'Then throw it out again!' Joey whined, the good nature that insisted we went through this palaver, rather than simply squashing the spider, hiding behind his fear. 'Maybe you could lean right out this time, make sure it's really outside.'

While I contemplated this impossibility, the spider took a couple of exploratory steps across the mat.

My teenage son screamed at a pitch that would have been unreachable if his voice wasn't currently breaking, and before I could react, the spider was pinned to the mat beneath two fork prongs.

We stared in awed silence for a few seconds. The spider waved one leg, like a feeble farewell.

'Joey, I can't believe you hit it from that distance. You are one impressive athlete.'

'I didn't mean to hurt it.' He grabbed my arm, distraught. 'It was, like, an automatic reflex thing.'

'It's pretty cool, though. Maybe you're actually a superhero and now you're thirteen your powers are starting to manifest.'

'A superhero wouldn't murder an innocent life with a fork.'

'They might kill a bug by accident while still learning to control their new capabilities.' I put one weak arm around him, as the bug in question assumed the classic death curl, as best it could while stabbed in two places.

'You're still going to put it outside, aren't you?'

'It's dead. Can't it go in the bin?'

'No!' Joey bumped against me, beseechingly. 'I'll know it's there. What if it's not really dead, and it recovers enough to crawl back out and drag itself up the stairs while I'm asleep, looking for revenge.'

'What revenge? Poking you with it's one remaining leg?'

'Mu-uu-uum!'

'I could post it out the letter box?' I didn't normally indulge my son like this. But I had my irrational fear, he had his ('*Really, Amy, is it really irrational to be nervous about going into a world where people get run over, mugged, mocked, detained by security when they accidentally steal a packet of tampons?*' my anxiety leered). When it came to patience and understanding, I owed Joey a lifetime debt.

He took one look at my face, then slumped away from me. 'It's fine. I'll call Cee-Cee.'

'No!' I fought to wrestle back the returning panic at the mere thought of opening the door again and reminded myself that feeling like I couldn't suck in enough oxygen to survive didn't make it true. 'Give me a minute, and I'll put a cup over it. Then I'll throw it out later.'

What? My anxiety snickered in disbelief. *Open the door twice in one day? Are you kidding me? You'd better call Cee-Cee...*

'I'll do it before dinner, and I'll be in here working until then, so I can promise you it won't escape. If it tries, I'll grind it into dust with my bare hands.'

Joey waited until the crumpled remains of the spider were under a large mug, with a dictionary, *Mary Berry's Complete Cookbook* and a box of washing-up powder balanced on the top. He backed out of the room, snatching a cereal bar and a banana on his way.

'This whole family is completely unhinged,' he pronounced, flipping from frightened child to all-knowing, melodramatic teenager the instant the danger was over, before thumping up the stairs.

I sighed, took another glance at the towering tomb and got back to converting a jumble of notes into something vaguely readable.

Once upon a time, a good day meant being the best in the world, appearing on television in front of millions of people, celebrating late into the night before catching a plane home to be met by cheering fans.

A bad day meant coming second.

Nowadays, a good day meant keeping both eyes open while I chucked a spider out the back door.

And as for a bad day? A bad day meant that when my son's greatest fear intruded into his home, the one place on earth where he's entitled to feel safe, he was confronted with the truth that his own mother could not – or would not – protect him.

Sometimes it takes just one terrible thing to finally force change after years of enduring the intolerable. For me, that day, it was an invitation, written on official notepaper. Even thinking about it made me feel as though I'd swallowed shards of broken glass.

I saved the document I was working on and opened up the internet.

It was time.

* * *

An hour and a half later, I reluctantly shut my laptop and tried to refocus on getting dinner ready. Dropping a handful of broccoli into the steamer, I stuck the lid on and glanced back at the cup. The thought of leaning outside to dispose of a spider corpse made my brain spin inside my skull. Moving the books, I wrapped the spider in a tissue and buried it under some carrot peelings in the kitchen bin. Yes, it was supposed to be 'time', but making the decision to research agoraphobia felt like more than enough bravery for one evening. Just reading about it on the internet had mentally exhausted me.

A minute later, Cee-Cee marched in the front door.

'Blowing up a storm out there. You should be grateful you're stuck indoors.'

I stopped, mid-poke of a carrot stick, and looked at the closest thing I had to a friend. Cee-Cee was flicking the rain out of her short grey hair, her down jacket and tracksuit trousers dripping onto the lino.

'Excuse me?'

She shrugged off her coat, dumped it on a chair and glanced around. 'Where's this spider then?'

'What? Did Joey message you?' Annoyance exploded in my chest like an airbag.

'He was worried you'd chicken out and sneak it into the bin.'

'I told him I'd sort it.' I drained the vegetables, burying my guilty expression in a cloud of steam. 'Joey!' I called up the stairs. 'Dinner's ready.'

'So?' Cee-Cee took three plates out of a cupboard and started setting the table. 'Can I reassure him it's safely outside or shall I empty the bin first?'

'*Safely outside*?' I snapped, just as Joey wandered in. 'Joey, go and fetch the dirty pots down from your room.'

'But you said it was...'

'Now, please.'

I closed the kitchen door after him and turned to Cee-Cee, who was lifting a tray of salmon out of the oven.

'I apologise. Poor turn of phrase,' she said, banging the tray on the table.

'In answer to your question, no you don't need to empty my bin, and I'm perfectly capable of reassuring *my* son. I don't need you acting as a go-between.'

'I'm here to help. Nothing more.'

'Can I come back in now?' Joey asked from the other side of the door. 'I don't want to be late.'

I blew out a sigh, reminded myself of everything Cee-Cee had done for us, and all that I needed her to keep on doing, and shrugged. 'I'm sorry. Once again, I appreciate your help.'

We ate dinner in awkward silence, and Cee-Cee left with Joey. She was taking him to a school start-of-the-year parents' meeting, because, if it hasn't already become apparent, I was a woeful failure as a parent. Or so I told myself, as I changed into pyjamas, before crawling under my duvet – the only place I could go to ease the weight of despair, frustration and self-hatred for a while. A failure who needed another woman to care for her child outside of these four walls. A failure who never saw her son grinning as he accepted an athletics award, or riding his bike with his T-shirt flapping behind him, or wide-eyed with wonder as he explored, discovered, embraced this big wide world I was too scared to be a part of any more. A failure who...

Ping.

Phew! My pity fest was interrupted by a message. Expecting Cee-Cee, or Joey – because really, who else would it be? – I fumbled for my phone and was surprised to see an unknown number. Curious, I wriggled out from under the duvet, and read.

Amelia, I'm sorry for contacting you like this, but you didn't reply to my email.

Damn it. How the hell did he get my number?

I automatically went to click delete. Then, realising that forewarned is forearmed, I ignored my heart, pounding with agitation and alarm, and carried on reading.

Can we at least just talk? I understand why you might hate me, but our child deserves the chance to know his father. Please don't punish him because I was an idiot thirteen years ago. I hope very much to hear from you, Sean.

Okay, so now I could click delete.

If only I could delete those words so easily from my brain. Along with deleting my number from his phone. This was not good. I threw my phone out of the bed and burrowed back under the covers, fighting an overpowering surge of dread-induced nausea and agonising memories.

Ten minutes of freaking out later, I prised my hands off the side of my head and flipped the duvet back.

'Enough, Amy!' I barked. 'A few hours ago, it was apparently "time"! What, a couple of stupid setbacks and you instantly revert to a pathetic mess? Get up, get the kettle on and get a plan together. You used to be a winner, for pity's sake. You have to get a winning plan again. *You have to!*'

So, amazingly, after thirteen long years of flailing, wallowing, eating way too much processed sugar, hiding and letting life kick me in the butt, I somehow found the strength to haul myself out of bed, arm myself with a cup of chamomile tea and give it a bloody good go.

* * *

The Stop Being a Loser Plan was beginning to take shape when Cee-Cee and Joey returned:

1. Do more research on how not to be a loser
2. Stop being a loser
3. Open front door
4. Walk/crawl/wriggle on belly out front door
5. Go somewhere
6. Don't die
7. Come back
8. Repeat

I quickly slid my journal into a desk drawer as they entered the kitchen and tried to find a neutral expression to hide how the effort taken to formulate the plan had reduced me to a pile of jitters.

'That was quick,' I said. 'How'd it go?'

'Fine.' Cee-Cee handed me a few sheets of paper. 'It's all here.'

'Great. I'll look this over with Joey later.' *When you're not here, so it doesn't hurt quite so much that you took my place yet again.*

'There's more. Joey – you've got maths questions to finish.'

We took a seat in the living room, Joey suspiciously willing to complete his first homework of the new school year. Cee-Cee took her time, making sure her mug was exactly in the centre of its coaster, adjusting her arthritic knee, fussing about with cushions. An ungenerous thought popped into my head, wondering if this was on purpose, if Cee-Cee was enjoying making me wait. Perhaps she was still annoyed by my comments earlier. Maybe she had sensed a change in my energy this evening, that I was on the brink of something. After all, Cee-Cee knew me better than anyone. *Or maybe she's just nervous,* I scolded. *Maybe it's bad news. Joey could be in a whole heap of trouble for all you know.*

'I had a call from an old colleague.'

'Okay.' A tiny warning buzzer sounded in my brain.

'He saw Joey at the meet last week. He was impressed.'

'Well, he's pretty impressive.'

The buzzing grew louder.

'He's been invited to try for the Gladiators.'

The buzzer upgraded to a furious siren now, drowning out all rational thought.

'What? No! You know I don't want him competing at that level.' I sat back, folding my arms tight against my chest. This was not open for discussion.

'They wouldn't ask if he didn't have potential.'

'You mean the potential to spend years sacrificing his whole life on the altar of swimming, only to realise that he's one-hundredth of a second too slow for it to count for anything other than a part-time job as a lifeguard?' I snapped, voice bitter.

'Why not let the Gladiators coach decide if he's good enough?' Cee-Cee's weathered face was a granite cliff.

'Because the coach won't factor in the cost to Joey! You know how I feel about this! Why are we even having this conversation again?' I banged my mug down on the coffee table.

'Don't punish him for your mistakes.' Her mouth turned down in disapproval.

'That is not what I'm doing! And I don't have to explain myself to you. If Joey wants to try out for a different club, he can talk to me about it. *I'm* his mother.' Later on I might stew about what Cee-Cee considered to be my mistakes. Right now I was too busy seething in a cauldron of fear, pain and resentment.

She narrowed her gaze. 'I'm the one who's seen him in action. Seen the drive and passion. Seen him win. Taken him training, to competitions. I deserve a say.'

I jerked back on the sofa as if I'd been slapped. 'That's what this is about. A second chance at second-hand glory. An *old colleague* called you, or did you call him?'

'Don't be ridiculous,' scoffed Cee-Cee.

'I'm sick of you undermining my authority as his mother—'

'What authority? You've not a clue what might be best for Joey. He's already said yes. I'm the one who insisted we tell you.' She shook her head, dismissing the point.

'Get out.'

Cee-Cee looked at me for another long, hard minute, before pulling herself up to go.

'Leave the key.'

She stiffened in the doorway, still facing away.

'We're done. You've controlled my life for twenty-three years. You will not do the same to my son. Manipulate him to go against my wishes...'

She twisted round, her face mottled. 'Your wishes are wrong! They're the wishes of a mentally ill, housebound, has-been. I don't control your life, fear controls your life. I saved it! I saved you both! We are not done. You need me.'

'I'm starting to realise that's just another lie. It's you who need us. You're the has-been. You were grateful to have us, after everyone else turned their back on you. Without Joey, you have nothing. But he isn't yours. And I'm taking him back. I'm taking both our lives back. Leave. The. Key.'

'I respected your wishes. Even now, I didn't tell him.' And with those words, the person who knew me better, longer, than anyone else in my life, who took me in when my partner, my parents, the world, didn't want to know, took the key to my house – my life – out of her jacket pocket, deliberately placed it on the windowsill and walked away.

Feeling numb, and weirdly detached from my body whilst at the same time more grounded, more solid than I had done in years, instead of crying or raging, I simply stared at the carpet for a long, long time and wondered what on earth we were going to do now.

* * *

I found Joey huddled behind his laptop.

'Here.' Swapping his laptop for a mug of hot chocolate, attempting to ignore my internal stampede of multiple deep, dark issues, I wriggled beside him on the bed.

'I'm sorry.' Tears hovered on his eyelashes. 'I wanted to tell you.'

I leant in and rested my cheek on the top of his head. 'I'm sorry, too. I shouldn't have made you feel you couldn't talk to me.'

He nodded, his soft blond hair rubbing against my skin.

'Will you tell me about it now?'

'You always say your problems mustn't stop me trying stuff. Or doing what I want to do. And I want to try out for the Gladiators.' He caught a tear that spilled over onto his cheekbone. 'But I knew if I asked, you'd say no.'

'Oh, Joey.' I wrapped my arms as tightly as I could around the torso I'd watched broaden into swimmer's shoulders over the past year, and reminded myself that this wasn't about me. 'It must have been rubbish, keeping something so exciting from me.'

'Yeah.'

'I'm worried Cee-Cee might have persuaded you to want this, without being honest about what it would actually entail. Do you really want to be swim training five or six days a week, often twice a day? You'd have to stop football, and cricket in the summer.'

Joey wiped his nose on his hand. 'I'd rather be swimming than anything else! When I'm swimming, it's like, I dunno, I forget all the other stuff going on. I feel free of everything. I feel invincible. Like I'm flying. Like I really am a superhero!'

'I understand, believe me.' I understood so hard, it was a searing ache in my chest, a burning behind my eyes. 'But why not carry on with the Brooksby team? Once you start training at Gladiators level, it's really hard to keep that feeling. It becomes about split-second timing and prac-tising until your arms nearly drop off, and teammates being rivals, because only the very best will make it to nationals. It's never being satisfied, always being pushed and pressured to be good enough.'

'But I *am* good. That's why it's awesome. This is my thing. Mum, I'm faster than every person in the club. I can beat everyone in our league without thinking about it. I want to do even better, to learn more. To be the best I can be at this. To see if I can be really good.' He sat up and looked at me, eyes wide, mouth trembling. 'What if I could be *really* good? You said I'm an athlete. I have to at least try.'

I took his hand and gave it a squeeze. 'It's getting late. We need to talk some more about this, after I've had a think. But – let me finish – I've heard you, Joey. I understand what you're saying. You know I love you and I want the best for you.'

'If that were true, you'd let me try!'

'Like I said, we'll talk tomorrow. But, I promise you we'll make any decisions together. You and me. Now, finish your drink and get some sleep.'

As if that was going to be possible for either of us, after the day that changed everything...

2

STOP BEING A LOSER PLAN

DAY TWO

'Come on, Amy, remember when you used to be a winner?' It was seven o'clock. I'd watched the minutes tick by through most of the night. Dozing had only led to jumbled dreams, ripe with yearning: the echo of the whistle, the exhilaration of the first dive, followed by the silent cocoon of water for that sweet moment until I burst up into the real world again. The tug of a swim cap. Lungs near exploding, muscles on fire, heart hammering as I strained to outswim the arguments bouncing off the tiled walls, the disappointment and the fifty-metre lane that became my prison.

I had been a winner, once. Funny how the memories still floating in my subconscious were all about losing.

I pressed at the ache in my temple, took a deep breath, and in some vain attempt to outrun what I was about to do, skidded out of the bedroom, tumbled down the stairs and threw myself at the front door. As I hauled back the bolt, which felt as though it weighed twenty kilos, my slippery hands grappling with the key, the panic caught up with me, freezing my fingers on the door handle. I remembered how I used to block out everything but my goal – shut off pain and stress and exhaustion and will my body into submission. So, I ordered it to open the door. Begged, pleaded, wept. Wrestled to overrule the paralysing fear clawing at my throat, whirling behind my eyes, screaming at me that I was dying, that if I opened that door one inch I would be destroyed.

'It's a panic attack,' I whispered to myself, even in the grip of it still aware of Joey sleeping upstairs. 'You'll be okay, you're not dying, it's just your crazy brain. You will be okay. Open the door. It's okay.' Still my hand gripped the handle, as I curled round into myself and slumped to the floor, arm sticking awkwardly behind me, refusing to let go. My whispers now punctuated with rasping sobs, 'It's okay, just open the door... open the damn door.'

My traitorous, stubborn, cowardly hand did not open the damn door.

* * *

When I had finally managed to claw myself back together, I got a bleary-eyed boy out of bed and off to school, reassured by the bounce in his step as I watched out the living room window to see him jogging up to the gangly gaggle of boys waiting across the road.

I showered, cried, forced down a mug of coffee, opened a couple of bills, remembered the glossy invitation and cried again. I felt as though I was being wrenched apart inside – one half desperate to take these first steps towards finally recovering my health, my freedom and some measure of control; the other part of me was, quite simply, terrified. Scared, alone and utterly beside herself at the risk of facing the world again.

I dragged myself through three hours of turning rambling drivel into what would hopefully be a successful tender for my current client, a storage company, and cut myself a quarter of a carrot cake.

Plopping down at the kitchen table, I stared at the cake. Looked down at my ex-world champion thighs, now flabby and blobby and weak, like my heart. Twanged the extra inches dangling beneath arms that were once solid and strong. Powerful and resolute.

I was thirty-two years old. I felt about a hundred and two.

What was I going to do? Would the fear or the hope win?

Closing my eyes, I took a deep breath in and threw the cake in the bin, for starters.

* * *

When Joey arrived home, I was in the living room. He hacked about half a loaf of bread into a gigantic cheese and turkey sandwich, surprised that for once I didn't join him in eating the other half, and threw himself down next to me in front of a cardboard storage box that took up most of the coffee table.

'What's this?' he asked.

'This is the real reason I'm scared about you joining the Gladiators.'

He took another bite of sandwich. 'Cee-Cee told me you nearly drowned, that's why you hate me swimming.'

'I don't hate you swimming. And I couldn't drown if I tried.' Opening the box, I let Joey remove the first object, unwrapping the thick blue velvet.

'A medal?' He glanced up at me, eyes lighting up. 'What's it from?' Peering closer he read the wording. '"FINA World Swimming championships". What? Is this a *gold medal*? Where did you get it from?'

'I won it.'

Joey's eyebrows shot up into his fluffy blond hairline. He jerked his head to look at me, then back at the medal. Back up, then down again. 'No way!'

Reaching into the box, I passed him a newspaper clipping: Piper pips competition to bring home the gold!

Joey scanned it greedily. He looked back at the medal, up at me, his grin a perfect mirror image of the one on the face of girl in the photograph, although her hair was chestnut.

'You won the world championships for 400-metre freestyle? In *Moscow*?'

'And a silver in the medley.'

'Why didn't you show me this before?' He delved into the box, glancing at other articles, certificates, medals and a couple of trophies. 'You were a world champion swimmer? Why would you keep that a secret? Why is this stuff in a box, not on the shelf? Why does that mean you don't want me to swim, when you won? I just... I can't believe this!'

Of course he couldn't. He could only remember me as his mum, without the prompts of photographs, stories or tarnished trophies to tell a different story. After all, this mum hadn't left the house in two years, three months and nineteen days. Had no friends and an invisible, online job. Ensured her time revolved around her son, making up for the lack of holidays or trips to the cinema with indoor picnics, movie nights, camping in the living room, an all-you-can-eat ice-cream factory in the kitchen.

And to imagine your out-of-shape, anxiety-riddled parent, who's about the worst example of strong and successful you can think of, as a champion. Well, I could hardly believe it myself, and I'd been there.

'Who's this?' Joey pointed at a photograph of me at the side of the pool, arm around another woman with cropped brown hair, both our faces exploding with joy.

I quirked one eyebrow at him. 'That's Coach Coleman. Known to her squad as Cee-Cee.'

'*What*?'

'Cee-Cee got me to the championships.'

* * *

'Is Coach Coleman not coming for dinner?' Joey asked a couple of hours later, getting out plates as I stirred a jar of pasta sauce into some penne. He'd been totally absorbed by the contents of the box, forgetting for the moment how my past career had impacted his current situation.

'No.'

'But I want to ask her about it, what you were like. How you trained.'

'I've asked Cee-Cee to give us a bit of space for a while.' Does *forever* count as a while?

Joey took his pasta, looking at me for an explanation.

I sat down opposite him. 'I've decided it's time to start facing up to my issues. I want to be a proper mum. Be able to chuck a spider outside. Go to your school meetings. Go out for the day. Watch you compete.'

'Mum, you're sweating even talking about it.'

'But I'm talking about it! That's one step better than yesterday. And, well, I think having Cee-Cee around to do things for me isn't helping. I kind of need to sink or swim with this.'

'Well that's good then, isn't it? No way you're going to sink!' Joey grinned, then paused with a forkful of pasta halfway to his mouth. 'It'll be weird not having her around, though.'

It would be more than weird. I could barely remember life without Cee-Cee. Try panic-inducing, gruelling, lonely, impossible... liberating.

We ate for a while, contemplating what might happen if I actually swam. It felt good to get the words out there – good, but equally horrifying.

'Are you angry with Cee-Cee about the trial?' Joey poked at the remaining pieces of pasta on his plate.

I took a slow drink of water. 'Honestly? I am a bit. Cee-Cee was my coach from when I was ten. I spent more time with her than anyone, even my parents. She told me what to eat, when to go to bed, how to train. She disapproved of any distractions, so I stopped piano lessons. She banned boyfriends, parties, even restricted exam revision. It sort of created a pattern. She made the rules, took all the decisions, and I went along with them.

'And then, when we lived with her, it just carried on. You know she's got no family, and coaching was her life. I don't need a coach any more, and even though she retired soon after I stopped competing, I don't think she knows how to be anything else. It'll be good for her to have a chance to think about herself for a change, maybe find a hobby and make some friends. And if we're going to find a way for you to take swimming more seriously, I want it to be with someone who can find a better balance so that it won't end up taking over.'

'But isn't she the best, at getting someone to be a winner, I mean? Won't I need someone to tell me how much to train?'

'She definitely used to be one of the best. But if you did join the Gladiators, then you'd need to listen to *their* coach. And hopefully in a way that means you can be a winner your whole life, not just for a few years in the pool.'

'You don't want Cee-Cee to turn me into you, you mean?'

I blinked back the sudden rush of tears. 'Cee-Cee isn't to blame for my panic disorder. Or my choices. But I still think we need a break from her, okay? And we need to find out more about the Gladiators before we decide anything. Even if it is the right decision, there's no way you can train all the way on the other side of Nottingham and still get to school on time.'

Joey's face fell. 'So, I can't do it then. Not without Cee-Cee to give me a lift.'

'Why don't we speak to your Brooksby coach, Mr Gallagher is it? See what he's got to say. We might be able to come up with some sort of compromise.' I said this, knowing full well the Gladiators would consider compromise a pointless, wimpy waste of time, not worth a moment's consideration.

Joey considered it, however, allowing the frown to morph into a slow smile. 'Gallagher's awesome. I can't wait to see his face when he finds out who you are.'

'Sorry, bud. That stays between you and me for now.'

'What? Why?'

'Because there's enough gossip goes on in this village without people discovering that the once celebrated Amelia Piper is now an overweight, scaredy-cat recluse living in a tiny little house in the middle of nowhere.'

'Mum, you're ill, not a scaredy-cat recluse.'

'I know that. But thank you.'

'You could do with losing a bit of weight though.'

'Sorry, what was that? "I volunteer to do all the washing up and tidy the kitchen, after bringing my beautiful mother a cup of tea"? Aw, thanks Joey, you're the best!'

In the end, he washed up and I tidied the kitchen, answering more questions about my glory days, while avoiding mentioning the terrible ones that came after, laughing about the antics his friends had got up to in science that day. Team Piper. I felt the tension in my neck and shoulders soften and clutched tightly to the spark of hope that dared to believe we would be okay without our coach.

STOP BEING A LOSER PLAN/PROGRAMME

DAY THREE/ONE

The next morning, after Joey had loped off to school, I sat and stared at the box containing the girl I once was until I found the nerve to have another go. After rescanning the notes I'd printed off the agoraphobia websites, I tried the back door this time. Opening out onto the enclosed garden, I reminded myself it was still part of my property – safe, secure, private. I stared defiantly at a point on the floor, as instructed, and attempted to lock my frenzied thoughts in neutral. Then, phone held ready, one millimetre at a time, I pushed down the handle and pulled the door towards me.

I made it about three inches. Slowly, slowly, I forced my eyes up to the crack in the door. Belligerently took in the narrow strip of the world outside – grass, still short from where Joey had mowed it the week before. The brown fence behind it, blue sky above. A thrush hopped into view, before cocking its head and moving on. I strained above the hammer of my heart to hear the distant sound of the traffic, a neighbour calling to a friend in the street. Dug deep, deep down to the long-buried grit that had won a FINA World Championships gold medal and held on to the door for dear life until I could squash the panic back behind my stomach. I opened up my lungs and found I could just about breathe. I even counted to ten, resisting the mounting pressure until, like a flood, the panic burst out again.

I clicked my phone, slammed the door, span around and collapsed on the mat, whimpering like an animal.

I glanced at the phone. 'Eleven point two five seconds. A personal best,' I gasped.

And yes, while the time to beat had been zero point zero zero seconds, it was a start. And doing what it took to beat my personal best was something I could be extraordinarily stubborn about.

I opened a new note app on my phone and tapped in the time and date.

This was it, day one. Watch out world, here I come!

It all seemed so obvious now. If there was one thing I knew how to do it was follow a training programme. I knew how to override stress and tiredness and intimidating opponents and do what had to be done. So, the Stop-Being-A-Loser-Plan had become a Stop-Being-A-Loser-Programme. Simples. I'd be cavorting around town in no time. I just needed a strong cup of tea and a good lie-down first.

STOP BEING A LOSER PROGRAMME

DAY TWO

Cee-Cee managed to stay away for three days. On the Saturday after I'd told her to get lost, Joey answered the front door, and she stalked in carrying several bags of groceries and sporting a nonchalant tilt to her head.

'Thought you'd be running low on a few things.' She opened the fridge door to find it packed.

'I did an internet shop.'

'Oh. Well. No need for that.' She creased her brow, disapproving and perturbed.

'Maybe not, but I did it anyway.' I turned away, closing my eyes and silently counting to ten through gritted teeth.

'Risky business. Online shopping. A stranger fingering your fruit. Palming the old veg off on you. Replacing organic granola with choco-late puffs of air as a substitute. And what a waste of a delivery fee.'

I ignored her, adding a grating of parmesan to the risotto I'd cooked.

'What am I meant to do with all this then?' she asked.

'I don't know, Cee-Cee. Return it. Eat it yourself. Donate it to the food bank.' I nodded at Joey to set the table.

'Rather ungrateful!'

'I've told you, it's time I did my own shopping. Now, seeing as you're already here, are you staying for dinner?'

'I will. Thank you.' The frown deepened.

'Then let's change the subject.' I talked a big talk, all cool and calm and collected, standing up to the woman who'd domineered me for so long. Pretending that asking her to give the key back didn't mean I meant to cut off all contact altogether. But, oh my goodness, as Cee-Cee and Joey chatted about the football season, his history project, how the heck she'd never mentioned the tiny matter of his mother being a world champion swimmer, my hands shook so hard, I could barely scoop rice onto my fork.

* * *

At eighteen years old, my life consisted of three things: swim, sleep, show-up-and-smile. The Athens Olympics were fast approaching, and I was the only hope the UK had of a woman winning a swimming gold medal since 1960. My manager and agent (once known as my parents, before being infected with the fame bug) were treating the run-up to the Games like an American presidential campaign, doing whatever they could to stir up media interest in between training sessions. I'd chopped ribbons with giant scissors, rabbited away on radio phone-ins and even fumbled my way through a couple of television appearances.

Cee-Cee was not impressed. I had become a puppet, my coach tugging on one arm, my parents-slash-entourage greedily pulling the other. Following orders, cringing beneath the verbal bullets whizzing between the opposing factions of Team Piper, the weight of expectation grew with every feature article, every jealous look from my squad. I was lost, emotionally exhausted, utterly strung out and desperate for some time to myself. If I still existed underneath all that pressure.

So, when I stepped out into the May sunshine following a particularly brutal early morning session where Cee-Cee had used callipers to show the team my microscopic gain in body fat, instead of heading for the waiting taxi, I turned in the opposite direction.

A shiny, happy, turquoise bus was pulling up to the nearby stop, and before I could think about the consequences, I hopped on.

'Where to, duck?' The driver shut the doors with a hiss.

'End of the line, please.'

'Two quid.'

'Ah. Right.' My ridiculous, micromanaged lifestyle meant I'd not even considered the need for money. After an awkward pause, I made a weak pretence at searching my tracksuit pockets for non-existent change.

'Ain't got all day. D'ya wanna ticket or not?'

'Um...'

'Come on, mate.' A guy called out from a few rows back. 'You can give a free ride to a future Olympic champion.'

'Eh?' The driver swivelled back to glower at the man, probably only a year or two older than me, who winked at me from beneath artfully mussed up blond hair.

'It's Amelia Piper? The swimmer?' He fixed dancing blue eyes on mine as he spoke.

'I don't give a toss if it's the bloody Queen. The fare's two quid. Otherwise, the pavement's that way.'

The doors hissed back open. Dropping my gaze, I wondered how far my manager was prepared to take the 'any publicity is good publicity' theory, and whether that included being thrown off a bus.

'Here.' A hand brushed my wrist, and I turned to see the man holding out a paper ticket, his face creased in a smile. 'To the end of the line.'

Mumbling my thanks, I slunk into a seat near the back, but he came and sat down next to me.

'So, Amelia Piper, what's waiting for you at the end of the line?'

I'd grown used to strangers acting as though they knew me, expecting autographs and photos as their right, and had grown wary of people overstepping. But even if this guy hadn't just saved me, his smiling eyes and soft voice made me want to answer.

'I don't care, as long as it's not a big rectangle of water, or another load of questions about how it feels to have the nation's hopes riding on my shoulders.'

'How about an ice cream and a wander up to the castle?'

'What?'

He leant over a little closer, dropping his voice even further. 'I meant with me, if that wasn't clear.'

'I don't usually wander about with strange men.'

His smile widened to a grin, and, honestly, every muscle I'd been hammering into solid rock melted like butter.

'Sean Mansfield. It's a pleasure to meet you, Amelia Piper.'

Oh boy. If I was still capable of rational thought, I might have realised that what was waiting at the end of this particular line was a whole lot of trouble...

STOP BEING A LOSER PROGRAMME

DAY THREE

Sunday, I had toyed with taking a day off from the Stop Being A Loser Programme. But the squeeze of sorrow and loneliness when waving Joey off to another gala had refused to be appeased with a book or Netflix. Instead, it was as if peering through some of the fog I'd been hiding in for the past few years had twisted the familiar ache to a sharp pain inside my chest and behind my eyeballs. I wrestled with the temptation to slump on the sofa and sob, but I pictured myself as that girl, fourteen years ago, how she would have dealt with the heartache, and instead I used the pain to propel me to the kitchen door and wrench it open. Teeth gritted, gasping frantically, I held my ground against the panic for forty-nine seconds.

A personal best, to go alongside Joey's four wins at the gala. We settled in front of the television that evening with glowing faces, giant smiles and plates of hot, oozing takeaway pizza.

'Did you tell your coach I wanted to talk to him about the Gladiators trial?' I asked, after swallowing my first bite.

'Yeah. But can we not have pizza any more? Cee-Cee says I should avoid unhealthy fats.'

'I don't think a pizza every couple of weeks is going to do much harm. You need to celebrate your success.' And for years we'd been doing that with a double pepperoni and sweetcorn. I felt a sharp twinge of agitation. Being cut off from so much of Joey's life, these little rituals had become disproportionately important. Even more precious, now that I had woken up from my stupor, and each day seemed even longer, emptier and more unbearable than the last.

'I'm happy with some chicken or something. Cee-Cee gave me a list. She said she'd stock up if I want.'

'Why don't we do an online shop together? You can tell me what you'd like, and I can show you what I used to eat when I was training.'

'Well, okay. But Cee-Cee says—'

'Cee-Cee never won a medal.' Ouch, Amy, jealous much? I took a deep breath and went back to my original question. 'So, does Coach Gallagher want me to call him?'

'He said he'd come round.'

'When?' That floored me a little. 'I'm happy to talk on the phone.'

'Yeah, but then I can't listen. I said you were always in, so any time's fine.'

Well yes, I might always be *in*, but sometimes I was also *in* my pyjamas, or *in* the shower, *in* bed freaking out under the duvet, or just generally *in* an otherwise unfit state to be welcoming visitors...

'He said he's got a full-on couple of weeks but will let me know.' Joey wolfed down another slice, contrary to instructions. 'So, I was looking you up online.'

Oh, crap. My mouthful of pizza turned to a concrete lump halfway to my stomach. I should have guessed this would happen and prepared Joey for it. Prepared *me* for it.

'Some of your races are on YouTube. You were awesome.'

'Thanks.' I held my breath. Braced myself.

'But that interview on breakfast TV was well bad.'

I took a careful drink of water to try and clear the lump. 'Anything else? Or was that it?'

'Nah, that's it.' He fidgeted in his seat, started pulling a piece of crust into tiny pieces. 'Only, I was wondering... did you stop because of me? I mean, you were like nineteen when I was born, weren't you?'

'No.' I sat up straight, looked my son in the eye. 'No! I'd already stopped when I got pregnant. It was nothing to do with you. Although, if you had been the reason – it would have been totally worth it.'

'Well, obviously!'

The doorbell rang, and I hastily adjusted my dressing gown while

Joey answered it. If it was Coach Gallagher then I might have to hide behind the sofa, which wouldn't be a great start.

'It's Cee-Cee!' he yelled, despite the front door being only a couple of metres from the living room.

Rolling my eyes, I stretched back out along the sofa again. For the first time, I felt a twinge of pity that Cee-Cee, who had spent all day with Joey, and now had the freedom to go and do whatever she liked, had nothing better to do than keep coming back here.

'I'm not staying.' Cee-Cee walked into the room holding out an iPad, a video paused on the screen.

'Awesome!' Joey stuck his head right next to mine. 'It's me crushing it, Mum. Look – watch that start. Aaahh – bad turn though.' He carried on commentating, analysing his performance against the other competitors, until he sat back, triumphant. 'The champion once again.'

I couldn't speak.

While part of me was aghast that I'd never thought to do this before, welling up with pride, overcome at the sight of his strong, sleek body powering through the water, so grateful to have seen it, another part of me was seething. I may have actually frothed at the mouth a little. How had I let this happen? How had I become a parent watching her incredible, beautiful, gifted child on a screen? How could I have allowed myself to miss years of galas, meets, championships? Football matches, school plays, trips to the zoo.

And I felt *pleased* about opening the back door for a few seconds? Like that was something to be proud of?

I pretty much hated myself in that moment. Had it been possible to suffocate in shame, I would have gurgled to my death then and there.

'Mum, are you okay?' Joey peered at me.

'You're doing that Gladiators trial. And I'm taking you.'

'Yesssssss!' He fist-bumped the air and flipped off the sofa, sprinting out of the room to do a victory circuit of the house.

Cee-Cee frowned. 'He can't be worrying about you losing it poolside. I'll take him.'

'Over my dead body.'

'Might well come to that,' she muttered.

'Excuse me?' I stood up, my anger swivelling round to lock onto a new target.

'Nothing. I'm just being realistic. Anyway, you need to sign this.' She pulled a form out of her pocket and handed it to me.

It was a consent form for an interschool athletics tournament. 'Why do you have this?'

'He got it Thursday. I gave him a lift after training. He mentioned it.'

'So why did you take the form, instead of leaving him to pass it to me?'

'He forgets.'

'Well, if you keep reminding him, he'll not learn to remember, will he?'

Cee-Cee ignored me, staring out of the window instead.

'How often are you giving him lifts?' I asked.

'It was raining.'

'How often?'

'Why is it a problem?' Cee-Cee barked. 'You've been happy enough with it the past thirteen years.'

'Because it's not just giving him a lift, is it? It's keeping hold of his letters and telling him what to eat. You know how precious our post-win pizza is. That's why you happened to call in when you knew we'd be in the middle of it.'

'I'll go then.'

'I think that'd be best. And next time, call before you drop-in to check if it's convenient. Even better, find something else to do, so you can stop obsessing over our lives and get one of your own.'

Since taking me in, Cee-Cee had gone above and beyond in treating me like the child she'd never had. The problem was, *above* had become too much, and *beyond* now felt too far. I wasn't a child, and if she couldn't get that, I had to redraw the boundaries, even if it did feel like ripping the bandages off a gaping, raw, anxiety-riddled wound, leaving it exposed to all sorts of infections and further trauma.

Cee-Cee, face taut, silently handed me another couple of school letters and then left. One about uniform, another to inform parents that a black car had been seen parked outside the school gates on several occasions, with the driver appearing to watch the children. While there was no indication that the occupier intended any harm, pupils had been told to report immediately to a teacher if the person approached or tried to speak to them.

See! my anxiety sneered. *Out there is dangerous, full of evil people and trouble waiting to happen. How are you possibly going to manage this on your own, without Cee-Cee? Are you crazy? You should ditch this stupid Programme before—*

'Oh, shut up!' I threw the letter in the recycling.

* * *

Later on that evening, I pulled a chair up to the window and watched the stars for a while. Blotting tears on my cardigan sleeve, I cranked the window open and leant out into the night. I sucked in the forgotten scents of earth and trees, letting the faint whiff of smoke linger in my nostrils. I pushed my face into the gentle breeze, eyes closed as it caressed my skin, seductive and intoxicating.

I hung there for a while, the crisp September air conjuring a thousand memories of late summer nights stretched out on picnic blankets, skinny-dipping in a moonlit lake with my squad, the prickle of damp grass under my toes as we ran for home…

Over the past few years, I had mentally and emotionally shrunk to fit a life behind four walls. Survived by making the best of things, banishing any thoughts or dreams of outside as much as possible, avoided total breakdown through focusing on what I had, where I was, not what I was missing. But things were changing.

The quiet of the night wooed me with the promise of safety beneath its thick canopy. I softly closed the window and padded upstairs to bed, wondering if soon I might accept its invitation.

STOP BEING A LOSER PROGRAMME

DAY FOUR

Monday was a bad day, riddled with anxious thoughts about a million things. I wittered through my work, trying to ignore the shadow of shame on my shoulder. I was feeling small and scared about the enormity of the challenges ahead and crushed with the grief at what I had lost. I needed to recognise how awful my life had become to keep going forwards, but at the same time that was gut-wrenchingly painful and left me feeling desperately exposed. My fracturing relationship with Cee-Cee meant that my security was crumbling away, too. Without her, I felt lost and alone.

And to add to all this was the guilt. Cee-Cee had taken me in, and then spent all these years helping us, being there. We'd become family. Was it right to suddenly change the rules, start putting limits on her time with me, and more importantly with Joey? Perhaps I was kidding myself, saying it was for her good as well as ours to move the boundary lines. Should I try harder to work things out, see if she could help me with the Programme instead of assuming she'd sabotage it?

The trouble was, I had no idea. No clue how healthy, functional families worked. And right then, I had neither the energy nor the strength to try to figure it out.

That evening, I held the door open for three seconds before slamming it shut in a fit of panic. A new personal worst.

STOP BEING A LOSER PROGRAMME

DAY FIVE

Joey watched me over the top of his breakfast bowl. 'You look well rough.'

'Thanks! I've not washed my hair yet.'

'No. I don't mean that. Are you sad?'

'I had a setback with the Programme yesterday.' I sloshed some coffee in a mug and came to sit opposite him.

He tipped out another half bowl of cereal. 'So, what did you do when you were swimming, if you had a setback? You didn't give up, did you?'

I sighed. 'I set the alarm for fifteen minutes earlier. Trained harder. Stayed longer. Made sure it didn't happen again.'

'There you are, then.'

* * *

I had planned on working late that evening. My client had changed their mind about how they wanted to address the contract they were hoping to win, and the deadline was zooming up fast. The boss of the tender company I freelanced for only tolerated me missing client meetings and training days because I reliably produced good work, on time. Maybe I would manage a meeting soon, but in the meantime I was heading for an all-nighter.

A few minutes after five, my phone rang.

'Amy? It's Lisa, Ben's mum.'

'Yes, hi. Is everything okay?' Joey had arranged for Lisa to give him a lift back from the athletics tournament.

'Joey's not here. Ben and his mates have had a good look around, but he's nowhere.'

A tentacle of fear uncoiled in my stomach and began slithering up my ribs. 'Has Ben called him?'

'It goes straight to answerphone. Sounds like the battery's run out. He left the changing room before Ben and no one's seen him since. The teachers are looking, I'm sure he'll turn up any moment, I just wanted to let you know, given that letter we had about the strange bloke hanging around.'

'I... um...' The tentacle reached my brain, clamping a sucker on so hard, I couldn't think. I tried to remember where the tournament was, how far away. Could I get there? For Joey?

'Could he have forgotten he was coming with me? Got a lift with someone else? Most of the other parents are still here, but we could send a text out.'

'Th... thank you. Yes. That's probably a good idea.' I could call a taxi. Ask Lisa to come and fetch me... pace the streets until I found my boy. I could do that, couldn't I? 'Should I come down? Help look for him?'

As if *should* would make any difference.

Lisa hesitated. She knew full well I was the crazy lady who never left the house. 'No, no, it's fine. There are more than enough people looking here. You'd better stay there, in case he turns up at home.'

'Right.'

'I'll keep you posted. I'm sure he'll appear in a minute and we'll feel like right wallies for worrying. I mean, that dodgy car was at Brooksby school.'

Lisa, God bless her, called me back every ten minutes. However, the initial surge of hope every time the phone rang was swiftly replaced with increasing anguish. The school grounds had been searched top to bottom. On the third call, having recovered my voice, I asked to speak to Ben.

'Hey, Ben. Did Joey seem okay today? I mean, had anything happened that might have bothered or upset him? Did he do okay in his events?'

'Yeah.' Ben's voice was huskier than last time he'd been round for dinner. I couldn't tell if it was his age or anxiety. 'The teachers already asked me. But he was just usual, you know? He was laughing when we came in to get changed and he said he'd see me in a bit when he left.'

'You're sure? You know it's really important to be absolutely truthful. If there's anything, even the tiniest thing, it might help us find him. If Joey's in trouble, or... or...'

'Nah, Joey's never in trouble. There's nothing, honest.'

By five forty-five, I started to consider if something genuinely terrible had happened. Instead of panicking me further, I fell into a surreal state of numbness, mentally listing the possible scenarios.

Joey was strong, nearly six foot now. And loud. Surely someone would have heard him if that man had tried to take him? Seen him struggle?

It goes without saying that being stuck at home had never felt as hideous as watching the minutes tick by between Lisa's updates. How could I be here, pacing up and down my living room and leave other people to find my son? People who liked Joey, some who even cared about him, but none who loved him enough to quite happily rip out her own heart if it meant he was okay.

Yet not enough to open a door and start looking for him yourself.

And that brutal thought was enough to try calling the only other person who felt anything close to my pathetic, impotent love. The one who had rocked him to sleep in the middle of the night when I was too exhausted to walk straight any more. Who had stood by my side as we waved him off into the classroom his first day of school. Who had introduced him to the love of his life in the Brooksby pool, before he could walk.

I gripped my phone and dialled Cee-Cee's number.

'What is the point of people having phones if NO ONE EFFING ANSWERS THEM?! This is the ONE TIME you decide NOT to be there when I need you!' I shouted, a minute later, hurling the phone across the room where it ricocheted off the wall. 'SHIT!' I scrabbled across and scooped the different pieces back together. If I'd killed the phone, then Joey, Lisa, the hospital, the kidnapper making ransom demands, no one could get in touch with me.

As I pressed the battery compartment back into place and switched it on, Lisa called again.

'Yes?' I gabbled, for the seventh time.

'Nothing yet. Amy, do you think it's time we contacted the police?'

The words hung between us, a huge chasm straddling 'oops, of course it was nothing to worry about, Joey you little monkey you scared us all half to death' to 'this is real, my son has been missing for nearly an hour and no one can find him. Least of all me, because I haven't made it past my front door in over two years'.

* * *

I was passing on a description to the very patient, sombre-voiced woman at the local police station when the door opened and Joey sauntered in.

With Cee-Cee right behind him.

Good job I was half blind with shock and rage, because with a slightly better aim, the vase I'd thrown would have made a serious dent in her head. I did have naturally strong shoulders after all. Joey, thankfully, ducked.

'What the hell?' he squeaked, and the look of confusion and fear on his face was enough to clear the black mist, leaving an eerie calm.

'Joey, please go upstairs.'

'What's going on?'

'I'll talk to you soon.'

I waited until his bedroom door had slammed shut before addressing Cee-Cee, my voice trembling.

'I've just been on the phone to the police. The whole school has been hunting for an hour. Ben's mum has been out of her mind—'

'What? What's happened?'

'Are you kidding me? You took Joey! That's what happened. You can't just take a child from a school and not tell anybody!'

Cee-Cee looked affronted. 'I always pick him up. How else would he have got home?'

'LISA WAS GIVING HIM A LIFT, AS ARRANGED BY ME, HIS MOTHER.'

'Well, you could have said.'

'Didn't *Joey* tell you?' I asked.

'He asked if I was supposed to be picking him up, I said of course.'

'It's a twenty-minute drive home. Where have you been?' My voice was ice. I don't know about Cee-Cee, but I was scaring myself.

'We picked up goggles from the sports shop on the ring road. I wanted to treat him, celebrate his trial.'

'You saw that letter about a weirdo hanging around the school gates! Didn't you think I might be worried?'

She shrugged. 'Not if he was with me.'

'Cee-Cee, this has to stop.' The adrenaline was fizzling into exhaustion now. 'I don't want you giving Joey lifts. Or buying him things. Or contacting him without speaking to me first. Please, we need a break. *You* need a break. Go and live your life. Let us live ours.'

'You need my help. For his sake.'

'No. No, we really don't. I appreciate everything you've done, more than I can say. But this is not helpful any more. I am not that vulnerable, broken girl any more. This time, I need to fix myself. And if you can't respect that, or my choices for my family, then I can't trust you to be part of it.'

Cee-Cee blinked, several times. It was the most emotion I'd seen in her in over a decade. 'Very well then. You're on your own.'

The door closed behind her. I closed my eyes, breathing in a deep lungful of regret, relief and utter terror. Firing off a text to Lisa to explain, I went upstairs to speak to my son.

* * *

More than a little unnerved by the evening's events, I ploughed through a load more work, most of which would probably read like drivel, and stood up to stretch the kinks in my neck. Digging through the pantry, I found a dusty bottle of red wine. I poured out a decent-sized glass and took a sniff.

'Okay, Piper. This is happening. It's time for stage two of the Programme.' I paused to remember the feeling of helpless horror from earlier that day, weighed it up against the anxiety now stirring at what I was about to do. 'No contest,' I announced, whipped the back door open and took a step out into the night.

'Okay, just keep breathing, nice and steady, in and out, you can do this, you're a champion, remember? You can do anything you put your mind to.'

I followed the technique I'd read about so many times in the past few days: found a patch on the garden path to focus on, waited for the swaying and the clanging in my head to ease, considered it objectively, as an irrational reaction due to a problem in me not out there. I'd read that panic attacks last five to twenty minutes.

'I'll stay here and endure this for twenty-one if I have to,' I gasped. 'Do your worst, pathetic panic, you're just chemicals and nerve signals and brain electricity. You aren't controlling me any more.'

After a while (I guess somewhere between five and twenty minutes, but honestly it could have been five hours), I managed to take a sip of wine. I took a quick look around at the garden, then tipped my head up at the sky. Another clear night. Without a pane of glass between us, the stars were so bright, they held me spellbound. If I had climbed next door's chestnut tree, I could have stretched up and caught one. Far enough from the city to be undimmed by light pollution, they spread so wide and high and deep, it seemed there was a star for every person on the planet. I spun slowly around, studying every one, their glorious, ancient beauty. A rustle from the bushes near the back gate startled me, but I kept my eyes up and remained standing until I'd finished my drink. It was maybe a little faster than if I'd been inside, but, hey, it wasn't quite a guzzle.

I didn't know why coming outside at night felt easier. Maybe the lack of people, maybe the lack of vision. But I had done it. I had breached the invisible barrier, once impassable as the widest ocean, as unreachable as those stars. Dizzy with emotion, I poured myself another glass and used the adrenaline to power me through the night to my deadline.

Tonight, one step into the garden. Next stop, the world.

STOP BEING A LOSER PROGRAMME

DAY THIRTEEN

Sean emailed me again. I deleted the message without reading it. I knew I was being unfair, but when it came to his son, fair meant nothing. The only good thing about that man was him living five thousand miles away.

Joey stumbled into the living room and fell face first onto the sofa. 'Dying,' he mumbled into the cushion.

I put down the book I was reading – having successfully completed my latest project, I'd given myself the day off – and went to have a look. 'What's up?'

'Feel,' he croaked, feebly draping one of my hands across his forehead.

'Ouch.' He wasn't dying, but it did seem like he was brewing a nasty infection.

I tucked him up in front of the television under a duvet, praying that a few hours of sleep would let nature do its thing. A miracle-requiring prayer, given that his swollen throat couldn't swallow the stockpiled paracetamol tablets.

'You have to call Cee-Cee,' Joey croaked, after gagging on his latest attempt. 'I need Calpol.'

Even if he didn't strictly *need* a good dose of strawberry medicine, he jolly well shouldn't have to go without it when there was a pharmacy in the village square half a mile away.

But no way on this earth I was calling Cee-Cee.

* * *

Despite my now nightly trips into the back garden, stepping out through the front door was like walking onto a ship in a raging storm. My rational self knew the evening was mild, the air gentle. But somehow the ground dipped and bucked, as the street ahead spun like the whole village had been chucked in a tumble dryer. I clung to the door frame, gulped in a wisp of oxygen, tried to find somewhere on the front path that would stay still for long enough to be a focal point.

Holding my arms out either side for balance, crouched low like a goblin, probably sounding like one as I wheezed and gibbered, I shuffled first one foot forwards, then the other.

'Go, Mum!' Joey cheered feebly from the sofa as I pulled the door closed behind me. 'I love you!'

Keeping my head down, I shuffle-squat-scampered to the gate post at the end of the garden, feeling like a piece of debris hurtling through open space. I grabbed on with both arms, taking a moment to steady myself. I had left at six-thirty. The pharmacy closed at seven. It was an eight-minute walk for a normal, functioning human. For me, in this state, it could end up taking hours.

Pressing on, I shambled along, clutching the fences that lined the path to the square, my body pressed against them, face turned in. Trying to push down the waves of nausea and wipe the sweat dripping off my forehead without letting go. I was still breathing, albeit in frantic, shuddering gasps. My heart most definitely continued to beat, thundering in my chest like a racehorse. I was actually doing this, one tiny step at a time.

And then I reached the road. And beyond it, the square. Fifty metres of wide-open space stretched out like the Kalahari Desert.

Crap.

'Come on, now. You can do this.' I closed my eyes, counted to ten in my head and prepared to make a run for it. A car suddenly roared past, music blaring, and I nearly disintegrated right there on the pavement. I opened my eyes again. Prised one hand off the fence post. Stretched out my feet closer to the kerb, until I couldn't go any further without letting go of the fence altogether. But I didn't let go. Instead I felt the panic begin to bubble, boiling over like a hot pan, so I retreated back to the fence. I crouched down, pressed up against the wood, vaguely aware that somehow, at some point, I had to pull myself together, get up and go somewhere. But helpless to do anything while the world spun all around me, I buried my head in my knees and tipped over into the abyss.

'Hey. Hi.'

I gradually became aware of a hand on my shoulder, pulling me back to planet Earth.

'Are you okay?' A man's voice. I clung to that sound like a lifebuoy as he continued to talk, asking me whether I was hurt, or ill, if there was anyone he could call.

Eventually, my head the weight of a rhinoceros, I dragged it up to see soft grey eyes full of concern as he crouched on the pavement.

'Panic attack,' I slurred, the all too familiar tsunami of shame bearing down, as the anxiety began to recede. 'Agoraphobic.'

'What can I do to help?' he asked. 'Can I get you home? Do you need a few more minutes first?'

'No!' My mission came flooding back to me, and I bolted upright. 'I need to get to the pharmacy. My son needs medicine,' I gabbled. 'Is it seven yet?'

The guy, who looked to be around his mid-thirties, glanced at his watch. 'Two minutes to.' He looked across at the rows of shops lining the square. 'I could run and fetch it for you, but I don't want to leave you here...'

'Can you walk with me?' There was no point worrying about my pride at this point. And as long as I could get there, then the mission wouldn't have been a total disaster. Everybody needs a little help sometimes, right? I'd done well to get this far, all things considered.

He helped me up, and we stood there self-consciously for a moment while I tried to figure out the best way to do this, bearing in mind my legs were about as helpful as Joey's old Slinkys.

'Shall I...? Um, does this help?' He put one arm loosely around my back, but it felt awkward and weird. I'd also been sweating pretty heavily for the past twenty-eight minutes.

'Would you mind holding my hand, instead?' I asked, and he jerked his arm away instantly.

'Sorry, sorry. I didn't mean to... Sorry.'

'No, it's fine. Honestly. I just want something to grip on to. It helps.'
There was no time to bother about how we were both melting with
embarrassment, or how when his face turned pink under his beanie hat,
he looked so gorgeous my heart froze for a second. No time to notice
how, despite me being taller than most men, he would have been the
perfect height to lean in and tuck my face into his neck. Not a second to
worry about how my hand felt safe, cocooned, wrapped inside his. And
how that made the rest of me feel safe too.

But, for goodness' sake, Amy, no time for that nonsense!

We sprinted over the road and across the square – or rather, I
sprinted, he barely needed to break into a jog. Arriving at the pharmacy
door puffing for breath, I didn't know if it was worse for him to conclude I
was completely unfit, or had turned to a wheezing wreck due to touching
a fully-grown man for the first time in, well, too long to think about.

'Okay?' He looked down at me, eyebrows frowning. 'Let me know if
another attack's coming.'

Ah, yes. Panic attacks. *That* explained the quivering knees and flapping mouth.

'Can I help you?' a woman in a white coat asked. 'We're about to
close.'

I got a mental grip on my brain and tried to hold it steady, to not
allow myself to become overwhelmed with being somewhere else, with
other human beings, where anything could happen, and quite possibly
would. 'Um, I need some Calpol. For my son.'

I hastily explained the situation, paid for the medicine and turned to
find my rescuer waiting for me by the door.

'Ready?' he asked.

The stranger offered me a tentative smile, and I couldn't tell if the
butterflies jiving in my midsection were because of the walk home, or
the thought of who I had the invitation to walk home with.

I spied the dusk approaching through the shop window and thought
about Joey at home, waiting for me. I felt neck-deep in humiliation.
Weak and pathetic, yet again. I could not allow this guy, with his giant
shoulders and kind eyes, who looked about ready and able to carry me
home if I asked, to help me. I could not dump Cee-Cee only to grab on

to whichever random stranger happened to be passing every time things got tough. That wasn't independence.

'Actually, I'm feeling much better now.' *Yeah, Amy,* my anxiety crowed. *That squeaky voice and manic giggle sound much better.* 'I can make it back myself. I only live down the road. But thanks very much for your help. I really appreciate it. You must have somewhere to be.' I nodded at his football kit, the rucksack on his shoulder.

He shrugged. 'I'll have missed kick-off anyway. I'll walk you home.'

'No, really, I'm much better in the dark.'

'I'm sorry, but there's no way I'm strolling off not knowing if you're okay or not.'

Yes please! the wimpy, pitiful, self-sabotaging part of me said.

I took a deep breath. 'If I take the easy way out now, then it becomes much harder to push myself next time.' So all the stuff I'd been reading told me. 'I can honestly manage once it's dark, so it'd be like chickening out if I accept help.'

And besides, I was beyond self-conscious at the thought of walking down the same pavement as someone so strong and sweet and normal, let alone having held their hand a few minutes ago. It was surely nothing to him, helping out a randomer in the street, but it was the most eventful thing that had happened to me in years.

He frowned. 'I really don't think you should be by yourself.'

'Look, walking home in the dark with a strange bloke is going to make me feel more nervous, not less.' I didn't add that this would be for embarrassing, amorous, love-starved reasons, not ones of safety. 'So, thanks for the offer, but I'd honestly rather do it alone.'

'This guy bothering you?' the pharmacist asked, frowning at him over her thick spectacles.

'No, it's fine,' I stammered back, mortified that she'd picked up on what I'd said and jumped to conclusions.

'Why don't you jog on home, sunshine?' she said, sternly, before turning back to me. 'I'm locking up in a minute, wait here and we'll leave together.'

'Right. Yes.' The guy, now looking beyond mortified, backed away towards the door. 'I honestly just wanted to help.'

'I know,' I called after him, cringing. 'Thanks again.'

I sat in the waiting area and boggled for a few minutes at the events of the past hour, while darkness settled onto the square.

I sent Joey a quick message to let him know I'd made it:

Mum you rock!

Did you get strawberry?

Orange makes me hurl.

I thanked the pharmacist as we stepped outside, and before she'd had time to roll the shutters down, I started running for home.

And while I may not have managed to run very far before a killer stitch forced me back to a walk, I did manage not to cry or freak out the whole way. I did, however, get the fright of my life when I stopped to pull the key out of my pocket and saw a huge person lurking in the shadows a couple of houses back.

That is, until he lifted one arm above his head and gave a quick thumbs-up before bounding off in the opposite direction.

* * *

I dosed up Joey, bundled him into bed and retired to the comfort of my own duvet, peeping out at the ceiling as a million thoughts whirled like a snowstorm in my head. What a humungous, momentous evening. I savoured the lingering buzz of endorphins from my race home, remembering how addicted I'd once been to my daily fix of happy hormones. How good it used to make me feel. Strong and purposeful and kick-ass. I wanted that feeling again.

And that other sensation, buzzing about inside, I poked it a couple of times to try to figure out what that feeling was, dug into my brain's dusty filing cabinet of positive emotions. *Ah – yes! I remember you from days of old: pride.* I felt proud of what I'd achieved that evening. And *that* felt so darn good, I cried.

And as long as I was feeling all those good feels, I could try to stop my thoughts loitering around soft grey eyes, a shy smile. The zap of electricity that I was pretty sure had nothing to do with chemistry and everything to do with being utterly bereft of adult male company for a decade. When human beings are attention – affection – and friendship-famished, it seems a random interaction with a stranger can lead to wild thoughts, outlandish fantasies and dreams that cause blushes to last right through breakfast.

Phew, I really needed to get myself a life.

STOP BEING A LOSER PROGRAMME

DAY SIXTEEN

Within a couple of days, Joey was bouncing back to school. The day after that, a Saturday, I set my alarm for six-thirty, wriggled into an old pair of leggings (fascinating how they managed to be both stretched to capacity and sagging all at the same time) and dug out a pair of Joey's old trainers.

I filled up a water bottle, tucked my phone and keys into my hoodie pocket and boldly whipped open the front door.

Oh. Too late! That was definitely dawn creeping up over the house opposite. I could manage a quick run anyway, couldn't I? Ten minutes up the road and back?

No. Apparently I couldn't. My feet remained frozen on the doorstep. I managed a giant hot chocolate and a cream cheese bagel instead.

Not part of the Programme.

I wondered about running at night, but when I wondered this out loud to Joey over dinner, he shook his head. 'I thought you were going to run in Top Woods so you didn't see anyone? You wouldn't let me run about in the woods at night. I'll be sat at home stressing about you.'

'I'll try again tomorrow morning.'

STOP BEING A LOSER PROGRAMME

DAY NINETEEN

In the end, it took three more days before I set my alarm early enough, and thanks to the same anticipation I used to feel when heading off to pre-dawn training sessions managing to overpower the simmering fear, I headed out.

I warmed up by walking until I hit the tiny lane that led to Top Woods. This comprised several miles of footpaths set across the old colliery site, weaving in and out of huge conifers and the more traditional English trees, interspersed with brambles and bracken.

'Right, here goes.' I clicked on the 'Awesome mighty warrior champion' playlist Joey had created for me, flicked on the head torch I'd bought online and got my flabby, neglected, scared little legs pumping. I discovered that one benefit from running in the near-dark is that I needed to concentrate so hard on not tripping over a root and snapping my neck, or stumbling off the path and down a sudden drop into black nothingness, that before I knew it twenty minutes had passed and I was back at the entrance to the lane. I estimated that I'd ran a third, marched another and limped the rest. Not bad for a first go.

To my simultaneous disappointment and relief, the woods had not been deserted as I'd expected. I'd passed three people walking dogs, their spaniel and labradoodles greatly intrigued by this huffing, puffing, lurching beetroot on legs. I was also overtaken by two men sprinting past. One of them twice, so I guess he lapped me. Well, maybe if I had their high-tech jackets, streamlined legging things and fancy-schmancy trainers I'd be overtaking them.

Or not.

I did so hate to be beaten.

I was going to have to do something about that.

Showered and changed, I rolled Joey out of bed and made us pancakes with blueberries and banana, grinning so hard I could barely chew.

It had been tough. My muscles protested, loudly. I had wavered between anxious, terrified and just about coping the whole time. I hated feeling weak. Clumsy. Uncomfortable. But the truth was, I'd been feeling all those things for years, I'd just buried it under an anaesthesia of robotic, mindless monotony. It was only as I staggered the quarter of a mile home that I acknowledged quite how taxing it had been, pretending things were not that bad, finding ways to live with the wretched reality of my condition, and all that it had stolen from me. Yes, I had cried – bawled – as I'd pounded through the trees. My pain and anger had combusted together to power me up and down the slopes. I had a mountain of grief and regret still to work through, but for now, this run was enough. After every race, before the analysis comes the celebration, embracing the sheer joy of having got up and at 'em and given your all.

I added a scoop of chocolate ice cream to our towers of pancakes.

Joey gaped at me. 'I think you should go running every day.'

'Really? I'm not sure this breakfast is on Cee-Cee's diet sheet.'

'Cee-Cee's not the one who won a medal.'

No. That was me. And right then, for the first time in forever, I remembered what that felt like.

STOP BEING A LOSER PROGRAMME

DAY TWENTY

Waking up to howling muscles felt simply glorious. Swatting away the memories, fixing my eyes firmly on the future, and the successful completion of the Programme, I hobbled back out of the house on my creaking legs – let's stop and marvel at this for a moment – BACK OUT OF THE HOUSE! FOR THE SECOND TIME IN TWO DAYS – and, feeling like an old pro, completed my loop of the woods two minutes quicker than last time. My limbs loosened, as I knew they would, and I ran with two minutes more confidence, purpose and joy. I'd spent years as a child learning how to shut down pain and forge on regardless, and then decades implementing this as an adult, as I trundled on avoiding confronting the utter crapness of my situation. Now, I embraced the pain and revelled in it. Pain meant I was waking up, coming alive again. I even managed to lift my head a couple of times, nod at a dog walker as I lumbered past.

Not the running men. I ducked out of the way as they sped by.

One step at a time.

Another email from Sean. Sorry, please, woe is me, terrible father, one more chance, blah blah blah.

Delete.

STOP BEING A LOSER PROGRAMME

DAY TWENTY-ONE

While on my third run-walk-limp, I thought hard about the glossy invitation in my desk drawer, wondering what to do about it. As I mulled over whether by Easter I would be in a position to accept, and whether, even if I could, I should accept, I spied a new runner heading towards me.

I guess it's to be expected that I'd spot new people out here, after all not everyone runs every day, at the same time, along the same route. But even so, this person felt like an intruder. I instantly hated his yellow running top and stupid red hat. The way that he sprinted up the hill like a mountain gazelle, with a face set in calm concentration rather than a sweaty, flaming grimace (honestly, my fluorescent pink cheeks mitigated any need for reflective clothing) made me dislike him even more.

Pah! to his natural running stride and broad shoulders.

Now. Hang on a minute. While my recent experience of men was somewhat limited, if I remembered correctly, they did all come in different shapes and sizes. They did on TV, anyway. I recognised those shoulders from my actual real life male human portfolio, mainly made up of dog walkers, the two runners and the pizza delivery guy.

And, of course, the man who'd found me as a blubbering puddle in the street a few days earlier.

'Hey!' He pulled up in front of me, just below the crest of the hill, a smile breaking out across his unflushed face.

'Hi,' I squeaked back, hoping the darkness hid quite how grotty I must have looked. I had slowed to an even slower walk, but he pulled out his earbuds and stepped closer, forcing me to either stop or act like a total ignoramus.

I stopped.

'So, you're running?'

I shrugged. 'Trying to, anyway.' I imagined my cheeks must be glowing like hot coals, throbbing veins lit up like rivers of lava.

'Well, good for you.' He nodded, seemingly impressed, as in, *I'm impressed a woman who couldn't even cross a road without clinging to a stranger's hand has made it out of her front door again.* 'How's your son?'

'Oh, he's much better, thanks.'

'Are you running by yourself? Do you think that's okay, I mean, safe? It's pretty lonely in the woods at this time... Don't you have a friend you could run with?'

Hah! A friend!

The heat of humiliation cranked up to nuclear. 'You're out here running alone. Is it safe for you?'

He quirked up his mouth in acknowledgement. 'Fair point. I'm a pretty fit guy though. I know how to take care of myself.'

'Unlike me?' To my fury, my voice cracked on the words. 'A completely unfit woman, who clearly cannot.'

I dodged past him, suddenly desperate to get away, and began to accelerate down the hill.

'Hang on, that's not what I meant!' he called after me. 'I'm sorry, that was a completely stupid thing to say. I didn't mean you. I'm an idiot... ah, crap.'

I slowed down enough to turn around and shout back, with a pleasing amount of breath, 'I'm a lot stronger than I look.'

Strong enough to not allow the brainless words of this self-proclaimed idiot to slow me down.

I decided to drag myself round for forty minutes, ignoring my anxiety's insistence on repeating the warning on a loop: *See, not safe! Alone in the woods! Not safe for a normal person, let alone a freak! What if you panic, fall and break your ankle, smash your head on a rock? What if a crazed rapist ambushes you from behind a tree – that big one up ahead? Murders you, leaving Joey motherless? What if that guy finds you curled up in a ball by the*

side of the path again, because a squirrel ran past or you heard a tiny rustle,
because that's all it takes to turn you into a snivelling wreck? Get back home,
where you're in control. You can't handle outside, remember? Remember what
happens when you go out?

I ran until I reached home, my miserable, bitter, whining anxiety
snapping at my heels the whole way.

I rewarded myself with bacon and maple syrup on my pancakes that
day. Men who couldn't keep their opinions to themselves could go and
run right off the top of a cliff, for all I cared. They didn't know anything
about me, or how I'd got there.

* * *

The day my home became my prison would be forever scarred onto my
soul. Things had been getting progressively worse for the previous few
years. Some ups, like getting my job as a bid writer through an old friend
of Cee-Cee's, eventually saving enough money to move Joey and me out
of her house and into a place of our own. Lots of downs: continuing to
be estranged from my parents, growing increasingly isolated as anxiety
dominated my decisions, struggling to make ends meet while juggling a
job and a small child, continuing to depend on Cee-Cee as my self-
esteem rotted.

It was all too easy to accept Cee-Cee's offers to organise things, or
take Joey to school. She'd never settled back properly into coaching once
I'd left the squad, grumbling about 'all talk and not enough talent', but I
suspected the truth was that my career ending had hit her hard, seriously damaging her reputation and rattling her confidence. And so
when she slipped into early retirement, we ended up propping each
other up with our mutual guilt – while I had ruined her only chance at
training an Olympic champion, along with her future career, I knew she
blamed herself for pushing me too hard, and losing sight of the girl
behind the ultimate goal, resulting in my current anxiety issues.

So, her way of making it up to me was by accompanying me out and
about more and more. Most people assumed she was my mum, and Cee-
Cee didn't bother to correct them. She had no family of her own to speak
of, and so in a weird way that was sort of what she'd become. Every eighteen months or so, I'd have a go at clawing back some independence,

knowing that most adult daughters don't need their mothers to come along to a routine dental appointment. Unnerved at how difficult I was starting to find it to do things alone, I would tell Cee-Cee we'd get the bus instead of accepting a lift. I'd have a feeble attempt at making my own decisions. Wonder if I could actually go about making a new friend or two somehow.

Then dawned the fateful Day of Doom.

I'd managed our current Cee-Cee holiday for five days. A record. It'd been tough, I'd nearly cracked more than once, but, like any addiction, I was praying things would get easier the longer we held out. Until something as simple as running out of tampons – an easy-breezy hop and a skip to the shops for most people (especially the women on those old tampon adverts; they'd whizz there on a skateboard, or hang glide to the square or something). To me, it felt, mentally, like a trek up Mount Everest. For a moment, I considered asking my ten-year-old son to go to the supermarket and buy feminine hygiene products. And then I had a brief flash, like a light bulb switching on, of just how low I'd sunk to even have that thought.

I threw on an old jumper and hurried to the shops. Joey was at football club, but the shop was packed with mums and children, teenagers in hoodies swarming around the snacks, pushchairs blocking half the aisles. My panic levels began to rise, adrenaline pulsing through my bloodstream in time with my pounding heart. I started to shake, felt the nausea slosh around in my stomach. Head down, I pushed past a cluster of kids, my aim to grab what I needed and get out of there.

It was as I reached for the blue packet that I heard it.

'It is. It's her.'

'Nah, can't be. What'd she be doing here?'

'She's buying incontinence pads! That's so hilarious.'

'Shhhh! It's not her.'

'It is! She just looks different cos she's got so fat.'

'Man. That's so tragic. And those clothes. What happened to all her money?'

'Well, it obviously didn't go on a hairdresser.'

'Just goes to show. What goes around comes around. She flaked out, and now she's an ugly cow who pees her pants.'

'Hey, take a photo. We could sell it!'

The floor of the shop bucked beneath me like an agitated bull as I turned and frantically headed for the exit. Lurching towards the door, I bumped against more people, all of whom had become a blur. My head clanged, drowning out any other sounds.

Including the sound of the two women who'd been slagging me off reporting me to the manager. And the sound of him ordering me to stop, not to exit the shop.

Even if I had heard, I don't think I could have turned around.

Until a grip on my shoulder forced me to a halt, dragged me back into the supermarket as onlookers gaped and gawped and gossiped and giggled.

Cee-Cee fetched me from the manager's office an hour later. She knew his sister, had been a loyal customer for years. Her concise explanation about my previous mental breakdown was enough for them to let the matter drop.

And while I may have suffered no formal punishment for my crime of stealing a box of sanitary products, the actual punishment had been two years, three months' imprisonment. My jailer, agoraphobia. Her deputy, panic attacks.

But not any more. I was currently rocking my parole.

STOP BEING A LOSER PROGRAMME

DAY TWENTY-SEVEN

The following Wednesday, Joey's swim coach called to ask if he could drop Joey home after training that evening and talk to me about the Gladiators trial. A man in the house!?! I squeezed into my least awful pair of jeans (slightly less squeezy than last time I put them on) and faffed about with my hair for an embarrassing amount of time. Make-up? Did I have any left anywhere? While for all Mr Gallagher knew, I wore make-up every day, Joey hadn't seen me dolled up in years. He might – *might* – be tactful enough not to blurt out a comment, but he'd notice. And I'd notice Joey noticing. I dabbed a blob of concealer under each eye and left it at that.

Feeling almost on the spectrum of respectable parent, I had positioned myself in a studious, professional, capable manner at my desk when they arrived.

'Hey, Joey. How was training?' I adjusted my smile to extra-normal and got up to greet them.

The smile went AWOL.

'Mum, this is Coach Gallagher,' Joey said.

'Nathan.' Coach Gallagher, otherwise known as hand-holding-but-also-patronising-man-who-haunts-my-dreams added, 'Nice to see you again.'

Should have gone for full face of make-up. At least some foundation to hide my flush.

'Amy. Um. Hi.' I stood there, for the life of me unable to remember the protocol for this. And by 'this', I mean interaction with a human being.

'I'll make a drink,' Joey said, rolling his eyes. 'Go and sit down and I'll bring it through. Do you want tea, Coach?'

'Just a glass of water, thanks.'

'Mum? Tea?'

'Right. Yes. Good idea.'

After a few more seconds, I managed to get my nervous system back in gear and led Nathan into the living room. We stood there for a moment, fidgeting, until deciding it was probably best to sit down.

'How's the running going?' he asked, after a few seconds had limped by.

'Okay.' Knowing I was appearing rude, which probably wouldn't help Joey in the long run, I tried to force my eyes over to at least his general direction.

'Look, I'm sorry about what I said.' He pulled his hat off, revealing mid-brown, mussed-up hair with streaks of natural highlights. 'I didn't mean anything... personal.'

I flapped my hand in what was supposed to be a dismissive gesture but ended up more like a drunken chicken impression. 'It's fine. Sore subject, that's all. I'm sorry I ran off.'

'Which time?'

Uummmm...

Nathan raised his eyebrows, but his mouth quirked up, managing to dissolve a smidgen of the tension.

So, yes, when I'd spied him running up ahead a couple more times, once with a group in matching sky-blue T-shirts, I may have bolted in the opposite direction. On Saturday, I'd possibly dodged him a total of four times, diving off the path into the undergrowth once or twice. It was almost as if he was following me. Except that would be impossible, given that an elderly slug would end up overtaking me.

Fortunately, before it became too obvious that I had absolutely no answer to that, Joey came in with the drinks.

'Have you decided anything?' he asked, stretching out across the carpet on his elbows.

'Not yet.' I picked up my mug, carefully, praying my nervous hands wouldn't drop it. 'I watched a video of Joey's race, from the county meet,' I said to a spot on the wall behind Nathan's head.

Nathan leant forwards. 'Joey's an extremely talented athlete. He's probably the best I've seen in ten years of coaching. At Brooksby, his only competition is against himself. I think he deserves a shot at the Gladiators.' He shifted focus to Joey. 'If you're up for the challenge, and the hard work that'll follow, I'd really like to help you get there.'

'I'm happy for him to do the trial. The problem is what happens if he passes. We don't have a car. There's no way he can get to early morning training and be back in time for school, and if he's trekking over there on the bus six nights a week, I'm worried about how that'll impact everything else.'

'They're starting training sessions in Greasby once the pool's reopened. It's, I don't know, maybe April, or the beginning of May?'

'It opens on Easter Monday. The last weekend in April.' My liver did a tiny quiver and I tried not to think about the glossy invitation.

'That's, what, a fifteen-minute bus ride? If the trial can be postponed 'til April, then Joey can up his training at Brooksby in the meantime. I'd be really happy to do some extra sessions, give him a feel for what it's like training every day, at that level. I've not coached anyone for nationals before, but I've spent quite a bit of time with the Loughborough Uni squad. What do you think, Joey?'

Joey sat up, resting his arms on crossed legs. 'I sort of want to get it done as soon as I can. I'll be years behind most of the squad already. But if I can get more training in and get in the best shape possible when I join, that's good.'

'I honestly don't know how else we'd work it,' I said. 'Even if someone gave you a lift every day, you'd not manage it. They won't tolerate two minutes late for training because the traffic was bad.'

He mused on this for a while. 'And by April it'll be easier for you to come. You'll be smashing the Programme.'

'The Programme?' Nathan asked, completely overstepping into none of his business.

'I'm working on my agoraphobia,' I muttered, before Joey could mention the actual title.

'Ah, okay. Is running part of the Programme?'

'Are we done talking about me?' Joey asked, standing up and

stretching until his fingers brushed the ceiling. 'Great. See you, Coach. Oh, and awesome. Thanks.'

They did some male fist-bump thing and Joey left. As in, left me and Nathan, the incredibly fit-looking guy who suddenly seemed to take up half of my living room, alone, together. In a previous life, I'd been conditioned to appreciate tall people with broad shoulders who loved swimming, but now I had no idea how to converse politely with a stranger in my house.

'Were you following me?'

Hello, Amy?!? THAT'S what you decide to blurt?!?

Nathan shuffled on the chair, picked up his glass and put it down again. 'Um, I'd prefer to call it keeping an eye on you.'

What?! He *was* following me? I gaped, unsure how to respond.

'I feel nervous seeing women running alone. Someone I know got attacked a few years ago.'

'Oh my goodness. That's awful. I'm so sorry. Was she okay? I mean, as okay as you can be, after...'

'She's in a wheelchair.' Nathan shrugged. 'Had a rough couple of years, but she's doing really well now. Married Chris, the guy who runs the café in the square?'

'Uh, yeah. I don't know him...'

'Right. Yes. Of course. Sorry.'

Please don't apologise for momentarily forgetting I'm a social freak.

'So, now you've taken it upon yourself to stalk random women about the woods to keep them safe?' I smiled, to show I got it.

'Precisely. I stalk the one random woman I've seen who's either crazy or audacious enough to run alone, in the dark, through the middle of nowhere. Anyone else joins my club.' He handed me a sky-blue flyer he'd pulled out of his tracksuit top.

'The Larkabouts?'

'An early morning running club. This time of year, we head out in the dark, so you should be fine.'

I scanned the leaflet. Wednesdays and Sundays, they met at Brooksby Leisure Centre at 6 a.m. A group of muddy women, arms around each other, grinned triumphantly at me.

'They're a really friendly, supportive group. You should come along, give it a go.'

'Thanks, I'll think about it.' I wasn't lying. I would definitely think about making sure my runs didn't coincide with the Larkabouts. Staggering through the woods in my hideous leggings and ratty hoodie, thighs wobbling and chest jiggling, sweat dripping, heaving for breath and flinching at imaginary danger was bad enough on my own. Throw in introductions, small talk about my non-existent life – or even worse, my significant past life – flailing around miles behind the rest, soon becoming the comedy member of the group. Yuk. No thanks.

'Great. I'll look forward to seeing you there.' Nathan's soft grey eyes crinkled up in a smile.

Now that comment was almost enough to make me change my mind. Or sprint hell for leather in the opposite direction. I couldn't decide which. I did wonder, after our slightly awkward goodbye, how many of the Larkabouts had suddenly found an interest in early morning running once they'd seen the head of the flock.

* * *

For some reason, after entertaining a man in my house, I decided to have a clear-out of my kitchen cupboards. Joey came down later, looking for supper, and enthusiastically joined in dumping anything that Cee-Cee called 'low-grade fuel', which basically meant all processed, sugary, trans-fatty, scrumptious food. We set aside anything non-perishable for the local food bank and dumped the rest.

'What's the deal with the pool at Greasby?' Joey asked, as he chucked a multi-pack of midget gems into the food-bank bag. 'You went all twitchy when Nathan mentioned it.'

'Coach Gallagher.'

'He said to call him Nathan! And you knew the date it opens again. Why would you know that?'

'He invited *me* to call him Nathan, not you. And I know the date because of this.' I tossed a dried-up packet of pepperoni in the bin and fetched the invitation out of my desk.

Joey took it from me, reading with interest.

'They've invited you to the grand reopening of the leisure centre? That's pretty cool!'

I waited for him to read a bit further.

'WHAT!? The AMELIA PIPER SWIMMING CENTRE!' He stared at
the card, mouth hanging open. 'They want you to give a speech and
present the prize for a sporting event to be confirmed at a later date!
Why didn't you tell me? This is unbelievable!'

'Weeellll...'

'No. Mum. You have to go. You are going, aren't you? Is this why
you've started the Programme?' He grabbed onto both my shoulders.
'Mum, you can't not go! This is like, so cool. Promise you'll go! You have
to promise.'

'I've not said I won't do it.'

'Muu-uu-uum! You won a gold medal!' He stepped back, waving his
arms about. 'You deserve this. It could be, like, your big comeback after
disappearing for all these years. And you'll do a killer speech and I bet
the Gladiators will be there and everyone will know you're not a weirdo
recluse woman, you're an awesome gold medallist. You won't have to
hide any more.' Tucking one hand under each of my armpits, he lifted
me up onto my tiptoes until our faces nearly touched. 'You have to go.
They're naming a pool after you. That's an amazing honour,' he said in a
voice like he was the adult, and I a truculent child.

'I know. I'm thinking about it, honestly,' I mumbled, as he dropped
me back down.

'And imagine how embarrassing it'll be if you don't show up. You'll
never be able to reveal your true identity then.'

'I'm not hiding my true identity, I just don't want to advertise it. And I
don't want you judged on who your mum is.'

'Yeah. I get that, I don't want any favourable treatment because of
you, either.' He absent-mindedly opened one of the 'reject' crisp packets
and shovelled a handful in his mouth.

Oh, Joey. I wasn't worried about the swimming world treating him
better if they knew who his mother was...

But he had a point, that things might be worse for him – and me – in
the long run if I didn't show. It was a mystery why they'd decided to
name a pool after me. Granted, I went to school in the village next to
Greasby, which makes me the most successful sportswoman in the local
area. But, still. Community buildings don't get named after someone
who turned out to be a national scandal. At least, they shouldn't.

I'd had hideous nightmares about me shuffling in, all my muscle turned to blubber. My hair self-cut, wearing an online outfit that, like most things you can't try before you buy, neither fit nor flattered. The courageous woman hiding deep down inside me knew that size, appearance, split ends, don't make a person, or determine their worth or success. But I was ashamed, not of my looks (okay, not *only* of my looks), but of the truth they represented: that the swimmer who never gave up had given up. On herself, on life, on having any purpose. I hadn't just let myself go physically, but emotionally, spiritually. I had literally let myself disappear into nothingness.

And besides: crowds, noise, a microphone in my face, journalists. And the likelihood that to ceremoniously open a swimming pool in my name, I'd probably be expected to go inside it. What if I panicked? *Surely* I would panic?

The very thought of it made my bones clack together.

I couldn't do it.

I couldn't *not* do it.

But, boy, I had some work to do in the meantime.

I put the invitation back in the drawer and ate a carrot.

14

STOP BEING A LOSER PROGRAMME

DAY TWENTY-EIGHT

The following day, there was another Sean message to mess up my head and boil my blood. I saved the document I'd been working on and hit Google.

If it turned out the absent father of my child had been wrongly imprisoned, or in a coma for the past decade, I might have felt a twinge of sympathy. But according to articles in online business magazines, and various conference speaker biographies, the managing director of Mansfield Recruitment, head office Denver, Colorado, needed sympathy from no one. I clicked on his website, teeth grinding at the staged image of him dunking a basketball (no boring sitting behind a desk for Sean Mansfield!). Ugh. Sean hated anything to do with sport. Apart from me, that was. For a while, anyway.

No mention of a wife or children. Mostly, it seemed he played golf, posed on aeroplane steps and made money. A lot of money. Sean Mansfield had recruited the heck out of Colorado. No surprises there. He was an expert at persuading people to ditch one career for, well, empty promises, broken commitments and a truckload of disappointment, in my experience.

And now, for some reason, he had turned his persuasive powers in the direction of my son.

Message deleted.

* * *

After meeting Sean on the bus, I started seeing him almost every day. Fitting a secret romance in between training and my parents' cashing-in-on-the-celebrity campaign wasn't easy. But the drama of sneaking off, defying authority and making my own decisions was part of the adventure.

The craving for normal – too young, too inexperienced to know that normal was an illusion – had burst out from behind my fierce ambition. I was sick of the weight of expectation. The relentless pressure to follow orders. Sean tapped into my deepest doubts about whether Cee-Cee and the other coaches, my parents, my sponsors, squad, even saw me as a person any more.

'You're a means to an end,' he told me, as we lazed on the grass in the university park. 'When was the last time they asked what you want, how you feel? Gold medals and hard cash. That's what they care about. They don't know the real you. If you never swam another stroke, you'd still be the most amazing person I've ever met. I love these shoulders.' He bent then, tucking the neck of my T-shirt back to kiss my bare skin. 'Your back, your incredible legs. Arms. Chest.'

I pushed him away, giggling, as after kissing each body part he made a pretence of going for my chest.

'But, to me, you're so much more than that. They want you for what you can do. I love you for who you are.'

Every ounce of air whooshed out of my lungs. I goggled at him, speechless.

He laughed. 'Well, you must know I love you. Why else am I here, not studying for my exams, like everyone else?' He gently pressed his nose to mine. 'You've messed everything up, Amelia Piper,' he breathed. 'I'm utterly under your spell. So you'd better love me back, or I'm in serious trouble.'

Oh yes, I loved him back. I loved the way he looked at me. How he casually took my hand whenever we were together, stroking it with his thumb. I loved that he always asked me what I wanted to do, and listened to my answers with a funny, furrowed brow. I loved the afternoons spent doing nothing, lying on a blanket watching the clouds drift by, dreaming, dozing in each other's arms. I loved that he never, not once, pressured me to do anything I didn't want to. Which, of course, made me want to do things I'd never have considered otherwise. Once exams were over, we swapped a picnic blanket for his bed. A girl prone to fierce obsession, my allegiance had changed. I no longer lived and breathed for the water. I lived, breathed, hoped, dreamed, dressed, lied and schemed for Sean Mansfield. And the more my lap times suffered, the more Cee-Cee sought to compensate with diet plans, gym workouts, video analysis, motivational lectures and the threat of actually losing, the further she drove me into his undemanding, understanding arms.

As the Athens Olympics drew closer, Amelia Piper, swimming hope of the nation, began to pull away.

15

STOP BEING A LOSER PROGRAMME
DAY THIRTY

I bought myself a new pair of trainers. I figured that stopping looking like a loser would help me to stop feeling like a loser, and as a result, stop me acting like one too.

Except I'd bought them online, of course, and they were slightly too big. The following Saturday, I stuck on an extra pair of socks and wore them anyway. The only trouble was, after three kilometres (mostly running, some walking, NO stopping!), I had what felt like blisters the size of beach balls beneath each ankle bone. I managed a hobbling sort of canter, wincing with every galumphing step as I decided to ignore the screaming agony and continue on for at least another K, but the combination of unsteady footing, pain-spawned sweat stinging my eyes and a particularly dark stretch of trees meant that my too-big trainer caught in a rabbit hole, sending me ricocheting head over bouncing-behind down a muddy slope and into the ditch at the bottom.

Oh, crap.

I half rolled, half scrabbled to a sitting position. Not an elegant sight, I'd imagine. I used my hoodie sleeve to wipe some of the mud from my face before gingerly bottom-squelching out of the ditch, which thankfully contained only an oozy dribble of actual water, and hoicked myself onto a rock and took a moment to steady my shaken nerves, forcing a wobbly smile in an attempt to laugh it off.

I was wondering whether to take my trainers off, and negotiate my

way home in sopping socks, when I heard footsteps crunching on the
path above me.

No. Don't be following me again. Don't have seen me tumbling down the
slope like a bouncy ball, squealing like a piglet...

'All right down there?' a woman's voice asked. 'That looked a right
tumble!'

Okay. This was somewhat better. I swivelled on the rock to see two
women peering at me from a few metres away. My heart accelerated at
their pale T-shirts, what looked like the silhouette of a bird, wings
outstretched, on the front. I'm no ornithologist, but I was guessing that
was a lark. Scanning around, I couldn't see anyone else, however, so
perhaps the incident could be contained.

One of the women asked, 'Do you need any help?' Judging by her
precise accent, it was the other, who had what appeared in the dusk to
be orange-squash-coloured hair, who'd spoken first.

'Um, I think I'm okay,' I said and made to stand up. Only to quickly
plop back down on the rock again.

Yowch.

I tried again, this time carefully putting all my weight on my right
foot, seeing as my left ankle appeared to be at the least sprained, and,
judging by the bolts of lightning now shooting up my leg, quite possibly
smashed into smithereens.

'I'm fine. Honestly,' I gasped, clearly not fine. 'I don't want to hold
you up.' Or attract further attention, like a big, strong male lark to toss
me over his shoulder and carry me back to the path.

Or did I? That image lingered in my brain long enough to confuse
the matter...

No! I didn't! Definitely not! No, no and thrice no.

No.

'Don't be crackers,' Orange Squash said. 'Yer not goin' anywhere.
Let's get you back up the slope first, then find some mobile reception
and call an ambulance.'

'No, really,' I winced. 'My son's at home by himself. I need to get
back. I'll be all right once I've walked it off a bit. Please. Carry on with
your run.'

Ignoring me completely, the women slid the last couple of metres
down the slope and tucked one of my arms over each of their shoulders.

Not so bad for the woman nearly as tall as me, but I had to stretch down several inches just to reach the top of Orange Squash's head. I hopped, swore, stifled a lot of sobs and somehow made it to the top. The taller woman, Dani, a red bandana framing dark skin, called for her husband to come and pick us up. Orange Squash, real name Mel, inspected my ballooning ankle with surprising tenderness. Her official diagnosis: 'Totally buggered.'

I insisted on hopping to the exit, where Dani's husband Derek could park his car, but had made it less than a few metres before he jogged up. Scooping me up in his arms, (impressively muscled, despite a full head of grey hair), he carried me the quarter of a mile back to his Land Rover and gently placed me on the back seat.

The sun was beginning to rise behind the treeline. I closed my eyes and counted slowly to ten. Then twenty.

'All right?' Mel asked, from about an inch in front of my face.

I opened my eyes, tried to summon up a smile. 'I'm fine, honestly. Thanks so much for your help.'

She hopped into the seat next to me, surprisingly agile for someone of her size – sort of teapot-shaped, short and stout. 'You keep sayin' yer fine as much as you want. Looks to me like yer gunna puke any second.'

Yep. A wise one, old Orange Squash Mel.

Thank goodness for wipe-clean leather seats.

* * *

My Good Samaritans saw me back home, propped up on the sofa with pillows and dosed up with painkillers, and then proceeded to... not leave.

Dani made a pot of tea and rooted about for the ingredients to cook a post-run breakfast (cheese and spinach omelette). Mel came downstairs with a pair of thermal pyjamas she'd found in my bedroom drawers and insisted on helping me change into something comfortable 'that don't reek'. She made an ice pack with frozen peas wrapped in a tea towel and used a bandage from one of Joey's old sports injuries to add compression.

'No ibuprofen for a couple of days, then use it to help bring the swelling down. Ice pack for ten minutes every two hours, no hot baths.

Stick it up in the air now an' again, too. You'll be right, it don't look too bad.'

When I asked if she had medical training, she laughed.

'I've got five kids, one of 'em with multiple disabilities. So, yeah, I guess so. They've 'ad more breaks and bumps and whatnots than I can remember. Spent so much time in the walk-in centre, we should get our own cubicle.'

'Shouldn't you be getting back to them?' I didn't want to seem rude, but I felt all twisted up and tense having strangers in my house. And no clue as to when they might leave.

'Nah, it's fine. Me mum's there.' She settled back into the armchair. Dani also seemed settled in for the morning, making another pot of tea after clearing up the remains of breakfast.

When Joey sloped into the kitchen at around nine, they were still here. 'Good morning, Joey,' Dani said, following him in. 'Your mother said you've a gala today, so let's get some good energy into you. We can do wholewheat pancakes. Or porridge. The others had an omelette. What do you fancy?'

'Um.' Joey sounded like he was wondering if he'd actually woken up yet. 'The others?'

'Oh, not all of us. Just me, your mother and Mel.'

'Right.' There was a pause. 'Who's Mel? And you?'

'Dani. Very pleased to meet you. Your mother tripped and fell off the top of Top Woods. We found her in the ditch at the bottom and got her home.'

'What?'

'I'm fine!' I called through. 'Just a mild ankle sprain. Nothing to worry about.'

Joey disagreed. As did, it would seem, everyone else.

'That's it,' my son instructed me, while scoffing a mouthful of scrambled eggs. 'You're not running in the dark by yourself again. I forbid it. What would've happened if Dani and Mel'd not been there?' He waved his fork at the pair, who'd somehow managed to take on the role of surrogate aunties in the half hour he'd known them.

'Then someone else would've come along. There are loads of runners and dog walkers about at that time.'

'Yeah, but if you'd smashed your head as you plummeted down, knocked yerself out and no one saw you, you could've been there for hours. Days!' Mel shook her head in imagined horror.

'What she said!' Joey agreed, vigorously.

'What do you want me to do, Joey?' I asked, the pain making me irritable. 'Stop running? Go back to how things were?'

'You could try running in daylight,' Dani suggested. 'Less risk of you falling, and more chance someone will spot you.'

Joey shook his head. 'She has to go when it's dark.'

'Eh?' Mel wrinkled up her forehead. 'What, you a vampire or summat?'

'I have an... anxiety condition that makes it easier for me to go out when it's dark,' I mumbled.

Joey did an enormous snort. 'Understatement.'

'Well, that leaves only one option,' Mel said, grinning. 'Yer'll have to join the Larkabouts.' She nodded at me, frowning. 'Once that ankle's better, o' course.'

Which I was rather hoping could turn out to be a very, very long time...

16

STOP BEING A LOSER PROGRAMME
DAY THIRTY-EIGHT

Or not, as it turned out. Pain that initially felt as though my ankle had been crushed in a vice soon faded to a mild ache. The swelling disappeared within a few days, and after a week I was itching to get out there again. Having caught the whiff of freedom in those woods, the thought of slumping back into captivity sent me frantic. The problem was, I'd hit a stalemate with my son.

He'd 'happened' to mention it to Nathan at the swimming gala. Nathan then 'happened' to give Joey a lift home instead of Lisa. So, obviously, then, he'd earnt the right to come inside to give me a lecture about the lunacy of running alone.

'I'm really sorry about your friend,' I said, once he'd paused to take a breath. 'But there are loads of people there, and I always take my phone.'

'No signal up there,' Joey said, butting in.

'I've weighed up the risks, and the chances of something awful happening are miniscule if I keep running. As opposed to *every day* being awful if I let fear win, and stay in this house. I won't waste any more time. And trust me, I'll be paying more attention from now on, I won't risk a moment's carelessness hurting me again.'

'Why not give the club a go? That way everybody's happy,' Nathan replied, running exasperated fingers through mussy hair.

'This may surprise you, but when it comes to my physical and mental health, I don't especially care if you're happy about it!'

'I meant you and Joey. And I really think you'll enjoy it. You've met Mel and Dani; the rest are just as nice. No one's going to judge you. Mostly. Well. Except maybe one. And you can ignore her. Everyone else does. There are tons of benefits to running in a group.'

'You might actually make some friends, for a start,' Joey said.

I glowered at him, still very miffed that he'd invited Nathan in while I was splayed out on the sofa in my pyjamas, body unwashed, hair unbrushed, face un-concealered, bra discarded onto the floor beside me. Thank goodness Nathan had stopped to take off his trainers, giving me time to shove the bra under the sofa cushion.

'You will make friends. But more than that, you'll have motivators, people to inspire and encourage you. Share tips. You'll get a professional programme, including warm-ups and cool-downs, the right variety in distance and terrain. Everyone's progress hits another level after joining a club.'

'I don't need motivation, or someone to encourage me. And I know how to warm-up and cool-down.'

Nathan tried again, 'But being part of a team is just... different. Special. Right, Joey?'

'I think Mum already knows that,' Joey replied, looking straight at me.

Once Nathan had left, Joey played his trump card: 'Give the Larkabouts one session or I'll tell Cee-Cee you're sofa-ridden.'

I do not tolerate blackmail as a way to conduct family business. I particularly hold no truck with children attempting to control or manipulate their parents.

However, I did pay attention to the distress in my boy's brown eyes when he said this. I gave serious credence to how he twisted up his T-shirt with worried hands and hovered around me for the few days it took to recover.

If I was going to get back out there again, and while I couldn't wait, I knew it was going to be tough again after a week in the haven of my house, it would be to join the Brooksby Larkabouts, 6 a.m. in the leisure centre car park.

Joey ordered me some running leggings and a jacket to negate the embarrassment of me wearing my old gear in public. His embarrassment, not mine. I gratefully accepted his choice of sportswear, even as I rued the fact that the trendiest gear in the world couldn't change or hide the woman floundering about inside it.

Only I could do that. Stop floundering. Change the woman.

17

STOP BEING A LOSER PROGRAMME
DAY FORTY

I knew I couldn't keep ignoring Sean's messages. Beneath the bluster, my accident had been a sharp reminder that however determined I was to become a fully functional parent, I was still only one person, and I couldn't guarantee that nothing would ever happen to affect that. Joey deserved to have someone else he could turn to, who would fight his corner and provide for him. And I didn't want that to be Cee-Cee again.

Would his father be any better?

Did I owe Joey, Sean – myself – the chance to find out?

And if I didn't reply, initiate some contact, would Sean take matters into his own hands? He'd found out my phone number, it wouldn't be hard to discover Joey's...

The thought of Sean charming Joey like he'd done me, only with thirteen extra years to perfect his techniques of entrapment and enchantment... it made my heart stutter in my chest, set my left eye twitching like a demented frog.

If Joey discovered I'd been keeping his father from him, he might be more easily persuaded to zip right off on one of those jets his dad liked so much. Off to a private Olympic-sized pool and masses of pocket money and family adventures that actually happened outside his new, enormous house.

Sean had relinquished any claim on his son through his absence. But did Joey have the right to find out for himself whether or not his father was a sleazeball? Even if that hurt him in the process? He was still a child. Who got to make that call?

18

STOP BEING A LOSER PROGRAMME

DAY FORTY-EIGHT

It was late October when I finally dredged up the courage to don my new gear and ready myself for the short walk to Brooksby Leisure Centre, having prepped myself with a few (secret) early morning walks to get used to being outside again. Knowing Mel and Dani would be there helped, a lot. Knowing Nathan would be there? I hadn't decided yet.

Joey had told him I was coming, mostly to make sure I didn't back out at the last minute – 'you have to go now, they'll be waiting for you'. That meant that when I saw Nathan waiting at the end of my street, I was barely surprised.

'You'll make people nervous, loitering about in the shadows,' I said, striding past without stopping, my breath a puff of steam.

It took about three smooth paces for him to draw alongside me. 'How's things?'

'So-so.' I didn't bother mentioning how my anxiety was currently trying to squeeze my breakfast back up again. 'How are you?'

We caught up on nothing much, managing to distract at least part of my mind from what lay ahead. I then asked how Joey was doing.

'I mean, of course he tells me training's brilliant and he's heading for imminent glory. I just wanted to check if your version matched his.'

'Honestly? He's incredible. If anything, he doesn't know how good he actually is. The trial is pushing him to work at his best, and it shows how much he's been coasting at Brooksby.'

I enjoyed the glow of pride, allowing it to shush my fears for the moment. 'Thanks again for giving him so much time.'

'It's a pleasure.'

We carried on walking in silence for another minute or two. 'So, who are you really?' I asked, as the leisure centre lights came into view.

'Excuse me?' Nathan peered at me through the darkness.

'Swimming coach. Running club instructor. Football player. Stalker of lone women. Who is the real Nathan Gallagher? Which of these do you concentrate on the rest of the time? Or is it something else altogether?'

'I'm a personal trainer. Mostly. I love coaching the swim club, and the Larkabouts helps me sleep at night. I've only ever stalked one woman.'

'By one woman, you do mean me?'

Nathan laughed. 'I've told you, you're the only woman crazy enough in these here parts to run solo at night.'

'While sober, anyway.'

'Fair point.'

'So what kind of clients do you have, Mr Personal Trainer?'

Nathan rolled his shoulders. 'All sorts. People rehabilitating after injuries or surgery. Wanting to lose weight for a wedding. Midlife crises. Quite a few who suspect their partner is having an affair. Or are recently divorced and trying to feel better about themselves.'

We entered the car park, where up ahead a group of women lounged against the wall of the centre, or sat on the steps outside the main reception. As they saw Nathan approaching, half of them stood to attention, or started doing stretching poses. Ones which seemed to focus on the chest or bottom area. Well, gotta stretch out those glutes before a good run, I suppose.

'And how many of them are female?' I asked, letting some mischief leak into my voice.

Nathan sighed. 'I get a lot of clients through the Larkabouts. Or mums of the swim club kids. And more women use personal trainers than men. Plus, more women tend to be free during the day, which is when I like to work.'

'All of them, then?'

'No! Not all of them. And I resent the implication that people only hire me because...' He trailed off.

'Because what?' I asked, all innocent. I'd spent many a long hour, once upon a time, hanging out with ridiculously fit, confident guys who oozed testosterone. Banter and jibes were the way we'd expressed sportsmanship, built team bonds. It felt weirdly comfortable slipping back into this role. Like being a teenager again.

Only Nathan was my coach, not my squad-mate. And I was not a teenager. I was a thirty-two-year-old mum who looked nearer to fifty. An unfit, messed-up, frumped-up, full-on failure.

Get a grip, Amy. Know your place!

'Hi, Nathan!' the Larkabouts chorused as we reached them.

'Who's this?' one woman asked, looking me up and down. She was probably one of Nathan's clients. Rail thin, apart from balloon boobs bursting out of her running top, with a massive dark ponytail, taut face and wrinkled neck.

Before I could coordinate my jellified legs to turn around and sprint right back out of there, never to return, I heard a familiar voice.

'Amy! Ey up! 'Ow's yer ankle?' Mel barrelled through the group, which took some doing given her girth, and reached up to give me a hug, holding on until my anxiety unclenched its claws from my lungs and I could breathe again.

'It's great, thanks,' I mumbled. 'I like your hair.' It was purple today, scraped into several teeny bunches all over her head.

'Yeah, the girls did it.'

I remembered from our previous conversation that Mel had two girls and three boys. Her girls were six and eight, the boys seventeen, thirteen and four. 'Five kids, four dads,' she'd scoffed. The first two were with her childhood sweetheart, who she'd married at eighteen. 'Then, that monster-evil cancer got him. And I plum lost me mind with grief. I was that lonely without him, I fell from one crappy mess into another. Only good to come out of them bad years were Taylor, Tiff and Tate. Then, with Tate being the way he is and all, I woke up. Pulled meself together. Started running and met people like Dani. So, family Malone're back on the straight and narrer now.'

'Is Gordon looking after them?' I asked. Gordon was the relief carer for her youngest son, Tate, who had a rare chromosome disorder resulting in multiple disabilities. I reckoned if Gordon was looking after all those kids at six in the morning, he might actually be an angel who simply moonlighted as a care worker for kicks.

'Nah. No point. They never wake 'til I get back. And if they do, Jordan'll stick *Love Island* on; they're addicted to that crap.'

'Jordan's the eldest?' I made no comment on my opinion about children watching *Love Island*. Who was I, mother of just one child, to judge?

'Yeah. I call him my lifeguard. Mostly I try to let him have a normal teenage life. You know, sleepin', eatin', on his phone, chasin' girls and gettin' inter trouble. But he always spots when I'm at the end of me tether. Runs me a bath or cooks dinner. "I'll be Mum today," he says. Gets the younger ones playin' *Minecraft* or summat. Him and the Larks, they're the reason I'm still sane.'

'Still sane?' a young woman with gorgeous black hair tumbling round her hoodie asked, in a strong Welsh accent. 'Who you trying to kid?' She turned towards me. 'Bronwyn. You must be Amy,' she said, and gave me a massive wink with huge brown eyes.

'Um.'

'Yeah, Mel and Dani've told us all about you,' she grinned.

Right. Not Nathan then. *No, Amy! Of course not!*

I wondered if Bronwyn was Nathan's client, too. I could imagine them in the gym together, him correcting her squats posture. Her dabbing at the sweat on her face and neck with a tiny towel...

'And this is everyone else. Everyone, Amy's finally turned up!' she called. 'I won't bother with names; you'll figure us out soon enough.'

Nathan started off by taking us through a few stretches, occasionally throwing out a pointer and ignoring the comments the women shouted back, one after the other like machine guns:

'You try doing that with your legs at my age!'

'Blummin 'eck, Nathan, I've given birth to five kids, I could 'ave a go at that move, but the results wouldn't be pretty.'

'I've had two and I'm not going there.'

'I've had none and I still don't think it's a good idea.'

'No one should be attempting that at this time in the morning, love.'

'No one should have to *watch* you attempt it...'

'At any time!'

And so it went on. Boy, these women could talk. While simultaneously jogging on the spot, sticking their faces down between their knees and, a short while later, their head torches bobbing down the old railway line towards the woods.

Except for one woman, I'd guess not far into her twenties, who was the only one apart from me to save her breath for the run. She was tall like me, too, but with a much more solid build. One of those bodies made to carry some curves. I guessed that in the right clothes, with the right attitude, she'd make a stunning plus-sized model. Slumped at the back in a tracksuit that looked borrowed from a '90s rapper, head down, shoulders hunched, face miserable, she appeared nearly as much of a lost, lonely loser as me.

'Audrey!' the woman with the massive fake hair and balloon boobs shrieked back at her every few hundred metres. 'For pity's sake, put some effort in. Even Mel's beating you. Do you want to be fat? Stay single for the next twenty-one years?'

'Shut up, Selena,' several of the women panted.

'It's not a competition.' Nathan had spent this first mile or so zipping up and down the line of ten runners, covering about five times the distance of anyone else, while still managing to utter words. And nice, encouraging ones at that. 'You're doing great, Audrey.'

I slowed down a little to run alongside her (only a little, but still – not the slowest, even having taken over a fortnight off). 'She seems a bit of a cow. Is she jealous?'

Audrey nearly choked on her own incredulity. 'Hardly! Look at her.'

'Looks like she's desperately trying to hold on to her past looks because without them all that's left is a mean and repugnant personality. What gives her the right to bitch at you like that? If I were you, I'd be tempted to get fit just so I could catch her up and shove her off the top.'

Ouch, Amy, who's the bitch now?

Well. That Selena woman had made me really mad. I felt substantial sympathy for crushed and cowering women who came last in their running club because they felt they deserved last place in life. Out of the all the Larkabouts, I thought Audrey might make a good, non-intimidating, non-invasive friend.

'She's my mum.'

Ah. Oh. Right.

Time to suddenly get too out of breath to speak for a while and shrink back into the shadows where I belonged. During which time my brain would try and fail to think of something to say to somehow remedy suggesting someone murder her own mother.

But by the time I'd thought of something ('sorry' – not much else I could say, really), we'd hit the steepest part of the hill, and Audrey dropped so far back I could only make out her head torch, pointing at the ground. It was impossible to stay with her without slowing to a walk. I would have swatted away my pride and walked anyway, only Nathan swooped back to jog alongside me.

'How's the ankle?'

'It feels a bit unsteady, that's all. I'm taking it easy.'

'Oh, this is you taking it easy?'

I considered the layer of perspiration plastering both my trendy bottoms and hi-tech top to my skin. Damp, straggly hair. Breath sounding like I was blowing into an invisible harmonica. Did I want Nathan to think this was my 'taking it easy' look?

'I've been resting for nearly three weeks. My fitness may have regressed slightly.' I glanced at Bronwyn, further up the hill. She was chatting away to the woman next to her, their hands gesturing like hyperactive shadow puppets. The other woman even found the strength to throw back her head and laugh.

'You're doing great. Just don't push it too hard the first week. I don't want you waking up so stiff tomorrow it puts you off coming back. Some of the group have been building their fitness for years.'

I felt a prickle of anger. One thing I used to be pretty darn good at was pushing myself to the very limits, refusing to acknowledge can't or won't, or never. Refusing to allow pain, or tiredness, or feeling *stiff* to stop me from being bloody amazing. How dare this guy label me as weak or flaky. How dare he patronise me like this, telling me I'm doing great as I gasp and hobble my way through a 5K run.

He knew nothing about me. What I was capable of. What was at stake. This is why I should have stuck to training by myself.

I nearly turned right around and sprinted for home. Only, I knew, with a few more plodding paces up that endless, evil mountain, that the emotion steaming through my blood wasn't anger, but embarrassment.

I used to be pretty good. Somewhere along the way, I forgot how. If there was a chance this group could help me, I would swallow my ridiculous, misplaced pride and do my best to let them.

* * *

It was seven when I straggled back into the village, ending up at the square instead of the leisure centre, as usually the club stopped for a drink or some breakfast in the Cup and Saucer café.

'We stink the place out, mind,' Mel told me. 'So Chris wants us out by eight to give the fumes time to disperse.'

We pondered that lovely thought for a few seconds, before I fudged my excuse about having to get home.

The faster women were already finishing off their cool-down stretches, with the exception of Marjory, who had appeared old and frail enough to need a walking frame until she'd overtaken me about thirty seconds into the run. Marjory had stretched, cooled and now sat in the café window, chugging a chai latte.

'Walking the last hundred metres doesn't make it okay to skip the cool-down,' Nathan called out, as the latecomers began drifting off. 'Stretches, people!' he yelled, seemingly at no one in particular.

'Sorry, Nathan, I'm due in court,' Dani shrugged, heading towards a sleek Audi parked opposite the square. 'Some serious human rights are at stake.'

'No can do, Coach, the minibeasts are awake and wanting their brekkie. I'll do me stretches as I go, look.' Mel started fast-walking in the opposite direction, flinging alternate arms over her head as she went.

Audrey attempted a couple of thigh stretches while Selena hissed impatiently, 'Watch it. If you lose your balance, I'm not risking putting my back out trying to haul you up again. You'll have to crawl home.'

I had very nearly used up every last drop of self-confidence in joining the Larkabouts that day. But, wow, how could any decent human being let that one go?

'How can you talk to your daughter like that?' I blurted, voice quaking. 'How is that helpful? You should be encouraging her, supporting her with love... and... and kindness and...'

'It's fine,' Audrey interrupted in a dull monotone. 'Mum's right. I have terrible balance.'

She trudged over to the café while I gaped in horrified disbelief and Selena smirked. 'It's called knowing your limits,' she faux-whispered, pulling open the café door. 'Try it sometime. Because you know what isn't helpful? Butting your nose into other people's business.'

She disappeared inside, leaving me rubbing at both arms as if that would help brush off the horrible words, before turning towards home.

'Nah-ah, Amy. Cool-down, first.'

Nathan jogged past, forcing me to come to a stop when he planted himself in front of me.

'If you skip it, your muscles will make you pay later.' He smiled, eyes glinting in the café lights.

I scanned the sky behind him. The sun wasn't up yet, but dawn was well on its way.

'I need to head back, make sure Joey's up. He wants an hour in the pool this morning.'

And I didn't want to spend one second in the village square trying to force my body into unnatural contortions in front of a highly attractive personal trainer who knew what a wimp I was. I did a mental shudder at the image of me being the one to lose my balance, having to crawl home after Nathan put his back out trying to haul me up again.

Nathan shook his head, wincing. 'Please don't go home and collapse into a chair without stretching out properly. You can trust me on this.'

'I know how to cool-down. And I know it's important. I might not look like it, but *you* can trust *me* on this.' I started to back away, picking up my pace as I reached the pavement. 'See, I'm not even finished yet. There's no point cooling down if I'm still running, is there?'

'I'm going to ask Joey later!' Nathan yelled after me. 'Five minutes minimum or next time I'll follow you to make sure.'

That's a big assumption, talking about next time, I huffed as I raced against the sunrise.

A gust of autumn wind hit my face. It smelled of crunchy leaves and muddy fields. Dirt and pure, wild freedom mixed together.

Who was I kidding? The run was the easy bit – hanging out with real life people for an hour, chatting with them, smiling, learning from them and not a single terrible thing happening to ruin it? Each one of the emotions powering through my bloodstream like a herd of marathon runners – jubilation, joy, worry, amazement, grief, hope, bewilderment –

showed up my recent existence as the numbed-up, limping, nothing of a half-life it really was.

Let alone that according to my cheapo imitation Fitbit, I had a new personal best to beat.

I couldn't wait to Larkabout next time.

19

STOP BEING A LOSER PROGRAMME

DAY FORTY-NINE

Thursday evening, Joey had a one-to-one training session with Nathan in Brooksby pool. I'd skipped a run that morning (no, I hadn't bothered with a cool-down, and yes my muscles were indeed making me pay for it) and was antsy after a day slumped in front of my laptop proofreading health and safety policies for a homeless charity. I decided to stretch both my physical (better late than never, right?), and my courage muscles, with a night-time stroll to the leisure centre. Arriving there nine minutes later, after the fastest stroll known to woman, I sidled up to the huge window that ran alongside the swimming pool and peered in, confident I'd go unseen due to the terrible outside lighting this side of the car park.

I hovered there for a minute, my eyes fixed on the body carving through the near lane only a few metres away, tantalisingly close, while frustratingly hampered by the steamed-up glass. I so wanted to see him clearly, to be able to make out his expression, admire his technique, be the proud mum marvelling at this incredible person I had made. But even the blurred sight of the pool was enough to cause my heart to pitch and toss like a tiny boat on the ocean of anxiety. I couldn't hear the echoing splash, or smell the chlorine, but my senses burned with the memories. I knelt down, huddling on the hard concrete, gripped the icy window frame, sucked in some sharp October air and tried to console myself that, for this evening, the window was a new personal best.

A few minutes before the end of the session, Nathan and Joey suddenly appeared right in front of the glass. I shrank back into the shadows and watched as Nathan, his back to me, used arm movements to demonstrate what looked like Joey's turning technique. Joey nodded, both of them gesticulating now, as they discussed whatever the issue was. As they appeared to reach a decision, Nathan ruffled Joey's hair, a gesture I'd stopped doing about four inches ago, and they burst out laughing before jostling each other back towards the changing rooms.

I slowly heaved my aching muscles up to a standing position and stared into the now empty pool, ignoring the cold seeping in through my coat. I felt blindsided. Blindsided by a ruffle. A jostle. A shoulder slap. Knocked sideways by the realisation of a thousand, a million, tiny inter-actions missed. Had another man ever ruffled my son's hair? Play-wres-tled him to the ground? Thrown him over his shoulder and carried him up to bed? Errr... no.

Never.

I thought Cee-Cee and I had done okay. Joey was, as he said, awesome. Happy, more often than not. Well-rounded, with a healthy dollop of self-esteem – didn't that say it all? Since those first few dreadful months, I'd never felt the lack of a father figure in his life. But now, when he had the potential for one in the form of his actual father, did I have the right to deny him the chance? While he might not *need* one, wouldn't anyone benefit from having an extra person in their life to love them? Someone else to cheer them on and pass on their wisdom? Laugh with them and ruffle their hair, in a way that says, 'I'm with you, I'm here for you, I believe in you and, no matter what, I'm on your squad'?

'Mum?'

Oh, poop.

I hastily swiped away the tears that seemed to be collecting on my face and sprang away from the window, summoning up a smile.

'Were you watching?'

'I had a quick glance, but it was too steamy to see much. I only got here a short while ago. But from what I saw, you looked brilliant.'

'Why didn't you come in? You could have sat in the viewing area.'

'Yeah. Well. I've not been that close to a pool since I stopped compet-ing. One step at a time.'

We started walking, my thighs protesting at Joey's easy long stride.

'You never told me why you stopped.'

'It's complicated. There were lots of reasons.'

'And? I'm amazingly smart, remember? I think I can keep up.'

'I have no doubt about that.'

'Was it because you got too anxious to swim?'

'No. If anything, it was the opposite.' I thought about it for a few more paces, trying to get some sort of hold on the choices that were made. I looked at Joey, his white blond hair glinting in the street light, and allowed myself to remember the man who had given it to him but chose not to stay and discover that for himself. 'Okay, let's get home and we can talk about it then.'

So we did. Episode one of how I got from there to here...

* * *

'Mmm.' I snuggled deeper into Sean's chest, rubbing my face against his shirt. 'I wish I didn't have to go.'

He gently tugged at a strand of my hair. 'Then stay.'

'Don't tempt me.' I half-heartedly pulled myself upright on the sofa, making a show of scanning about for my shoes. 'If I miss training with only two weeks to go, Cee-Cee would probably handcuff me until we land in Athens.'

'No.' Sean spoke softly. 'I mean *stay*.'

Something about his voice made me look up. 'You mean... stay the night?'

His eyes shone as a smile began to creep across his mouth.

I stared harder. 'What? What did you mean then? *Longer?*'

The smile broke into a grin.

'It's going to be bad enough when I plod in fifth or something as it is, but I need to at least look like I've tried.'

Sean sat up quickly, taking both my hands in his. 'If you can't win a medal, why put yourself through that? The pressure of the build-up, the disappointment, having to answer stupid, obvious questions live on TV. Cee-Cee and your parents acting like you've let *them* down. Let the squad down. The whole country! This is your life. You're the one who's made all the sacrifices, put in all the work... just because you wanted it before, doesn't mean you have to go through with it now.'

'Ten years, Sean. I've got two weeks left. I can't throw all that away.'

'You were a kid then. You're a woman now. Dreams change. People grow up, want different things.' He stopped smiling. 'Don't you? Isn't *this* what you want?'

'Yes. But it can wait a few weeks, can't it? If I bomb the Games, then I'll have the perfect excuse to retire...'

'But why go at all? Right now, this situation is making no one happy. Going to Athens and coming in last won't make it any better.'

I had to admit there was some truth in his words. Although I still cared enough to feel riled at the suggestion I'd come last, it would be an understatement to say that all was not well behind the bright smiles and clichéd sound bites of Team Amelia. While doing my best to alleviate suspicion by turning up on time and nodding my head in the right places, my heart had left the pool and firmly set up home in Sean's grotty student digs. And this, along with the guilt, the embarrassment, of my slipping times, the arguments, the scrutiny, the strain of constantly lying, the pressure of supposedly carrying the hopes of a nation (who, looking back I can see mostly weren't all that bothered), feeling like a total fake: all this combined into a swirling cauldron of resentment and anger and hurt that only found peace inside this house, in this person's arms.

I was buckling. Drowning. Heading for certain doom.

Could I really just walk away? Just not *go?*

Okay, I'd given ten years to this. One goal, one hope, one dream. But did that mean I had to go through with it for the sake of it? For everyone else's sake?

It took another week of agonising. The lack of sleep and monstrous inner turmoil didn't exactly help my training times. One day, a local news reporter was waiting outside the pool for my comment on a local man who had got a life-size tattoo of me wearing an Olympic gold medal on his back. I blurted something about how amazing it was to have such fantastic support, then barely managed to make it back inside before dissolving into tears.

I was eighteen years old. I had no one to talk to about this except for a business student I'd known for three months, who was more than a little biased. While I dithered and panicked, ranted and cried, as everything I'd known, the person I thought I was, began to crumble, he planned a future for us that sounded idyllic.

In the end, I didn't walk away because of anything as selfish as my own happiness, or anything as pathetic as a teenage infatuation. It had become a choice between getting on a plane to Athens, or keeping my sanity. It was the only way to protect my mind and body from full-on implosion, to save my poor, tender self from a force I was not equipped to handle.

Would I have been okay, had I not got on that bus and met Sean? Would I have made it through all the pressure and the intense build-up intact, and brought home the gold? Or at least the pride in knowing I gave it my all? Would I have gone on to have a glittering career, smashed it at Beijing, even London? Ended up a sports pundit, appearing on *Strictly Come Dancing* or gone on to train the next British champion?

With the benefit of hindsight and maturity, I can safely say I haven't a clue.

What I do know is that I wouldn't have Joey.

So it's no contest, obviously.

* * *

I gave Joey the PG version: pressure got to me, lap times started to drop, fell in love, ran away.

Not my proudest moment, telling my son that I bunked off the Olympic Games at the last minute. Cee-Cee missed the plane waiting for me to show up. My parents reported me missing to the police. Thanks to all the recent cringey publicity stunts, the press went bonkers: had I been murdered by a rival, kidnapped for ransom money, held hostage by a crazed fan? One of my commercial sponsors offered a ridiculous reward for news of any sightings, adding to the frenzy.

Hiding away in Sean's family's holiday cottage in Devon, it was five days before I realised what was going on.

Unable to face calling Cee-Cee in my current state, I made a hideous, horrendous, heart-breaking phone call to my parents.

In response, my mum and dad, or should I say my manager and agent, wrote and published a book, filed a lawsuit and publicly disowned me, their daughter.

They never spoke to me again.

* * *

Joey stretched out on the living room carpet, taking a few moments to think about this before coming out with the inevitable question:

'So, this Sean is my dad?'

When this subject had come up in the past, I'd gone for a brief explanation about how his dad had needed to work in America when he was a baby and hadn't been able to come back yet as he'd been really busy and plane tickets were so expensive. Lame, yes, but the truth was even lamer. How do you tell a child that his father abandoned him, fleeing to another continent and choosing never to return?

'Yes.'

'You gave up swimming for him?'

'No... I think I would have had to do that anyway. Sean maybe sped up the process. Or helped me realise? He also gave me a safe place to go. My parents were really, really angry and I couldn't stay with them.'

'So, what happened? Why didn't you stay together?'

'We were very young. I'd never had a serious boyfriend before and kind of rushed into it because I was looking for an escape. Then, as time went on we just realised it wasn't going to work long-term.'

Sort of true. If *time* actually referred to *the moment I told him I was pregnant*. And, to be fair, him disappearing off to America a month later did help me realise that things weren't going to work.

'Has he never tried to contact us? Or did you stay in touch, but things fizzled out, like with Fenton's dad after he went to Scotland?'

Whew. Can this wait until morning?

I looked at my son, trying hard to balance a cool, casual mask on top of a lifetime's accumulation of desperate hope.

I guess that's a 'no' then.

Telling him that his father had got in touch with me a whole seven weeks earlier was one of the toughest things I've ever done.

Answering the stream of questions: why now, where did he live, why didn't he ever call or email or visit before, what was he like, was Joey like him, did he have any other children... that was even tougher.

Joey understood why I hadn't instantly responded to Sean's emails. I tried to keep my answers based in fact, brief and to the point, not filling in gaps with assumptions or attempted explanations. Even if that made half of my replies 'I don't know'. But if I didn't know, there was only one man who did.

So, the crunch question:

'Can I speak to him?'

'Look, this has been a huge amount of information to take in. Can we sleep on things, take a couple of days to process before we make any decisions?'

Joey propped himself up on his elbows, all the better to glare at me. 'How is there any way in this universe that I would come up with the decision *not* to contact my dad?'

I took a deep breath. 'Okay, but I want you to have considered some of the potential outcomes, so you're prepared.'

'Seriously? You don't think that in the past thirteen years I might have considered every single possible option, Mum? You think I might just have considered, in one of the endless, infinite variations I've imagined, the strong possibility that a man who hasn't got around to contacting his son in all this time might be a total loser? Or that he might make a great show of being the world's best dad and then disappear again as soon as he gets bored, or spooked about the responsibility, or a more important phone call comes along? Or he might try to buy my affection with stuff, or scam *me* for stuff because he's a waster? Or that it might hurt you for me to start a relationship with him? Or might end up really, really hurting me?' Joey fluffed up his hair, so like Sean's, with vigorous hands. My heart was being wrung inside out. 'I don't *need* a dad who's been nothing to me. But I deserve to decide if I want to know him. Considering he's not, like, a serial killer or a terrorist or anything.'

I blotted the tears currently streaming down my face. They were instantly replaced with another torrent.

'Can we take some time to at least think about how we do this?'

I offered Joey the soggy tissue, but he swiped at his eyes with his sleeve instead, before nodding.

How long could I eke out some time *for?* I wondered. *How long would it be fair to drag this out, given Joey's been waiting over a decade?*

'You'd best get to bed. School tomorrow.'

'Training tomorrow.' He gave me a pointed look as he clambered to his feet.

'Well, see how you feel.'

'How I feel has nothing to do with whether I train or not.'

I smiled feebly.

'I love you, Mum.' He bent down and kissed me on the head as he walked past, this beautiful, wise, compassionate man-in-the-making.

I hoped he was right, that whatever happened – with Sean, with the Gladiators trials, with the absence of Cee-Cee and my ongoing mental health battle – he would not be destroyed, or damaged. I hoped he wouldn't get hurt at all, but wasn't that every mother's wasted prayer?

20

STOP BEING A LOSER PROGRAMME
DAY FIFTY-TWO

Sunday morning, I jogged to the leisure centre to join the Larkabouts for the second time. I may have felt a twinge of disappointment that Nathan wasn't waiting for me at the end of the road, but it couldn't dent the joy of being greeted by the Larks as if I was an old friend. I powered through the warm-up with a not-altogether unpleasant combination of nerves and excitement.

Look! Me! OUT! Outside, with OTHER PEOPLE! Pretty much smiling, letting out a giggle every now and then and not all of them faked!

Inside my brain, I wrestled with the constant current of anxiety that could so easily take over my body, too: *Well yes, you might look normal now, but what happens if you start to panic? You can pretend your heart isn't racing and your lungs aren't wheezing like broken bagpipes, but I'm still here, waiting to strike, to find the worst possible moment to drag you to the ground.*

What if a car pulls out too fast, a nasty dog jumps out at you, someone asks you an awkward question about where you like to go or what you like to do or if you are the disgraced swimmer Amelia Piper or whether you just look like a sad, washed-up version of her...

But in another corner of my mind, I lunged and squatted and star-jumped with glee. Two months ago, the thought of jogging across a car park in the freezing dark, surrounded by laughing, chattering women, would have seemed beyond impossible. In this moment, being here, I had a victory. The reams of advice I'd read as part of the Programme research told me not to let fear about what might happen next ruin that.

During one of the walk-periods (most of us mixed up running and walking, with one notable exception being Marjory, who, at seventy-five, could have lapped us all without breaking into a sweat), I found myself alongside Orange Squash Mel. Or, rather, Cherry Coke Mel this morning, hair piled up like a pineapple.

'Bloomin' 'eck, I'm strugglin' today,' she wheezed. 'Got next to no sleep. Tate's got another one of his chest infections. Thought it might be a trip to A&E at one point, but he settled towards mornin'.'

'Maybe you should have stayed at home, got some rest.'

'You kidding?' She wiped her forehead with a mottled arm. 'Nights like that, I need this the most.' A few steps later, she added, 'But Gordon's with him, in case he takes another turn for the worse. If he's still right by the time we've finished, I'll stop and have a brew.'

Before we had to start running again, I just said it: 'Do your younger three ever see their dads?'

The split second it took Mel not to answer was enough to get my anxiety stirring.

I hastily tried to explain the intrusive question. 'I'm sorry, I know that's none of my business, it's just, well, Joey's dad has been in touch and I'm entering new territory here, trying to avoid any hidden mines. You don't have to answer, in fact, please forget I asked.'

Mel tossed her pineapple hairdo. 'Come off it, it's hardly gunna be a secret if my kids see their dads or not. And, to answer your perfectly acceptable question, Taylor sees hers once a fortnight, they go out for pizza or play footie or summat. The man who happened to provide the sperm for Tate, not a chance. Even without all the extra problems, he wasn't interested. And Tiff, well, she won't ever get to know who her dad is, thanks to my shockin' behaviour at the time. I couldn't pick him out in a line-up. And I've got to live with that, which is fair dos, but she has to an' all, which is disgusting, and a regret I'll carry until I'm gone.'

We picked up the pace a bit, in response to Nathan's hand gestures from a few hundred yards up the track.

'Well, you were in a tough place, and...'

'And I had three kids at home, who depended on me as their only parent, and had no right getting smashed out me face on vodka shots and going off with a strange man, riskin' a whole lot worse than a baby. I was in self-destruct mode.' She pumped a few more hefty strides. 'I had no right. But nothin' to be done except do me best today and tomorrer.'

Wise advice.

Of course, it would help to know what my best actually was.

'But you want to know about your lad. Whether he should meet his dad or not,' Mel said.

'He lives in America, so that's not currently an option. It's whether he contacts him at all that I'm freaking out about. And whether that might end up with him wanting to go and meet him. I mean, he's not dangerous or anything. But, well...'

'Far as I can tell, danger comes in a lotta different disguises. A word here, broken promise there. 'Specially hard when there's so much at stake, every bitty thing counts when you've all that catchin' up to do. You've done the hard work, now you're worried this fella gets to swanny in and suddenly his opinion'll count for everything, Joey'll be tryin' to impress, prove his dad wrong for ignoring him all them years. Dad'll be offering the moon, no matter if he can follow through or not. And where does that leave you? The boring, always there, rule-enforcing, reality-checking, taken-for-granted, must-be-partly-to-blame-for-all-the-years-of-absence, mum!' Another few huffs and puffs. 'Well, listen to me, bletherin' on, it's your lad, your ex-fella, what do I know?'

Um, everything, it would seem?

Nathan was waiting for us around the next bend, jogging on the spot, his sleeveless T-shirt revealing rock-solid arms that almost succeeded in distracting me from fretting about the subject in hand.

'If you can make conversation, you aren't pushing hard enough. Save the gabbing for the Cup and Saucer, and get those legs moving.' He trotted backwards as he spoke, the flash of a grin as he turned to sprint back up the hill lessening the telling-off.

'I can think of worse incentives to get me up this mountain,' Mel sighed, as she made a token effort to increase her speed, for about six steps. 'Like a greyhound after a rabbit, following that fine specimen. Now, what was we talking about? Oh yeah, Joey's dad. Well, I've said all I'll say, except this: you've spent thirteen years loving that boy, helping shape him into best he can be. Nurturin' him, body, mind and soul. All that input, that's what'll last when the whizz-bang of speakin' to his dad has fizzled out. This is a scratch he has to itch, a missing piece needs fill-in', and who knows, with the grace of God, it might end up brilliant – I'm all the proof you need, people can change for the better – but if not, he's a good lad, mostly thanks to you, and he knows that.'

'Thanks, Mel.'

It's quite a challenge, running with your nose blocked with snotty tears, and a much shorter woman's arm gripping your waist. Timewise, it was not my best run. But it was absolutely my favourite.

* * *

'Coming in?' Dani asked, gesturing to the café with her neat afro as Mel and I reached the gaggle of runners already waiting outside the door.

'Um, not today. Joey will be up for training soon, he'll be wondering where I am.'

'Send him a text then,' Bronwyn chirped, head between her impossibly long legs.

A faint sheen of watery blue pushed at the darkness above the buildings surrounding the square. My anxiety peered out at the increasing visibility, the lessening shadows, revealing the vast, unpredictable, complicated world stretching out with a squillion terrifying possibilities.

'Maybe next time,' I managed to squeak out between chattering teeth.

Yeah, or maybe in the dead of winter, when I'll have time to knock back a cup of tea before the sun comes up.

Quickly turning to go, I saw the last woman home trudging towards the square, Nathan alongside her.

'Come off it, Audrey!' I heard Selena screech behind me. 'Have some dignity! At least pretend like you have some!'

Audrey continued walking at the exact same pace, head down, shoulders slumped, her feet scraping along the pavement with each step.

'Let her be, Selena,' someone said. 'Nathan knows what he's doing.'

'Not enough for her to have lost any weight in the past four months,' Selena snapped. 'Not enough for her blood pressure to drop, or her blood sugars to get out of the screaming danger zone. Not enough for her to be able to fit...'

Thankfully, Selena's voice disappeared, presumably due to someone shoving her inside the café before her daughter came within earshot. I wondered if Audrey would buy a massive, fat, squishy cake and eat it one deliberate mouthful at a time while Selena tried not to choke on her hot water and lemon.

Part of me hoped she did. The other part felt sad that Audrey allowed herself to be dragged along with the Larkabouts at all. Then I watched Nathan, his slow pace matching hers as he made sure all his team were home safe, and I thought that maybe, two hours a week spent with non-judgemental, uncritical, respectful people who put it all out there, in every sense of the word, made the hour of hell worth it.

Maybe Audrey was the one doing the dragging, because she hoped it might end up changing Selena. In two sessions of the Larkabouts, I already suspected that the work being done here was as much to do with the inside as the outside. Which suited me just fine.

I allowed myself one glimpse back at the warm lights of the Cup and Saucer, nestled between the dark frontage of the shops either side. Saw the silhouette of an arm gesturing madly, heard a hint of raucous laughter in the brief second Audrey opened the door to enter. One day, I would sit and drink tea, eat a wholemeal blueberry muffin or an egg on rye toast. Gossip and joke and maybe even tell a story or two. The wide-open space would be an invitation, not a torment. The world wouldn't tip and sway and there would be no clanging in my ears or erratic thumping in my chest. I would dig a deep, dark grave for my anxiety and bury her there, along with my shame and my guilt and the wasted, wretched years that these three tyrants have ruled over me.

But first, home, a shower and a conversation with my son.

'Amy!' Nathan called across the square, jerking me out of my contemplation. 'Hang on a minute.'

I pointed at the hint of sunrise on the horizon, not bothering to turn around. 'No time.'

I wasn't surprised when he caught up with me. 'If you want to stay for a drink, I could walk you home afterwards.'

'I think I'll pass on you somehow manhandling my sweat-drenched, retching, panic-ridden jelly of a person home in broad daylight on a Sunday morning, thanks.'

His eyes grew startled. 'Okay. Fair enough.'

At some point, we'd stopped walking. Nathan appeared to have been frozen by the image of me as a retching jelly. My anxiety snickered in the background. I really had to get home. 'Was there something else?'

'Oh! Um, yes.' Nathan held up the gift bag in his hand, as if he'd forgotten it was there. 'I brought you this. Just in case.' He offered it to me, wincing a little bit, as if he was afraid I'd throw it back in his face. 'I'm an optimist.'

'I guess you have to be, in your line of work.' I took the bag. Was I supposed to open it now? While I was growing to genuinely like Nathan, and my heart had done a double flip in response to being given something, my churning stomach and trembling legs had other priorities right then. 'Thanks. I'll look at it when I get home.' The press of panic grew strong enough to override my attempt at a normal conversation, wrenching me across the road.

'After your cool-down!' Nathan shouted after me.

'Yes, yes, after my cool-down,' I muttered, hoping he wasn't stood there watching the sunrise bounce off my wobbling backside. Unsure about how much my impressive pace was due to the frantic need to get home safe, and how much my desire to see what he'd given me.

Cool-down be damned, I fell onto a kitchen chair and yanked open the gift bag, pulling out a sky-blue T-shirt. Size medium. I examined it for a moment, feeling a mix of I don't know what at the realisation that Nathan had thought about what size clothes I wore. He'd written on the bag's tag: *Welcome to the Larkabouts. Great to have you on the team.*

Well. Of course it wasn't a personal gift, a ha ha! Ha ha ha! Nathan was my son's coach, sort of my coach now. That would be utterly unprofessional. AND TOTALLY NEVER GOING TO HAPPEN ANYWAY, I reminded myself, catching sight of my drooping reflection when stepping into the shower. Ugh. Please. Nathan spends all day with women who have self-respect. And confidence. And... *perk.*

Get over this stupid attraction to Nathan, I ordered my mind, body and emotions, trying to scrub off the growing crush along with the morning's mud and grime. Being starved of human connection meant I had homed in like a traction beam on the nearest male. Lots of Larks flirted with Nathan, it was natural to be attracted to an attractive man. But those women had other lives going on, maybe boyfriends or husbands or wives. For them, it was a silly bit of fun. I added a new task to the Programme:

Talk to more human beings. Male ones, in particular.

Who knows, once I was well again, I might even end up genuinely connecting with one of them.

What I hadn't anticipated, and should have been more prepared for, was the next available handsome man I spoke to being the ex-lover, first-lover, heart-breaker, life-ruiner, father of my child.

A sure-fire guarantee to end in trouble.

But in the meantime, I had a whole lot of blubbing to be getting on with in the shower about that T-shirt. Putting the giver of the item to one side for a moment (harder than it should have been), I had a *team shirt*. I was part of a team. For better or worse, in fitness and in health, for fitter for poorer... I belonged to a squad again. I dried off, buried my head in the shirt and wept some more, finally able to acknowledge another layer of the harrowing loneliness that had scraped against my heart like sand-paper for the past thirteen years.

I wasn't going to mess it up this time.

I hoped.

* * *

Later that day, once he'd dissected his training, spent two hours in mortal combat with his friends on the Xbox, eaten his own body weight in cereal plus lunch and dinner, Joey came to find me. I was lying on the sofa, pretending to read while ignoring my muscles wailing and thinking black thoughts about cool-downs and stretches.

'Can we talk about me contacting my dad yet?'

I tried to sit up, instantly regretted it, lay back down again. Joey waited patiently for me to stop yelping.

'Maybe we should start with me emailing him, work up to a phone call. Take it steady,' I suggested.

'Why? You sending messages isn't going to change who he is, or what he wants. Why string this out any longer? I really want to talk to him.'

I tried to think of a decent reason for waiting, other than everything else was changing, shifting under our feet, and I needed more time, more chance to get my head straight, get strong enough to deal with speaking to Sean again... tried to think of a reason that didn't revolve around me, and actually put my son's needs first. I came up with this stunner:

'I just need a bit more time, Joey.'

'Time to do what? Freak out? Change your mind? Watch me suffer?'

I whipped myself upright, then. 'That is not fair. Taking a week or so to adjust to this, me making some initial contact can't do any harm. If he's serious about forming a relationship with you, he'll wait.'

'Oh, so that's it? You're hoping he'll give up and move on to something else if you can put this off long enough? Maybe one of his other abandoned kids, which we don't even know if he has because you won't let me talk to him.'

'No! I just don't want you to be disappointed. We don't know what he wants yet.'

'Maybe he doesn't know what he wants! Maybe we don't have to have everything for the next twenty years figured out, either! We aren't discussing where I'm going to spend Christmas, or whether I go there for my summer holiday! It's one email! And why does what he wants decide what happens anyway?'

I took a deep breath. Tried not to clutch at my hair. *Christmas!* 'I would feel much better once I've spoken to him first about his intentions, what's made him get in touch now. Then, depending on his reply, we'll make a decision about the next step.'

'You can't do this!' Joey was shouting now. It was the first time he'd yelled at me since his voice had broken, and given the subject matter, it rattled me how much he sounded like his father. 'He's *my* dad. You have no right to stop me contacting him! I'm not a little kid.'

'I'm not going to.' I tried to keep calm but had to raise my voice to be heard above his yelling. 'I just want to wait a bit, that's all.'

'Well, screw what you want!' he threw back at me. 'This isn't about you for once.'

'Joey, I know that.' I stood up, reaching out to take his arm, but he jerked it away, face twisted with fury.

'You're jealous. Just like with Cee-Cee. You want me all to yourself because you have no one else. However bad my dad is, I bet he's not a screwed-up, selfish bitch.'

While I stood there, reeling as if my own son had punched me in the face, which honestly would have been preferable, Joey grabbed his ruck-sack and stormed out of the house into the frosted sunshine, where he knew his screwed-up mother couldn't follow him.

* * *

Joey hadn't come home by dusk. The clocks had moved back an hour that morning, and it was dark enough by five-thirty for me to stop pacing up and down the living room, shrug on my trainers and head out.

The leisure centre was open for a public swim, and it was easy to spot the extra-fast blur of boy streaking through the water on the far side. I leaned my forehead against the glass in weak relief. Perhaps I knew my son better than Cee-Cee thought. Or, at least, I knew the one place I'd have headed at thirteen under similar circumstances. Any circumstances.

I also knew me finding the guts and gumption to wrestle my way inside and interrupt him wouldn't help. I found a bench to huddle on, pulled the old woolly hat I'd dug out from the back of my chest of drawers down further over my forehead and prepared to sit it out. The pool closed at seven, so I knew I wouldn't freeze to death.

The cars dotted around the car park gradually disappeared as a group of older men carrying squash rackets, then gym users and most of the swimmers trickled out. One car stayed in the far corner. The shadow behind the wheel was clearly waiting for someone. Probably their kids using the pool, or maybe a staff member. From the lights clicking off around the building, it appeared the centre was shutting down for the night.

Seven came and went. A family of three children and their dad left on foot, hair dripping. Seven-thirty. Hands and feet numb with cold, I prowled up and down. The car was still here, so someone else mustn't have left yet. I wondered again about trying to go inside. Changed my mind. Changed it back again. And then, an agonising length of time later, Joey appeared at the main entrance, together with a young guy wearing the centre uniform. I shrank back into the shadows while the guy locked up, unsure what to do next but sure that it didn't include approaching Joey while he was with someone else.

Heart thumping, I waited while the staff member wheeled a bike out of the communal rack and cycled off. Joey adjusted his rucksack and turned to where I had so cleverly concealed myself beside a metal tool shed.

'Are you walking back?' he asked, voice subdued.

'Yeah.'

'Sorry I called you a bitch.' Not screwed-up, or selfish.

'Thank you. I'm sorry I've handled everything so badly. I'm sorry that I allowed my issues to make me act selfishly.'

He nodded, once, in acknowledgement, and turned for home, hands in his pockets, eyes straight ahead, mouth set.

I felt so angry with Sean Mansfield I could have swum to America and strangled him.

Most of all, of course, I just felt angry at myself.

And with all that anger, it was only the next day, when we got another text alert about the creepy black car creeping about near school that I remembered the car at the leisure centre car park. Waiting for, it turned out, nobody.

I shook off a prickle of unease. There were a dozen, perfectly plausible explanations for someone to be sat in the dark in a village leisure centre car park for over an hour. Like, maybe a man was waiting for his secret lover. Or had been kicked out of the house when his wife discovered the secret lover, and he didn't know where else to go. Maybe he had a nasty wife and a gang of uncontrollable children and he pretended to go swimming every week even though he couldn't actually swim, just to get a couple of hours' peace and quiet, finding sitting alone in a cold car park preferable to being in his own house.

Maybe.

Maybe I would start meeting Joey from training more often.

21

STOP BEING A LOSER PROGRAMME

DAY FIFTY-EIGHT

I had never been so aware of my feet as during these past few weeks. So many things I had forgotten, tiny things, everyday nothings to the millions of people who open their front door, stride out and go somewhere without thinking twice about it every single day.

Shoes, for starters. I hadn't worn anything sturdier than slipper socks for two years until that first evening under the stars. The flip-flops, trainers and work pumps felt like long-lost friends as I dusted them off, tested them out, tried to get used to them again.

I stepped in a puddle early one morning, up to my ankle in freezing water. Oh the thrill of squelching along, toes tingling, sock sopping, mud-spattered trainer well and truly out of retirement.

And the ache! From where overgrown nails pressed against the edge of my trainer, through soles, arches and heel, right up into the ankle. My throbbing, attention-demanding, hard days' graft, worn-out muscles and tired bones gloriously ached.

I soaked them in long, hot baths, tears plopping onto the bubbles. The clamour from the physical feelings were continuing to wake up deeper – soul-deep – feelings kept carefully dormant for years. They stirred and stretched: thick, black grief rose alongside disappointment. Curiosity brought with it joy. *Joy.* Hope's sister. The antidote to despair. It seemed these feelings were a package deal: fear and loss, wonder and anticipation. There were so many of them, the only way to make room for them all was to let some out: to cry and wail, laugh and sing.

I stored them up on my morning runs, my occasional night-time walks, and once Joey left for school each morning, I would let the feelings come, embrace the agony and the exhilaration as they swirled and ripped right through my heart and soul. To feel was to be alive.

I was living once more. Not a measly portion of me, a skin-deep, just-about-enough-to-survive part of me. Every blood vessel, tendon and cell hummed with life.

And, oh, I would feel it all.

* * *

I was now running every Wednesday and Sunday, and walking Joey home from training four weekday evenings. Each foray out was a new adventure. Although, like any real adventure, still scary and daunting and sheer hard work a lot of the time. I saw a fox, one evening. It stood and watched me from the opposite pavement, eyes glowing in the reflection of the street light.

As the nights grew longer, I started setting off a little earlier, walking different, longer routes. One evening, I made an extra detour to post a letter. Another day, I braved the local greengrocers, meeting Joey with a paper bag full of plums I had chosen myself, gently squeezing each fruit to check its ripeness, just because I could.

On a particularly bold Saturday evening, Joey and I walked to the square to get fish and chips for tea. We hadn't talked about Sean again, but I knew it wouldn't be long before Joey decided he'd been patient enough and a decision would have to be made. Until then, I was enjoying some uncomplicated mother and son time. This was a dream come true for me, heading out together to do something normal like actually taking away our takeaway, instead of having someone else deliver it. I squeezed my hands, stuffed deep inside my pockets, with glee.

'He was, like, a giant, Mum,' Joey marvelled as we crunched through the frost. 'Taller than Nathan. And *built*. I was faster, but his turns were unbelievable.'

'You don't sound massively disappointed.' A new competitor had pipped Joey in one of the races at a regional swim meet.

'I have graciously conceded defeat to a superior athlete.' He glanced at me. 'This once. Next time he'll be choking on my backsplash.'

'That's a solid attitude for someone who just lost for the first time all year.'

'Yeah, well, it's like that part in the film where the hero gets beaten by a stronger, fitter enemy. He might mooch about for a bit, but then he gets his head back in the game, decides he's got to... Hang on, is that Cee-Cee?'

Up ahead, crossing the square, an old woman shuffled through the decaying remains of autumn leaves. Before I could react, Joey had sprinted over and skidded right in front of her.

'Hey, Cee-Cee,' he beamed.

'Joey.' She nodded, stiffly.

'How's it going?'

'Fine.' Woah. She did not look fine. Even in the dark, I could see the bitter lines etched across her face. 'Raced today?'

'Yeah,' Joey was still smiling. 'I came second in the backstroke.'

If possible, Cee-Cee's frown sharpened even further.

'But it's cool, gives me more incentive to dig that bit deeper next time.'

Cee-Cee took a long moment to silently express what she thought about that lackadaisical attitude. The eyebrows said it all. 'And your mother?'

Joey pointed me out, foiling my attempt at passing for a new Brooksby Square art installation. 'Woman frozen in guilty horror', it would have been called.

Cee-Cee's face flinched, the equivalent of anyone else fainting with shock. 'Right. Well. I won't keep you. Nice to see you, Joey.' She paused, managed a strangled, 'Amelia,' then shuffled off, considerably faster than before.

'That was a bit weird.' Joey bounded back up to me, where I was still imitating the frozen woman. 'Did she seem different to you?'

I pressed one hand against my heart, as if that might get it back under control, and sucked in a slow, deep breath.

'I mean, not old exactly. Like she'd sprung a puncture and the air was slowly leaking out. Do you think she's okay?' he asked.

Another long, slow breath. 'I'm sure she will be.'

But I wasn't at all sure. I also wasn't sure that it was not my problem. Should I go after her? Call her up and invite her round for tea? Give it one more chance? The thought of letting Cee-Cee back into our lives still filled me with dread. I knew I wasn't strong enough, still had too many difficult days to resist relinquishing control again and slipping straight back into our old pattern. But was it right to sacrifice the woman who had saved me, saved Joey, for my own freedom?

'Let's get food, Mum. I'm starving.' Joey tugged on my arm, snapping me out of my thoughts and reminding me of one thing I did know: I had to get well, for Joey's sake as much as my own, and in order to do that I had to put my needs first for now. At the moment, the Programme was working – I was here, after all, in the village square on a Saturday evening, and Cee-Cee would respect that I couldn't risk messing that up.

I followed my son into the batter-filled warmth of the chip shop, sucking in a delicious lungful of salt and vinegar as the door jingled shut behind us.

'All right?' the woman behind the counter said. Kelly, her name was, or Kayleigh. Something like that. Her daughter had been in Joey's class right through primary school. 'Ain't seen you in a good while. 'Ow you keepin'?'

'Good, thanks. How are you? How's Lucy getting on?'

A three-minute chat with Kelly (Kathy?). Handing over the money myself. Watching Joey blush when Lucy appeared.

I was keepin' good.

I couldn't contact Cee-Cee. Not yet.

22

STOP BEING A LOSER PROGRAMME

DAY FIFTY-NINE

Cee-Cee was still shuffling about in my head the next morning. I trundled along near the back of the Larkabouts flock, trying to ignore Nathan's concerned glances.

So, when Dani made her usual invite to stay and have a drink in the Cup and Saucer, safe in the knowledge that dawn was a good hour away, I overruled my needling anxiety and said yes.

The fear was there, even as I ordered coffee and a cranberry granola square and found a seat with a decent escape route to the door. Chuntering in the background as Mel worried about Jordan's new girlfriend ('she's all about herself, that one, Jord should know better') and Dani showed off the photos of her niece's Nigerian-style wedding (five hundred guests, and a whole lot of party), I did my best to ignore it as Selena loudly berated Audrey.

'Sprinkling a few berries on the top doesn't magically dissolve all the fat and sugar,' she sneered. 'It's like you *want* to hear Dr Cooley tell you the prediabetic is no longer pre.'

Audrey carefully cut her waffles into twelve little squares, then deliberately proceeded to eat, seemingly deaf to Selena's tuts and disgusted sips of beetroot coffee.

'Looks great,' I said, quietly. 'I've not had waffles in ages.'

Audrey swivelled her eyes in my direction, briefly, before repositioning her plate a couple of inches away from me.

Right. Okay...

Thoroughly rebuffed, I nervously looked to Mel on the opposite side of me, hoping to slide back into her conversation, but she was already standing up to go.

'Gotta get back to the rabble.' Mel jammed on a turquoise bobble hat, stuffing her strawberry milkshake ponytail inside. 'See ya later, everyone!'

I briefly debated getting up and joining Dani, now showing the photos to a different table, but before I could decide whether to leave Audrey alone with her waffles (despite that appearing to be her preferred seating arrangement, it would still seem rude to everyone else), Dani slid her phone back in her pocket and also made to leave.

'Sorry, I have to run, too. Four incredibly brave young women are counting on me sending a particularly nasty piece of work to prison this week. I need time to perfect my killer lines.' She blew us all a kiss and was off.

Great. I hunched awkwardly in the chair as Audrey worked on her second waffle. The other table laughed riotously as Bronwyn told a joke about some new guy she was seeing. I eyed the escape route, desperate to ditch the rest of my granola square and make a run for it.

But, then, if I left now, would I ever dare come back? My heart began to speed up, the all too familiar dizziness tossing and tumbling behind my eyes.

Stuff it, my mouth was too dry to eat the stupid square anyway.

I jerked back my chair with a screech, tried to find enough air to at least say goodbye to Audrey, hoping I could slip past the others without them noticing. Rallied the exhausted muscles in my legs. Closed my eyes, started counting to ten. Got to about six and then forgot what came next.

'Hey,' a soft voice said, from somewhere close by. 'Aren't you going to finish that granola?'

I opened my eyes. Nathan was in Mel's vacated seat. He gestured towards the plate with his chin.

'It's important to refuel after pushing your muscles so hard.'

Unable to speak, let alone find the coordination to pick up a piece of crumbling grains and berries, I simply stared back at him, aware my eyes were probably bugging half out of my head.

'You're doing great,' he murmured. 'Just keep breathing, nice and slowly. Take your time.'

Easier said than done.

I tried to unscramble my brain and catch hold of one of the techniques that had been helping me so much lately. Breathe, yes. What else? Find a focus. Yes. I could do that. Find something to focus on. Come on, Amy, there must be something here. Concentrate.

'So, Audrey, are you still in the bridge club?' Nathan turned away, breaking the eye contact which had been keeping me tethered. I felt another flood of panic rolling up, but before it overwhelmed me, a warm hand gently prised mine off the arm of the chair and clasped it.

For a few moments, as my neurons righted themselves and my heart skittered back to a speed in the range of non-critical, I could focus on nothing else.

Nathan supplemented Audrey's one-word answers about her bridge club with pleasant conversation and thoughtful questions for another few minutes, until Selena barked something about a microneedling regeneration appointment for her upper arms and they both left.

Once Audrey had trudged out the door, Nathan gave my hand a soft squeeze, then dropped it.

'Better?'

Um...

'You said it helped, having a hand to hold.'

Err...

'That time when you needed to get to the pharmacy.' His eyes grew wide with concern. 'You said holding a hand helped. When we were crossing the road... I saw you starting to panic and I thought it would help. I mean, you were, weren't you? Beginning to have a panic attack? Not that I hope you were, except, well, if you weren't, and I just grabbed you for no reason in the middle of a café, then, honestly, I'm really sorry. And next time, please just pull your hand away, and tell me to get lost, or, I don't know, slap me or something.' His face creased up into utter horror and dismay.

Phew, Amy, get some air moving back through those vocal cords at some point today, can't you?

'Yes.' I squeezed my own hands together now, hoping it might help.

Stared at the remaining chunk of granola, a much safer and altogether more appropriate focal point. 'It helped. Thank you.'

If by *helped*, I meant *was the loveliest thing that has happened to me in forever*. Or, perhaps, *felt like I had found my true source of gravity, and all my haphazard, helpless, swirling through time and space could rest for a moment, that moment, tucked inside your hand.*

'Granola,' Nathan said, thankfully intercepting the runaway thought-train.

'What?' Was this an impromptu word-association game? 'Should I say something like "Bird seed" or "Veganuary"?'

'You can say what you like, as long as you finish your post-run breakfast.'

'Oh, for goodness' sake. Do you ever switch off?'

He looked at me, as if baffled.

'Kick back and relax, break a few rules, do something naughty but nice? Indulge in a guilty pleasure?'

'I don't see what breaking rules has to do with being relaxed.'

'That depends on what kind of rules you follow.' I deliberately pushed away my plate, signalling that, no, I was not going to finish my post-run, refuelling, muscle-regenerating breakfast.

'I believe in the rules I follow. Adhering to them means I can relax, happy I've made healthy, positive choices.'

'I disagree. Following some rigid system of rules all the time, with complete inflexibility, might ensure physical benefits, but it isn't good for you mentally or emotionally.'

And I speak from experience, ladies and gentlemen.

Nathan frowned, sitting back as the café owner brought him a plate of two eggs on thick-cut rye bread. 'The usual, mate. Sorry about the wait.'

'Cheers, Chris.'

I don't know where it came from, quite possibly some residual ooomf from the hand-holding, but I caught Chris before he went back to the counter, 'Excuse me?'

'Yes?' He glanced at my plate. 'Is the granola okay? It was fresh this morning.'

Sheesh, I was never going to order granola again.

'Does Nathan order the same food every time he comes in?'

Chris grinned. 'He doesn't need to order, we just plate it up, soon as he's finished his pint of water. Breakfast: two eggs on rye. Lunch: chicken and avo salad. If he pops in for a client meeting, green tea and a gluten-free, dairy-free, processed-sugar-free date and banana bite.'

'Thank you.' I turned back to Nathan as Chris wandered off again, my eyebrows raised in vindication.

'I don't see your point. What's wrong with eating well?' He shuffled in his seat. He saw my point.

'Eating well, or eating to an exact, rigid, robotic, Mr Boring spread-sheet of no fun?'

'You're calling me boring now? You, with the jam-packed, thrills and spills, whirlwind of a social calendar?'

If Cee-Cee had made that comment, I might have jabbed my teaspoon up her nostril. Instead, I had to fight back a smile. It had been a long time since anyone except Joey had teased me. At some point, Nathan had strolled on into the 'knows me well enough to banter' zone. I liked him being there more than was sensible.

'At least I'm working on my issues.' I pointed at him, accusingly. 'What do you eat if you're at a party? Or a wedding?' Dani could prob-ably have made use of my cross-examination skills in court today. 'Do you eat chicken salad for Christmas dinner, while lecturing your family about refuelling and post-present-unwrapping cool-downs?'

He smiled at that. Then frowned again.

'Seriously, do you ever eat something just because it tastes good, or you feel like it, or it brings back a lovely memory, or is a fun way to mark a special moment?'

'I think what I eat does taste good.'

'What did you eat on your last birthday?'

'I can't remember.' Nathan shovelled in a forkful of eggs, stuffing his mouth too full to speak.

'Either you ate what's on the spreadsheet of boringness, or you didn't. Don't pretend you can't remember whether you sometimes commit food crime or not.'

He chose not to answer that.

Intrigued, I waited until he'd swallowed the last mouthful, then pushed a little further. 'When was the last time you did something spon-taneous?'

Nathan sat back, eying me suspiciously. 'Is this interrogation some kind of revenge for that second hill?'

I pressed one hand to my chest, as if shocked and affronted. 'Interrogation? I'm just making conversation, trying to pick up some life hacks from my coach. Now I'm wondering why that question makes you feel uncomfortable.'

'It doesn't.' He shifted, uncomfortably. 'I like order and routine and following a system. I'm cool with that, and if the situation called for it, I could change my plans.'

Chris came back at that point to clear our plates. 'Nathan, change plans? Maybe if there was a meteor strike. Or a terrorist attack. If he broke both his legs halfway through a training session, he'd drag himself through the rest on his backside.'

'I can change my plans,' Nathan said, his face turning an interesting shade of pink.

'That's like your mate Harry saying he can go a whole night out without a drink, he just can't provide a single example.' Chris winked at me and started to walk away. Then he froze, and backed up again. 'Hang on, I just remembered. A few weeks back. The match. We thought you must have been hit by a bus or something.'

'Okay, thanks, Chris,' Nathan interrupted. 'I think you've got a customer waiting.'

Chris glanced back. 'There's no one there, mate.' He turned to me. 'We were seriously worried. Nathan never misses a warm-up. He's never even been late. To bunk off the first match of the season? Against our arch-rivals, Houghton? Couldn't believe it. We lost, as well. The lads've changed his shirt name to No Show.'

'Bye then, Chris. Thanks for breakfast.' Nathan did not sound very thankful.

'And he lost the captaincy. Gotta have a damn good reason to decide you're going to change plans for the first time in your life under those circumstances.'

He whisked away before Nathan could say anything else.

'It's fine,' I said, wishing I'd never brought it up. 'I'm not going to pester you to tell me.'

Nathan huffed and shook his head, picking at an imaginary spot on the table. 'It's not a big deal.'

Hmmm. Sounded like it might be.

We left then, along with the rest of the Larks, who made me promise to join them another time. I jogged home through the mist, mercifully keeping the threat of sunrise from snapping at my heels.

And then, because I'm a nosy, emotionally stunted woman pretending she isn't growing increasingly and dangerously besotted with her running coach, I had a good rummage around on the internet for Brooksby FC.

According to the list of team fixtures and match reports, the (ex)captain missed the first game of the season, against their biggest rivals Houghton, on Wednesday, 19 September.

September 19 was the day Joey came home from school with tonsillitis.

The day a strange man found me collapsed in a heap in the street, helped me get to the pharmacy, waited outside after I'd rudely rejected his offer to walk me home and made sure I got back safely anyway.

Nathan, the responsible, reliable man who never broke his rules had broken them for me.

Yep. Besotted.

23

STOP BEING A LOSER PROGRAMME

DAY SIXTY

Monday was 5 November. Bonfire Night. Gunpowder, treason and plot. Or, in my case, hot chocolate, warm hat and watching the Brooksby Grace Chapel firework display from the back garden. Joey brought me back a toffee apple – pretending to leave his friends early because of training the next morning, but in reality carrying another kitchen chair outside to join his mother.

'Looks better from out here than the upstairs window,' he pronounced, grinning at me from behind his scarf.

I breathed in a deliciously chilly lungful of smoke that had drifted over the fences, blended with the faint aroma of popcorn and hot dogs, and turned to gaze at my gorgeous son, cheeks rosy, eyes bright. 'It certainly does.'

'It's even better from the field. And a lot warmer if you get near the bonfire.'

Pink and green and blue rockets of light whizzed above our heads with a loud crackle.

'Maybe you'll come with me next year?'

I blinked, hard, and vainly tried to swallow the broken lump of love wedged in my throat. We watched another rapid succession of whooshing explosions.

'I don't think so.'

Joey tensed in his chair.

'Mum tags along with fourteen-year-old son and his friends at a bonfire display? I can find my own friends to hang out with, thank you very much.'

He let out a relieved laugh. 'Well, I thought it was only polite to ask.'

'Maybe we'll go on holiday or something together instead.'

There was silence for a few moments. When Joey replied, his voice was soft enough to crack my heart. 'That would be awesome.'

It truly would.

24

STOP BEING A LOSER PROGRAMME

DAY SIXTY-TWO

The car was there again, in the leisure centre car park. Crouching in the furthest space from the building, half-hidden in the shadows. I'd walked over to meet Joey after his early morning swim, another success to tick off on the Programme, but hadn't managed to cajole myself as far as the swimming pool window this time, sticking to the bench instead. I checked the time – nearly eight. Late enough to message Lisa:

What make is the car hanging around school?

Black merc. That's why people noticed it. Think you've seen something?

I peered through the darkness. Quickly googled Mercedes, to double-check.

Leisure centre car park. Joey says it's been here a few times

Report it

I knew I should report it. The school had asked us to call the non-emergency police number. I thought about that while switching my gaze from the car to the leisure centre door and back again. Thought about the police arriving, asking me to wait. Imagined an interview, a methodical police officer going over things, one careful question at a time, as the strip of pinky-blue peeping over the horizon spread. Thought about how much I hated being this person, still so weak and messed up, as I turned and hurried home.

Once Joey had gone to school, I phoned the leisure centre and left an anonymous message. The guilt held me hostage in the house for the rest of the week. I scuttled between my desk and the duvet, my anxiety jeering in the background the whole time. My shame piled even higher. My self-loathing rose to lung-deep.

25

STOP BEING A LOSER PROGRAMME

DAY SIXTY-SIX

Sunday, I was jolted awake at eight-thirty by the doorbell. After a moment's consideration, I decided the best course of action was to bury my head under the pillow and go back to sleep.

The doorbell rang again, a few seconds later. Followed by a knock and, to my indignation, what sounded like a vigorous rattle of the handle. Huffing and chuntering, yet baffled enough to investigate, I pulled a sweatshirt on over my pyjamas and cautiously descended the stairs.

I saw a head-high blueberry cloud through the shadow of the glass, a much taller, darker blob beside it.

'Amy? You in?' Two hands poked the letter box open, and an upside-down mouth somehow managed to speak into the gap, less than a foot above the ground. 'It's Mel and Dani. From the Larks.'

Well, yes, I had figured that one out, thanks, Mel. Could I sneak back upstairs and pretend I was out? Ignore them, with a who cares if I'm in or not, it's eight-thirty on a Sunday morning and I'm having a lie-in for once...

Did I want to do that? The boulder of self-pity I was dragging around with me voted yes, make them go away. Why should I have to face strong warrior women who rocked at life, who met troubles and suffering and just waded right on through? I was a crappy mess, and I didn't need that being rubbed in my puffy face on my day off.

But before I had a chance to self-sabotage the situation, the front door popped open and Mel strode through.

'What?' I garbled.

'Amy! There you are.' Mel grinned at me from the bottom of my stairs. 'We weren't sure if that flashy car outside meant you had company. But seeing them pyjamas, I'm assuming it's a no. I'll put the kettle on, shall I?'

Excuse me?

They bustled down the tiny hall into the kitchen, Dani calling, 'Are you up to eggs? Or we've got raisin toast. I brought a selection of pastries too. Nathan said not to get granola, so it's all the unhealthy stuff.'

'I...'

'Goodness, it's nippy in here. I'll get the fire on.'

I rubbed the sleep from my eyes, tried to slap a bit of life back into my face and endeavoured to remember if this was actually my house.

Once I'd established that, yes, this was my home, and no, I hadn't invited Mel and or Dani into it, I forged confidently into the breach to get some answers.

'Nathan said you ain't been well. You're a single mum without a Gordon, or a Jordan, or a mum around,' Mel shrugged, spatula in hand, as if it was obvious. 'So, we stocked up at the Cup after running and 'ere we are.'

'Most people wait to be invited in.'

'Oh. Honey,' Dani laughed. 'We are not most people.'

'How did you open the door?'

Mel winked, giving the spatula a wave. 'We've been around, picked up some skills.'

So once again, Joey woke to find these self-appointed aunties in his kitchen, one of them cracking eggs, the other ironing school shirts, despite my protestations that, a) Joey could iron his own shirts and, b) I was fine and really didn't need their help.

'Joey should be saving his strength for the gala,' Dani tutted. 'And he will be exhausted when he comes home.'

'And, no offence, but you need someone's help. Might as well be ours,' Mel added, sliding an enormous omelette onto a plate for Joey. 'This kitchen looked worse than the inside of my wheelie bin when we got 'ere.'

I would have been offended at that, but after my three-day slob-fest, it was probably true. And I was simply too tired to bother feeling insulted.

'Right,' Mel said, once she'd seen Joey off, 'we can give yer bathroom a good going-over, change yer bedding and whatnot. Or, we can stick on a film, 'ave a good laugh, a good cry and eat the rest of them pastries. See if that 'as you a bit more like yerself.'

At that, I decided for us by immediately going for the good cry. Very good, in terms of number of tears, intensity of blubbering, volume of retching sobs and how much better I felt afterwards.

'I'm terrified this *is* myself,' I'd wheezed. 'I think I'm doing better. So much better. Like this is the new me. But then I act like an idiot and the old me comes back. What if the old me is the real me, and she'll always be there, just waiting to spring out again? I can't get rid of her, and I hate her wimping guts.'

Mel and Dani had no answers, no advice, no platitudes or reassurances that it would be okay. They knew as well as anyone that sometimes things were far from okay, and not every ending was a happy one. But they had love, and care and hugs and soft hands to stroke my hair, and somehow that felt even better than if they'd waved a magic wand and banished old Amy forever. I clung on to my friends' strength, their unspoken promise to keep turning up if they were worried about me, breaking in if necessary. And I found hope there. So I sucked up their kindness, and as I applied some of that kindness to myself, it shrivelled my self-hate and shooed away my shame.

Before Mel and Dani left, we watched six episodes in a row of a cheesy reality show where brides- and-grooms-to-be who'd all been through horrible life situations, like cancer or having their house burn to the ground, got an amazing wedding, along with extras like replacement houses thrown in.

Cue more blubbering. Times three.

I would need to go out and get more tissues.

Only I couldn't, because despite all the encouragement and support, despite my recommitment to getting back on the Programme, my determination to keep pushing forwards, to celebrate my progress so far, I was still trapped. My prison had expanded, yes. Considerably, compared to what it had been. But it was still infinitesimal compared to the great, big, wonderful world out there. I remained a hostage to the night.

Stepping out into the sunshine of a summer's day still seemed as impossible on day sixty-six of the Stop Being a Loser Programme as it had on day one. Cutting the ribbon in front of a crowd of people, inside the Amelia Piper swimming centre? Cheering at the side of the pool while Joey competed in the Gladiators trials? For a woman who couldn't even get to the corner shop to buy more tissues? Well, that made me need a tissue more than ever.

26

STOP BEING A LOSER PROGRAMME

DAY SIXTY-SEVEN

Early the next morning, I broke my pact with Joey and bullied my reluctant bones out the door for a solo run. Dani had offered to go with me, but I declined.

Stepping back out onto the front path was hard, but I breathed and focused and turned the volume on my running playlist up to max and I kept on going. I found my stride in amongst the pine trees at the top of the first hill, scampering alongside an early morning squirrel. Sucking in as much of the icy air as my lungs could manage while gasping for breath, I savoured the whip of the wind against my burning cheeks, imagined all the places it had blown through on its way here. Frozen fjords? Churning oceans, humpback whales cavorting below? Whizzing between mountains, ruffling the bracken as it sped past. Over moors and meadows, carrying eagles and sparrows, buffeting fishermen and farmers, foxes and field mice. And I was out here and a part of it. I celebrated the fresh air, the leaves tumbling past me, the muddy squelch of every joyous step. I relished muscles aching, feet pounding, chest heaving. A body flowing, a soul awakening, a heart thundering with life.

I slowed down to a walk at the end of my road, feeling deliciously spent and ready for a hot shower and a bowl of porridge before work. I nearly stopped when I saw the black car parked three doors down from my house. A Mercedes. There was a shadow in the driver's seat.

I ordered my stiff, stilted legs to keep moving. I didn't have to pass the car to get inside, but still got close enough to send my anxiety into hyperdrive. Stumbling down my path, I fell through the front door and somehow managed to close and lock it before collapsing onto the hall floor.

'Tough run, Mum?' Joey wandered into the kitchen doorway, bowl and spoon in hand, tiny dribble of milk running down his chin due to speaking through a mouthful of cereal.

'Eat at the table, please,' I wheezed back, lifting my cheek off the laminate. 'And great run, actually.' I could have mentioned the car to Joey, but if it was still here I knew he'd be outside, knocking on the driver's window while still chewing on his peanut butter clusters.

Despite the ridiculous rumours, at no point had the mysterious Mercedes driver of Brooksby done anything to harm anyone. Certainly nothing worth hiding in my house peeping through the blinds and panicking over.

What would a non-loser do? I asked myself.

I listened to my gala-winning son belting out an indistinguishable rock anthem from the bathroom, and added a new step to the Programme:

Next time I see the Mercedes, go and find out who it is.

27

STOP BEING A LOSER PROGRAMME

DAY SIXTY-EIGHT

There is a difference between brave and reckless, I chided, as I scribbled that new step out the following day.

I'd had another email. Not from Sean, but equal in its power to stir up nauseating memories.

The email was from a journalist, Moira Vanderbeek. She'd become aware of the Amelia Piper Swimming Centre and thought the public would be very interested to hear my story, finally revealing the truth about why I gave up competitive swimming, what happened next and how I'd rebuilt a new life for myself away from the spotlight.

My mind jumped back to an enquiry from a potential client a few days ago that suddenly went cold. My phone number was on the bottom of my work email signature. Surely it wouldn't be too hard for a journalist to find out where I lived.

If it wasn't too hard thirteen years ago, when I wasn't working for a company that handed out my details willy-nilly, and no one in the world save my boyfriend and his brother knew my temporary hideout, I was pretty sure that they could manage it now.

I wondered if Moira Vanderbeek drove a Mercedes.

I pondered whether she'd hang out in the local leisure centre car park hoping to catch the ex-world champion going for a swim, maybe get the zoom lens out and start snapping her cellulite. I considered whether she'd snooped about in the local swimming club circles until discovering that the best swimmer in the league, scouted by the Gladiators, who attended Brooksby Academy, happened to have the surname Piper.

At that point, I threw up, cleaned myself up, sent an email begging my boss to take my details off the company website and spent the rest of the morning wondering what the hell I was going to do.

My conclusion? I was going to keep pressing on, working harder, fighting through and putting one trembling foot in front of the other. I would keep on pounding my way up and down those glorious hills, keep breathing in the fresh, autumn air and not let any journalists, ancient ex-boyfriends or anyone else stop me. This time, it would be different.

* * *

After running away from my Olympic dream, I spent five blissful days in Sean's family summer home in Devon before the bubble burst. Living on cheese sandwiches, young lust and the sea breeze, we swam, slept, sunbathed and did a whole lot of other things beginning with s.

The mistake we made was venturing out into the local village for ice cream one afternoon, not for one second imagining the media circus currently spearheading the 'Search for Amelia', until I spied the headlines in the newspaper.

Sean bought six different papers and we scurried home, our 99s dripping onto the pages as reality sank in.

Calling my parents was the hardest thing I've ever done. I dialled the number on the cottage landline with trembling hands, my breath frozen in my chest, stammering so badly, I could barely get out an explanation. Their reaction didn't make things any better. 'What the hell are you going to do now? No one will ever trust you again. You'll be bankrupt by the time the sponsors' lawyers have finished with you.'

Yowch.

Their solution? Get a PR firm on the case, sell some story about an illness, or a mental breakdown, whatever, that wasn't important, get myself on the next plane to Athens, win the gold, all is forgiven, and there'll probably be a film deal in it for us to boot.

My stammering counter-offer of a sincere apology for all the time and trouble, a brief explanation of the reasons behind my disappearance, paying the sponsors what I owed them under the contract terms and leaving it at that did not go down well.

I hung up the phone while my mother was mid-screech, hands shaking so hard that I couldn't place it back in the receiver. Curling up in Sean's lap, I filled him in on what my parents had said, the weight of my actions starting to sink in.

Sean shook his head in disgust. 'What they really mean is what the hell are *they* going to do now. Did they even ask if you were okay, or if you needed any help? Did they stop screaming for one moment and actually listen to what you had to say?'

He was right. But they were still my parents, and I loved them, needed them, and prayed that they would forgive me. That is, until they called me selfish, self-obsessed and ungrateful on breakfast TV. After that, I turned off the television, hired Sean's brother to act as my solicitor and got a job working in the local café under a fake name.

Six days after my parents publicly disowned me, the paparazzi found us, and the nightmare siege began. When Sean's parents realised what was happening, they threw us out of the cottage. We holed up in an apartment in Exeter, but for days, every time I left the building I was followed, photographed, bombarded with questions, jostled and hassled and, on one occasion, knocked off the bike I was riding.

Already on the brink of a breakdown, utterly adrift in my isolation and despair, I retreated inside, hunkering down behind drawn curtains. My anxiety flourished, and my utter loathing and fear of journalists grew with it.

Which is why, right then, I would have preferred a crazed pervert to be lurking inside that car, rather than Moira Vanderbeek. I would not be returning her calls.

28

STOP BEING A LOSER PROGRAMME

DAY SIXTY-NINE

Wednesday, to avoid the whirlwind of my own thoughts sucking me into despair, I skidded through the frost to join the Larks again. Mel was at home with her daughter, Tiff, who'd broken her collarbone thanks to two older brothers, a chestnut tree and a game of dare.

Because the pavements were icy, Nathan insisted we stick to a brisk walk until we reached the more sheltered woods. This meant that for the first time I was able to keep up (just about) with Marjory, the oldest member of the group.

We chatted for a while about our respective families, my work as a bid writer and her former job as a PE teacher, making the most of having enough breath to make conversation.

And then Marjory sucked all the air out of my lungs with one horrifying question:

'Do I know you from somewhere? You look familiar.'

It took about ten paces before I could shut my anxiety up long enough to formulate a reply. It was a good one:

'Um. No.'

Marjory kept her eyes straight ahead, arms pumping. 'I don't mean from around here. Are you well known?'

C.R.A.P.

I stumbled on a non-icy patch of pavement, arms pinwheeling as erratically as my thoughts. For half a second, I contemplated allowing myself to smack face-first onto the asphalt in order to avoid answering, but Marjory's super-strong hand caught one elbow while her arm braced my back, righting me.

'Okay?' she asked, one eye narrowed.

'Yes, fine. Must have hit a patch of ice.'

The other eye joined it.

'Wow, Marjory you are impressively strong, as well as fast. How are you so crazy-fit?' I asked, as we approached the footpath leading into the woods.

'Well.' She bent down in one smooth motion to adjust her laces. 'I did run for England once or twice. And don't worry.' She straightened up again, leaning in close. 'I won't tell anyone.'

A wink, a knowing nod, and she left me standing there, stunned, in her dust.

* * *

Three miles, four buckets of sweat and an embarrassing fall on my backside later, I cradled a hot cup of tea with frozen fingers and tried to appear semi-normal, rather than a gibbering sack of flopping, floundering nerves.

To make matters worse, Mel had turned up, having left the kids with her care assistant Gordon. Of course, Mel being there in itself was fab, it was the flyer she'd brought along that was the problem.

And by problem, I mean, *reason why I wanted to sprint home, pack a bag, jump on the next flight to the middle of nowhere and never return.*

'We totally have to do this,' Mel said, voice loud enough to catch the attention of all three tables of Larks, the rest of the café patrons and probably Bronwyn, currently in New York with her new boyfriend.

'What do you think, Nathan?' Dani asked, waving the flyer in his direction. I'd deliberately sat as far away from him as possible, still feeling flustered about knowing he missed the match to help me, and more importantly how I was ever going to look at him again without blushing thanks to the feelings that accompanied this knowledge. Unfortunately, this meant sitting not only next to Audrey again, but Selena on the other side. Feeling trapped between a granite wall on one side and a pecking vulture on the other had not helped defrazzle my mood.

'Sounds like a great idea,' Nathan replied. 'Having something to aim for can increase cardiovascular capacity and mental resilience.'

'Hello, did you see the flyer? See that big word in orange letters across the top? That says FUN. Let me know if you need further explanation.'

Nathan shifted awkwardly. 'Yes, but I'm just saying, it can also be a great tool to build self-discipline.'

'Yeah? 'Ow about it can be a blummin' good laugh, and summat to talk about next time that snooty cow at playgroup goes on about how awful it must be to have a child like that, and 'ow tired and crappy I look.' Mel stopped and blew out a long breath. 'Sorry. Bad day all round yesterday. And I really missed me run.'

'Well, whatever the reason, I'm in,' Dani said, enveloping Mel in a slender-armed squeeze. 'There's nothing I love more than winning.'

'It's not all about winning,' Marjory said, winking at me.

'Speak for yourself,' Dani retorted. 'If I'm on your team for once, instead of running against you, I might actually stand a chance.'

'Winning? In a *triathlon*?' Selena let out a caustic cackle. 'You do realise that would mean us getting on a bike.' She glanced around, but no one was sharing in the joke. '*All* of us.'

'No, actually,' Mel said, speaking in a slow voice as if to one of her smaller children. 'If you put your bifocals on and bother to read the flyer—'

'Bifocals!' Selena choked on her radish smoothie. 'Hardly!'

'Whatever. It clearly says you can enter as many in your team as you want, but different people get to do different bits. So, people who are good at ridin' can do the cyclin' part. Some of us can run, and if any of us are good at swimmin', they can do the mile in the pool. It's five months away, yet. We've loads o' time to practise.'

'When is it?' Nathan asked.

'It's for the opening of that new fancy pool, in Greasby. Easter bank holiday Monday.'

'What do you think, Amy?' Dani, asked me.

Think? I couldn't breathe, let alone think.

'Mmm.' I tried to contort my lips into something not too far off a smile. Tried and failed, judging by the disconcertion on my clubmates' faces.

'Don't put yourself down, love,' Mel said, coming over to my table and patting me on the shoulder while simultaneously stealing the remains of my cinnamon whirl. 'You've come on great these past weeks. By Easter you'll be smashing it.'

Well, that was the plan.

But how could Amelia Piper chop the ribbon, or however these things worked these days, give the big speech, present the trophy, while Amy Piper slogged her way through a 5K run, or a 10K bike ride or – possibly worse – swam a mile in broad daylight, with a massive crowd of people – including Nathan AND Moira Vanderbeek – while wearing, most probably, because she'd appear even stranger otherwise, a swimming costume.

My anxiety was positively rapturous.

I made my excuses and bolted.

If I could move that fast on triathlon day, we might stand a chance at winning.

* * *

I was so blummin' fast that I was nearly home by the time Nathan caught up.

'Hey.'

'I think we've already spoken about the wisdom of sneaking up on women in the dark.' I slowed to a walk, too exhausted all round to keep running while Nathan tried to talk to me.

'It's barely dark, Amy. Hadn't you noticed?'

I glanced up at the clouds all around us, definitely more grey now than black. 'Yeah, well. I've got other stuff to worry about.'

'Will you let me help?'

I stopped walking.

'Why would you pick on me, out of all the Larks, to help? Audrey is way slower than me. I wasn't even in the slowest three this morning. By April I'll be able to hold my own without extra tuition for the out-of-shape, fat girl, thanks.'

Underneath his beanie, Nathan's gaze was steady. Authoritative.

Slightly intimidating, actually. 'I don't help Joey because he's the slowest. Or out of shape.' He shook his head, slightly, as if in disgust. 'And "fat girl"? Really? Like anyone in the Larks ever makes an issue about size.'

I crossed my arms, fat-shamed in a whole new way. 'So, why am I the one you chase down the street to offer help to?'

Even as I asked it, my heart was about to explode inside my chest, spattering idiotic, hopeless, fantastical feelings everywhere.

It's not that reason, Amy!

Nathan shrugged, opened his mouth and closed it again a couple of times. Kicked at a non-existent stone on the pavement. Looked up and about as if the encroaching dawn would supply the answer.

'Because I really want you to be at that triathlon.'

Because...

'Because it would seriously bother me to think any of the women I coach and train had to miss out on a club event because they couldn't face it. It bothers me that you can't relax at the café because you're so worried about missing the sunrise. That you can't get your son medicine without having a panic attack in the street.'

'And I'm working on those things. Making really good progress.'

'So, with Joey's trials, what are you thinking about? How you want him to do well, how you'll be there to offer him your one hundred per cent support? Your... issue...'

'My mental illness,' I ground out, like dirt under my shoe.

'Your illness means that a really big moment in Joey's life isn't about him but becomes about you.'

'Joey knows that I'll be there! Offering him my undivided attention and support.'

Nathan looked at me. It was my turn to kick at the pavement and scowl at the horrible strip of bronze above the rooftops.

'Do you think he doesn't worry about it? About how hard it might be for you? Do you think that he might want you there with him *every* time he competes, cheering him on like only a parent can?'

Dammit. I did not want to hear this. But then, how could I not hear it, unless it really was all about me, and not my child?

'I don't think he's ever going to know how good he is until you see it. Until you say it. Until then, it's like it's not even true for him, because your opinion is the only one whose really matters.'

'I do say it,' I choked out, past the jagged ball of shrapnel in my throat.

'It's not the same.' His voice was soft, eyes kind. It didn't make the words hurt any less. 'Watching on a screen hours later. You know it's not the same.'

I did know. Oh, how I knew.

'I'm working on it. I have a plan, and it's working.'

'But when it means this much, why wouldn't you accept help, when someone who just genuinely cares is offering it?'

I was too overwrought right then to consider whether he meant he genuinely cared about Joey, helping me or possibly, perhaps just... me. 'I don't need dietary advice or training techniques. Being able to run is great, but it's not really the issue.'

'Amy, about ten per cent of my job is about diet and exercise. Every single woman I work with knows that if she wants to get fitter she needs to eat less cake and move more. It didn't take many clients for me to realise that what they really need is to get some confidence in who they are. To learn to love themselves better, and not let other people's expectations or judgemental asides or passive-aggressive Instagram comments hold them back.'

'Okay. I'm listening. But I need to continue this conversation inside.' I scurried for the door, a sort of power walk, while at the same time being so far from powerful it was a joke.

Nathan followed me into the kitchen, and I distracted myself with filling up the kettle, even though I'd had a massive pot of tea less than twenty minutes earlier.

'My problem isn't confidence. I wish it was that simple.'

'I get that. But I think I could help anyway. Research shows that everyone does better when they work with someone else. It's why people pay for piano lessons, even though you can find videos online to teach you how to play, or go to language classes instead of just using an app.'

I finished making the drinks and brought them over to the table. 'What do you have in mind?'

'We pick different targets, and I'll help you do it. Maybe start with getting out in the day. Being able to come to a gala, go on a bus. I don't know, we can figure it out as we go.'

I thought about this. Imagining facing those challenges with Nathan was dangerously appealing, and agonising at the same time. I didn't know where the line lay between being dependent on someone else and being helped by them. I didn't know if I'd been working things out on my own long enough to trust myself with that. But then I heard Joey's footsteps thumping about above me.

'I can't pay you.'

Nathan frowned. 'I wouldn't accept it if you could. I love Joey. And, in a weird way, I actually kind of think of you as a mate...' He attempted a sheepish grin. I resisted the urge to lean forwards and topple into his lap.

'So, how about this?' I asked. 'We do some challenge days together. But you have to complete a challenge too.'

The frown returned. Phew, much safer territory.

'Look, *mate*, I'm not the only one with issues.' I looked pointedly at his drink. 'You would consider it actual torture to drink caffeinated tea, with cow's milk.'

He picked up the mug, prepared to take a sip, then sighed and put it down again.

'Don't worry. It's Redbush. But on challenge day, maybe it'll be a chocca-mocha freak-shake with marshmallows and caramel sprinkles and full-fat ice cream.'

Nathan squared his shoulders. 'If you can accompany me to a café, in the hours of daylight, I will drink that shake.' He held out his mug, waiting for me to tap it with mine in a toast.

'Challenge accepted.'

'This was supposed to be an offer of help. How come with you everything ends up a competition?' Nathan asked as he was leaving, a few minutes later.

Maybe one day I would even tell him about that.

* * *

The whole new head-spinning addition to the Programme had left me in what Mel would call a right tizz. So, when I saw the black car parked a pathetically non-inconspicuous four doors down from my house (yes, I'd been peeking out the windows), I waited until it was near enough twilight, grabbed a torch for temporary-blinding purposes, tucked the hood up on my jacket and went to give Moira Vanderbeek a world exclusive.

As I approached the car, to my surprise, it pulled off. With just enough brain in gear to switch the torch on, I caught the glimpse of a baseball cap as it accelerated past. I stood and watched it disappear up the road, then stood for a whole lot longer, until I could trust my legs to wobble me back inside.

If that had been a journalist staking out my house, he or she was an astonishingly crap one. I had googled Moira Vanderbeek. She might be more *Gossip* magazine than BBC, but she wouldn't have driven away when the one person she was trying to interview approached.

And if she had been secretly watching me, she surely had enough wits about her to park further away, on the opposite side of the road so she could drive off without having to pass me.

So, if it wasn't the honourable Ms Vanderbeek who was hanging around my son's school, lurking outside the leisure centre, now blatantly staking out my house, who the fish-and-chips was it?

29

STOP BEING A LOSER PROGRAMME

DAY SEVENTY-ONE

After two days of twitching my curtains and straining my ears to wildly interpret every creak and knock as the return of the Baseball-Capped Killer, Joey's cricket bat accompanying my woeful charade at sleeping, I was so grateful to receive Nathan's text, I would have probably said yes to whatever wild and crazy challenge he'd presented me with.

Challenge 1: breakfast at the Cup and Saucer tomorrow

That's it? Was expecting something a bit more interesting. If you eat breakfast there every Saturday, and this is just incorporating me into your robot routine, then I'm highly disappointed.

Have eaten breakfast there about 4 Saturdays since it opened. Thought a familiar place would help you get started.

Don't pretend there isn't a spreadsheet listing precisely how many Saturdays. I'll meet you there at 9.

Thought we could meet in the dark, leave in the light. Maybe 7.30?

Are you trying to stunt my progress? Or hoping if you're easy on me I won't present you with a decent-sized challenge in return? Cos that's not how I roll. And I'm ready to kick some butt, might as well be my own.

See you C&S, 9.

30

STOP BEING A LOSER PROGRAMME
DAY SEVENTY-TWO

That night consisted of precisely seven minutes sleep, seventeen thousand grabs of the cricket bat and seventy-hundred hissed arguments with my anxiety.

When I finally gave in and messaged Nathan at 6 a.m., he replied instantly.

I snatched about fifty-three seconds more sleep and finally dragged myself into the bathroom just before seven-thirty.

'Ouch!' I winced at the wild-woman squinting at me from the mirror. 'This is going to take some time.' And about two days more sleep. And a professional hairdresser. And more make-up than I had worn in the rest of my life all smeared together. And a miracle.

By eight-fifty, when the doorbell rang, I was a good twelve per cent of the way to looking in a fit state to be seen out having breakfast with Nathan Gallagher. Helped along by a non-terrible blue shirt dress from my pre-hermit days, I did my best attempt at casually sauntering downstairs, and opened the door, almost as if it wasn't bright November sunshine outside.

'Ready?'

I closed my eyes. Took a deep breath. Remembered I was on high alert for a crazed stalker and quickly opened them again. Nodded. Took a great big step out onto the path. Stepped back in again and decided I'd probably best put some shoes and a coat on first, as there was a wicked frost out there.

Only, by the time I'd put my boots on, I was ready to change my mind again.

Nathan said nothing. He crinkled his eyes at me in a sort of smile and held out his hand. I ignored that gorgeous temptation, taking a tentative step outside and then stopping again.

'There's been a complication.'

'Okay.' He watched me, steadily, eyes still crinkling.

'I didn't ask you to meet me here because I was wimping out of walking by myself. That car, the one the school warned the kids about, I've seen it a few times at the leisure centre, and for the past week it's been hanging about the street, here.'

'Seriously? How often?' Nathan quickly turned to scan the road behind us.

'A few times. I went out to confront them on Wednesday—'

'*You did what?*'

'They drove off when they saw me coming.'

'Have you seen them since?'

I shook my head. Nathan's apparent concern was enough to allow the thoughts which had been keeping me awake most of the night to not seem so melodramatic after all. I was overtired, overwrought and totally lost inside my own head. It was hardly surprising that a big, fat tear squeezed out and rolled down my cheek. If anything, I was impressed it was only one.

'Come on, let's get inside. It's freezing out here.' Nathan took me by the shoulders and gently steered me into the kitchen, guiding me to a chair.

'I don't want to cancel the challenge. I'm not failing right at the start,' I said. At least, I think that's what it was, it was hard to decipher, what with all the sniffing and sobbing and sappy loserness going on.

'Nothing wrong with adapting the challenge to suit new circumstances.' Nathan was rummaging around in my fridge. 'If you had flu, or a broken leg, or something came up with Joey, you'd do it.' He pulled back out again, a carton in one hand. 'Eggs Benedict?'

'I'll cook it.' I straightened my shoulders, found a tissue in my pocket and did a weirdly elephantine blow of my nose. 'I might have forfeited the right to force Danish pastries and hot chocolate on you, but I'm not letting you get away with cooking some Mr Natural version of eggs, either.'

He hesitated. Because he wanted to cook me a nice, comforting breakfast or himself a horrible, healthy one, I wasn't sure.

'Fine. You cook. I'll set the table.'

And he did. After dragging it outside into a dazzling patch of sunshine in the back garden first.

* * *

Deep breaths. Counting to ten, slowly. Finding a focal point. I refused to hold Nathan's hand. No way on this earth we were going to eat breakfast while holding hands across the table. Especially with my son's window overlooking the garden. So, yes, the focal point did appear to be Nathan's face, but that was okay. It's generally considered normal to be looking (*staring intently!*) at someone's face when making conversation, isn't it?

And making conversation seemed to work, too. Especially when I talked fast and loud enough to drown out my anxiety, which did entail talking without registering any thoughts. Probably not the best conversation style, but, hey, Nathan was here to help.

'You replied to my message fast. What were you doing up at six on a Saturday?'

'I was heading to the gym.' Nathan poked his breakfast, dubiously.

'Do you go every day?'

'Not Wednesday or Sunday.'

'What do you do there? I mean, I don't need your whole routine. But weights, cardio, Zumba? I heard they did a new booty bounce class on weekends.'

'I was working.' He carefully sliced off a tiny corner of his pancake – the only slither not drenched in maple syrup.

'Working what?'

'A client.' He froze, fork halfway to his mouth. At first I thought it was his muscles refusing to cooperate with the pancake. 'I mean, I was training a client. At work. Not working a client...' His voice trailed off and he stuffed the chunk of batter into his mouth.

'Yes. I got that.'

Nathan had turned the same colour as the bacon balanced on top of his pancake stack.

'I don't even know what *working a client* would mean.' I could kind of guess, but this was getting interesting, and interesting went a long way in helping me not to tip the table over and run inside screaming.

'Nothing. It means nothing. As far as I know.' He shovelled in another forkful, not even trying to sneakily let the syrup drip off his fork onto the grass. My suspicions grew.

'Who were you training?' I asked, oh so cool and breezy.

'I don't discuss client information...'

'Is she pretty?'

'Um, not, well. I...'

'Ugly?'

'No!'

'Pretty then.'

'I haven't noticed.' Another mouthful firmly eaten, as if that would end the subject.

'You haven't noticed? But it's your job to notice her physical appearance. To watch carefully as she does all the personal training moves. Check out how her body's improving.'

'Bloody hell, Amy. I get enough of this from the lads at football.' Nathan shoved his plate away. I didn't point out the piece of bacon still resting in a pool of syrup, choosing instead to concentrate on pouring myself another mug of tea. 'I'm a professional. I've studied anatomy and physiology. I observe every client to ensure they maximise the exercises and avoid injury with the same level of objectiveness. I'm no more going to be focusing on whether a client is *pretty* than if I was their doctor, or physiotherapist. I maintain a professional relationship at all times.'

'Even when they come on to you?'

I didn't know why I was still talking about this. Nathan was clearly miffed, and I didn't especially want to discuss how he spent all day *observing* women's bodies. It was like some twisted attempt to remind myself of the sort of woman Nathan had to compare me to. While I admired his strictly-business-only attitude, that meant that surely he'd keep a business-only attitude with me. Which was good to know.

Except that he'd told me I was a friend, not a client. Did that still count? Or was him calling me a friend also setting a firm boundary:

friend, not potentially more than friends, just in case I got any wrong ideas.

'If they come on to me, I deal with it. If I have to, I pass them on to another trainer.'

'So, who do you date, if you can't date clients?' I asked, my mouth still seemingly unable to resist returning to this topic like a fly buzzing round a cream bun.

'I don't have a lot of time for dating.'

'So... no one?'

'Not currently.' Nathan sighed, but it seemed exasperated rather than angry, so I kept on buzzing.

'And how long has *currently* been going on for?'

'A couple of years.' He shrugged. 'And I'm fine with that. I've got a great life, I'm not lonely, or unfulfilled. Why would I look to change that?' There was a slightly too long pause. Nathan blinked at the table, running one hand through his hair as he answered. 'Although, I suppose having a girlfriend might have stopped Selena from trying to eat me alive. She hasn't always shown due respect for the no-client rule.' He glanced up at me then, and after a split second the crinkles were back.

'*Selena?*'

'She got the hint. Eventually.'

Yeah. Me too.

* * *

Nathan stayed for an hour or so, heading off to burn off all those evil extra calories once the challenge was complete and my courage exhausted. Following the weird start, I had managed to maintain a decent conversation. I was definitely getting back into the swing of the whole chatting thing, helped by Nathan being a really easy person to chat to. It would have been even better if I wasn't avoiding an entire baggage trolley worth of subjects – my childhood, family, Cee-Cee, Sean, the triathlon, how I'd ended up in this state in the first place...

The couple of times Nathan gently steered towards my past, I deftly responded by ignoring the question and changing the subject. I had a huge amount of work to do before being ready to handle a genuine friendship with a man I found so darn attractive. My urge to open up to him, spewing all the ugly secrets and unflattering truth about who I really was, and had been, was precisely the reason for keeping firmly on the polite side of friendly.

I spent the rest of the day cleaning, reading, glancing out the window into the back garden and smiling to myself at my momentous achievement while not at all thinking about Nathan's eye crinkles. When Joey took it upon himself to make us fajitas for dinner, I should have known he'd heard me belting out Beyoncé while scrubbing the shower and decided to cash in on his mother's uncharacteristic good mood.

'To celebrate that you're feeling better,' he pronounced, tipping a pile of chicken and peppers out of the frying pan onto a serving dish. 'And managed a giant leap forwards in the Programme today.'

'Thanks, Joey. This looks great.' It sort of did, too. I was sure the charred bits of chicken would merely add to the flavour. 'Are those baked beans?'

'I'm really glad Nathan's helping you. He's such a quality coach.' Joey grabbed a wrap and started loading up. 'Beans are a superfood, and they're the only type we had.'

'I'll have you know, I'm helping *Coach Gallagher*, too.'

'You are?' He boggled at me. 'What, like giving him training tips? Have you told him?'

'Absolutely not.' I shook my head. 'I'm just helping him to loosen up a bit. He's got so entrenched in following all these rules for optimum fitness, and, well, I know that kind of controlling lifestyle doesn't always end well.'

'Cool.'

We ate in silence for a while, until Joey couldn't contain his twitchiness any longer.

'So, if you're feeling better, can we talk about my dad now,' he blurted, my last bite instantly congealing inside my mouth.

Well, I should have seen that one coming a mile off.

I somehow forced the ball of now tasteless mush down my throat, helping it along with a slow drink of water. My brain was racing at a hundred miles an hour, but somehow still couldn't catch up with a single coherent thought.

'Only, it's been ages, and I've been really patient, and I still want to speak to him just as bad, but if you really aren't going to let me talk to him without you emailing first, can you please hurry up and do it. Like, this evening. If you aren't doing anything else.'

I sat there for a while longer, the longing in my child's voice ringing in my ears, before replying with the only word I could find right then. 'Okay.'

'What?!' Joey nearly fell off his chair, choosing instead to fling himself across the table at me, sending sour cream flying.

'Your jumper's trailing in the salsa,' I mumbled into his shoulder.

'Don't care.' He gripped me tighter. 'I love you, Mum.'

'I love you too. Now, while we clear up this mess, I'd better fill you in a bit. Knowledge is power, after all.'

Washing-up abandoned, we sat and went through Sean's company website, plus anything else we could find about him online. No social media, except for a long-abandoned Twitter account. I recounted what little I knew about Sean's background. Joey lapped up the knowledge that he had an uncle and grandparents, while expressing a mix of relief and disappointment that we failed to find any siblings.

I refused, unequivocally, to show him any of the emails. I didn't need to argue about the other messages, as I hadn't mentioned them.

'When was the last time he sent you one?' Joey asked, biting the last shred of his nail to the quick.

I thought about that. 'A while, actually. There was a flurry a few weeks ago, but nothing in the past month.'

Joey looked at me, fear in his eyes. A twinge of anger.

'Hey, don't panic. If your dad meant any of what he said about wanting to get to know you, a month isn't going to have changed that. He probably thought it best to give me a bit of space.'

Joey said nothing, unconvinced.

'Well, I guess there's only one way to find out, isn't there?' I opened up my email, then, before I could type anything, shut the lid on the laptop altogether. 'Before I do this, can I tell you how it ended?'

Was this the right decision? Would it help Joey – help protect him – to know this? Or was it one last stab at making sure I remained the good guy, that history wouldn't repeat itself, and my boy, so like his father, wouldn't abandon me too?

As someone who earns a living by taking crappy information and turning it into something positive, I did a pretty good job of softening the blow and making it sound not quite so appalling. After all, Sean had been young back then.

What a shame he'd done nothing to make it any less appalling for me, even younger, and without him, utterly alone.

* * *

Sean and I had ridden out the hideous weeks following the Search for Amelia scandal behind the drawn blinds of the flat in Exeter. Once the paparazzi had found another poor celebrity to persecute, Sean charmed his way into an office job which paid enough to cover the bills. For some reason, he chose to put in increasingly long days in the office, rather than come home to his emotional wreck of a girlfriend. When this became accompanied by regular after-work drinks, dinner, joining the department bowling team, my loneliness, boredom and excruciating neediness only grew. An obvious solution was for me to get a job, but by the time all the legal issues with the sponsors had been settled, I could barely get out of bed. And who would employ Amelia Piper, the most famous quitter in the country?

So, we fought, sulked, felt guilty, made up again. Each time, the cycle left us a little more weary, mistrustful, resentful. And I watched the clichés disprove themselves before our eyes. Love, if that's what it was, could not conquer all. Instead our love was being resoundingly thrashed by immaturity, isolation, rent arrears, profound insecurities and hidden depression. I had thrown away everything – tossed aside my entire identity, along with my future, career, family and friends. The person Sean had loved had gone, and the unkempt, dreary, pitiful shambles emerging as her replacement was not quite his type.

And then, six months after we had run away together, I started throwing up. My breasts grew swollen and sore. I became even more exhausted from my days of doing nothing than I had before. I snuck twenty pounds out of Sean's wallet and bought a pregnancy test. Then I stole another twenty and did it again. Praying for a different result, while clinging onto it as potentially what might save us. At least I would have something to live for now.

I gave myself a week to absorb the shock, then, in between dashing to the bathroom to empty my battered stomach, I prepared a lasagne and chocolate fudge cake. I showered, changed into my nicest dress and tried to cover up the haggard fear on my face with some leftover make-up from my celebrity days. I dredged up some remaining energy to tidy the flat, change the bed and light the candles I'd bought from the pound shop.

I phoned Sean at work to tell him I had a surprise, and to please be home for dinner. He promised to be home by seven. When he finally rolled in at nearly nine, I plastered on a smile, dolloped the dried-up remains of his favourite dinner onto plates and relit the candle stumps.

'This is nice,' he managed, the waft of beer fumes causing my stomach to contract dangerously. 'Are you feeling better? Because if you are, there's an advert in the newsagent's window, looking for a cleaner. I know it's hardly your dream job, but it at least gets you out the house and earning.'

'Now's not a good time,' I interrupted.

He threw down his fork. 'Really? Is there a better time for you to get a job than when you're spending all day sat on your arse nagging me about mine? Please, do tell me about a better time to get a job than when we owe two months' rent?'

'I...'

'You, what?' he sneered. 'You might as well get a job, darling, because you are a disaster as a housewife.' He pushed his plate away. 'This is inedible.'

'It was perfectly edible two hours ago.' I swallowed back the lump of nausea and tears threatening to overwhelm me.

'Don't you dare criticise me for earning us money. You have no idea what a real job entails. In the real world, you can't swan off home because your girlfriend's feeling lonely.'

'No, but you could perhaps manage to come home instead of going to the pub, considering you promised. And the only person to wish me a happy birthday so far is the creepy man at the Asda checkout.'

Sean looked at me then, his face a mixture of guilt and dismay. 'It's your birthday. Why didn't you say something?'

'And... and I'm pregnant,' I sobbed out. 'There. That's the surprise.'

I threw down my paper napkin and ran off to the bathroom.

When I came back, twenty minutes later, having cleaned myself up and changed into sweatpants and a hoodie, Sean hadn't moved.

I sat down opposite him, feeling more alone, more terrified, more desperate than ever before. 'There's cake if you want it,' I squeaked out.

'Are you sure?' he asked, his lips barely moving, eyes fixed rigidly on my stomach.

'Yes.'

'How the shitting hell did this happen?'

I took a deep breath. He was shocked, of course he was. I had been, too.

'I don't know. I guess nothing's foolproof.'

'Especially when someone behaves foolishly.'

'What?' I sat back, stunned.

'Have you been taking the pill properly?'

'Well. Yes. I mean, I might have forgotten the odd one or two, on the days when I wasn't feeling well. But that shouldn't have been enough to stop them working.'

He held up his hand, in a 'stop' gesture. 'I have one more question.'

I propped my head on my hands, in a futile attempt to stop it from spinning.

'Did you do this on purpose?'

'How could you even ask that?'

'Oh, come off it, it's the age-old desperate woman's trick.'

'I don't need to trick you, we're together! You love me!'

'You still haven't answered the question.'

No, I hadn't. Because I knew that, right then, waiting for the answer was the only thing keeping him there.

I closed my eyes, tried to claw back my body from the brink of panic. When I opened them again, he had gone.

He came back, of course, two days later. We had one conversation about 'my choices', and their bearing on 'our future'.

Another three weeks of long silences punctuated by rigid small talk followed. I slept, wept, threw up, stocked up on folic acid and lost half a stone in weight. Sean hid at the office, the pub, behind a frozen mask. Four times he stayed out all night.

Then came the day he packed his bags. 'I've got a transfer.'

'What? To where?'

'Colorado.'

'When do we go?' I asked the question, even though I knew the answer.

'I'm going tomorrow. Alone. We both know this isn't working. And if you're going to keep the baby, it'd be better off not growing up in a home where its parents can't stand each other.'

Can't stand each other? When did that happen?

'If I go now, it'll never miss me. We can have a fresh start.'

'Sean. What? What am I supposed to do? We're three months behind on the rent. I can't live here by myself. What about when the baby comes?' I bent double, clamouring for air, the pain ripping through my guts like a meathook.

'Here.' He tossed a wad of notes onto the table. 'That'll help get you started. Get to Citizens Advice, or whatever. There's good benefits these days for single mums. I'm sure your parents will help. They'd probably be pleased to know they're going to have a grandchild.'

I was aghast, speechless.

'This is your decision, Amy. You took risks with your contraception. You decided not to work. You chose to keep a baby. I'm just not ready for this. I can't be a parent at my age and I'm not going to spend the next eighteen years paying for your mistake.'

'YOU'RE not ready?' I screech-wheezed, finding some kind of voice at last. 'I'M NINETEEN!'

'Like I said, your choice.' He swung his bag over his shoulder. 'I wish you all the best.'

And that was the last time I saw the scumbag wastrel otherwise known as Sean Mansfield.

* * *

The version I gave Joey was somewhat sanitised. Somewhat. I would do whatever I could to spare my son a twinge more pain than was necessary, but at the same time, my sore heart felt little obligation to protect the man who'd left me alone, broke and pregnant, and in doing so, leave Joey unprepared. And how do you pretty up, 'yes, he knew I was pregnant when he left, and, no, he made no contact with me to ask about my child until now'?

'You still want to go ahead with this?' I asked.

Joey nodded, his frown uncharacteristically grave. 'Warning noted. Dad was once a loser – but, hey, we know better than anyone that losers can change, right?'

I took a deep breath. 'Right.'

I kept the email short, simple:

Sean,

I am considering your request. Can you please provide more details about what level of contact you had in mind, and what you hope to achieve? Clearly, my first priority is protecting my child.

Amelia

Three minutes later, as Joey pretended to watch TV in the living room and I sat at my desk watching videos of pandas rolling down hills to calm myself down, a reply pinged through:

Amy,

Thank you so much for getting back to me. I can't tell you how much this means. I totally understand you want to protect Joseph. I'm happy to proceed as you see fit and take it as slow as necessary to rebuild trust. My aim is simply to get to know my son, to do whatever I can to make up for not being there. I know there's nothing that can replace the years he had to go without a father, but he doesn't have to go the rest of his life without one. If he doesn't want that, I get it. All I'm asking for at this stage is the chance to say how sorry I am, and to at least try.

Sean

'That FUDGING CUSTARD!' I growled, while noting, with a sense of pride, my impressive self-control in neither swearing when my thirteen-year-old son was in the next room or hurling my laptop out of the window.

How the FUDGE did he know my son's name? And, actually, he chooses to be called JOEY.

How DARE he imply that somehow Joey missed out from not having that worthless piece of SHITAKE MUSHROOM in his life?

He doesn't have to go the rest of his life... like it was some CHUFFING accident or unpreventable tragedy that stopped him from picking up the phone or sending an email up until now.

Like I wasn't enough?

Like he had the power to make Joey's life better?

I wanted to yank out every single one of my eyelashes with frustration, because even in my blinding rage and soaring anxiety, I knew that it might be true: having a father, a parent without a squillion freakoid big-bad-world-out-there issues, could make Joey's life better.

However, I knew that having Sean Mansfield step in to try playing Daddy could also make our lives a whole lot worse.

Blugh. Even the baby panda going down the slide in a straw hat wasn't enough at this point.

I shut down the laptop and dragged my stressed-out bones to bed.

31

STOP BEING A LOSER PROGRAMME
DAY SEVENTY-THREE

The following morning, unable to bear thrashing around under my duvet torturing myself with increasingly disturbing potential Sean-scenarios for one more minute, I set off extra early to meet the Larks.

I decided to kill a bit of time with a dawdled detour along Foxglove Lane, past a row of decrepit cottages and a brand-new barn conversion. At the barn driveway, I paused to ogle the huge window spanning both storeys of the building. There was a light on, and I have to confess to a teensy bit of nosying at the gallery balcony inside, admiring the beautiful furnishings and rustic-yet-contemporary kitchen. I mean, if you're going to put in an enormous window, and no blinds, you have to expect passers-by to take a sneaky peak. You probably *want* people to appreciate your magazine-worthy interior. So, when the front door swung open, accompanied by several exterior lights flashing on, there wasn't really any reason for me to jump behind the nearest bush.

Having found myself there, however, when footsteps began scrunching down the gravel drive towards me, I realised that reappearing out from behind the undergrowth now would require some sort of explanation for why I was lurking behind a bush right outside their house at six in the freezing cold morning. Either that or I'd have to run away, and despite recent improvements, my current fitness levels could in no way guarantee the footsteps wouldn't catch up with me.

I edged deeper into the foliage as a horror-show flickered through my head, involving being restrained by the house owner until the police arrived, Moira Vanderbeek hot on their tail, swiftly followed by a front-page exposé on Amelia Piper's descent into a life of petty crime.

The footsteps crunched closer. I held my breath, my anxiety rendered speechless for once.

And then they rounded the corner of the bushes, straight into the glow from the nearest lamp post.

Well.

All the pent-up air burst out of my lungs, immediately followed by a strangled wheeze-in to compensate.

The person wheeled round in my direction, the radiant grin which had meant it took a couple of seconds to recognise her instantly replaced with a wary scowl.

'Who's there?' she stammered.

I should have run. There was no way Audrey would have caught up with me. Especially not in those heels.

'I know someone's in the bush,' Audrey said. 'The leaves are rustling.'

Well, perhaps it's a squirrel, up early to gather nuts. Or a wood pigeon? A badger? Come on, Audrey, use your imagination.

'I can see the reflective stripes on your trousers!'

Darn Joey's health and safety obsession! A woman can't get any decent privacy any more.

'Audrey? Darling?' a man's voice wafted down the drive.

Darling? My ears must have grown a good few millimetres, they were straining so hard. More crunching footsteps.

'Is everything all right? You need to get home before your mother wakes up.' Through the bushes, I saw the man come to stand by Audrey, placing one hand on her shoulder. He had white hair, a bushy beard, and appeared to be wearing a dressing gown and wellington boots. Was this Audrey's dad? I knew Selena was divorced – maybe it had been so acrimonious that Audrey had to visit him in secret. Slightly strange, visiting before six in the morning. But perhaps she'd ended up falling asleep on the sofa last night, and, well, I could understand Audrey going to extreme lengths to avoid yet more hassle from her mum.

'There's someone hiding in that bush.'

'What?' The man whirled round to face me, peering closer. 'Who is it?' he demanded. 'Come out at once or I'll call the police.'

Oh, no, please... an innocent peep at some nice decor was spiralling into a nightmare.

'Be careful,' Audrey rubbed her dad's (grandad's?) hunched shoulder. 'Don't provoke them. Think about your heart.'

I braced, tried to force my legs to move out into the open, but they had frozen stiff like two stripy glow-in-the-dark ice pops.

'You get on home, darling. I'll call 999. No one needs to know you were here.'

'Except the peeping Tom. I'm not going anywhere, what if something happens to you?' Audrey replied.

And at that point – ooh, I really hoped this was not one of Audrey's relatives – she flung both arms around his neck, plastered her mouth against his, and judging by the writhing and moaning, stuck her tongue halfway down his wattled throat.

I was about to make a break for it, when she abruptly pulled away. 'Ooh, Graham, I love it when you act the hero. Remember the power cut?'

'Oh, sugar-pumpkin,' he breathed, tugging her back towards him with stiff arms. 'How could I forget? Come *here*!'

'Hello!' I called out, the consequences of being exposed waaaaaay preferable to witnessing the aftermath of Audrey undoing Graham's dressing gown cord.

They abruptly broke apart, Audrey steadying her lover as he wobbled.

'It's you!' Audrey's eyes reflected the glow of the lamp post like a white-hot laser beam. 'Were you spying on me?'

'You know this woman?' Graham asked. 'Shall I call the police?'

Audrey shook her head in resignation. 'No. She's harmless. Weird, but harmless.'

I was aware I should probably say something.

'Um, your dressing gown.' I waved feebly in the general direction while trying to keep my eyes a good foot above the strip of bare Graham where the gown was flapping open.

'You keep your eyes off him!' Audrey snarled. Believe me, I was trying. That was a lot of bare belly to avoid.

'Never mind that, darling. If she was sneaking a look at us *in flagrante delicto*, it wouldn't be the first time my potent virility has driven a woman to break the law.'

'That is not what I was doing.'

'Oh no? So why were you hiding in Graham's bushes in the dark?' Audrey retorted, sounding uncannily like her mother.

'It's stupid, honestly. I was on my way to meet the Larks, and I happened to glance in your very large window and notice your gorgeous interior as I walked past.'

'Oho, so *that's* what the kids are calling it these days,' Graham chortled.

Swallowing back the urge to barf, I ploughed on. 'I need to redecorate my living room, so I was just admiring your colour scheme when the door opened and I panicked.'

'She does do that a lot,' Audrey said, lasers boring into my skull.

'I have an anxiety condition,' I replied, flapping my hands in a '*Duh, what a silly-billy!*' kind of way.

Graham didn't look convinced.

'I do strange things to cope. But, honestly, I really couldn't see much at all from back here. And I certainly couldn't see you two. The only light on was in the big window.' I forced out a smile.

'That is true.' He nodded, considering.

'Look, this really is much ado about nothing, and I don't want to miss the run, so, um, sorry again for scaring you, Audrey, and I'll see you later.'

And on that note, I broke all of Nathan's warm-up rules and sprinted the heck out of there.

Arriving just in time to join the Larks jogging out of the car park, I seamlessly inserted myself about halfway down the pack, beside Dani. Less than a dozen steps later, our coach caught up with me.

'You need to stop and warm-up before going any further. Club rules. Warm-ups are not optional.'

'What if I'm not running with the club today, I just happened to be going in the same direction at the same time?' I puffed. 'Are you going to stop me running along a public road?'

'If you're not running with the Larks, you need to remove your T-shirt,' Nathan replied, his smooth strides barely breaking past a walk.

I nearly stumbled head over heels into an oncoming dustbin lorry.

'You can change in the cabin.' He gestured across the road to the village park, where a rusted, graffiti-riddled door was swinging off the female loos from one hinge. 'Zip your jacket up and no one will know.'

'Or, I could zip up my jacket anyway, covering up my T-shirt without having to remove it.'

'One, it's not your T-shirt, you are hereby suspended from the Larks running club until complying with the rules and regulations. Two, when you have to call an ambulance because your knee ligament is ripped to shreds, the Larks T-shirt will make me liable, damaging my reputation and harming my business.'

'Nathan, it's a warm-up. I've been running now for at least three minutes, look at my face. I'm warm.'

'Three. I'd be gutted if you injured yourself and had to stop running with us. Or needed to postpone the Sort Nathan's Obsessive Control Issues plan. Or suffered any unnecessary pain. Especially when I could have prevented it.'

'Okay. Right. Well. I actually warmed up before I got here.' What impressive technique I maintained, keeping my eyes straight ahead, not even twitching my neck an inch to look at Nathan and try to figure out if there was any hidden meaning behind that comment.

'Stretches?'

Did squatting in a bush count?

'Stretches. Now go and bother someone else, I know how to train properly.'

Plus, that stuff about me suffering had successfully stolen the miniscule amount of extra breath enabling me to continue the conversation. I put my head down and tried to focus on putting one step in front of the other, not infuriating emails or flapping dressing-gowns or personal trainers who made me want to get personal. And I almost managed it. My champion's brain was shaking herself awake and remembering how to do this. How not to be a loser.

I finished sixth.

Now, that deserved a hot chocolate to go alongside my French toast.

* * *

I took a seat with Mel and Bronwyn, able to avoid hunching beside Audrey for once as she hadn't turned up, having told Selena she had a migraine. I also felt a scrambled mix of relieved and disappointed that Nathan wasn't there, having gone to take a call from a client. Mel was explaining how the latest change in the benefits system meant that she couldn't afford to take Tate to his hydrotherapy sessions at the fancy pool on the other side of Nottingham.

'They reckon we can manage fine on the bus, no need for a taxi.' She shook her head in disgust. 'I told 'em, it's two buses, with a twenty-minute wait in between and over half-hour pushing a pushchair and carryin' all his stuff. The pool's busy all the time with lessons for normal kids, who can lift themselves in and out the water. Or them Gladiators are hogging it. It's only available nine-thirty in the mornin' – which means somehow dropping the kids at school and catching a bus in town at the same time – or Monday and Thursday evening. I said to 'em, "Have you even read his notes? Seen where the specialist doctor who's been caring for my son for the past three years says he can't be outside for any length o' time in the winter, because of a severely elevated risk of pneumonia. Let alone when 'e's just come outta soppin' wet swimming pool."

'I pointed to it on the page, with both hands, just in case they'd missed that, with all the other pages of notes about my son's extensive disabilities and life-limiting conditions. I asked 'em, "Perhaps I read it wrong, do please tell me what the world-renowned expert Dr Wu wrote'll happen if Tate catches pneumonia? Because I thought that on page four, paragraph two, it said there's a significant risk of death."' Mel tossed her raspberry red hair extension over one shoulder. 'And I sat there waitin' until they confirmed that, yes, through a process of logical deductions, it's not an exaggeration to say that Tate catching the bus to access the hydrotherapy that will help keep him alive could end up killing him.'

'Woah,' Bronwyn gasped, around a mouthful of walnut muffin. 'Did they reinstate the money?'

Mel's shoulders slumped. 'Nah. Said they couldn't, their hands were tied. But one of the women and the man interviewing me cried while they said it. And one of 'em slipped a card in me pocket with the number for a discrimination lawyer.' She blotted one eye with a napkin, leaving a smear of sugar from her doughnut across her cheek. 'As if I could afford a lawyer, when I can't even spring a taxi for something as important as Tate's therapy. As if I could find the time and energy to fight this, in between hospital appointments and meetings and cookin' and cleanin' and carin' for four wild and crazy kids along with my severely disabled son.'

'Oh, Mel, the whole thing stinks,' Bronwyn said, coming around the table to hug her friend.

'Yeah, it stunk even more when I snuck in and stuffed Tate's dirty nappy behind the radiator in the office of the boss woman who shoved Tate's case notes at me and said if it was that important I'd find a way.'

We laughed at that, long and loud. Sometimes life is so darn stinky you have to laugh, or else you'll never stop crying.

'What about when Greasby pool reopens?' Bronwyn asked, after we'd dried our eyes and recomposed ourselves. 'Where we're doing the triathlon. Will Tate be able to do hydrotherapy there?'

Mel shook her head. 'I've already asked 'em. With all these cuts, it can barely afford steps, let alone a hoist.'

'That's total crap,' Bronwyn announced, her Welsh accent deepening with passion. 'It's plain idiotic. It'll cost far more to treat Tate's condition if it worsens than pay for a hoist, surely? You should write to our MP.'

'Our MP thinks people like Mel should get a job and pay for their own taxis,' I said. 'We'd be better off raising the money ourselves.'

'Amy!' Bronwyn rounded on me, her enthusiasm loud enough to catch the attention of the remaining Larks who'd not slipped off to enjoy the rest of their Sunday yet. 'You're a genius. Let's do it. Did you hear that everyone?' she called across the café. 'Amy's had a fab idea. We're going to run and swim and whatever else it is you do in a triathlon to raise money to get a hoist for the new Greasby pool, so Tate can still do his hydrotherapy even though the government's stolen his taxi money off him.'

Um, are we?

'You'd better get one of them fundraising web pages sorted, Ames.' Bronwyn winked as the café erupted into excited chatter. 'We can get it out there on social media. Maybe tell the *Nottingham Post*?'

'Or the radio?' someone else suggested.

'What about Notts TV?' Dani chipped in. 'They're always looking for local-interest stories.'

'There you go, Mel.' Bronwyn grinned. 'We'll have a hoist sorted in no time.' She took a satisfied slurp of coffee. 'What are we looking at, anyway? What does a decent hoist cost? Only the best for Tate.'

Mel cleared her throat. 'Well, the best one's a PoolPal...'

'So how much?'

'Thirty-thousand pounds.'

'Right.' Bronwyn downed the rest of her coffee and stood up. 'I'm off. I will say this before I go though: you've got guts, Amy, to take on a project this size. I wouldn't have thought you'd got it in you, but I stand corrected. Total respect, and we're with you all the way. Go Tate!'

She whirled out the door in a gust of wind, leaving me gaping and gibbering in her wake.

'Don't worry,' Mel said. 'She'll have forgotten about it by next week. You don't have to do this.'

The trouble was, I looked in her eyes as she said it. A mother, on her own, like me. Who'd made mistakes, like me, with gargantuan consequences. Who would swim down to the depths of the ocean, cycle up to the moon if it would help her child, if it would help make his life less bone-grindingly tough and bring some much-needed happiness into it instead.

'I know.' I smiled. 'But I want to.'

Mel dabbed another sprinkling of sugar on her face – both cheeks, this time.

'I'm not doing any press, though,' I added. 'I can organise it, but I'm not appearing in the paper or on the radio. And definitely not on television. You can do that bit, show everyone how gorgeous Tate is.'

'Oh, come on now, Amy.' Dani stopped on her way out and put her hands on my shoulders. 'Don't you want your fifteen minutes of fame?'

'I most definitely do not. Fame's not all it's cracked up to be.'

'I'll do the media side of things if Amy doesn't want to,' Selena said from the table behind us. 'I mean, for little Tate, of course. Someone has to do it, and it might as well be someone with no—'

'Brain?' Dani muttered as she made to leave.

'Capacity for human kindness?' Mel whispered, eyebrows raised questioningly.

'Chance of actually donating any money herself unless she has something personal to gain from it?' Dani added, earning herself a discreet high-five from Mel before she sashayed off.

'Confidence issues,' Selena finished abruptly, sensing that she was the butt of a joke but not sure what it was.

'Please, feel free. I'm well aware that I'm nowhere near confident enough to be on television,' I replied.

Marjory peered around Selena's brittle ponytail and winked.

Oh boy.

* * *

Despite all the buzz about Bronwyn's idea, which had somehow in everyone's head become my idea, I made it outside while it was still twilight. Bright enough to give myself a complimentary pat on the back, while still dark enough that I could wrestle my anxiety back inside its cage without too much trouble.

Also dark enough that when a shadowy figure loomed out of a doorway at the edge of the square, I let out a strangled squeal, jumped about eight inches off the ground and felt exceedingly fortunate to have emptied my bladder only moments before.

'Audrey! What the hell?' I felt almost pleased to see her, so relieved at it not being a man in a baseball cap. 'It's not okay to jump out at people in the dark.'

She stood in front of me like a mousy-haired mountain. 'Should I have hidden in your rhododendron bush instead?'

'I don't have a rhododendron bush,' I responded, feebly.

'This will have to do, then.'

We stood there and glowered at each other, as the sun inched closer towards the horizon, and Selena inched closer to leaving the café and finding her daughter lurking in a doorway instead of in bed with a migraine as she'd been led to believe.

'Have you told anyone?' Audrey said, eventually.

'No, of course not.'

'Really?' She narrowed her eyes.

'I know what it's like to be gossiped about. And who you choose to spend your time with is none of my business. I'm not going to mention it to anyone.'

One eye unnarrowed itself a micrometre.

'I promise. If you hadn't noticed, I'm trying to be your friend, Audrey. Which, if successful, would make the grand total of my friends four. I really don't have the capacity for enemies.'

'If you told the other Larks, then it would be a funny story and you'd make more friends. Nice ones.'

'The kind of people who would want to be my friend because I told them the private business of a fellow Lark for a cheap snigger do not count as nice.' I rubbed my face, exasperated. 'Look, I have to get back. All you can do is take my word for it. But if I was going to tell them, surely I'd have already done it. There's Mel leaving, why don't you ask her?'

Audrey shifted from one foot to the other, still unsure. Then, her gaze focused on someone behind me and a hint of a smile twitched at her pale lips. 'If Nathan heard you'd been spreading rumours, he'd think you were a right bitch. Probably ask you to leave the Larks. Definitely stop giving you the special treatment.'

'Okay, well, I don't know what you're talking about, but if it makes you feel better to think you've blackmailed me into not spilling your secret, rather than choosing to believe I'd not say anything because I'm a decent person with a shred of integrity and not, actually, a right bitch, then... Whatever, Audrey. I'll see you around.'

And with that retort reverberating around the square, I stomped home and proved I wasn't a right, or a wrong, bitch by emailing Sean and telling him he could communicate with his abandoned son, as long as he had a phone conversation with me about it first.

* * *

An almost instant reply. Did this man do anything apart from sit at his computer waiting for emails to ping through?

It asked if I would be prepared to meet him face to face.

What!?

I answered almost as quickly, before I had time to think about it:

How? Aren't you in the US?

Three seconds:

I can be in England in ten hours. Just tell me when and where.

Don't even go there, I instructed my non-bitchy self, who was starting to seriously waver. *No point wondering why, if it's that easy, he hasn't been here before. Count to ten, think of Joey and be prepared to give him a chance to explain.*

Joey speaking to Sean on the phone, messaging – even FaceTiming was bad enough. Meeting face to face? That was a completely different level of stress migraines, queasiness and spiralling day-mares. Sean, here, all real and hugging Joey and taking him to places I can't go and telling him things that I can't like, 'Call me "Dad"!' and 'I'm proud of you, son,' and being actually, really *there.*

It was my worst nightmare. And I've got some bad ones.

Joey's dream come true.

I might not be able to sleep, eat or think straight until it happened, and possibly not until he was safely back on the other side of the Atlantic, but it was time to get over my own fears and harrowing memories and put my son first.

I would give Sean Mansfield a chance to meet the child he abandoned. But I decided to wait a bit longer than ten hours before I told him when and where.

32

STOP BEING A LOSER PROGRAMME

DAY SEVENTY-FOUR

Monday afternoon, I spent a jittery one hour, thirteen minutes and four seconds in the back garden. It was a glorious new stage of the Programme: Time Outside During Daylight. To begin with, I pressed myself against the wall of the house and simply waited for the ground to stop spinning like a demented merry-go-round. But after a while, I noticed a humungous dandelion growing in a bare patch of dirt near the back fence. Inching towards it, arms out for balance, because planet Earth was clearly moving faster than usual that day, I wobbled down to a squat and yanked it out with a satisfactory cloud of damp soil. But there, a couple of feet away, was another one. Hardly a surprise. Cee-Cee had always tidied up the garden, and the weeds weren't going to pull themselves up out of respect for her memory.

I sucked in a nose-full of wet earth, mingled with the scent of rotting leaves. Stood up again and observed how the light reflected off the droplets still clinging to the grass, the richness of the autumn foliage – so many shades of orange and gold, bronze and russet. Sunshine yellow and deep chestnut brown. There was a slug on the concrete fence post. Fat and glistening, its back patterned like the bark of a tree. If I focused in small, to about a square foot, I could do this. If I gave myself something to do, kept my mind and my eyes and my hands working together, I could block the anxiety, keep it waiting at the top of the slide into panic.

And I did. For nearly fifty minutes, I pulled weeds in my little haven. Cee-Cee had kept shears and a fork in a small storage box in one corner, and once the weeds were mostly gone, I started pruning back the bushes. Whether they needed pruning, or how to prune them, I had no clue, but the point was I had both feet firmly planted on outside territory, the gentle kiss of November sunshine on my skin, and I was, quite literally, reclaiming ground.

Until, suddenly – maybe I'd simply used up my courage for that day – I couldn't. Unable even to divert the few feet to put the shears back in the box, I bolted inside, slamming the door behind me.

Still, I reflected later, when safely under my duvet, it was a magnificent step forward. That brief time outside had begun restoring something askew in my soul. Working on something tangible, soaking up the sunshine, marvelling at the vibrant colours of the plants, the details in the leaves and bright contrast of the berries had been like a balm to my frayed heart. The air felt different in the daylight. Clearer. Richer. More alive. And, to my joy and wonder, in a deep, soft place below the buzz of the anxiety, I had felt those things, too.

* * *

I was roused from my brief celebratory snooze by the thumps and crashes of multiple hungry teenagers marauding through the house in search of snacks. Hauling myself out of bed (being brave apparently used up a lot of energy), I tidied myself up and went to say hello, dodging the mound of giant school shoes and black rucksacks in the hallway.

'Mum, have we got more popcorn?' Joey yelled.

I followed the scent of hormone-infused body spray into the kitchen. 'Hi, Joey, how lovely to have you home. How was your day? Oh, and I'm great, thanks for asking.' I grinned at the other boys. 'Hey, everyone. Popcorn's in the cupboard where crisps used to live. Are you guys okay?'

Joey's swim club friends were all various stages of okay, ranging from 'sound' to 'awesome'. I began hustling them into the living room, so I could get some admin done at my desk, but while they were still bottle-necked in the obstacle-ridden hallway, I heard one ask, 'Did you tell your mum about the scout?'

The hair on the back of my neck pricked up. No offence to the others, but there was only one member of the Brooksby swim team worth scouting. And he'd already been scouted by the best club in the region.

'Shut up,' Joey hissed. I poked my head round the kitchen doorway and found him shoving the others into the living room as fast as he could. 'Of course I haven't. Stop stirring.'

He banged the door shut, muffling the sound of boy banter, and I hesitated for only a moment before settling down to my accounts. Pursuing this now might mean a better chance of finding out the truth from the other boys, but then secrets might end up being revealed on both sides. And mine would result in far wider consequences.

I could grill Joey once his friends had left, inviting accusations of earwigging and potentially a total clam-up. Or, I could try another tactic altogether.

* * *

I'd barely spoken to Nathan the day before, since he'd arrived at the café just as I was leaving. But when he texted me that evening, it made my cheeks warm up and a tiny sparkler fizz away inside my heart.

I made myself wait one minute and thirty-five seconds before I read the text. There is no significance to that number, except that ninety seconds seemed reasonable and it took another five seconds for me to stop fumbling with my phone and open the message.

You snuck off yesterday without arranging challenge 2. Feeling chicken?

Feeling busy! I had to get home for a conference call.
Yet you had time to stop and chat to Audrey. Or should I say CLUCK to Audrey?

Ha ha (if I knew what emoji indicated sarcasm I'd add it now – as I don't, I'm sending this one of fries as I'm guessing that will irritate you the most), I'm not discussing our challenge in front of the Larks. We'd never hear the end of it.

What's it to be, then? Lunch in the café?

I thought about that. I desperately wanted to conquer spending some daylight hours in public, after my victory in the garden. But there was something I wanted – needed – to conquer more.

I want to watch Joey train. From the right side of the window.

A speedy response:

Cool. Tomorrow evening?

Okay. And we'll go somewhere random and spontaneous afterwards. My choice.

A much slower response to that:

Deal.

It might require a shirt. And non-trainers. I haven't decided yet.

I'm looking forward to it

(a row of chicken emojis).

I could have asked Nathan about the scout, but I didn't want to go behind Joey's back if I could help it, especially when his relationship with Nathan meant so much. And I was the expert here on sussing out a scout. I'd go along to training, find an inconspicuous spot to spy from and draw my own conclusions.

Well check me out! All going along *and* drawing my own conclusions! *Goodbye begging for scraps of Cee-Cee and Joey's conclusions and good riddance!*

33

STOP BEING A LOSER PROGRAMME

DAY SEVENTY-FIVE

The following morning, I phoned Antonio Galanos, Head of the Notts County Council leisure department, and introduced myself. Mr Galanos fussed and fawned and waffled on about all the amazing shiny new facilities at the Amelia Piper Swimming Centre, and how he really hoped I would be their guest of honour at the grand opening and I was very welcome to bring my family and friends along, they would have a wonderful time and be very well looked after.

'What about my friend Tate? I could invite him along to see this fantastic, incredible pool. But then, Tate is disabled, and he can't get in the water without a hoist. So, all he'd be able to do is see it. I'm not sure quite how fun it would be for him to sit at the side and wave at his two sisters and two brothers splashing around in the intelligent thermostatically controlled water. What do you think?'

'Um.' There was a brief silence as he fumbled for a reply. 'We do have a wheelchair accessible café area.'

'If he wanted to go to a café, he'd pick a nice one, like the Cup and Saucer in Brooksby, which is also accessible and isn't a bus ride away. Incidentally, the café owner's wife, Gill, also uses a wheelchair so can't use your amazing new pool facilities. Would you like me to invite her to the grand opening? Will she be very well looked after as she watches from the café area?'

'Um.'

I breathed out a loooong sigh. 'Look, I know it's not your fault personally. I don't want to make you feel bad, but surely, as the Head of Leisure Services, you could have done something? Maybe, before splashing out on a smartphone-controlled LED lighting and music system, gone for a pool that more people can actually get into? I'm not sure I feel comfortable endorsing a facility that is so non-inclusive.'

A gulp came down the phone line. 'The signage has already been ordered,' he stammered. 'We can't possibly change the name now.'

'I wonder if the newspapers would be more receptive to my opinion?' I pondered. 'Come to think of it, a national journalist has been in touch recently, wanting to do a "where is she now?" story. Moira Vanderbeek. Perhaps you know her?'

'Um, I don't think...'

'Funny that, because you're friends on Facebook.'

'Well...'

'I'm guessing not friends enough that she'd ditch a story like this to protect your smart little swimming pool.'

Antonio Galanos took a couple of deep breaths. He hadn't risen through the ranks of the Nottinghamshire County Council and made it to Head of Leisure Services for nothing!

'Look, I'm aware that the lack of a hoist was an oversight. But these things cost money and there isn't any left. What I *can* do is invite you to meet with our team and discuss a hoist budget for the longer term.'

'That doesn't really help Tate and Gill now though, does it?'

'I appreciate that, Ms Piper, but really, I'm not sure what you want me to do.'

'Well, I'm very glad you've asked.'

Fifteen minutes later, I had a guarantee (to be confirmed in an email by five o'clock that evening) that the council would give their full backing to the PoolPal campaign. I wanted banners, flyers, marketing, encouragement to every team entering the triathlon to consider raising money, all profits made from their wheelchair-accessible café area on the opening weekend and a generous donation to the JustGiving page from Antonio Galanos as a demonstration of his personal commitment.

That was for starters.

But the price was not cheap.

Amelia Piper was opening the swimming centre. This included

giving a speech and presenting the triathlon trophy, along with a gazil-
lion photos and meet and greets with local sports clubs. That I had been
prepared for. The point at which I had to squinch my eyes shut and
think very hard about Tate was when Antonio asked me to do an interview with Moira Vanderbeek. I would have said no, but I'd just threat-
ened him with the same thing. Plus, I was pretending to be a badass.

It was my turn to gulp. I did remember to hang up the phone first.

I sat back, made a congratulatory cup of tea and shook my head in
wonder that the woman who'd coolly negotiated such a fantastic agreement with the council moments earlier was actually me. If I carried on
at this rate, forget pretending, I'd be a badass for real.

And when I thought about it, in a secret spot in my own mind, I was
maybe starting to like myself a little bit. Enough to know that liking
myself, feeling proud of who I was becoming, was okay.

* * *

At seven o'clock that evening, Nathan met us at the Brooksby Leisure
Centre door. I eyed his trainers and tracksuit with a questioning
eyebrow.

'I've got a change of clothes in my car.'

Speaking of cars... yep – there it was. Skulking in its usual corner. I
wasn't surprised. At some point in the past twenty-eight hours, my head
had clicked two connecting thoughts together like Lego bricks: mysterious fancy car, often found loitering in the leisure centre or outside my
house, plus a scout scouting out my son. The car was stalking Joey. Full
on stalking might seem extreme to those who haven't lived inside the
world of ultra-competitive sport, but I knew different. If a big-time agent
wanted a new client, they would be thinking about sponsorship,
endorsements, celebrity appeal. They would be asking who this athlete
was – did they have a stable family life, were there any unsavoury secrets
that could pose a problem in the future, were they susceptible to taking
performance-enhancing drugs – or party-enhancing drugs? Were they
constantly getting into trouble with authority?

If it was a big agent, and they were doing their research, they would
surely have connected Joey Piper to Amelia Piper.

Joey was thirteen. Even if he joined the Gladiators and looked set to make it to the national squad, I'd be insisting on no agent for a long while yet. If ever. And come the Easter bank holiday, my cover was blown anyway. All I had to do was stall this scout until then.

For now, getting a decent look at him would suffice. From the inside of the leisure centre, which is where I presumed he was, given that the car was empty.

'Right. Let's do this!' Joey grinned, pumped that his mum, the ex-world champion swimmer, was seeing him train at last.

'Yes,' I said. Or tried to say. It came out more like a dying chipmunk's final breath.

'We'll see you in there,' Nathan said. 'Your mum might need to take her time.'

Joey frowned, reluctant to go in without me.

'Don't worry, I promise I won't let her run off. She's coming in even if I have to carry her.'

I flapped my hand, anxiety sign language for 'what he said', and Joey nodded once before jogging inside.

'Amy – you need to breathe,' Nathan said.

'The smell, though,' I whispered, using as little breath as possible.

A woman pushed open the door to leave, releasing another blast of warm, wet, chloriney air that churned up a tornado of nausea and dizziness, while sweat popped out from every pore on my body. My hand groped blindly behind me for the entrance railings, as the all too familiar panic clamped down on my chest.

Don't fall, Amy.

'Of course you're going to fall,' my anxiety screeched. *'You can't breathe. Your heart is exploding. You're about to collapse and smack your head on the concrete and a whole crowd of people will gather round to watch you bleed.'*

If I could only reach the railings, grip onto something. Anything...

And then my flailing fingers brushed something solid. And warm. And soft and strong all at the same time, and whatever it was wrapped itself around my hand and held on tight.

And, hallelujah, I *was* thinking. And breathing. And my heart was decelerating to a pace where I could distinguish the individual beats again. Because I knew that hand. I was learning to trust it, almost as much as I liked it.

'I'm not dying,' I croaked.

'Nope,' Nathan agreed.

'Just feel like crap.'

'I sort of picked up on that.'

And then it hit me.

This feeling – which to be fair, was overpoweringly horrendous to the point that it genuinely did seem as though I was dying – was it. There was nothing terrible inside the leisure centre. The monster I feared was *this*. Was here. Inside me. I was panicking because I was afraid of a panic attack. Afraid that the panic would make me collapse, or throw up, or act hysterical, or not do something I needed to do, like show up and act normal. A fear that was justified, considering in the past it had made me do all those things.

But it was the *fear* that made me do it. Not the place, or the people, or the chemical smell or the echoey tiles or the squeak of a swim cap.

And I couldn't feel any more afraid than I had thirty seconds ago.

And I was not going to let a *feeling* stop me from keeping a promise to my son.

I slowly straightened upright, lifted my head so that I could see more than my shoes. Wiped the perspiration-snot-tear combo off my face with a tissue and adjusted my woolly hat.

'Let's go,' I declared, face set like flint.

'Lead the way,' Nathan grinned.

I looked back down at my feet, doing their best not to let the team down but not quite ready to be leading this stage of the Programme just yet.

'Could you lead the way?' I asked. 'I'll follow.'

Nathan's eyes did that kind, crinkly thing again and he gently tugged me forwards a couple of steps. 'Let's do it together. That way I can catch you if you pass out.'

'Good plan.'

And it was. I shuffled along, gripping my anchor, keeping my breaths as shallow as possible as we made it up the stairs to the viewing area, which overlooked the pool below. I lowered myself into a plastic chair and finally unclenched my hand from around Nathan's.

'You can open your eyes now,' he said.

I did. His were still crinkling away. 'You look inappropriately pleased to be witnessing someone suffering a panic attack.'

'That would be inappropriate. But I'm witnessing someone over-coming a panic attack, and seeing that has made my day.'

Oof – it seemed my poor, frazzled heart had just about enough energy left to do a weak flop in response.

'Do you want a coffee or anything?'

'I've water in my bag.'

'Right, I'd better get down there.'

'Thank you,' I called, as he reached the stairwell, managing to squeeze the words through the giant blob of tears balled up in my throat.

He spun around and paused there for a moment. 'Well done.'

Two little words, but he spoke them as if one of his squad had won the gold. Like he was proud of me. I tucked those words inside my heart and used the warm glow to power me around to look down onto the vision of my past a few metres below.

My past. My son's future. He was even more astonishing than I'd imagined. I wondered if me being there helped. Scrap that. I *knew* how much it helped. The number of times he glanced up at the viewing area told me that. Mesmerised, I barely blinked the whole time, so desperate was I to not miss a second of it.

Different swimsuits and shorts, a lot less bellowing and bullying from the coach, but not much else had changed. It was all so familiar, yet it felt as though a lifetime of avoidance and denial, secrets and cover-ups, had built an impenetrable wall between my present world and this one. I watched, and wept, and let the adrenaline gallop through my system, but, most important of all, I stayed.

It was incredible. Me, here at last. Watching my boy. I pushed aside the weight of regret, and shame and anger and hurt, and grasped hold of what consolation I could at the certainty that this was a new day, I was here now, and I would be here from now on. I had made it.

Twenty minutes before the end of the training session, a man wearing a dark brown baseball cap pushed through a door below and hurried over to one of the poolside benches where a few of the parents were watching their kids below me. He sat down, one arm placed on each knee, head twisting from side to side until he spotted Joey, powering along the far lane.

He didn't look like a scout. Scouts wore tracksuits and trainers, not jeans, thick sweaters and heavy boots. And the agents who didn't go for sportswear dressed in suits.

Who was this man?

I clattered down the stairs in a mix of anger and terror, wheeling along the corridor to the door leading to the pool. As my brain finally caught up with my agitated body, it produced this thought: *What are you going to do when you open the door, Amy? Accuse him of stalking in front of everyone? What if he knows who you are? What if the one time you turn up at Joey's training you cause a scene and embarrass him?*

Jerking to a stop, I crashed into the door, sending it flying open as I stood there behind it. Every pair of eyes belonging to everybody on the bench swivelled to look at me. In the split second before the door swung shut again, my own eyes locked onto two of them. Which was precisely enough time to realise who they did in fact belong to.

'Sean Mansfield,' I exclaimed. 'I should have known.'

I stood there, my nose an inch from the closed door, my whole being in suspended animation. Before I slipped completely into an insensible stupor, the door creaked open and Nathan appeared.

'Are you okay?'

'Probably not.'

'Were you trying to brave it poolside? If you wait ten minutes, I'll give you a hand.'

'No. Thank you. I'm going to sit out here and wait for the other parents to leave.'

Behind what I hoped was my cool exterior, I began plotting grue-some murder.

'Amy, are you sure you're okay?'

'Yes.' I rotated myself around and jerked down the corridor towards the reception desk. I had approximately fifteen minutes to get a grip and decide how the hell I was going to handle this without upsetting Joey or breaking the law.

Fourteen minutes and thirty seconds later, my plan consisted of don't upset Joey and don't break the law.

Every gracious thought I had been trying to summon up in order to allow that man to meet my son had evaporated in a cloud of steam tooting out my ears.

I waited on a plastic chair while the other parents and the lifeguard strolled past. Some of the faster club members began to filter out of the changing room door on the other side of the reception desk. Was Sean going to hide in there until the leisure centre staff locked everything up? Did he really think that—

Apparently not.

Sean Mansfield scurried into the centre foyer and straight past me, head down, cap pulled low, as if I wasn't even there.

'Take one step out through those doors and you will never meet your son.'

Well, that did the trick. He froze for a few seconds, then swung slowly around as I sucked in a long, careful breath, trying to calm my heart from its frenzied scrabbling.

I dug deep for the few remaining scraps of courage that would help me meet his gaze, head up, jaw set, shoulders squared.

'Amy.'

'You've been stalking Joey. For weeks.'

He pulled up the side of his mouth. The familiarity of his '*I'm sorry but, hey, I'm charming, so you can't help but forgive me*' expression was like being punched in the stomach with a thousand memories. 'I'm not sure it's technically stalking if it's your own child.'

'I'm not sure he's technically your child if you abandon him before he was born and wait thirteen years before bothering to try and contact him.'

'I thought about him. And you. Every single day.'

'No. You didn't.'

'I regretted what happened—'

'What you chose to do.'

'...from the moment I left. I realised that however tough being a father would be, it couldn't be as hard as knowing my child was growing up without me.'

I laughed, then. At least, it started out as a laugh and twisted into a sort of enraged snarl.

'You thought about your child every day? I thought about him every second. Loved him and cared for him. Found a way to provide for him after you left us with nothing. I was there, with him, doing whatever it took to be a mother and a father to my son. That you could even suggest that sparing him the odd thought is somehow harder than putting in everything I had, than making everything I did be for him, just confirms that you have no idea what it is to be a parent, that you have no right to call him your child. If your biggest concern was that he didn't know you, rather than whether he had a roof over his head, or food to eat, let alone was happy or safe or healthy, then you are no father.'

I vaguely registered a collective gasp from the parents and children gathered, enthralled, in the foyer.

'I did worry about that,' Sean mumbled, his eyes pleading. 'But I didn't know where you were. I was young, and broke.'

I wasn't the only one who let out a loud snort.

'I knew I'd messed up, badly. And I kept thinking that I needed to sort myself out, get a decent job, some money saved, show you I'd grown up, that I deserved to be allowed back into his life...'

'Back in?'

'I was young, Amy. I was an idiot. I've told you that in the emails, apologised. But, like I said, I'm here now to put it right.'

'Why now? You've been running a successful business for six years.'

'I don't know... by the time I felt ready, it seemed like too much time had passed. And then, well, like you said, I have a business to run. I always thought that soon I'd do it, in a few months, once we'd negotiated that contract, completed the next project, and before I knew it, years had passed. And honestly? I felt terrified. I knew if you'd told him the truth about me, he'd probably hate me. I hate myself for what I did.'

'So, it was easier to do nothing. It's a good job utter terror and self-hatred didn't stop me from being there for him.'

Sean took a couple of steps closer. 'I can't excuse it. But please give me a chance. I'm here now.'

'Yes, you are. And how long exactly have you been here, sneaking around and scaring people, Sean? Are you sure your business is coping without you?'

'I've been here since the end of August. And I'll stay for as long as it takes.'

'Oh, please. For as long as what takes? For you to stop feeling guilty?'

'This isn't about me.'

'Yeah, right,' one of the dads behind me retorted.

I automatically glanced back, the realisation hitting me that a dustbin-lorryload of mine and Joey's personal issues now lay scattered across the reception before a crowd of onlooking scavengers.

'You need to go before Joey gets here.'

Where the hell *was* Joey? I scanned the crowd, but the only pale blond mop in the room was Sean's.

'Are you still going to let me see him?' Sean spoke quickly, his eyes imploring. 'At least tell him I'm here, let him decide...'

'Get out of here now, and I'll tell him.'

I mean, I would have to, wouldn't I? The trick would be doing it before half the swim team and the smattering of overly competitive parents told him first.

'I'll wait for you to message me. Or... or call... or shall I call you?'

'Go!' I practically shrieked, only waiting long enough to be sure Sean had actually exited the building and was out of sight before pushing my way through the crowd. In blatant disregard of swimming pool etiquette, child protection issues and quite possibly the law, I burst into the male changing room, eyes frantically searching for Joey, my legs nearly collapsing when they found him, sat on a bench with Nathan.

'Mum? What's happened?' Joey stood up, understandably alarmed. 'Are you having a freak-out? I'm really sorry, only Nathan wanted to talk about changing the training programme.'

'I'll leave you to it.' Nathan gave my arm a reassuring squeeze as he passed.

'Thank you,' I whispered.

He nodded, once, and let the door close behind him.

'Firstly, you were magnificent,' I said. 'It took my breath away, watching you fly through the water like you were made for it. I'm so grateful I got to see that, so thrilled and delighted and awed, I don't want to waste any more time feeling devastated about how much I've missed. I'm beyond proud, Joey.'

'Thanks. But can you hurry up and tell me what's second, because you've not even given me a hug, so I know it's something bad.'

I sprang forward and wrapped my arms around him, speaking into his shoulder. 'It's not bad. At least not totally bad. But I think we'd best talk about it at home.'

He peeled himself away from me. 'Let's go then!'

* * *

We talked for a long time that night. And then spent more time sat side by side on the sofa, not talking. Until way past a sensible bedtime for a thirteen-year-old who is supposed to be training at seven-thirty the next morning before a full day of school. Joey was shaken to know that Sean was in the UK, let alone that he'd been following him about for the past few weeks.

'He should have told you.'

'Yes, he really should have,' I agreed.

'I guess if you've never parented before you don't know about being appropriate and stuff.'

I didn't reply that any adult should know that stalking people is never appropriate. And certainly not stalking a child.

I knew that the only way for Joey to have any peace, let alone sleep, was to arrange a meeting. I texted Sean and asked him to be in the Cup and Saucer at five-thirty the next day. Not an ideal choice of venue, it being one where there would be other human beings, some of whom might even know Joey or me, but it was the only place in the village where we could have a drink that wasn't a pub, and it would feel weird taking my son to a pub to meet his dad for the first time, on a school night. While able to feel some gratitude that this whole thing had happened once I had been able to go anywhere, I wasn't ready to think about catching a bus, or getting a taxi, to somewhere new.

Eventually, I pulled rank and called it a night, bundling Joey up the stairs. 'Come on, let's at least pretend to try and get some sleep. And I think it would be wise to skip your early training tomorrow.'

'What? I seem to remember you going on about how if I was going to be serious about swimming, I couldn't skip training because I was tired, or had a bad day, or had other stuff going on. "You have to get up and show up and give it all you've got, no matter what."'

'Hmmm. Well. You're not in the Gladiators yet.' I opened his bedroom door, winced at the mess, and gestured for him to go in.

'No, and I never will be if I decide to lie-in every time some little thing happens like my dad turning out to be the village stalker. What would Nathan say?'

'Coach Gallagher would say that you should trust your mother when she tells you that if you want to make the distance as a swimmer, you need to make some occasional allowances.'

'I do trust you. But I'm also not you.' He flopped onto the duvet, flinging one arm over his face, no doubt to block out all sight and sound of his annoying mother.

'I'll let Nathan know that you might not be there. He'll understand. Good night.' I quickly backed out, pulling the door shut behind me.

'He'll understand that at the first sign of pressure I need my mum to step in and start taking over like I'm some little kid!' he yelled through the wood. 'Stop fussing, I'm not tired! You're so irritating!'

'I love you, Joey!' I sang back, as irritating as ever. 'Try to get some sleep.'

34

STOP BEING A LOSER PROGRAMME

DAY SEVENTY-SIX

'I wasn't sure you'd be here,' Nathan said when I arrived in time for the warm-up the following day. 'Thought it might be a sleepless night.'

'It was, so I decided to come and run before I started using up my nervous energy smashing plates or throwing stones at cars.'

'How's Joey?'

I leant against the leisure centre wall and began stretching out my leg muscles. 'As you'd expect. A dozen different emotions all bubbling together inside the brain of a half-child, half-man.' I swapped to the other leg. 'Insists he's coming to training though.'

Nathan nodded. 'I can see why. It's as good as running to get rid of some of that nervous energy, shut down the manic thoughts for a while.'

'That's true.'

Nathan twisted round in the shadows and bent his head closer to mine so that the other Larks couldn't hear him softly say, 'And by the way, I forgive you for standing me up last night. It had only taken about an hour to find a decent pair of shoes, on top of the time it took to figure out how to iron a shirt.'

I dropped my foot from the thigh stretch I'd been doing. 'I completely forgot!'

Nathan smiled. 'Like I said, I forgive you. And I also understand if you need to put the Programme on hold, given the extenuating circumstances.'

'Err – hang on, buddy. I went inside the pool last night. You ironed a shirt. Screw extenuating circumstances, you owe me a sweaty, awkward, challenging evening.'

'My, my,' Bronwyn exclaimed, as she strolled past. 'Can I come?'

'It's not what you think!' I called after her, following a frozen moment of horrified silence.

'Oh, Amy, you have *no idea* what I'm thinking.' Bronwyn looked me up and down in the amber glow of the car park lighting. 'Then again, maybe you do!'

'Bronwyn, you know the policy on my relationships with club members,' Nathan hissed.

'Yes, but policies were made to be broken, isn't that right?' she drawled, somehow making it sound a million times more suggestive than any sentence containing the word 'policies' should be.

Nathan looked about ready to combust, pulling at his hat with agitation. 'No! I'm helping Amy with some private coaching.'

'I bet you are!'

'Of a perfectly respectable nature, well within the policy! And in return, she's... helping me to overcome a few of my own...'

'*Policies?*' Bronwyn couldn't help laughing, high-fiving the woman next to her at the same time.

'Issues,' Nathan choked out.

'Ah, Nathan, I'll help you with your issues,' someone shouted from the shadows. 'You can call on me anytime.'

As the catcalls continued, I slunk off to one side, glancing over to see Nathan clenching his jaw, eyes on the ground, hands firmly planted on his hips.

'That's harassment in the workplace,' Dani pronounced, as she swung past him. 'You should give me a call sometime, I'll sort this lot out. For a reasonable fee.'

'A reasonable fee?' Nathan shot back, eyes dancing in the darkness. 'That's the funniest thing I've heard all morning. Right. Time to stop gabbing and get moving. And, Amy, I'll see you tomorrow night after Joey's training. Now, stretch up...'

* * *

Inevitably, it somehow happened to be both the longest day while at the same time whizzing towards five-thirty like a speeding space-shuttle. I faffed about on a new project, made a half-hearted attempt at some cleaning, flopped on my back under the duvet, fretted, worried, agonised and stayed as far away from external doors and windows as possible.

Of course, when Joey came home from school it only got worse. We flitted around the house like mosquitoes in a heatwave, and I don't think I was the only one who changed my outfit more than once before we headed out.

'Is it weird, seeing him?' Joey asked as we walked towards the square.

'Very,' I replied, voice muffled from behind my scarf. 'He's different in some ways – obviously he looks older. But his voice and his mannerisms haven't changed at all.'

'Do you hate him?'

'No.' And I wasn't lying, either. 'I do feel angry, and have some painful memories about what happened. But he didn't deliberately try to hurt me, and he's the one who missed out.'

'I can't help trying to imagine what it would have been like if he'd not gone, and I'd grown up with a mum and dad around. Is that okay?'

I took a few strides before answering. 'Yes, of course it's okay. But we wouldn't have stayed together even if he hadn't gone to America.'

'He'd still have been around to do stuff with me. Take me on holiday and things.'

Come on now, woman. Don't start crying before you've even got there.

We waited for a car to pass before crossing the road onto the square.

'But there's no point wondering what might have happened, is there? Because it didn't, and we can't change it. And if he's the kind of dad who left before I was born, it might not have been that great having him around anyway. At least now I'm old enough to figure out for myself if he's worth bothering with or not.'

Oh, Joey.

I hoped so.

* * *

Sean was waiting at a corner table. He jumped up when he saw us come in, brushing his hands against a black pair of jeans.

Joey walked right up and held out his hand.

'I'm Joey. It's good to meet you.'

Sean reached out and tentatively shook it, unable to take his eyes off Joey's face. 'It's *great* to meet you,' he said. 'I've looked forward to this for a long time.'

Joey nodded, pulling out a chair and sitting down. I joined him facing Sean, although it was already clear that my role in this meeting would be that of silent partner.

The next hour passed in a blur. I gripped my coffee mug, made sure my lungs re-inflated every few seconds and focused on the sturdiness of the oak table in front of me. Joey had that confidence in talking to adults common in only children and, after a hesitant start, was soon making conversation with Sean about school, his various sports clubs, what computer games he played, films he liked. He also quizzed Sean about his life in Colorado, and I managed to absorb enough to learn that he had been engaged in his late twenties, had no children and lived in what sounded like an excessively large ranch-type house for one person.

And then came the question we'd all been waiting for:

'Why did you want to meet me?'

Sean swallowed. He must have been prepared for this, but I enjoyed watching him squirm all the same. A bit different looking your own child in the face and answering that than it must have been practising it in the mirror.

'I... You're my son. I'm only sorry we didn't meet earlier.'

'So, why didn't we?'

Sean sighed. 'Because I was an idiot. And a coward. For a long time, I didn't know how to even start, we live so far apart.'

'Although you didn't know where I lived. I could have been anywhere.'

A short pause. 'I guess I assumed you were in the UK.'

'How did you know we even had somewhere to live?' Oh boy. I held my breath, waiting to see how this turned out.

'I knew your grandparents would take care of you both.'

'Mum's parents wanted about as much to do with me as you did,' Joey replied, while I tried to unclog the broken shards of heart from my windpipe by sheer force of will. 'They've never even met me.'

All the colour drained from Sean's face. Even his lips were white. 'What?' He looked at me, aghast.

'You knew they'd sued me and then published a book about it. Why on earth did you think they'd want to take on my baby?'

'But how could they leave you to fend for yourself? Their own child?' he stuttered.

'Bloody hell, Sean!' Oh dear, this conversation appeared to have caused my swear-translator to malfunction.

'What, like you did, you mean?' Joey said.

Sean dropped his forehead into his clenched fists, barely managing to stop his jaw from scraping the table. We sat there, Joey and I, and calmly waited for him to pull himself together.

Eventually, after much face rubbing and slow head shaking, Sean rose from the depths of the table. 'I'm so sorry. I just never thought.'

'Well, no, that would have presented you with a quite inconvenient truth, wouldn't it?' I said.

'What did you do?' he asked, voice hoarse.

'We coped,' I snapped back, suddenly exhausted with the whole conversation. Part of me wanted Sean to grasp quite how tough it had been, being hurled across the chasm from Sports Personality of the Year nominee to homeless, jobless, single teenage mother in such a short space of time. The other part – a mix of pride and wanting to protect Joey – wanted to stick my chin up and pretend I'd managed perfectly fine, thank you very much, and here is the amazing proof, sitting right next to me.

And it was for Joey's sake that I summoned up enough strength to bite back the thirteen years of angry accusations jostling to be heard, squished my outrage down beneath my clenched intestines and took a slow, deep breath.

'So, where are you staying? Have you managed to see much of Nottinghamshire while you've been here?' I asked, valiantly omitting 'or have you been too busy stalking us?'

Sean blinked a couple of times.

I picked up my slice of lime and courgette cake, waving it breezily. 'If you can get out into Sherwood Forest this time of year, I've heard the trees are spectacular.'

It took another minute or two of blatant changing the subject before

Sean got the hint that I was moving things along from grotesquely painful to bearably bland. He tried to chat with Joey for a few more minutes, but the mood had shifted from nervously expectant to strange and tense.

'I think it's time we made a move,' I interjected after an awkward anecdote about Sean's brother (Joey's uncle!). Joey sprang from his seat before I'd completed the sentence.

'Right, well. It was wonderful to meet you.' Sean stood, too. He was the exact same height as Joey. 'I really appreciate it. And I hope we can do it again soon.'

'I'll let you know,' I said, snapping on my woolly gloves as if my insides weren't a crumbling pile of wreckage. 'Joey's very busy with school and swimming at the moment. As you're aware.'

'I wish I could tell you how sorry I am,' Sean blurted, just as we began to leave.

Joey turned around, and the brief flash of anguish and confusion was a perfect mirror of the face behind us.

'I wish I could make it up to you. Prove I'm not that selfish, immature jerk any more. I know I have a huge amount of work to do before I can earn your trust, let alone your respect or affection. But I'll do whatever it takes. Whatever you need. I hate that I wasn't there for you. But I'm here now. Please give me a chance.'

Bleuch! 'That's enough, Sean. I said I'll let you know.' Fully immune to his charms, I placed my hand on Joey's elbow and steered him out of the café. But I knew it was too late. Desperate for a dad worth knowing – worth forgiving – with the simple faith of a child, Joey decided to give Sean a chance.

And I couldn't blame him. I knew I mustn't try to change his mind, that I shouldn't allow my feelings on the matter to influence how I handled Joey's. But, ooh, how I wished that smooth-talking, drops-in-now-it's-convenient, not-even-a-part-time-dad had never come here. I couldn't wait for him to go back.

35

STOP BEING A LOSER PROGRAMME

DAY SEVENTY-NINE

I had been invaded. Again. Only worse. It was nine-thirty on Saturday morning, Joey had headed off for an early football match, and I'd planned a lazy morning to combat the stress of the day before. However, somehow my house had become the headquarters for the Amelia Piper Swimming Centre PoolPal campaign. Maybe I should have known that sending Mel the link to the JustGiving page I'd set up would result in half the Larks plus associated children and elderly mother turning up on my doorstep, but I was still getting used to this whole friends thing.

An hour after Mel and Dani's arrival, I was still pretending that the ratty, oversized leggings and long-sleeved T-shirt I'd worn were my outfit for the day, not that of the night before. Mel's two older boys, Jordan and Riley, were at home in bed. Taylor was spending the weekend with her dad, so Tiff and Tate were now in my living room watching one of Joey's old Disney DVDs while Mel chose a good publicity photo of Tate. Marjory and Bronwyn were sat at my desk, designing a logo, and Dani was trying to put together a couple of paragraphs to pass on to the press that managed to tug on heartstrings without pulling so hard they made people cringe. Bronwyn's mother, Gwen, was assembling mince pies at my kitchen table.

'It calms her down, see,' Bronwyn had told me, unloading a mountain of ingredients when she'd first arrived. 'She's got dementia. Early onset – it's why I joined the Larks. My dad can manage first thing, but once he's at work she needs me around. It's fair dos, he takes the evening shifts while I'm working. But anyway, she was a Saturday girl in a bakery, back in Swansea, and she's not lost her touch, have you, Mam?'

Gwen didn't answer, but she smiled faintly while adding a handful of orange peel to a huge metal bowl.

I did my best to smile back. While Joey had often invited whole groups of friends over in the past, this was the first time I'd ever had a houseful. Seeing my kitchen crammed with people – *Teammates? Friends?!* – discussing and joking and working together, was incredible but overwhelming. I didn't know the rules, didn't know how I felt about them rooting through my cupboards, moving my stuff and taking up all my space. Then I thought about the quiet, lonely tomb my house had been for the past few years and decided I felt flippin' well over the moon about it.

'Where do you work?' I asked Bronwyn, while putting the kettle on, a genuine smile on my face now.

'Oh, security at Outlaws. The new venue in Nottingham?'

'Security?'

Bronwyn grinned, and flexed her muscles. 'I'm the best bouncer they've got. Ever been there?'

'No.' But I'd heard of it. The rumour was that the doormen (and women, as it turned out) were checking that you'd got a suitable weapon before letting you in, rather than the usual way around. Even if I had a social life, was ten years younger and had the energy or the money for a night in Nottingham, I would have had to be a genuine outlaw before venturing inside Outlaws. And Bronwyn was in the paid employ of the crooks who ran the place. Gulp.

She wrinkled her tiny, pert nose. 'Yeah, I know it's not one hundred per cent morally sound, but I need the money, and they pay *good* money. One day Mam might need full-time care. We don't know how much longer Dad can work since his stroke, and forget a rainy day, I'm saving for the crapstorm I know is heading our way. Once I've got enough saved, I'll be back in an office somewhere.'

'If you live that long,' Dani said, looking up from where her laptop rested on top of my hob.

'Well, the only other way I know how to earn this much a night involves stuff that would make my Daddy cry if he ever found out. And if it all turns ugly, I know a good lawyer.'

'You better not need this lawyer,' Dani frowned. 'I wage courtroom war against some nasty pieces of work, but I would consider retirement before I messed with those Outlaws. The clue is in the name.'

We were interrupted by a knock at the door. Strange. If it had been another Lark, they'd surely have just swanned in. All my friends bar one (who I knew was working all morning) were here already, plus extras. That left ex-boyfriends, pushy journalists or one of Joey's friends. And Joey's friends didn't call round unannounced at this time of the morning.

While I was still wondering who it might be, hoping it would be someone who wouldn't want to come in – I had hit my physical, mental and emotional capacity for guests about four guests ago – Marjory answered the door.

'Oh, hello!' she said. 'Long time no see.'

'Marjory,' a voice I knew better than my own mother's replied.

Oh no.

Who do I even introduce her as?

How do I explain knowing her?

I'mnotreadytotellthemyet. I still want to be Amy for a while longer.

PLEASE don't tell them.

Marjory stepped back to allow Cee-Cee in, and any panic that my secret was about to be exposed or annoyance at her uninvited appearance dissolved at the sight of her dishevelled state and grey complexion as she scanned the occupants of the kitchen with shrunken eyes, before they came to rest on me.

'I'm sorry. I didn't realise you had company. I'll come back another time.'

Of course she didn't realise. Apart from Joey's friends and the odd repair man, she'd been the only company in this house since I'd moved in. Until I joined the Larks.

'No, it's fine.' I tried to ignore the pulse pecking at the inside of my skull. 'We can talk in the garden.'

'What?' Cee-Cee glanced out the window at the sunshine, probably wondering what alternate reality she'd stepped into.

'Don't be daft, we're moving.' Bronwyn gave Marjory and Dani a pointed look, gently taking her mum's hand.

Two seconds later, they had joined Mel and the kids in the living room. My kitchen suddenly seemed very empty.

Cee-Cee lowered herself onto one of the chairs, wincing. 'You don't need to look at me like that. It's just arthritis.'

Are the side effects of arthritis lank, unkempt hair and giant eye bags? Does it cause extreme weight loss and sagging shoulders where a curtain rod used to be? A surge of compassion welled up in my throat as I took a seat beside her, rendering me speechless.

'I see you've been busy.' *Replacing me.*

I poured her a tea from the pot and sat down. 'It's Redbush.' Because, yes, I had wondered if a certain non-normal-tea drinker might pop in after finishing work to see how things were going. 'I joined a running club. We're starting a campaign to raise money for a disabled hoist at the new Greasby pool.'

'Right.'

We sat there for a moment in awkward silence.

'How do you know Marjory?' I asked.

'Mexico '68. We became... very good friends.' *What does that mean??*

'You competed at the Olympics?' *And never told me!?*

For a startling moment, I realised how little I actually knew about Cee-Cee's past. She had always been Coach Coleman to me. But she was also a woman, had been a girl before then, with hopes and dreams and hobbies and homework. My guilt jumped up a gear as I realised that the context of our relationship meant that I'd always thought of Cee-Cee in terms of how she related to me, and then Joey. I had considered her my closest friend for thirteen years, and I didn't even know her real first name. My illness had reduced me to a horribly self-obsessed person. A terrible friend. If Cee-Cee had been a mother to me, she had endured a spoilt brat for a daughter.

Before I could begin to convey any of this, Cee-Cee shook her head, impatiently. 'She ran the eighteen hundred metres. I was with the coaching team. Things were more... flexible then.'

'Maybe you could tell me about it sometime.'

She scoffed at that. 'No point dredging up the past.'

'I think Marjory might do some dredging. She knows who I am.'

'Don't the rest of them?'

'They only know me as Amy.'

'And now you're spearheading a campaign for the Amelia Piper Swimming Centre.' Something akin to a smile flitted across Cee-Cee's face. 'How do you expect that will turn out?'

'I'll tell them before the opening. Once I've regained enough self-respect that admitting it won't make them pity where I've ended up.'

She nodded. 'You think that's likely?'

I shrugged.

'Maybe you should aim for enough self-respect that you won't care what they think.'

We both drank some more tea, listening to the lively buzz of chatter from the living room.

'Was there a reason you came over?' I cringed as I asked, still finding confronting her hugely difficult.

'Heard Sean had turned up. Thought you might need some moral support.'

I took another sip of my tea, considering that. Was I ready to welcome Cee-Cee back? I ached for some support, but could I accept it from her, or would moral support soon morph into her controlling and undermining me? With everything else going on, I didn't think I had the energy to fight her. But looking at Cee-Cee, she wouldn't be putting up much of a fight, either. And I was not the same woman I had been a few months ago. I took a deep breath, drew a mental boundary that would not be crossed, and nodded.

'Have you got any plans for Christmas Day?'

Cee-Cee took a careful sip of tea, avoiding my eyes. 'Not as yet.'

'Will you join us for dinner?'

'Yes. Thank you.' Her chin tipped up then, and I saw something of my old friend glinting in her eyes. 'I'll come early and help you prep. You can tell me what needs doing.'

So that was that – Cee-Cee was back. I hoped I was ready. I hoped I wasn't to blame for her shabby appearance and hollowed-out cheeks. I hoped that we could start again, on an equal footing, and build a genuine friendship this time. I hoped that one day the shard of icy guilt now sawing through my guts would stop and let me enjoy one of Gwen's mince pies, which turned out to be a miraculous combination of fluffiness, buttery crumbliness and warm, spicy Christmas all in one.

Bored of campaign prep, by noon everyone was in the living room surrounded by empty cups and pastry crumbs, chatting about who would be doing each section of the triathlon. Nobody seemed in a hurry to leave, or to have considered the possibility that I might actually have plans other than entertaining a houseful of unexpected guests for the day, and when Selena and Audrey turned up, I started to wonder how I was going to rustle up lunch for eight women, two children and the bottomless teenager currently stripping my fridge bare like a locust.

Perching on an old beanbag in her pencil skirt and towering heels, thanks to everyone ignoring her hints to give up their seat, Selena proudly showed us her plans for the social media part of the campaign. 'Facebook for the oldies, Instagram for the rest of us. Hashtag PoolPalforPiper. We'll link to the JustGiving page, have updates of how much money we've made, how the triathlon training's going and include some sweaty shots of Nathan for sex appeal. Who's liaising with the council? We want to make sure they reference PoolPalforPiper every time they mention the leisure centre, especially when promoting the grand opening.'

'Amy's on council liaison,' Mel said, before breaking into a grin. 'Eh, this is like being on *The Apprentice*, in't it? Reckon I might get one of them tight skirts, Selena. I've seen one in Primark.'

'No you haven't,' Selena replied. 'And are we sure Amy is the right person for that role? I can't help wondering if it needs someone with more... presence. No offence, Amy, but it's going to take brains, panache and twenty-six years' experience in the marketing industry to get us anything past a token gesture. They're going to chew you up and spit you out before you can say hashtag PoolPalforPiper.'

'For mercies' sake, Selena, we get the hashtag. Congratulations. We're very impressed. You don't need to mention it every two minutes,' Dani said.

'We should all be mentioning it every two minutes! That's how a campaign goes viral and Tate gets his hydrotherapy! Now, are we all agreed I'll step in and handle the council?'

'I've already secured their full backing,' I said, examining my fingernails in a deliberately nonchalant manner.

'Eh?'

I reeled off the generous agreement I'd made with Antonio Galanos, including poolside café profits and masses of publicity, never mind his personal donation of one thousand pounds.

Selena narrowed her eyes. 'Are you screwing him or something?'

'This may come as a surprise to you, but not everything is about sex,' Dani scolded. 'How dare you imply that Amy doesn't have the brains and the panache to get the council on board without prostituting herself! And, *no offence,* but I'm not sure five decades of playing at marketing in your daddy's firm will be of that much use when it comes to actual marketing.'

'Five decades!' Selena squeaked, as if that was the most insulting comment in that statement.

'Speaking of Nathan's sweaty sex appeal—' Bronwyn interrupted.

'Bronwyn, that was ages ago, keep up,' Mel said.

'Yes, but at the time I couldn't get a word in, and then Dani said sex and that reminded me. Plus, this is good, so let me finish. Speaking of Nathan, and sweaty sex.'

My heart plummeted, while somehow still pumping copious amounts of blood to my cheeks. I knew from the wicked twinkle in Bronwyn's eye where this was headed. Would it be bad manners to ask everyone to leave immediately?

'Amy hasn't told us about her *personal, out-of-hours, late-night, sweaty* training sesh the other night. With Nathan.' She pointed, triumphant, as everyone else's heads whipped round to face me.

'Why would you want to know about my training session?' I asked, as if I didn't know. 'Nathan coaches lots of people, I don't see why mine would be any different.'

'Well, if it's all so innocent and fitness-related, you can tell us everything, can't you?' Dani asked. 'Maybe we'll pick up some tips for the triathlon.'

'Maybe if the triathlon events were flirting, snogging and seduction,' Bronwyn smirked.

Every woman craned her neck closer. Even Audrey, plonked on a cushion next to the fire, seemed to be listening.

Ah, what the heck, I decided. Every moment we'd spent together, from leaving training to Nathan dropping me off at my front door one-hundred and seven minutes later, had been replaying in the back of my mind like a loop for the thirty-eight hours since. Maybe if I told the

Larks, saw them sag with disappointment at the obvious nothing-to-be-excited-about it might help me to stop boring myself with it. And for goodness' sake, it was a huge deal for me to be finally growing myself the tiny shoots of a life. And not only did I have a life, I had people to talk about it with. How could anyone resist blabbing under these circumstances?

'There was none of that,' I laughed. 'And I don't think wine, cheese and dancing are in the triathlon either.'

'How can you even begin to class that as a training session?' Selena asked. 'Even one of those three would constitute a date.'

'Hear, hear,' Mel agreed, along with everyone else.

'It's not what it sounds like!' I protested, wishing I'd never said anything. Panicking at what Nathan would say when the women started making comments. 'Nathan's helping me with my anxiety. I'm getting over severe agoraphobia. And because despite living as a recluse with no friends for the past three years, I still have a smidgeon of pride dragging along with me, I insisted I return the favour.'

I went on to explain how the wine and cheese night was a challenge for both of us. I actually put on a dress (another online order, but I'd ordered five dresses in the hope one would fit, which this did), blow-dried my hair, got in a car and ventured more than a mile out of the village, to a place that I would never have been able to contemplate going without Nathan.

Nathan wore a shirt and allowed me to direct him to a local country club, famed for its snobbery and snootery. He sampled all six types of full-fat, pure-dairy cheese, only two of which were organic, and every time he noticed my anxiety popping up, he took my mind off it by eating something else. We had to ask the waiter for an extra plateful.

And then, after we'd spent an hour or so (fifty-seven minutes, if we're clock-watching) chatting and trying to distract ourselves from freaking out by making up stories about all the other guests, I insisted we dance.

'Oooh,' Bronwyn sighed. 'I bet Nathan's a smooooooth dancer. Did you swoon in his arms?'

'It was the end of the night. They were playing "Livin' on a Prayer".'

'That is so romantic!' Mel clasped one hand to her chest. 'Me and Mr Malone walked down the aisle of Grace Chapel to that when we were eighteen. It were our song!' She let out a honky sob. 'Only 'e didn't make it, no matter how hard 'e sweared. Or prayed. And 'e did both. A lot. We did only get halfway there, thanks to the shit-evil cancer. See, I'm swearing just thinkin' about it. Close your ears, kids.'

'That's enough to make anyone swear, poppet,' Marjory said, next to Mel on the sofa. She offered her the box of tissues from the coffee table, and by the time we'd passed it round, I hoped we'd moved on from my extracurricular activities, especially given how they didn't seem to think it was as innocent as I'd thought they would.

'So, was it romantic?' Dani asked, blotting her mascara smears. 'Did you sway in his hunksome arms?'

'I told you, there is nothing romantic about this! If Nathan thought there was, he'd ditch it in a heartbeat. And even if there was the slightest bit of interest on either side, you lot know he's one hundred per cent professional.'

'That's true,' Selena said, nodding her head like one in the know. 'However much chemistry Nathan has with one of his clients, he won't budge an inch. He's like a robot.'

'I can fully concur with that. It was the most robotic I've seen anyone move while not trying to dance the robot,' I agreed.

'Boo!' Bronwyn said. 'I can't believe he's a rubbish dancer! That is SO not what I imagined!'

'I can't believe you're surprised,' I replied. 'He's hardly Mr Uninhibited.'

'That's a good point. Maybe when he's able to let his guard down, the super-sensuous-sexy Nathan slinks out.'

'I would not like to meet that Nathan.' Mel pulled a face.

'Please, ladies,' Marjory huffed. 'Show your coach some respect. We do not need to discuss Amy's date like schoolgirls.'

'So, what happened after you danced?' Mel asked, giving Marjory a friendly nudge.

I shrugged. 'We chatted a bit more, then he drove me home.'

'Without the tiniest hint of frisson as he said goodbye?' Dani asked. 'Did he run round and open the car door? Walk you down the path? Linger on the doorstep and tell you what a lovely evening he'd had, his voice slightly rough, his expression one of wonder?'

'He did not. He pulled up, said "See you Sunday" and drove off once

I'd summoned the strength to open the car door and heroically got myself down my own drive.'

'Ah, well. We can always dream,' Dani sighed.

'You lot need to get your own love lives, stop inventing ones involving Nathan,' Selena scoffed.

'Says her!' Mel whispered, loud enough to cause every single person to duck their heads and hide their smiles, apart from Selena, who suddenly became very engrossed in what appeared to be an enraging phone message, and Audrey, who shot me a lightning-quick worried glance before hastily continuing to stare at a blank space on the wall as if completely oblivious.

* * *

Everyone left shortly after that, to my great relief, as stomachs were beginning to rumble and there were only three mince pies left. Having my first ever houseful of guests had been exhausting, but as I curled up on the sofa with a mug of butternut noodle soup, the chatter and the bustle still faintly echoed through the empty rooms. I had been an adequate hostess, I reflected, and hadn't even embarrassed myself or visibly freaked out. I thought I had made everyone feel welcome. More importantly, I couldn't believe that these women had chosen to welcome *me*. To count me as one of their own. It was so overwhelming, so stunningly wonderful, that it almost stopped me thinking about Nathan and our evening together on an endless, revolving loop of mushy drivel.

Almost.

Once Joey got back, no doubt after discerning that I'd had an unusually good day, he succeeded in interrupting my thoughts where I'd failed by bringing up the subject of seeing his dad again. This time, without me there to 'make me feel guilty for not thinking he's Despicable Dad'. Sean posed no threat, physically at least, and I didn't think a couple of hours after school could cause Joey any lasting emotional harm. But, oh, it was hard. A first, tiny, step towards co-parenting my child.

36

STOP BEING A LOSER PROGRAMME
DAY EIGHTY-FOUR

That Thursday, I took another step forward in the Programme. Sean had picked Joey up from school and taken him to a local pub restaurant that offered a 'create-your-own rotisserie experience'. I thought there were probably better experiences than thirty combinations of cheap chicken and sides, but it was a darn sight better than the non-existent places I'd taken Joey in the past few years, so I couldn't really comment.

I could, however, use my angst at the father-and-son meal to propel myself into the Brooksby Leisure Centre and firmly plant myself on a bench, *poolside,* ready for training. And I only needed to hold Nathan's hand for the actual stepping through the door into the pool area. After all, there couldn't be anything worse in here than Sean, and I'd already handled that challenge. Once I was in, I strolled on up to that old bench as if I sat there three times a week alongside all the other normal parents. Lisa, Ben's mum, came and plopped herself down next to me a few minutes later.

'Hey, Amy,' she exclaimed. 'Great to see you! You're looking well.'

By which we both knew she meant: *you're looking OUT OF YOUR HOUSE!*

It was none of her business, but she'd definitely have heard about last week's spectacle. There was no point fudging the issue.

'I'm here to spy on Joey's dad.'

Lisa nodded. 'I guessed as much. For what it's worth, the odd time I've stayed for training, he's done nothing weird.'

'You don't usually stay?'

'Nah. Only when I haven't got the twins with me. And I don't really watch. It's just an excuse to sit down and do nothing for an hour. It's not like Ben cares whether I'm here or not.'

'I thought all the parents stayed.'

Lisa rolled her eyes as a gaggle of mums pushed through the doors and started tottering towards us on heels that would have been a health and safety risk on a dance floor, let alone the side of a swimming pool. 'Only this lot. And they aren't here to watch their kids.'

I followed the tilt of her head to the other side of the pool, where Nathan was laughing with the lifeguard.

'Or the lifeguard,' she added.

Between the revelation that my guilt at not attending training had been for nothing, and the sight of five women so blatantly offering themselves up to the man I had been trying to keep in the mental friend zone, I was rather flummoxed.

'I know,' Lisa tutted. 'It's pathetic. As if he'd be interested in such a blatant attack of bored, middle-aged-crisis mums.'

I managed a vague, sort of snorty squeak in reply.

'Not that there's anything wrong with being middle-aged, or a mum, of course. I personally consider my forties to be my finest decade.' She wrinkled her nose in thought. 'I think it's the desperation that's so grim. Like, their radars lock onto every fit and attractive single male in the village, irrespective of what he's like as a person, or whether they have anything in common.' She put on a high-pitched robot voice. 'Must make man fancy me. Prove still able to get man and therefore not worthless as woman.'

I might have considered that a bitchy statement, had I not personally been wincing at the pouting and preening, flicking hair and prominently displayed body parts. David Attenborough would have had a field day in here. No wonder the swimming pool glass was steaming up.

Nathan, to his credit, didn't even give them a second glance.

He did, however, give me a questioning look, responding to my tentative thumbs up with a grin and a nod, as if he'd known all along that I'd be fine.

After that, Sean slithered in and took a seat beside me on the bench, and by the time I could see something other than a raging-red cloud, Joey was in the water, and, despite my own possible, not-quite-middle-aged-grim-desperation, I couldn't possibly look anywhere else.

'He's incredible,' Sean said, as Joey powered past us for the dozenth time, glancing at me after a few seconds when I failed to reply (I still wasn't quite ready to agree with Sean on anything, and I could hardly disagree with that comment). 'It's uncanny. As soon as he hits the water, it's like watching the male version of you.'

'You never saw me in the water,' I replied, in a tone that made it clear I wasn't falling for any of Sean's lines this time around. 'You hated me swimming.'

'I didn't hate you swimming,' he said, softly. 'I hated how it made you feel. How the pressure was affecting you. Swimming wasn't the problem. The supposed hopes of the nation being strapped to your shoulders? That I had a problem with.'

We watched Joey in silence for a while. I'd been doing a reasonable job at making this evening be about him, pushing the avalanche of memories to one side by focusing on the here and now. Getting myself here was a huge deal, and I really didn't need Sean Mansfield tossing reminders at me like snowballs.

'Do you regret it?' he murmured, shifting a couple of inches closer to me on the bench, making him now at least eight inches too close. 'Walking away from it all? I mean, looking at Joey, I guess you can't wish it had been any different.'

'Oh, shut up.' I got up and went to stand beside a woman in a skintight purple dress cut so ingeniously that she was actually showing more flesh than the girls in the pool. Next to her, I felt like even more of a washed-up frump than usual, which only made me more annoyed with Sean than I had been already. Ugh. This was going to be a long however-long-he-was-going-to-be-here-for.

What annoyed me the most? How when he leant towards me and lowered his voice, it still had the power to trigger a faint echo of the way those eyes, that gentle smile, had made me feel fourteen years ago. I was a woman careening down a mountain in a bobsleigh after years trapped in the ice palace at the top. Every sensation, every person, every new (and old) experience was overwhelming. I couldn't trust it. I couldn't trust myself yet to handle, well, anything much at all beyond a run in the woods with some kind women and a chance to sit and watch my son swim.

I wanted to be there for every second that Joey and Sean spent together. To observe, analyse, intervene as necessary. The prickle that skimmed down my arms when he'd quirked the side of his mouth up made it clear that it would have to be long-distance surveillance wherever possible.

37

STOP BEING A LOSER PROGRAMME
DAY EIGHTY-FIVE

By the hundredth time I'd heard, 'Dad said...' I knew I needn't worry about keeping up to speed with their relationship. I did my best to brush off the pain that everything Sean said was new, and exciting, and utterly brilliant and obviously right. Joey deserved to enjoy this. And the only time I let him see me cry was when he leaked a few tears of his own, at breakfast the next morning.

'I called him, "Dad,"' Joey told me, his voice hoarse, while round eyes made him appear a little boy again. 'It was weird. But then, not. Do you think it's weird? He looked weird when I said it. Oh, farts. Do you think it freaked him out? Should I have waited until he asked me to call him that?' He paused, sniffed. 'I just. I can't believe he's here. I can't believe I have a dad. I wanted to see what it felt like to say it. And now I've probably ruined everything. He'll be like, "Dude, we only just met, enough with the pressure!" What if he doesn't like me, I'm not what he expected, and now he's totally panicking because he doesn't want to be my dad?'

I placed a hand each side of his face, smudging away the tears with my thumbs. 'He left his whole life behind to come and hear you say that, Joey. If he looked weird, it's because you just made his dream come true. In all those years he's been imagining what you're like, it couldn't have come close to how wonderful you are. He told me at the pool that you're incredible.'

That had the reverse effect than I'd intended, as Joey cried even harder.

'And trust me, I know when he's telling the truth or not. He loves you already, Joey. How could he not love you?'

We clung on to each other until we decided we'd cried enough for one morning, and I accepted again that no rich, cool, exciting, long-lost parent offering a myriad of adventures could ever come close to replacing thirteen years of tears dried, breakfasts shared, a million tiny moments that create a life lived together.

But, honestly, the whole thing left me exhausted. There was so much to process. I swapped my run for the duvet that day. I felt too weighed down with the memories, the questions about where Sean had been and what him turning up here would mean. A thousand 'what-ifs'... what if I'd tried harder when we were together, coped better, been less demanding – would he have stayed? What if I'd laughed off those stupid girls in the supermarket, instead of allowing their thoughtless cruelty to crush me? What if I'd got help earlier, been to counselling, stopped allowing Cee-Cee to empower my decisions to retreat from life? What if I'd been stronger, braver, wiser? Better? I'd been this way for so long. What if I couldn't be strong, brave, or wise enough now?

I stayed in bed most of the next day. And the next. And before I realised it, the rest of the week. Sean turning up had coincided with the echo of my younger self emerging in a jawline, cheekbones – most of all the spark in my eyes: hopeful, determined, a gleam of confidence. It terrified me. I felt haunted. Did I regret what happened, the woman I'd been? Sean had asked me, as if regret meant I wished my son had never existed. I hadn't regretted it since the moment I knew he was there. Did I regret *how* it happened, and what happened after that? Like a slap in the face each time I caught my changing reflection in a mirror, or a darkened window. And the hurt and the shame were too much to bear.

So as December slipped past, I stopped running.

Ate biscuits.

Worked at my desk in ratty leggings and a giant hoodie.

Hung Christmas decorations, ordered food and presents for Joey and Cee-Cee online.

And I used every spare ounce of energy pretending that the Stop Being a Loser Programme was just on a break.

38

STOP BEING A LOSER PROGRAMME

DAY ONE HUNDRED (DAY FIFTEEN SINCE QUITTING)

They waited two whole weeks.

'Enough wallowin', Ames.' Mel told me, in no uncertain terms. 'Time to get yer armour back on.'

After fobbing off their texts and phone calls with excuses about a massive work contract, a bad cold, general Christmas busyness, of course Mel and Dani had turned up at the house, barrelling their way in before I could say, 'I'm actually about to go out.'

'I'm actually about to go out,' I mumbled, as they each dumped a shopping bag on the kitchen table.

'We get that Joey's father turning up is a significant life event to have to cope with,' Dani said, looking me up and down. 'But your strategy of completely letting yourself go, retreating back into your cave and shunning your best friends clearly isn't working. We're staging an intervention.'

Best friends?

'Nathan told us.' Mel, her hair red and white striped plaits like a candy cane, pulled a ginormous watermelon out of a bag, whipped a knife off the rack on the wall and began hacking away. 'We knew Joey would've filled 'im in so we harassed and terrorised 'im until 'e were worn down.'

'He refused to give up any details, though. Despite my superior court-honed interrogation skills. So...' Dani jerked the top off a bottle of fresh orange juice, while giving me a steely glare. 'You can fill us in while we prepare you a self-respect-restoring, excuse-eliminating, return-to-real-life-with-the-support-and-solidaritory-of-your-friends-enabling brunch.'

An hour and a half, two mimosas and a healthy yet humungous pile of food later, we were all filled up and filled in. Mel and Dani, on Sean and Joey's chicken Thursdays, how Sean had cheered Joey on at a regional gala I hadn't even bothered trying to attend, how the memories were bombarding me like slow-moving shrapnel from a bomb detonated over a decade ago, how I had lost the courage to keep going with the Programme and regressed to the crappy coping mechanisms that had been consistently failing me for years. And I had been filled in on Bronwyn's newest new boyfriend (although details were scarce, making Dani suspicious that he might be one of the Outlaws crew), Selena's new hairstyle (bigger than her whole head in every direction, à la 2010 Katie Price, according to Mel) and the real reason they'd come round that morning.

'I don't think I should go,' I told them, once they'd confessed.

'You can't not come!' Mel protested. 'All the Larks'll be there, and their fellas – or women or whatever. I hardly ever have a night out.'

'Which is one reason why I won't come. I'll panic, and cause a scene and spoil somebody's night when they end up trying to take care of me.'

'Maybe our night will be spoiled by you not being there in the first place,' Dani threw back at me, patting my hand to counteract her tone. 'Unlike Mel, I go out all the time, so if you start to feel overanxious, I'll whizz you home and be back at the party before anyone's missed me. Any other reasons not to come? No? Great, Derek and I will pick you up at seven-thirty.'

'I feel uncomfortable leaving Joey here alone all evening. He's not done that before.'

'You've got a phone, haven't you?'

Right on cue, Joey clattered down the stairs and into the kitchen. 'Oh, hey, Mum. Hi, Mum's friends. Dad asked if I want to go to the cinema this evening. Maybe get a burger or something before. I'll be back at ten-thirty. Can I go?'

'Well, that's perfect, then in't it?' Mel beamed. 'You can stay out 'til ten, Amy.'

'Are you going out?' Joey asked, a spark of hope in his eyes.

'I'm thinking about it,' I said.

'Where?'

'The Lark's Christmas bash,' Dani replied. 'Only the best night out of the year. She's going *out* out.'

'Since when was the Cup and Saucer out out?' Mel asked, bewildered.

'Since we'll be there.'

Mel and Dani vigorously pooh-poohed my final excuse, insisting I must be able to find *something* to wear, even if it was just a nice pair of jeans and a shirt. In the end, they forced their way upstairs and had a good riffle through my wardrobe, Dani triumphantly brandishing the one half-decent item in there.

'What about this? It's lovely, and looks new.'

I willed, with every muscle in my body, not to blush. 'I wore that to the wine and cheese evening.'

There was a half-second beat of silence while she processed my point. 'He won't notice it's the same dress. But I understand, a woman has her pride. No worries, this is my size.' She eyed me up and down. 'I'll pick you up at seven-twenty, with a few options for you to try. Right, we'd better get you back to your sweet little Christmas angels, Mel.'

'I'll think about it,' I mumbled to a pair of backs clattering down the stairs and straight out the front door.

There was no way I was going to that party.

* * *

'There's no way you're not coming to the party,' Nathan told me, at six that evening, leaning against my front door frame in his running gear.

'Are you going to drag me there like this?' I retorted, releasing a smidgen of the tension that had been spreading through every nerve and sinew as the clock ticked closer to party time. I'd expected Dani to ignore my cowardly, cancelling text, deliberately changing into my pyjamas so that when she turned up, she'd realise I was serious. I'd also planned on not answering the front door. Although that hadn't stopped her in the past, picking the lock would at least give me enough time to gather my defences.

So, when I opened the door, the sight of Nathan, eyes crinkled beneath his beanie hat, hands stuffed in his jacket pockets, was the visual equivalent of a giant hug after a day fraught with frittering.

Then I mistakenly allowed an image of him taking me to the party to pop into my head, releasing a burst of warm, sparkly, Christmas feelings that were not helpful.

Get a grip, Amy, my anxiety cackled softly.

Nathan held up a carrier bag. 'From Dani.'

'I can't do it.' I couldn't seem to stop shaking my head. 'See? I'm already panicking.'

'Amy, two weeks ago you made it all the way to the country club. This is just the café. With all the people who are in the café every time you go.'

'I haven't been out since then,' I confessed. 'Joey's at the cinema with Sean and I'm not in a fit state...'

Nathan ducked to meet my eyes, waiting until my bobble-head slowed down enough to lock onto his gaze. Oh my. Could we just stay here all night instead? Those grey depths looked like solid rock, hewn from the side of some ancient mountain. Strong enough to hold me steady when the rest of the world was bucking like a rodeo.

'This is what's happening: you're going to go upstairs and change into your running gear, then we're heading out as if it's 6 a.m., and after our 3K run we'll stop at the Cup and Saucer and hang out for an hour or so. Have a drink, eat some fruit and oats or eggs or,' he pulled a face, 'pancakes. We'll talk, the Larks will tell stories, make jokes and take the mickey out of me as much as possible. Then, once the post-exercise endorphins have worn off, I'll walk you home. And you will be so damn proud of yourself for going, in the morning when your courage muscles are sore and tired along with your body, every twinge will make you smile.'

I blinked, sniffed, felt around in my dressing-gown pocket for a tissue. 'That is not how the scenario in my head plays out. And I've been thinking about it all afternoon. There are multiple options, like those choose-your-own adventure stories. None of them end with me proud, or smiling.' I let out a watery laugh. 'More like embarrassed and pathetic. Possibly covered in vomit or passed out in the back of an ambulance.'

'I don't like your scenarios. Let's go with mine instead.'

'Is this another one of my challenges?'

His eyes crinkled. 'Do you want it to be?'

'If that means I can pick a challenge for you.'

He shrugged. 'Hit me with your worst. Nothing can beat "Livin' on a Prayer".'

'I'll have you know, Mel walked down the aisle to that song.'

'Like I said, you can't beat it.' Nathan grinned, my heart liquified to molten mushiness, and that was all it took.

'Give me five minutes.'

* * *

Ten minutes later, having changed, brushed my hair and teeth and darted randomly around my room for a bit, I found Nathan stretching his arms over his head in my kitchen. Whew, he was tall. A glimpse of flat stomach where his T-shirt had ridden up sent a rush of heat to my face and nearly made me forget the very important question which had occurred to me while fumbling to tie my running shoelaces.

Ah yes, that was it...

'If we're going straight to the party from our run, I'll be sweaty and dishevelled and gross. And I don't want to turn up wearing these when everyone else is all done up in their party gear. I'll be self-conscious enough as it is.' *So there!* I didn't mention the alternative plan jigging about inside my brain, that Nathan and I keep on running right past the café and come back here for a party for two. Honestly, I really had to get back out in the real world and remind myself that other male humans did exist.

'We'll take it easy, not get too sweaty. And by the time we get there, the party'll be in full swing, everyone else will be just as bad and having too much fun to notice or care. And Dani's bag is in my rucksack, you can change when we get there. Now, come on, warm-up.'

'Thirty seconds.' I sprinted back upstairs, coming down again with a handful of make-up and a hairbrush shoved into an old washbag. 'Will these fit in?'

Nathan sighed, rolled his eyes and stretched round to stuff them in a side pocket.

'Oh, and my phone. And I'll need some money. Definitely tissues. And shoes! I can't wear muddy trainers. House keys. Anything else?'

Nathan stood there fidgeting while I added the extra items as they occurred to me.

'You know what? We'll walk the first quarter-mile, make that the warm-up.' And he bundled me out the door before I could protest about the importance of proper pre-run stretches...

* * *

An hour later, I staggered through the door of the Cup and Saucer, a pungent combination of icy numbness and steaming heat. For goodness' sake, as if Amelia Piper could exercise alongside a man she found increasingly disturbingly, pointlessly and humiliatingly attractive and *take it easy*. The only way for me to face what lay at the end of the run was to push so hard I didn't have enough spare oxygen to think about it. It was the first time I'd run alone with Nathan, and it felt unexpectedly intimate, pushing up and down the wooded slopes through the darkness, the only sounds the twin squelch of our footsteps – and my laboured breathing (it is really quite distracting, trying to run as fast as you can while not wheezing and panting like an asthmatic warthog). I could have kept running right on through until sunrise. Possibly a little bit further than that. If I didn't have a stitch by then.

Nathan, on the other hand, strolled in behind me as if a taxi had dropped him right outside. He handed me the rucksack, threw me a wink and promised to bag me a spot at my usual table. I tried to slink to the ladies' room undetected, while at the same time aware that every pair of eyes in the room was on me, or my personal trainer. Probably swivelling in glee (or rage) between the two of us, jumping to all sorts of impossible and ridiculous conclusions. None of which (*ALL OF WHICH!*) I'd been imagining while pounding the footpaths, a million stars above our heads.

To no one's surprise, least of all mine, my disappearance into the ladies' room coincided with a mass urge to powder noses. When I came out of the cubicle, the tiny space in front of the sinks was jam-packed.

'Can I wash my hands, please?' I asked, attempting assertive and unbothered, succeeding at nervous and uncomfortable. My anxiety eyed all those women and smirked, giving me a nudge in the ribs sharp enough to make my lungs stutter.

Thankfully, not all those women were gawkers. Dani and Mel were crammed up against the door.

'Oy!' Mel yelled, probably loud enough that everyone in the café could hear above the blare of Michael Bublé. 'If you ain't here to use the facilities, show a bit of Larks' solidarity and get on wi' yer. You all know Nathan's bin givin' Ames some personal trainin' – and no, not that type o' personal, Miranda Jones, you ain't fourteen, please stop actin' like it – ain't nothin' remarkable about them turning up 'ere in running gear. If they'd waltzed in 'ere all done up and flushed from a cheeky pre-drink somewhere, then you'd 'ave cause to raise yer drawn-on eyebrows, Isobel Martin. But even then, it'd be none of yer business. Nathan can date oo 'e likes.'

'Actually, that's not true,' Selena, rammed up against the other cubicle door, said. 'He's not allowed to date clients. And even if he was, he won't, however tempted. So unless this is also Amy's leaving-do, you can rest assured there's no reason for you to be squashed in here like sardines scavenging for plankton.'

'You're in here!' Bronwyn called from her perch on the edge of a sink.

'I came to check if she was all right!' Selena barked. 'Not to scrump for gossip!'

Ugh. I felt as though I had fallen into a volcano. Suffocatingly hot, dizzy from the lack of air, the outside music distorting into a cacophony. I needed space, quiet, cold water on my wrists and face. To find a focal spot and remember how to get my chest moving properly. And most of my head was taken up with the overwhelming urge to grab onto the strong, gentle hand that had become my anchor.

I leant my arms against the spare sink, closed my eyes and cursed this whole stupid enterprise. At some point, which could have been anything between a few seconds and half a lifetime, I felt a different hand – wonderfully cool and firm, press against the back of my neck.

'Come on,' a voice with an unmistakeable thread of steel said. 'Time to buck up and stop giving those jealous cows something to gossip about.'

I debated that statement for another few seconds.

'Here. Get changed, then I'll sort your face.'

Dani's bag bumped against my arm, and I opened my eyes to see Selena rummaging through my make-up bag, her nose wrinkling at the measly contents. I picked the carrier bag up, twisting it in my hands while attempting to clear the freezing fog from my brain.

'Tonight's a big deal for Nathan. If you skulk off now, then he won't be able to enjoy all the Larks who *did* make the effort, sorted babysitters, bothered dressing up and dragging their other halves out to honour everything he's done for us this year. He'll just feel crap about the one Lark who flaked.' Selena pointed an ancient lipstick at me, 'You are not going to make Nathan feel crap this evening. If Audrey has to pin you down while I wrestle you into that dress myself.'

The thought of Audrey getting involved in this scenario was enough. Less than a minute later, I was leaning against the sink as Selena tried to work a miracle with my gunky old mascara. 'You care a lot about Nathan,' I observed, risking a good, hard poke in the eye.

The tip of the wand hovered for a fraction of a second, Selena's gaze fixed firmly somewhere around my eyebrow. 'I've met enough scummy men to know the value of a good one.'

'Why don't you leave the Larks and investigate where that chemistry might lead?'

She jabbed the mascara back in its lid. 'If I don't come, then Audrey won't. And believe it or not, the club is the closest thing she's got to having friends. She spends all day by herself, cleaning empty houses for women who have the confidence to do something with their lives. Apart from playing bridge with a few pensioners, she doesn't see another soul. And while she might act like she hates it, in the past few months she's started running most days. Actually getting off her backside and doing something positive.' She started dabbing some gloss onto my top lip. 'She comes back glowing. I knew she'd learn to appreciate it if I dragged her along enough times.'

'Right.' *Wrong!* 'You're sacrificing your feelings for Nathan for the sake of Audrey.'

'Oh for pity's sake, don't try twisting it into something noble. No mother wants a fat, lazy daughter with no friends and no prospect of ever moving out. If she can scrabble together some self-respect, we all end up better off.'

I could have said that if she showed Audrey some respect it might help, but seeing as she was currently in charge of my face, I'd save it for another time.

'Besides, while Nathan and I might have undeniable physical magnetism, when it comes to a relationship, he is so not my brand. And however spectacular our no-strings nights would be – and they would be – in the morning I'd miss my run with the girls. Nope, Nathan and I are one of those doomed cases of pure, raw passion destined never to be.' She leant forwards, her bronzed cleavage squishing against my cheek as she fiddled with some stray strands of hair. 'Still, he knows that I know what's running through his head when he sneaks a peek at me limbering up.' She straightened up, spinning me around to face the mirror and lowering her voice to a purr. 'Pure. Magic.'

'Wow.'

'I know. And look, with a bit of effort you've not scrubbed up too badly, either. You could almost justify the rumours about you and Nate. Dim the lights, wait for him to chug a few beers and it's not so far-fetched to think he could offer you a second glance.'

'Thanks, Selena. I think that's the nicest thing anyone's said to me in years.' I might have managed to pull off the sarcasm a little better, had that statement not actually been true.

'He doesn't drink alcohol though. So I guess it'll still be all eyes on me.'

And with that, she swung out the door, giving me a much-needed minute to look in the mirror and wonder who on earth blinked back, in that pretty black jumpsuit with the pink and blue flowers that somehow transformed chunk to curves. This strange young woman with her smooth skin and bright eyes got a second glance from me, and that was all that mattered.

'Right then, whoever you are, time to find out whether you like to party or not.'

And wouldn't you know it, she did.

And, while Nathan may have only offered me one glance as I stuck back my shoulders and did my best attempt at a confident strappy-heeled stroll over to Mel, it was long enough for his eyes to crinkle up and his smile to spread to a surprised grin, and it lit me up all the way to the buffet table. What mattered was not whether or not it contained any physical magnetism, or pure, raw passion (I'm ninety-nine per cent sure it didn't), but that he knew I knew what he was thinking anyway: Nathan was happy for me, and proud of me, and pleased as the cinnamon punch that I had made it.

So, Selena had been right about that, if nothing else.

I spent the remaining two hours before Joey was due home listening to my friends (*my FRIENDS!*) laughing and telling stories and winding each other up, while sipping on cheap wine and inwardly goggling at the fact that I was at a party, and not even hating it. When, about an hour or so in, my anxiety stirred, Dani tucked one arm through mine and winked, effectively clonking it on the head with a sledgehammer. I joined in the quiz, and cheered along when Bronwyn dragged Nathan onto the tiny dance floor, because 'we've heard you're a legendary groover'.

'Good job her new boyfriend isn't here,' Dani pouted, making the word *boyfriend* sound like something she'd found floating in her toilet.

'Not his scene, apparently,' Mel replied, flinging some of her own shapes beside us as Taylor Swift pumped out of the speakers.

'Because the closest thing to illegal drug use is Audrey puffing on her inhaler,' Dani sniffed back.

Mel shimmied closer. 'Plus, Isobel getting a speeding ticket is the Larks equivalent of a crime lord.'

'It's not funny, though. If Bronwyn doesn't extricate herself from this situation soon, I'm going to seriously worry. Either that or start digging up evidence to get him banged up somewhere very far away.'

'Do you know for sure it's one of the Outlaws?' I asked.

'I know for sure her previous boyfriends' names, jobs, favourite holiday destinations and brands of underwear,' Dani said. 'And most of them only lasted a couple of weeks. If he's not an Outlaw, she's got another very good reason for keeping him a secret. And I can't imagine it's anything good.'

'Unless it's him!' Mel giggled, as the door to the café opened and a man stepped in. 'Maybe she's decided to go for a more mature man after that last fella turned out to be a teenager.'

Only, Bronwyn wasn't the only Lark keeping her love life under wraps, of course. I watched, and waited, dying to say something but determined to keep my promise. The elderly man, who had fortunately swapped his dressing gown for tweed trousers and orange waistcoat, comedy tiptoed across to where Audrey sat, her back to the room, like a grumpy Christmas gnome. He might have gone largely unnoticed, everyone was so engrossed in having a whale of a time, except that he crept up behind Audrey and placed his hands over her eyes, in that never-ever-in-the-history-of-ever-funny 'guess who I am!' manoeuvre. She let out a shriek like a Nazgul, jumping back and flailing around so hard that it caused a domino effect of toppling people that was only stopped by the buffet table. Here, the last domino knocked the punch bowl flying and drenched the initial domino's mother from the top of her giant hair extensions to the bottom of her designer *Grace Tynedale* shoes.

Oops.

'Who's that?' Mel asked, mouth agape, as people scrambled to their feet, and Chris and his waiting staff rushed to mop up the mess.

'That, is Graham.' I suspected Audrey's secret was out at this point.

'Isn't he the guy who lives in that massive house on Foxglove Lane?' Derek, who had smoothly arrived at Dani's side at the first hint of trouble, asked. 'Had a thing with the woman in the Post Office?'

'Graham Giggs?' Mel shook her head in wonder. 'I didn't recognise him with a beard. And he was carrying on with Elaine Moody, at the library, not Post Office Paula. They used to slip into store cupboards thinkin' no one would notice. Caused a right problem before them self-service machines got installed.'

'It was both of them,' Marjory chipped in. 'And half a dozen more besides. The thing about horrid little men who think they're God's gift to womankind is that they always seem to home in on those gullible enough to fall for it. Women with no self-esteem and no purpose. Who are looking to escape a hostile home environment, where they are belittled and bullied.'

'Audrey does seem to really like him,' I ventured.

'Really?' Dani quirked one eyebrow. 'I can't see it, myself.'

Audrey was currently looking more animated than previously appeared possible, waving her arms as she clearly explained to Graham what she thought of him turning up at the party.

'How do you know Graham Giggs?' Selena, dabbing at her white dress with a damp cloth, asked, her snarl echoing through the otherwise silent room. 'Is he one of your bridge group?'

'Yes,' Audrey replied, at the same time as Graham said, 'What bridge group?'

'Because if he was, I'd have banned you from going.'

'You can't ban her from doing anything!' Graham retorted, grabbing Audrey's hand. 'She's twenty-two years old, she can do whatever she likes!'

'You keep out of this, you old fart!' Selena shouted, her face turning crimson beneath the orangey bronzer. 'I'm her MOTHER, if I say she's not going, she's not going. Audrey – you are no longer going to the bridge group.'

'Well, ban away, Mother, there is no bridge group!' Graham laughed. No one else joined him.

'Mum,' Audrey said, her eyes wild, entire body trembling. 'Graham and I are together.'

All the red drained out of Selena's face, leaving it whiter than the remaining clean patches on her dress. 'What?'

'You can't stop me! He makes me happy. Isn't that what you want, for me to find a man and be happy? That's why you made me join the Larks.'

'You dirty old pervert.' Selena's voice was ice-cold venom. 'If you touch my daughter again, I will personally slice off your disgusting, droopy old—'

'MUM!' Audrey shouted. 'Why do you never listen to me? Graham and I are in love. He's asked me to move in with him.'

'You do know he'll be dead before you're thirty?'

'That's all the more reason to make the most of the time we have now.'

'Is that what he told you?' Selena took in a huge breath, scraped the punch-soaked tangles of hair back from her face. 'Did he also tell you that none of the other women counted, the only reason he's slept with half the village is because all these decades he was searching for you, his true soulmate, whose inner beauty is enough to make the years between you meaningless?'

'Selena,' Graham warned. 'Don't say something you'll later regret.'

'If you don't stop talking, I'm going to punch you in the face,' Selena replied, coolly. 'And I promise I won't regret it; I've wanted to do it for sixteen years.'

'No,' Audrey said. 'You stop talking! You have nothing to do with this. You are not going to spoil it. You have everything and I have NOTHING but this and him and… and our love and you are not going to have had that too. You are NOT GOING TO TELL ME YOU'VE HAD HIM TOO.' Stricken, distraught, as though all the emotions that had been brewing behind that blank mask were bursting up and out and into life, Audrey pulled Graham towards her, wailing through her tears. 'Yes! Yes I'll move in with you. Now. Tonight.'

'Audrey…' Selena gasped, as Graham beamed with glee.

'I never want to see you or speak to you again.' Audrey stomped across the Cup and Saucer, Graham shuffling behind as fast as he could manage, while the Larks and their assorted guests watched, mouths open, for the first time ever their hearts cracking with sympathy for the frozen, punch-splattered figure in front of them.

After what seemed like a horribly long time, Marjory broke the silence. 'You know how this goes. She'll be back once he gets bored, you haven't lost her.'

Selena blinked twice and shook a purple droplet from her hair. 'Oh, I've no doubt he'll dump her as soon as another foolish, lonely girl catches his eye. If he doesn't drop dead of a fornicating-induced heart attack before then. But I have to disagree with your last point. If I hadn't already lost her, she'd never have fallen for the slithering pus-ball.'

Nathan brought Selena her coat and handbag. 'Come on. I'll take you home.'

'Right, show's over, people,' Dani called out as they left. 'As much as we love Selena and Audrey, and all loathe Graham Gags, there's nothing we can do about it now. It's nine-thirty, we've still got an hour and a half of serious partying left. And I haven't danced to Beyoncé yet. Mr DJ, would you do the honours?'

It took another couple of songs, but, boy, Dani's moves were infectious, and once Marjory and her partner started jiving, we had to clear all the tables to the edge of the room anyway.

'Come on, Amy!' Mel yelled, throwing an imaginary lasso to tug me into the crowd. 'Time to stop spectating, start participating!'

I looped the lasso over my head and tossed it back to her. 'Maybe another time.' I'd had a good night, mostly. Had overcome another massive hurdle, done some genuine participating. But it was now nearly ten, and I was mentally and emotionally running on empty.

Bronwyn flossed over to where I stood. 'If you dance, you can go to bed tonight knowing you aced it. A-star. Gold medal. Were utterly bold and fearless and brilliant in every instance. If you don't, you'll go home knowing you let fear win, even if just in this one small thing. Come on, let's totally smash the party.'

'Maybe in a minute, okay?'

Before someone else came and made getting Amy to dance the new focus of the evening, I dodged round the edge of the café and slipped into the bathroom. Whew. The Amy in the mirror was a far cry from the last time I'd been in here. I looked as though I'd been *out* out. For a woman who'd been in in for so long, that felt like an A-star to me. And when I returned to find Nathan back, strutting to 'Uptown Funk' like a drunken robot chicken, I figured what the hell, if I was dancing with him, then it would give me an excuse to look right at him, rather than ogle from the sidelines.

'Is it wrong that I find that sort of sexy?' one of the younger Larks I didn't know very well whispered out the side of her mouth, as Nathan jerked about.

'If it's wrong, then I don't want to be right,' Bronwyn laughed, breathless. 'But don't tell my boyfriend I said that!' she added, coming to an abrupt halt. 'Like, seriously. Please don't.'

'Are you scared of your boyfriend?' I asked, as she started bopping again.

'As if! I'm a hardcore bouncer, remember!' She grinned and twirled away, but not so fast that I didn't see the flicker of a lie behind her smile.

A couple of songs later, I quit the dance floor and checked my phone. A missed call from Joey. Four texts that rambled on for several paragraphs each. The summary: could he stay the night at Sean's Airbnb?

Crap.

Could he? I reviewed the numerous reasons he gave for this last-minute change in plans. Took a deep breath, ducked into the bathroom and called Sean.

'Hey, Amy. How's the party?'

'Was this your idea?'

'It was...' I could hear the cogs turning in Sean's head as he tried to decide what answer would be more likely to make me say yes. 'Sort of, came to us both at the same time.'

'Right. Fill me in on the details, then.'

'Well. There's a spare room in the apartment. I've got an extra toothbrush. I'll drive him straight to the gala in Leicester in the morning, stay and watch him race. That way you don't have to rush home and can lie-in tomorrow.'

'He needs his kit.'

'Yeah, we can pop by and pick it up on the way.'

'You already have it, don't you?'

Silence.

'If this is going to work, you need to stop playing me. I'm not nineteen any more and I won't be manipulated or controlled. This kind of crap just stops me trusting you.'

'Yeah. Sorry. I hear you, and I'll make sure I talk things through with you in future. But Joey's really excited and...'

'Again, emotional blackmail is not going to help. I'm totally comfortable with disappointing him or coming off as the mean parent if I believe it's in his best interest. You're the one who got his hopes up, not me.'

'Right. Sorry. I'll bring him straight home. Tell him it was my fault, I should have discussed it with you earlier.'

The door to the bathroom crashed open as Bronwyn and another runner tumbled through, sweaty and laughing, accompanied by the sound of a roomful of partygoers giving their all to 'Livin' on a Prayer'. 'All right, Ames? Nathan's looking for you, wanted to dance.'

I thought about that for a couple of seconds. Did one of those lightning-quick parental calculations, assessing the pros and cons and deciding that I didn't actually have a good reason for making Joey come home now, just to be picked up by Sean first thing in the morning. Pretended it had nothing to do with me dancing with Nathan. Decided that even if it did, so what? It was about time I wanted to stay out and have some fun for once.

'No, he can stay. But I'm serious about ditching the games, Sean.'

'Thanks, Amy. I can't tell you how much it means to us...'

So they were an *us* now, Sean and Joey. Was there any of that cinnamon punch left?

STOP BEING A LOSER PROGRAMME

DAY ONE HUNDRED AND ONE

Three glasses of wine later, the remaining few Larks sat strewn amongst the debris, as the staff attempted to clear up around us. Mel, despite giving up alcohol when Tate was born, was nevertheless drunk on communal dancing, sleep-deprivation for all the best reasons, and a truckload of endorphins.

'You lot!' she exclaimed, leaning her head on Dani's shoulder. 'Are the best Larks a woman could wish for. I can't believe all what you're doing for my little boy. That triathlon is going to be one of the best blummin' days of my whole life. All these years, it's been all up ter me. Meetings and phone calls and appeals and fighting to get my kids what they need. All the while knowing that if I drop the ball, if I mess something up or get it wrong, it's me kids who will suffer. And now. Now... I'm not on me own any more. I just can't tell yer...' She dabbed her eyes, hiccupped and did an enormous sniff. 'Right, someone change subject for goodness' sake. It's supposed to be a party. Eh – I know – did you hear that Amelia Piper is gonna be there on the day to open the centre?'

Oh no. My heart froze.

'Really?' Bronwyn leant in. 'Wasn't there some massive scandal about her, ages ago?'

'Oh, yes,' Dani nodded. 'She went MIA. Never turned up to the Olympics. What year was it?'

2004.

'2004,' Marjory said.

'There was that whole Search for Amelia thing!' Bronwyn exclaimed. 'And then it turned out she'd just run off with some bloke, and she got sued by her own parents.'

'Oh yeah, I saw them on the telly...'

I made it three steps out the café door.

Nathan found me, slumped against the freezing cold wall, wiping the vomit off my chin. He handed me a napkin, waited while I cleaned up, then held out a glass of water.

'Are you okay for a minute while I sort you a lift? It might take a while to get a taxi this time in the morning.'

'No.' I cleared my throat, tried again. 'No, I can walk. It was just the heat and the wine and everything. I needed a minute to clear my head, but I'm fine.' Hah. If fine meant my vital organs were disintegrating.

He studied me for a moment, unconvinced.

I pushed away from the wall and stood as straight as I could manage, chin up, swimmer's shoulders back, hands raised in a 'see?' gesture, using everything I'd got to override the chaos in my ribcage. 'And I don't need you to walk me home, either. It's eight minutes. I'm feeling great now. You shouldn't just disappear without saying good night to everyone.'

He shook his head in mock frustration. 'I've already said good night. And I can follow you like last time, or we can walk together. Either way, you know I'm seeing you home.'

Underneath my complete freak out, I did know that. 'Okay then.'

He held out a hand. 'Would it help?'

I nodded. Nathan gently took hold of my hand, and, honestly, as long as I focused on that, it felt as though nothing else could touch me. Like being at home, in the safety of my bed, only infinitely better because I was still outside, breathing in cold, crisp air as opposed to stuffy duvet fumes and walking beneath the light of a billion stars.

Halfway home, Nathan spoke again. 'You know that if you want to talk about it, I won't tell anyone.'

'What is there to say? It just got too much. I've been out for seven hours.'

We walked a few more steps. 'Joey filled in a parental consent form to join the club.'

'And?' I frowned, my wrung-out brain trying hard to follow this new conversation.

'Amy Piper.'

We had nearly reached my house. I stopped anyway, my hand dropping from his. 'How long have you known?'

He looked down, kicked at a wonky slab in the pavement. 'I told you I trained with the Loughborough Uni team.'

'I need to get inside.' Hurrying past Nathan, I virtually ran down my front path, scrabbling at the lock with my key until he gently took it off me, opening up and letting me practically ram him out the way to get to my sofa before my knees gave out. 'Carry on.' I waved a hand at him, impatiently. My anxiety was out of its cage and on the rampage.

Nathan took a seat on the chair opposite me. 'I watched you compete a couple of times. We even trained together once. I ate lunch at your table in the café. Asked stupid questions about your diet because I couldn't think of how else to start a conversation.'

'I don't remember.'

'Of course you don't. I was nobody, you were Amelia Piper. I'd never seen anyone so focused and strong and brilliant. You were captivating. I was in awe.' He pulled a wry smile, running his fingers through his hair. 'You were my first major crush.'

I clutched my stomach, praying there was nothing left to throw up. 'So how did you recognise me? I bear absolutely no resemblance to that person.'

Nathan's voice was gentle. 'You're far more like her than you think. In all the best ways.'

'So, you've known all along?'

'I wondered, when I saw the name on Joey's form. When I saw him swim. But then, you never came to training, or to the meets. I guessed you might be trying to avoid stealing his limelight, wanting him to be judged on his own merit. And, of course, your career hadn't ended well. But to never turn up, when swimming had been everything to you? I decided it was a coincidence, similar name, or maybe you were distant cousins or something, that's it. And then, when I saw you in the street, as soon as you opened your eyes... I was seventeen again.'

'Why didn't you say anything?'

'I got why you wanted to stay anonymous. It wasn't my secret to tell.'

'All that fuss about the triathlon, the whole publicity thing...'

'I remember what it was like for you. How everyone who came near you had an agenda. Resenting your talent, or worshipping you for it. I didn't want you to think I was one of those people. Only interested in what your name and fame could bring us.'

I shook my head, even managed something close to a laugh. 'Well, I did a pretty good job of using my name and my fame to get what I wanted from Antonio Galanos at the council.'

Nathan smiled. 'I did wonder.'

'Bloody hell, Nathan. You must have been dying to say something. How could you resist trying to wangle it out of me? All those times we talked about warm-ups and training.'

'Being stiflingly self-disciplined can come in useful sometimes.' He paused. 'As I'm sure you know.'

'Mmm.'

The momentousness of the whole conversation filled the room.

'You probably should tell the others at some point.'

'I know. I've agreed to open the centre.' I sighed. 'I'm just not ready to talk about it yet. The Larks have been... everything. Once they know, it'll change. You heard them just now. Even if they pretend to be all nice and understanding, I know what they really think.'

'Late-night idle gossip. You're talking about the single mother of five kids, one of whom will never know who her father is. A human rights lawyer who was the only black woman in her Oxford college, and the girlfriend of a local mafia boss. They aren't going to judge you.'

'They've already convicted Amelia Piper.' I shook my head. 'It's been so good being accepted as a loser, rather than a failed winner.'

'Well, if it's any consolation, I won't be treating you any differently. And I hope that's not been like a loser or a failed winner.'

'You've been nothing but professional at all times, Coach Gallagher.'

Nathan beamed, suddenly, all white teeth and eyes like stainless steel.

'What?'

'Amelia Piper, calling me coach.'

'Keep being nice to me and I might sit with you at lunch sometime.'

We chatted for a few more minutes about nothing much, Nathan only going home once it was clear the shockwaves of the past half hour had settled, leaving me with about enough strength to drag myself upstairs, brush my teeth and crawl into bed. Maybe other women would feel ashamed to wake up in last night's clothes, face a smeary mess and hair smelling of Prosecco, but as a one-time-only thing, partying past midnight was a whole step up on the Programme. I showered, wolfed down a mountain of tea and toast and spent the next six hours in full-on information-processing mode. Trying to spend more time focusing on the fact that Nathan knew who I was, rather than replaying over and over again that I was captivating, he was in awe, first major crush. That, combined with AS SOON AS YOU OPENED YOUR EYES, I WAS SEVENTEEN AGAIN, equalled feelings that didn't only break Nathan's rules, they stomped them into smithereens.

40

STOP BEING A LOSER PROGRAMME

DAY ONE HUNDRED AND THREE

One side effect of being mentally imprisoned within your own house for over two years is an acute case of talking to minibeasts, television characters, inanimate objects and, inevitably, myself. Another, I realised the week before Christmas, is an ability to stretch a modest income from one payday to the next. On top of my usual outgoings – rent, bills, Joey's mammoth calorie requirements, his membership of various sports clubs and associated equipment costs – I now piled on my own running club fees, the additions to my wardrobe and shoe-rack, plus multiple orders of pancakes, fancy coffees and more variations than I'd have thought possible of eggs and avocado. Add on drinks at the Christmas party and my night out with Nathan and by the time I finished the Programme, complete with full-on outside life, Amelia Piper would be reduced to selling her story to the likes of Moira Vanderbeek to avoid plummeting into the washed-up-celebrity bankruptcy cliché.

I clicked shut my online bank statement, booted out a horrible thought about Sean and child support, then listened again to a saved voice message from my employer, Grant Winlock, who ran the bid company I worked for.

As one of the most productive and long-standing bid writers at Winlock Tenders, I had been offered the position of senior bid writer several times. One of the current three senior writers was retiring in the New Year. The job was mine if I wanted it. Oh, and providing I could attend an informal interview to demonstrate my ability to present myself to major corporate clients as a non-gibbering wreck in the flesh.

It would be a significant pay rise. Enough to pay for a whole lot of power breakfasts to fuel my meteoric rise as a business professional.

I had no doubt that I could talk the talk as a senior bid writer. I had managed more than a few conference calls and video meetings without embarrassing myself (apart from the time I knocked my laptop, revealing my ratty old pyjama bottoms to the director of a flashy PR company). But could I walk the walk? Bus the bus? Catch the train to meetings with high-level management staff, march into boardrooms wearing a swanky suit and swing my laptop bag onto the conference table as if I belonged there?

I had until the end of January to decide whether or not asking Sean for financial help was preferable to a nice promotion.

I opened the front door and stared at the December grey until a gust of wind caught my hair, sending a shudder through my bones. I whipped the door closed. Swore. Counted to twenty, focused on my breathing, opened the door again and then shut it, this time at what I hoped comprised a normal, unhurried, well-balanced person's speed. One day soon I would step out there into the midday sun.

One day.

Soon.

I emailed my boss and told him I would think about it over Christmas.

41

STOP BEING A LOSER PROGRAMME

DAY ONE HUNDRED AND SIX

It was the best and the worst day of the year: 21 December, the shortest day. I snuck in an extra-long run, enjoyed a full pot of tea at the café and even ambled home afterwards. By half-past four I was out again, calling in at the bakery, the newsagents and the library, on a glorious, glittering roll. I strode home, dumped my bags on the kitchen table, waved off Joey for the school Christmas party and whizzed back out to meet Mel at the chapel near the square to watch Tiff and Taylor perform in a deliciously dimly lit carol service.

Check me out – *whizzing.*

Singing.

Popping back to Mel's afterwards for chilli-smothered nachos and the noisiest game of charades ever.

Walking home.

I had smashed the winter solstice. But tucked up in bed later, blissfully opening one of my new library books, I realised with a start that the shortest day meant tomorrow my confinement would start lengthening again.

Where would I be in six months' time, on the summer solstice?

Cowering inside until ten every night?

Pretending that I was fine sitting in my own garden, rather than trapped like an animal in their zoo enclosure?

Waving Joey off on holiday with his fully-functioning parent?
I had better not be. I'd better not be blubbing like I was now, either.

42

STOP BEING A LOSER PROGRAMME

DAY ONE HUNDRED AND SEVEN

The Saturday before Christmas was another challenge day. Nathan's turn this time, following my successful conquest of the party. Joey was spending the weekend with Ben, and I had assembled all the required components of the challenge. Nathan was not happy.

'This is a complete waste of a day.'

'How can doing something fun and relaxing be a waste?'

'It's not... achieving anything. It's totally unproductive. I thought you were going to take me to the Christmas market or something.' Nathan tugged at his hair in distress.

'Wrong! It's producing happiness and achieving relaxation instead of seasonal stress. Spending a day enjoying yourself has to be the least possible waste of time. How often do you get to completely chill out for a whole day?'

'This isn't relaxing for me. It's gross. Chilling out is hiking in the Lakes or kayaking down a river.'

'Organising a nutritional spreadsheet? Creating an ultra-marathon training programme? Lining up your running shoes in order of tread-wear?' I raised my eyebrows.

'What's wrong with that?'

'Nothing, if you can balance it with occasionally letting things go, being spontaneous and indulgent once in a while, too. If you don't find relaxation relaxing, then you need more practice. Here.' I handed him a pair of men's pyjamas. 'Get these on, and the challenge will commence.'

It may have been a little mean, going for stripy, gentlemen's night-wear, but I figured Nathan probably wore a lot of jogging bottoms and T-shirts at home, and I wanted him to feel as out of his comfort zone as I had in Dani's jumpsuit. And besides, the look worked, he looked danger-ously cute and ruffled, slouched on one end of the sofa, arms crossed and brow tense.

'Help yourself to snacks,' I said, handing him a plate, my own 'pyjama day' wear consisting of a pair of checked lounge pants, fleecy hoodie and fur-lined slipper boots.

'Thanks.' Nathan took the plate, put it on the coffee table, then glanced at me standing there, hands on my hips. He sighed, picked up a fistful of salted caramel popcorn and dumped it on the plate. I cleared my throat, waiting until he'd added a square of brownie and a couple of crisps before loading up my own plate and taking a seat on the other end of the sofa.

'Now, prepare to embrace a whole different type of marathon.'

I clicked play.

* * *

'Have you ever been married?' I asked, as the final credits rolled for the first film.

Nathan glanced at me before looking back at the screen. 'No.'

'But?'

'But what?' He picked up a chocolate truffle and ate it, confirming the definite existence of a 'but'.

'You tell me. Or don't, if you'd rather not. You do kind of know all my embarrassing secrets, though.'

He sighed, brushing at the crumbs sprinkled on his pyjama top. 'I was engaged for a few months.'

'I'm guessing from the look on your face that she ended it.'

'Yes. But it was the right thing to do. Didn't stop me feeling like a complete failure, though.'

I pulled a cushion onto my lap, waiting to see if he wanted to share more.

'The woman I told you about, Gill, who was attacked?'

'Oh, no.'

'We were engaged at the time. Although things hadn't been right for a while, I'd been dealing with it badly, by spending more and more time doing my own thing. The day it happened, I was supposed to be meeting her for a run.' He paused, taking a couple of deep breaths before carrying on. 'I tried to keep things going, afterwards, pull myself together and be the man she deserved. But it turned out that instead of deserving a man who stayed with her out of guilt – and by *stayed with her*, I mean, literally, too terrified to leave her alone for five minutes – she deserved a man who loved and respected her.'

'Chris?' I remembered Nathan telling me his friend who'd been attacked had married Chris, who ran the Cup and Saucer. Knowing she'd been engaged to Nathan first shed a whole new light on things.

'She married him less than a year after we'd split up. Turned out he'd been in love with her for ages and was just hoping I'd do the right thing and find the courage to end it before the wedding.'

'Wow.'

'Yeah.'

'And you've made sure there's no room for dating on your weekly activity spreadsheet since.'

Nathan shook his head, offended. 'Not because of that! Spending my time doing things I enjoy rather than giving in to the must-be-in-a-relationship propaganda is a positive lifestyle choice. If the right woman happened to move next door or something, then fair enough, but I'm not wasting my time hunting for something I'm perfectly happy without, just because it's popular opinion.'

'Good to know. And according to rom-com scriptwriters everywhere, that's exactly the way it's meant to happen. As demonstrated in our next instalment of Christmas feel-good joy.'

'There's another one?' he groaned.

'This is a marathon, Nathan. You should know better than most that there's hours to go yet.'

'My marathons last well under four hours.'

'Well, what kind of challenge would that be?'

Nathan sank back into the sofa and stuffed a cushion over his face. I smiled, grabbed a handful of popcorn and pressed play.

* * *

Halfway through the third film, at the point where I wondered if I would start amalgamating with the cushions if I didn't move soon, I heard a gentle whiffle. Surreptitiously swivelling my eyes across, I found Nathan, eyes closed, *slumping* into the squishy old sofa, head back, mouth slightly open, crumbs from his tipped-up plate sprinkled across his lap.

I distracted myself from the sudden rush of longing to shuffle up, snuggle into his chest and drape his arm around me by picking up my phone instead. Incriminating photos taken, plate transferred to a more stable surface, the urge to rest my head on his shoulder and pretend for a few seconds that I had someone to curl up on the sofa with had refused to abate. I left Sandra Bullock gazing doe-eyed at a far less lovely sleeping man and went to heat up a lasagne.

Nathan found me twenty minutes later, hair comically fluffed up and pyjamas rumpled. I concentrated hard on chopping up a yellow pepper, hoping the word '*adorable*' might have stopped crashing about inside my brain before I needed to look up again.

'I think I might have dozed off for a moment.' Nathan sounded bewildered.

'The snoring would indicate that, yes.'

'*Snoring?*' He tried in vain to smooth down the feral tufts of hair. 'I do not snore.'

'I bet you don't sleep in the afternoon, either.' I took a garlic and rosemary focaccia out of the oven and dropped it onto a bread board.

'Once. After a twenty-four-hour race.'

'Coach Gallagher, I think you might be getting the hang of this relaxing thing.' Scooping two slices of lasagne onto plates, I carried them over to the table. 'Either that or you're getting old.'

* * *

After our very late lunch/early dinner, even I had to agree that we were Christmas rom-comed out, so we switched to Scrabble. And while, yes, the professional writer in the room may have had a slight advantage, Coach Gallagher could hardly object to his clients exhibiting some competitive spirit. After losing twice, and nearly losing more than just the game over a decidedly dodgy use of a triple word score, he concluded that for the sake of our client-coach relationship we should probably stick to playing on the same team, and moved on to general lolling.

We checked into the PoolPalforPiper JustGiving page. Donations were steadily creeping up, but there was a huge way to go before the target would look achievable.

'It's fine,' I said. 'We'll make most of the money on the day.'

'Maybe Amelia should get publicly involved with the campaign before the day, get her official endorsement behind it.'

'That might well have the opposite effect.' I pulled my blanket up around my ears, burrowing deeper into the armchair. 'Being that Amelia Piper is a national loser.'

Nathan peered at me over the top of his phone. 'Why would the council name a leisure centre after a loser?'

'It's not the whole centre, just the pool. And who else did they have? The only other famous local is a convicted serial killer. It was probably a close vote.'

'You were a top UK athlete. People loved how you connected with them. And at eighteen, under enormous pressure, you handled a very difficult situation as best you could. If that makes you a national loser, then I dread to think what it means for the rest of us.'

I shook my head, refusing to be coddled. 'I'm worse than a loser.' Nathan frowned as my voice broke. 'At least a loser actually takes part. And I don't just mean the Olympics. What am I supposed to say when Moira Vanderbeek asks me where I've been all decade?'

I squinched my eyes shut, furiously trying to force the tears back inside my head where they belonged.

'Okay, so I don't know who Moira Vanderbeek is, or what she has to do with it, but look at all you've achieved the past few months, Amy. How can you still think of yourself like that? This is putting a serious dent in my professional credibility.'

I whipped down the blanket. 'Getting dressed and going outside under the cover of darkness is not an achievement. "Walked around the village, and even once – *once* – left the village to visit a nearby club" is hardly going to make it onto my Wikipedia page.'

Nathan was quiet for a while. 'Over 1.3 million people in the UK suffer from panic disorder. Around a third of them will develop agoraphobia. I think that they, and their families and friends, all the health professionals working in mental health, would be really interested to hear what you've overcome.'

Note to self even while in midst of frenetic battle with inner anxiety monster: Nathan Gallagher has been doing his research.

'I'm hardly a poster girl for mental well-being.'

'You will be.'

I pulled a tissue out of the box on the coffee table, unwittingly dragging out about six more with it. 'This isn't about me, though. It's for Tate, and for all the other people who long to go outside and get stuck into life but are constantly hampered and obstructed by a society designed with them completely left out of the equation or the budget. They deserve this to be about them, not me providing fodder for TV panel show comedians.'

'So answer the obvious questions, don't make living a quiet life in the countryside, taking care of your son and doing a job you enjoy a big deal. Then shift the focus where it needs to be. You make a living out of persuading people to believe in companies and organisations. That must include skimming over the less desirable aspects and bigging up the stuff you want them to notice.'

'I'm pretty sure your ancient crush has coloured your perspective. But thanks for the encouragement. I'll think about it.'

And I did, for half the night. My anxiety feeding me impressively creative worst-case scenarios, one of which resulted in Joey moving to Colorado, refusing to answer the letters scrawled from my hospital bed. But I knew that while I continued to hide, the fear of being exposed, judged, ridiculed and rejected still held me in its power. What was the point in being able to go anywhere, anytime, if inside my head I constantly looked over my shoulder in dread of someone finding out who I really was?

I had to face this at some point. And I knew where to start.

* * *

The other half of the night, it goes without saying, I thought about a whole twelve hours spent with another person, who wasn't my son. I thought about how there hadn't been one moment where I felt uncomfortable or inadequate, or *anxious*. For so long, so many of my thoughts and feelings had stayed in my head. With Nathan, I was learning to let them out. To laugh about them, and weep over them. I was remembering the value of listening – to someone else's opinion, and to stories and problems and circumstances outside of my own boxed-in world. Nathan had this incredible ability to make me feel like his equal, not a client trying to get to grips with basic life skills. I supposed this was what having a friend felt like. In summary, it felt blummin' gorgeous.

Phew. I hoped those *other* feelings – the ones that tap-danced in my stomach and frolicked up and down my ribs before oozing dreamily through my arteries like warm caramel – I hoped they didn't go and ruin it all. If past experience was anything to go by (and let's face it, what else did I have?), allowing those feelings any credence, any say at all, would not turn out well.

43

STOP BEING A LOSER PROGRAMME

DAY ONE HUNDRED AND TEN

Christmas Day was, well, different.

Joey had a whole list of reasons prepared about why his dad should spend the day with us, rather than alone in his apartment. Shuffling through Christmas Eve, too tired to argue and deciding that another man in my life could only help in the Battle to Annihilate the Stupid Feelings, Joey was bamboozled by how easily I gave in.

'It's a Christmas miracle!' he assured Cee-Cee, as they helped prepare lunch. 'Who'd have guessed my dad would be here!?'

'Not me,' Cee-Cee muttered, ferociously scraping a parsnip. When the doorbell rang, she ignored it, despite me being elbow-deep in chestnut stuffing, the corner of one eye twitching as she scraped harder.

In actual fact, the day wasn't terrible. Sean brought presents, and after a couple of glasses of fizz, I decided I might as well enjoy them. He gave me a fitness watch – an expensive one, which played music, workouts and probably the pipe organ alongside monitoring my steps and distance.

'Easy-to-read calorie counter?' I mused. 'Are you saying I need to lose weight?'

But I knew that he wasn't. And the wry smile confirmed quite the opposite – this was Sean encouraging me. Acknowledging the woman I really was, underneath my illness. Offering a token recompense for his contribution to her demise. To Joey, he gave the predictable far too many, far too expensive things. To my surprise, I shut down Cee-Cee's tutting disapproval with a glare: it was Christmas. Joey had spent enough years being grateful for the paltry presents I carefully selected to stretch my budget as far as possible. He was owed thirteen years of successful-business-owner dad presents. And like Mel had said back when I first freaked out about the thought of Sean, Joey was not going to be spoiled by a few flashes of a credit card.

Sean insisted on Joey helping him to do the post-lunch clean-up before they went out to play with his new drone, leaving Cee-Cee and me to undo the top buttons on our jeans and fall into a calorie-induced trance on the sofa.

'You need to be careful,' Cee-Cee said, after a while.

Not interested in another row, I pretended to be dozing.

'Closing your eyes and trying to ignore it won't help.' She snorted. 'A Christmas miracle! Next he'll be setting you and Sean up on dates and some such nonsense.'

I groaned. 'Joey has no illusions about me and Sean.'

'Wise up, Amelia. And Joey won't be the only one getting his hopes up if you carry on indulging his game of happy families.'

'You're being ridiculous.'

'You're being naïve.'

'Please remember it's none of your business.'

'Just don't get sucked into something without realising it.' She sighed, adjusting her position on the sofa. 'He's not as terrible as I remembered. It might be more tempting than you think.'

If I hadn't been quite so annoyed, I might have paid more attention.

* * *

It was later on, when we were trying to stuff cheese and crackers into stomachs still bloated with dinner, that I was startled into wondering if Cee-Cee might be right. Joey was badgering us for stories about when we first met, and I remembered faking a hair appointment for a magazine photo shoot while I was actually with Sean, my parents then pretending to like the dreadful hack-job he'd done.

'I did wonder, once the horror of my butchering skills began to emerge, whether to just shave it all off and make something up about aerodynamics.' Sean couldn't stop laughing.

'I overheard Mum and Dad arguing about it when they thought I was getting my make-up done. She wanted to sue the hairdresser, but Dad insisted it must be some new noughties trend they didn't know about. She was all, "Gareth, if ugly, backward mullets with random chunks of hair missing had suddenly become fashionable, I would have one by now."'

And then it happened again. A repeat of when we'd been watching Joey train together. Our eyes met, and a spark of warmth, camaraderie and shared history flashed between us. Instantly, the distant memory of first love, the intensity of summer nights drenched in passion and promise felt a whole lot less far away. I hastily looked down, shovelling a cracker in my mouth. But I could still feel Sean's gaze on me, lighting up every nerve ending on my skin.

Get a grip, Amy! I berated myself later, once Cee-Cee and Sean had left. *Stop acting like a hormone-riddled teenager who's been locked up in a basement for thirteen years, snarfing up crumbs of attention from the first two men to pay her any attention. Actually, forget about getting a grip, how about getting some standards?*

It was a relief to realise I might not be falling for Nathan after all. Unless I was also having legitimate feelings for Sean. Which made me want to rip off my own skin and prise out my heart with a carving knife, so probably not.

44

STOP BEING A LOSER PROGRAMME

DAY ONE HUNDRED AND TWELVE

During the twixtmas funk, fuelled by leftovers, chocolate and way too much slobbing around with nothing to do, I repeatedly came back to one thought: ploughing on with the Programme, forcing myself outside was not enough. At some point, I had to confront the root of it all. I would have loved to talk to Nathan about it – to get an outside opinion from someone who knew who I was, but he was in the Alps with a crowd of adventurous, fun and attractive women (okay, so some men too, but it was the women in his Instagram pictures that I noticed – an excellent reminder of the off-duty Nathan's world and the kind of people he had things in common with).

In the end, I just picked up the phone.

'Mum. It's me.'

A horrible silence. 'One moment please.' *Was this her, or her voice-double now employed as a secretary?* I then heard my mother, the one who had publicly disowned me at eighteen years old during the middle of an emotional crisis and privately rejected my weeping, pregnant, homeless self a few months later, frantically whispering to my dad: 'It's her! On the phone! What do you mean, who? Amelia! Here. You deal with it.'

A broken, stuttering heartbeat away from hanging up, I heard my dad take the phone. 'Amelia?'

'Yes.' It took everything to get that one word out.

'How... Is everything all right?'

I pressed my free hand to my forehead, trying to stop my brain from trembling. Was there even an answer to that question? 'Yes.'

'I mean, you're not... ill, or anything?'

Does raging nausea, cramped lungs and a shattered heart count?

I took a deep breath, counted to five in my head. 'No, Dad. I just thought I'd call. See how you were.'

'Oh. Right.'

Another count to five.

'How are you both?'

'Fine. We're fine. I suppose. Your mother's keeping herself busy with tennis and lunch club. And I'm still managing the shop. Part-time, now. Have to watch my blood pressure after the stroke.'

'Stroke?' *Oh. Oh. Oh my goodness.* I slumped back in my office chair. My parents had grown old without me. My own blood pressure careened upwards in response.

'Just a tiddler. Nothing to worry about. You'd never know, except they have me on that many pills I rattle.'

The endless possibilities of the past decade flashed in front of my eyes – all this time, anything could have happened. Just because my life had consisted of the barest remnants of nothing much for year after year, why had I assumed the same for them?

'But you're all right?' Dad asked. 'And what about... your little one?'

'He's six foot now. Not so little.'

'Ah, got his mother's genes then.'

'He's the most amazing swimmer,' I blurted.

'Of course he is. You get to find out what it's like from the parent's side, now.'

'Dad, I wanted to say I'm sorry. For what I did, and the way I did it. I was young and confused and I panicked. The pressure of competing was bad enough, but then with all the TV stuff, the appearances and inter-views, I felt trapped and lost all at the same time, if that's possible. I couldn't think clearly and I didn't consider properly the effect it would have on you.'

A well-known kind of apology is the one where you say sorry in order to get an apology back. I hadn't realised quite how strongly this fell into that category until my dad replied.

'Right. Well. I appreciate that.'

I waited. Filling in the silence with what I so desperately needed to hear... *No – we're the ones who are sorry. You have nothing to be sorry for. We were greedy and selfish and bitterly regret abandoning you when you needed us. The only reason we haven't tried to contact you is that you are better off without us. We think of you every day...*

'And I am glad to hear you're all right. Keeping well.'

Keeping well? At what point in the conversation did we discuss how I was keeping?

'Right. I must get on. Nice to hear from you. Bye then.'

Oh. My. Goodness.

I stared at the phone as if it was the font of all knowledge, holding the very secrets to life itself.

Because following that conversation, it was pretty darn close to it. The secrets to my life, anyway.

The secret?

My parents were crap.

Beyond crap.

It explained a lot.

And while it would not be an excuse, as I pondered and raged and pounded through the frosted forest later that day, it did allow me to release a little of the shame and the guilt along with my cloudy breath. It did convince me that I would strive to not let my past control me any more. I would choose to no longer define myself by my worst mistake.

I am Amelia Piper. My friends call me Amy. And I have as much right to be here, walking, talking, running, sweating, taking up space and oxygen and vital resources as anyone else.

I am here.

It was time I bloody well started acting like it.

STOP BEING A LOSER PROGRAMME

DAY ONE HUNDRED AND TWENTY-ONE

The first Saturday of the new year, Nathan sent a text, which was absolutely no reason for my heart to skip up and down my ribcage, given that he'd sent it as a group message to everyone in the club:

First pre-triathlon practice run tomorrow. 8K so allow for an extra 30min, depending on how fast you run

What!? How utterly outrageous. The texts pinged back. Didn't Nathan know these Larks had work to do, ill mothers and young children to take care of, church to attend and spas to relax in? Every woman had a reason why she squeezed an hour's run right at the start (or, in Bronwyn's case, the end) of her day. All of us had a lifeful of people and pressures needing our time and energy. Except for me, of course. And Marjory, who sent a short sharp reply reminding us once again to respect our coach, that winning took commitment and if we couldn't spare an extra thirty minutes on a Sunday morning we might as well give up now. And where would that leave Tate?

There was an hour or two of radio silence while calls were made, schedules adjusted and rotas rearranged. The Larks would be there. By hook or by crook, we women would do what it took. Except, for goodness' sake, Nathan, please could you give us a bit more notice next time?

Great. An extra thirty minutes. I was the only person not to respond.

Say yes, and that meant risking sunrise on a country path with nowhere to hide. Say no, and I was basically saying no to the triathlon, to the campaign.

I could plead a migraine, a stomach bug, a groin injury fifteen minutes into the run.

Nathan knew where I was at with this. The Larks was supposed to be a safe, non-judgemental place. Who was he to decide when and where I faced my next hurdle? Let alone who with. He didn't even know that I'd spent the past few afternoons scuttling down my front path and back again, daring myself to linger for longer each time at the gate.

He's your coach, the message from Marjory reminded me. *And your friend.*

I waited until ten that night. Joey was staying with Sean and I had spent the evening typing out and deleting messages until my thumbs ached. Sick of once again finding myself in this loop of despair and nervous panic, I went and stood in the garden, span around looking at the stars, the treetops and the cat from a few doors down until my skin had cooled off, my nerves stopped jerking about and I typed a momentous, 'see you then'.

Nathan replied two seconds later. Not a group message, this time.

OK?

Not really. But I'm doing it anyway.

I added on a chicken and a giant lollipop.
He replied with a picture of a lion.
Oh boy.

STOP BEING A LOSER PROGRAMME

DAY ONE HUNDRED AND TWENTY-TWO

Early the following morning, I headed out into the delicious darkness. It was far too cold to hang about waiting for the rest of the Larks at the leisure centre, so I took my favourite detour down Foxglove Lane. The house with enormous windows was completely dark. I thought about Audrey, hoped she was doing okay. Muttered a heartfelt prayer that Graham was genuine, and that if he wasn't, Audrey would realise it in time to leave the relationship on her own terms rather than be discarded by someone else who thought she wasn't good enough.

The women who gathered in the car park were half optimistic buzz, pumped on New Year's resolutions, rejuvenated by the break and eager to take on the extra challenge. The other half were pale-faced, half-assed, comparing notes on how much weight they'd gained and how little they'd moved in the past few weeks.

'I'm literally running on cheese and chocolate right now, Coach,' Bronwyn moaned.

'Are you going to whinge the whole session?' Selena snapped. 'Because some of us have come here with a New Year PMA and don't want to hear about your crap choices.'

'If that's a positive mental attitude, then it must have been a ho ho happy Christmas at Selena's,' Dani murmured, stretching her quads out beside me.

'She went to her brother's,' Mel said, silver bunches bobbing as she jogged on the spot. 'Wanted to get away, what with Audrey not being there.'

'Hmmm. I suppose we can extend a little grace. For now. But at some point that woman has got to learn the art of healthy communication. Otherwise she'll be spending a lot more than Christmas alone.'

'And I'm not going to whinge!' Bronwyn called across to Selena. 'I'm just prepping Coach that if I collapse halfway round, he'll need to carry me the rest of the way.'

'How's he going to manage that after stuffing yourself with cheese?' someone yelled, their head between their knees for a hamstring stretch.

'Fireman's lift?' Bronwyn purred, flicking her hair at Nathan. 'Cradling me like a knight bearing a fair maiden to safety, or a groom sweeping his bride across the threshold, I'm not fussy.'

'I don't even like cheese, Nathan,' someone else said. 'If I get tired, will you carry me?'

And so it went on, Nathan studiously ignoring the catcalls and the borderline harassment as he led us through the rest of the warm-up, while I pretended my irritation was down to moral decency and respect for my friend-slash-coach, not possessiveness and jealousy because even if I wanted to ask Nathan to 'sniff my new non-cheesy body spray', I couldn't. And I wouldn't, because unlike most of the women safe to hoot and holler at him, I probably would collapse for real if he leant in to catch a whiff.

'Right, let's take it steady now, we're doing an extra 3K today, so pace yourselves. Especially those of you who consider Christmas a good time to fuel your body with toxic waste and then stew in it. And for those of you who seem to have forgotten the Health and Safety policy, if anyone collapses, then the designated First Aid Officer will secure a safe means by which to evacuate them to the nearest appropriate medical facility. If they are unable to walk, then this will be via a stretcher, or ambulance if necessary.'

Nathan's face was a mask. I had no idea if he was playing along with us or not. Then he turned to me, and for the briefest of moments his eyes crinkled up as they held mine. A rush of warmth swooped up my chest and neck, catching my heart and sending it spinning.

It was a tough run, up and down and through the forest in the freezing early morning, warily skimming the horizon for signs of sunrise while also attempting to avoid tripping over a root or a stray bramble. But the hardest part of that hour was trying to stop the grin from splitting my face in two every time I remembered that crinkle.

It's okay to enjoy a private joke, I told myself, even my thoughts huffing with exertion. *It's been a really long time since I had fun with people, and it's perfectly normal given the circumstances that it would feel as though the moon had reached down from heaven and wrapped its soft, strong arms around me...*

Yeah, you keep telling yourself that, Amy.

* * *

At what my thighs reckoned was probably around the twenty-six-mile mark, but my new watch insisted was only 7.5K, we were still nowhere close to Brooksby. My wavering anxiety, kept at bay by the memory of a crinkle, began to stir. A thick line of bleached-blue now crowned the field to the east, as we shuffled along the edge of the woods, and the winter stars were fading one by one, swallowed up into the dawn. I knew this was coming. I had prepared for it. Was ready. But what I was ready for was to sprint down the hill, along the road into the village, with every ounce of my being fixed on the sanctuary of home. Lost on a hilltop in the wilds of Sherwood Forest was not how I had planned to do this.

To give my anxiety even more of a boost, up ahead people appeared to have decided this was a good point to take a rest. Half a kilometre before the finish line.

It was now light enough that I saw it, several metres before I reached them.

A silhouette of camping chairs, stretching along the brow of the hill. A table, behind them all, with two huge flasks and an array of breakfast food. I lumbered up to where Marjory, one damp curl on her forehead, was slicing up a pineapple.

'Stretches, people,' Nathan ordered the stragglers.

I ignored him. 'What is this?'

'Looks like breakfast to me,' Bronwyn said, helping herself to a yoghurt.

'The café's closed today, Chris and Gill are away.' Nathan watched me carefully.

'Did everyone else know about it?' I asked, my voice managing to span a good couple of octaves in one sentence.

He shook his head, before turning to where the other Larks were crowding like pigeons round the table. 'I know some of you have pressing commitments this morning, feel free to grab a snack and then go. It's a fifteen-minute walk if you follow the fence back through the wood. But, for the rest of you, feel free to stay and support Amy in her next challenge.'

'What?' someone asked. 'How is a picnic breakfast a challenge?'

'Oh, do be quiet,' Selena retorted. 'Honestly, some people notice nothing any more unless it pops up as a notification on their phone.'

'Some people might say that's better than being a nosy cow,' Dani said, smiling sweetly before taking a sip of tea from a cardboard cup.

'Some other people, and by that I mean me, think we should stop bickering and start considering Amy's feelings.' Mel pointed at me, which was about the last thing my feelings wanted right then. I felt as though a grenade of stress hormones had exploded in my chest, blurring my vision and sending my head reeling.

'Where do you want to sit, Ames?' Bronwyn asked. 'You plonk yourself down and I'll bring you a cuppa.'

Um, on my own sofa at home? Buried under my duvet?

'Stretches first,' Nathan said, as if he'd never held my hand as I flailed about on the street like a dying haddock.

How dare he do this without asking me first? How dare he expose my worst fears in front of these women I respected? How dare he keep pushing and prodding me forwards when I'm not ready, as if trying to prove that I'm incapable of deciding these things for myself?

I somehow resisted the urge to stretch so effectively my fist connected with his face, even as he stepped closer, head bending towards mine.

'You're ready for this. Studies prove that by tackling your fears with a supportive community of trusted people around you—'

'Not everybody here is supportive. And I don't trust most of them.' Right now, I didn't feel like I trusted Nathan much, either, and that showed in my voice's bitter crack. 'I'm not going to sit here while they ogle me like the post-run entertainment.'

Nathan was stern. 'This group is not like that, and you know it. Who's been ogling Selena and Audrey, or gossiping about Bronwyn's hitman boyfriend? This is your *team*. We're sitting here with you, and watching the sunrise. Whether you like it or not, we're in this together.'

'Well, for the record, I don't like it.' That wasn't quite true. I got the team part, I had lived by those rules, once. I knew that being part of something – a team, a tribe, a community, a family – was everything. And expanding my team beyond my son and my old coach in the past few weeks had changed my life beyond recognition. What I didn't like was how the sky just kept on getting paler, causing my heart to thump increasingly erratically, and how I didn't really know where I was, or if I was going to tumble into a full-blown panic attack. Being part of a team had been great when I was the strongest member. Letting everyone see that I was the weakest felt about as pleasant as stripping off naked in front of them all.

In the end, everyone stayed.

'Larks forever!' Mel chanted, until she noticed that I was crying, so instead she jiggled her chair right up close to mine and gave my shoulders a squeeze.

So, what else could I do but stay with them? I had ranted on at myself that it was *time* for several days now. I could either put up or shut up – or run home and hate myself even more than I had three months ago. Instead, I pressed myself into the back of the chair, one hand clenching a mug of tea, the other enclosed perfectly inside the loveliest, safest hand in the world. I focused on a tiny tractor chugging across a distant field, and I breathed in the crisp, clean air, and by some miracle, despite the fact that my internal organs felt on the brink of liquification, I kept on breathing out again.

'A lark!' Bronwyn whispered, as a lone bird began cheeping in the trees behind us.

'Chiffchaff,' Marjory said.

'Well, there's no need to be rude!'

'No, that's the name of the bird, it isn't a—'

'Shhhh!' Dani interrupted. 'Look.'

And there it was. The light had been getting brighter for a while now, as pinks and reds mingled with gold along the horizon. But now a slither of deep orange crested the brow of the hill. We watched, in silence, no one slurping their coffee or scraping their bowls any more, as the shadows fled and the glorious sun rose to meet us, streamers of light celebrating the arrival of the new dawn with a spectacle that outshone the greatest of human endeavours in every way.

A new day.

'My God, it's amazin',' Mel sighed, and it was a prayer not a blasphemy, as we all silently echoed our 'Amen'. 'Which reminds me,' she whispered, 'I'm on refreshments rota at chapel this morning. Best get home and jump in the shower, sort the kids out.'

The enchantment broken, the rest of the group started collecting up the plates and divvying out the leftovers, gradually drifting off in twos and threes down the trail.

'How are you going to get these chairs back down?' Dani asked, one of the last to leave. 'And for that matter, how did you get them up here? Were you camped here all night?'

Nathan grinned. 'I stored them in an old bird hide in the wood along with the food. Only took me three trips. Carried the flasks up first thing.'

Dani raised one eyebrow at me, and I knew full well what it meant: *what a lot of effort, all to help you face the morning.*

'Do you want help carrying them back down?'

'It's fine, thanks.'

'Right then, I'll leave you to it.' And with that, she blew me a kiss and disappeared into the wood.

I stayed in my chair while Nathan put everything back in the hide. Not because I was still annoyed at him, or feeling lazy, but because I couldn't take my eyes off the view and was gulping in the grand, sweeping beauty stretching out below me like it was oxygen. There were copses of trees dotted amongst the brown winter fields. A flock of birds wheeled across the far end of the valley, their shadows chasing across the earth below. Next to a stream, a blip of yellow bobbed beside a black and white dog splashing through the sparkling water. A procession of cows swayed across a meadow, and as I watched, my heart slowed to their gentle cadence. The crisp air flowed deep into the far, neglected corners of my lungs, my stomach sighed and settled, and I couldn't even cry, because my soul was soaring over that valley, carried on a gust of hope and untarnished happiness.

I was here. I had made it. And I had stayed.

Somewhere, during the past twenty years or so, I had forgotten the sheer beauty and the wonder of being alive, in a world teeming with life. I promised myself in that moment that I would do my utmost never to forget that again.

'While I don't want to intrude on the moment, if you end up frozen to the chair, it's going to be a pain getting you back down the hill.'

I blinked, took a couple of seconds to come back to myself, and realised I was stiff with cold, my fingers grey claws. 'What time is it?' I sounded like a bad ventriloquist – my whole face was numb.

'Just after nine-thirty,' Nathan grinned.

'Why didn't you say something?' I scrabbled off the chair, nearly ending up on my backside as my limbs struggled to get working again.

He shrugged. 'This was the whole point of us being here.'

'I've taken up half your morning. It must have totally messed up your plans.'

'Nope.' He folded the chair and swung it over his shoulder in one deft move, starting to walk towards the path back to the village.

'Don't pretend you don't have a whole day of productive, meaningful activities scheduled.'

Nathan paused to allow me to catch up with him. 'Oh, I do. But I allowed some flexibility in the schedule, given that I'll be doing them with you.'

'Excuse me?'

'Did I forget to mention? Breakfast was only part one of the challenge.'

I was speechless as I kept walking, the brilliant after-effects of my hour in the sunshine haemorrhaging onto the muddy path behind me.

'Don't panic.'

'Then tell me what the hell you're talking about.'

He reached out and grabbed my hand, face serious, but those crinkles betraying his excitement. 'A whole day, sunset to sunrise, out.'

'Urr.'

'Come on, you're here now, might as well keep going for a few more hours. And once you've finished, you'll be ready to conquer anything.'

I stopped, fighting the urge to bend over and retch into the bracken. 'No, thank you.'

Nathan took my other hand, ducking his head to look me in the eye. 'You can do this.'

'You don't know that.'

'You didn't think you could eat breakfast out here in broad daylight, and you smashed that.'

'And that was really, really enough for one day. I know my limits, Nathan, I am freaking out right now. Just getting myself through the village, into my house and under my duvet is challenge enough. How the hell am I supposed to manage a whole day?'

'One minute at a time.'

'That sounds like a very long day,' I virtually screeched at him. 'Can I at least know what's going to be happening?'

'First, we need a shower.'

Well, my anxiety was somewhat bamboozled by that statement.

Nathan's mouth fell open as blood flooded his cheeks and neck. He dropped my hands as if they were electric eels. 'That came out wrong.'

I actually laughed. 'I should hope so.'

'Crap.' He tugged at his hair in agitation. 'I had planned on us getting... changed... at mine, but now it seems... inappropriate.'

'If I was a football mate, or another personal trainer from the gym, would it be appropriate?'

'Yes. But I don't let my clients even know my address.'

'So, we'd better make a decision.' What a bizarre conversation to be having on an ice-cold Sunday morning, the words echoing through the woods around us. 'Am I your client, or a friend?'

Nathan hesitated, looking around as if the answer lay buried in the brambles or swinging from a branch. 'What do you want to be?' he asked, haltingly.

'Right now? I really want a shower.' *And I really NEED to get inside a solid building*. 'Maybe we can temporarily suspend our client-coach relationship until we've left your house again. I'll pretend I don't know where you live and forget it ever happened.'

He frowned at the path, then up at the clear sky, before his non-crinkled eyes settled on me. 'I suppose it's no worse than spending the day together in pyjamas.'

We resumed walking.

'You could always make some amendments to the rulebook, draft a new contract or whatever, for clients who also happen to be friends,' I said, a few minutes later.

'No point,' Nathan replied, two steps behind me. 'I'm not planning on this happening with anyone else. And any rules I come up with, you'll just bend to suit you anyway.'

I looked over my shoulder, about to throw a witty, unbecoming retort back at him, but before I had a chance to think one up, my body, still mainly facing forwards, stepped out of the treeline onto the main road and simultaneously *oofed* into another person.

'Watch it, you idiot!'

My brain decided that now would be a good time to succumb to the cold weather and freeze completely solid.

* * *

Ten minutes – an age, an epic expedition later, with numerous pep talks and pauses to steady my breathing and bone-crushing grips of Nathan's hand later – I finally reached the sanctuary of what turned out to be a tiny cottage on the edge of the village. About as functional and staid as I would have predicted a Robo-Coach's house to be, I collapsed onto the leather couch, and immediately sprang upright again, rubbing my arm.

'Okay?'

'You really need some cushions in here. What kind of person buys a sofa with metal arms?' Focusing on Nathan's house rather than the dissipating panic helped reassure my scrambled head that I was now safely indoors.

'The kind who doesn't slob out or pass out unless he's in bed, at the intended time.'

'Or watching cheesy Christmas films in the middle of the afternoon,' I smirked. 'Maybe you should get a cushion in case a friend comes round and wants to be able to sit comfortably.'

He ignored me, holding out something that looked suspiciously like Joey's old sports bag. 'A change of clothes, and... ahem... whatever-else-you-need-I'm-sorry-this-is-still-weird-for-me.'

I took the bag. Weird for him? This was so off my radar, I was in need of a search party. I steeled my shoulders, made a feeble attempt at wrestling whatever hormones were making my nerves thrum back into whichever gland they were gushing from, and reminded myself that we were client-coach-friends. 'Is the bathroom upstairs?'

'Um. Yes. Yes, at the end of the landing.'

And for reasons of personal pride and general dignity, the less said about me being naked in Nathan's shower cubicle, the better.

* * *

The best day of my life was when I was twelve years old. I know it's supposed to be the day my son was born, but after sixteen hours hoping and praying that my mum would turn up, being yelled at by Cee-Cee about focus and self-discipline, on top of the pain and effort required to push out a ten pound baby, by the time Joey arrived I had no energy left to feel much at all.

But at twelve, on the day of the Regional Championships, I hit the side of the Ponds Forge Olympic pool in Sheffield, turned to see my arch-rival, Georgie Bannister, a good three seconds behind me, and in that moment, dripping, exhausted, lungs raw, I knew I had what it took. The confidence and the drive that won me a gold medal took root that day, as my squad, a mixture of envy and pride, argued about who got to sit next to me on the bus home. My coach patted me on the shoulder (which is more affection than she offered me in labour). A blushing Benji Simons gave me his Snickers bar, and my parents gushed the whole evening about agents and sponsorship, my mother drafting a resignation letter for her joke of a job as an entertainment consultant.

It was a milestone of a day, as I left one era behind and stepped boldly into another. In my mind from then on, there was only before and after. When I was just Amelia, a girl who was mad on swimming and loved the Sugababes, and Amelia Piper, future world champion.

My day out from sunrise to sunset was something like that day.

First of all, Nathan took me to the Grace Chapel in Brooksby, where I'd been for the carol service. It was a different place in the daylight – light and warm both at the same time, full of colour and energy and smiles and children running about chasing each other with catapults (which apparently was a one-time thing, linked to their Sunday school class, and definitely not happening again after a muffin from Mel's refreshment stall was catapulted into the face of an elderly gentleman with cataracts). I hummed along to songs I didn't know and cringed while the minister spoke about the power of forgiveness, including forgiving yourself, and how mistakes from our past can hold us back from our future. I didn't dare glance up at Nathan, who seemed to be sniffing more than is socially acceptable for someone who hasn't even got a cold. While at first a room full of strangers made my bones quake, I soon spotted people I recognised from the carol service and my school-gate days. Joey's friend, Ben, was there with his mum, Lisa, who came over to chat, and, to my surprise, Marjory was right in the thick of it. Even those I didn't know smiled and said hello, most of them presuming, for an awkward, lovely minute or two, that Nathan and I were a couple – understandable, given that he was holding my hand when we walked in.

After that, we changed pace at a local farm shop. Nathan hustled me round the fruit, vegetables, and delicatessen counters, insisting I squeezed, sniffed or sampled the produce as my anxiety buzzed in the background, as though trapped behind a pane of glass. We then moved next door to the farm café, gamely trying to fit in a huge bowl of parsnip and apple soup on top of all the free samples.

'Am I really witnessing Nathan Gallagher eating bread, made of actual wheat?' I asked, spreading my own slice with freshly churned, organic butter, glimmering with salt crystals.

'Am I really seeing Amelia Piper, out in a public place in daylight, enjoying herself?' he replied, before ripping a huge hunk off with his teeth.

And if that wasn't enough, he ordered us both pear crumble for dessert. While we ate, I distracted myself from my anxiety by talking, determined to ignore the taunts that a random stranger would recognise me by focusing on the person right here. I relayed the phone call with my parents, the wise words from the sermon that morning still resonating. And that naturally led on to other things, like what had happened with Sean, and the years after Joey was born, and before I had time to finish my coffee, Nathan had somehow found out everything about me.

'So, what about your family? I hope your parents aren't as crap as mine.'

He shrugged, fingers tapping on the side of his green tea (one step at a time, people!). 'They're decent enough. Work too much, aren't exactly demonstrative when it comes to affection. My dad loves sport, when he finds the time, so we always had that in common. Used to go to Trent Bridge for the test matches together, or down to Leicester for the rugby.'

'Used to?'

He took a sip of tea before answering. 'When Gill got attacked, I sort of went into survival mode. Head down, spending every day taking care of her, ticking off my lists so I knew I wouldn't mess up again. Then, once she ended it, I suddenly had all this time to think, and none of those thoughts were good. I didn't know how to handle the guilt and the shame at failing at something so important. I would cry or lose my temper in the worst places. My nephew's first birthday party, or a family barbeque. So when I started staying away more, distancing myself, I think they were relieved. And then, as I built my business, I got busy. It's easier, I suppose, to keep going as we are now.'

'The easier route is rarely the best one. I should know. And so should a personal trainer and sports coach.'

He nodded. 'Hearing about your parents makes putting in a bit of effort with mine seem not such a big deal.'

'Your next challenge. Maybe you should invite them to the triathlon.'

'Maybe I will.'

I took another sip of coffee. 'Interesting how you dealt with your out-of-control emotions by compulsively controlling everything else.'

'Being self-disciplined when it comes to making positive lifestyle choices has nothing to do with it.'

My BS detector rejected that statement.

'Pastor Dylan of the Grace Chapel would suggest that if you haven't done so yet, going back and taking a look at what caused those emotions is the only way to get free of them. He might suggest it's time you forgave yourself.'

'What happened back then is not relevant to how I choose to live now.'

'So, what enabled you to get over it?'

'I don't know! I just moved on, moved past it. Gill's happy with Chris. I barely think about it any more.'

'Yet it shapes your whole life. Your work, your family relationships. Chasing strange women through the woods to browbeat them into joining your running club.'

'A terrible thing happened, and I did something positive in response.' He waved briskly at the waitress, 'The bill, please.'

'As long as you haven't shut down all your healthy emotions, along with the scary ones, I guess that's fine then.'

Exasperated, he chucked a few notes on the table and got up to leave.

'And if you can still manage deep and meaningful relationships, with friends, family... people you're attracted to, people you *can't control*, without having a list of rules to ensure a manageable distance is maintained, then fantastic, no problemo.'

He marched in stony silence to the car. Once our seat belts were safely on, Nathan gripped the wheel and blew a long, sharp breath out of his nose. I surreptitiously checked – no smoke, so I figured he hadn't quite blown a gasket, I was okay.

He opened his mouth a few times as if to speak, before finally getting to it. 'What happened with Gill, that did drive me to bury my head in work. But my motivations readjusted themselves a long time ago. I don't do this as some sort of penance. I love my job, I enjoy achieving my fitness potential and I like things how I like them. I also just had dessert for the first time in forever, so maybe give me some credit for recognising my tendency towards being inflexible and allowing you to browbeat me into working on it. And, trust me, my emotions are not shut down right now.'

He revved out of the car park in a spray of gravel. A point well made.

Next, Nathan really surprised me. We ended up on a suburb at the edge of Nottingham, where a young guy handed me the keys to a tiny Kia.

'What is this?'

'A test drive.'

'I haven't driven in six years. I'm not insured.'

'Jase is a driving instructor, the car's insured for anyone.'

'Six years, though.' I held the keys like they'd been plucked out of the sewer.

'Do you want to be stranded in Brooksby for another six?'

'I'm not sure I can afford a car.'

'No one's expecting you to buy it, just give it a go and see what you think. But if you do decide that the freedom of having a car is worth the money, you won't find a better deal than this one.'

In the end, the thought of having a car to hide in, rather than face public transport, coupled with the irresistible promise of newfound *freedom*, swung it. And it *was* an excellent price. I spent over an hour pootling around the roads between Nottingham and Brooksby, my confidence growing until I grew tired and made a couple of stupid mistakes. By the time I had swapped the car for Jase's contact details, and the assurance that he'd hold it for a week, the sun was a white disc in a sea of molten copper.

'Home time?' Nathan asked, standing next to me on the pavement.

'Yes, please.'

We wound our way back to Brooksby through the twilight. I watched the sky melt through Prussian blue to thick black with fluttering joy and wonder. I had only gone and done it.

After spending the drive home phrasing and rephrasing multiple times in my head how to invite Nathan, coach-friend, in to help me celebrate by washing down some of the farm-shop purchases with a glass of wine, he saved me the bother.

'You made it.' He parked the car outside my house.

'I still can't believe it. Today's been like a dream. Beyond anything I could have dreamed of, to be honest.'

'Well done.'

'Thank you for persuading me to do it. It made all the difference, you being there. And, I'm astounded to say, I really enjoyed myself. And the planning – I can't tell you how much it means, you bothering to do that.'

'Well, planning's kind of my thing.' He laughed, awkwardly, glancing across until his eyes hit mine. And there it was – pow! A bolt of intensity, like a traction beam locking our gaze. And suddenly we were enveloped by velvety darkness, as the car filled with soft, heart-thumping silence. My chest seized, but this was nothing like the anxiety which had been mumbling in the background for most of the day. This was good nerves. Positive Panic, which I probably just made up, but for goodness' sake, Amy, stop wittering and do something adorable or sexy or preferably both. But don't use your hands because they're sweaty and gross. And watch the handbrake. Maybe try leaning in and—

On second thoughts, maybe not.

Nathan abruptly whipped his head back to face the road. 'You must be exhausted. And I'm meeting a friend later, so I'd better get on.'

'Right. Right! Yes, of course. And Joey'll be back any minute. I can't wait to tell him.' I fumbled at the seat belt, continuing to blether on until

I'd managed to extricate myself and figure out where the handle was on a door I'd been opening quite merrily all day.

Nathan waited for my malfunctioning mouth to pause for the briefest of breaths, engine already running. 'Enjoy your evening.'

'You too! Enjoy your... friend. Thanks again. See you Wednesday. If not before, who knows – I'll probably be all over the place now, could turn up anywhere.' Thankfully, at that point, my body took over, slamming the car door and allowing Nathan to drive off before I sprinted down the path to safety.

He did wait at the end of the road until I'd made it inside, but hey, that's just the kind of guy he is.

* * *

Two glasses of wine, an enormous salad and five different types of cheese later, I texted my boss, saying I'd be delighted to accept his invitation to discuss the senior bid writer's role – name a time and a place and I'd attend the heck out of it, in person, face to face, in actual bodily form, all present and correct.

He replied shortly afterwards, inviting me to his office on 11 February and congratulating me on my use of synonyms.

After a slice of cake made with local, organic carrots, some quick-fire bartering, and a longer online loan application, I had bought myself a car.

STOP BEING A LOSER PROGRAMME

DAY ONE HUNDRED AND TWENTY-FIVE

I shouldn't have been surprised that the following Wednesday morning, more than a few of the Larks seemed to have chosen me as their pacemaker. Not only had Dani left Nathan and me on top of the hill together, Mel had winked at me so many times across the chapel, someone had asked if her eye needed praying for.

I kept up a steady too-breathless-to-speak pace, but not saying anything only piqued their curiosity, and by the time we reached the Cup and Saucer, I was like the popular girl in an American high-school movie cafeteria scene, there were so many chairs squashed around my table. Nathan didn't help by leaving straight after the cool-down.

Giving in, I offered a boring as possible summary of the day, pretending that my Cheshire cat grin was down to conquering a day outside, not the company while I did it.

'Well, I reckon it's fab that you two are friends,' Mel said. 'Nate's everyone's mate, no one's friend. He could do with someone to get a bit more real with.'

I nodded vaguely. He'd barely said three words to me all morning, and not even asked whether I'd been out again (yes, on both days, around the village and even inside a couple of shops), so I was pretty sure I'd been bumped back from the friend zone to client. At least Mel wasn't insinuating we were more than friends, like there'd been a lust-filled moment in his car or anything.

'Enough about that,' Selena flapped her hand, as if discussing the second-best day of my life was beyond boring. 'We need to plan the triathlon. It's only three months away, and we haven't even decided who's doing what.'

'If nine or more of us are taking part, the rules say we need at least three in each race,' Isobel announced from the next table.

'Thank you, Isobel, for pointing out what we all already knew,' Selena droned back. 'The crucial question is, who does what?'

We then entered into a brief debate, involving everyone talking over everyone else and saying the same thing, which was that Marjory should run. By process of elimination, we then determined that the three women with a bike would have to cycle – Dani, Isobel and a woman whose name I hadn't found out in the acceptable window of asking time and would now remain an awkward mystery until someone else joined the Larks and got introduced. I called her Mystery Woman One, to distinguish her from the other woman whose name I'd failed to learn or remember — Mystery Woman Two.

Selena was the only one who wanted to swim.

'No way,' Bronwyn declared. 'My fella might come, and he won't be happy if I'm parading about in a cossie.'

'It's a swimming pool!' Dani barked. 'What does he expect you to wear?'

'He expects me to wear running gear, and run,' Bronwyn huffed back. 'He has to put up with men trying to paw at me every night at work, asking for my number and sending drinks over to the hot bouncer. The least I can do is spare him that on our days off.'

'Nobody is going to be pawing at you during a triathlon,' Marjory said, brow furrowed.

'No, but they'll be gawping. I mean, come on, it's only natural.' She pointed down at herself, trying to make a joke of it, but nobody was laughing. 'Look, he's the jealous type, but nobody's perfect. And I happen to think it's quite romantic, wanting to keep me for his eyes only.'

In the end, Mel agreed to swim, given that she was probably a better swimmer than runner.

'On the same basis, Audrey can do it,' Selena said. 'She's not swum in a while, but it can't be worse than her running.'

There was an awkward silence, while several of the team suddenly felt the need to check their phones.

'Selena, darling,' Dani placed a hand on her arm. 'I'm not sure Audrey will be there.'

'And if she's not coming to training, should she even be allowed to take part?' Mystery Woman Two asked.

'She's missed three weeks!' Selena snapped back. 'If she hasn't come to her senses by Easter, I'll drag her out of that viper's nest myself.'

'And what else can we do?' Mel asked. 'If we haven't got anyone else.'

'I'll swim.'

That got everybody's attention. Mine, included.

'You?' Selena replied, as if I'd just offered to do her pre-pool bikini wax.

'I heard you had a phobia,' Isobel said. 'That you had a meltdown watching your boy swim, started screaming at a sports agent looking to sign him up.'

'That's not true.'

I twisted my clammy hands together under the table, reminding myself that however hard my heart might thud, it could not and would not actually break a rib and erupt out of my chest.

'But it is true you avoid swimming pools,' Mel added, gently. 'It'd be good to 'ave someone swim who can smash out a couple of lengths now and then. You're comin' on great at the running, Amy, I think you'd do the team proud if you ran.'

'I'm a better swimmer.'

Marjory chortled. 'Let her swim. You might be surprised.'

No one looked convinced. They even went as far as to offer to pop in on Audrey and talk her into coming back.

Okay, heart now trying an alternative escape route up my windpipe, knees knocking against the table leg, I went for it: 'My surname is Piper.' A mix of blank and sympathetic looks. 'And Amy is only the short version of my first name.'

Dani got it first. 'Oh. My. Days.'

'Shut the fudging fridge!' Mel stood up, and shouted. 'You are going to frickin' well win this race for my Tate!'

'Eh?' Isobel asked. Nobody was listening.

Selena immediately plunged into PR overdrive, bombarding me with instructions about press releases and Instagram and contacting Notts TV.

'Are you even allowed to race though?' Bronwyn asked, causing a moment's worried pause in the conversation.

'She's Amelia bloomin' Piper!' Mel roared. 'It's her pool! If she wants to race, she'll bloomin' well race!'

'Does Nathan know?' Dani asked, eyes wide with interest.

'Two Olympians on the team – he'll be ecstatic,' Bronwyn cooed.

'One Olympian,' I said, bracing myself.

'One World Champion gold medallist, and an Olympian who came home empty-handed,' Marjory said.

'Fahitas, fajitas, you're both bloody brilliant,' Mel cried, banging her spoon on the table. 'We're all bloody brilliant!' She yelled even louder. 'HASHTAG POOLPALFOROURPIPER!'

'Actually there's no "our" in the hashtag. That wouldn't make any sense.'

'Give it a rest, Selena,' Dani rolled her eyes.

'If we want it to go viral, we need to ensure people hear the phrase correctly every single time, it's crucial that the exact wording becomes second nature... Is anybody listening to me?'

STOP BEING A LOSER PROGRAMME

DAY ONE HUNDRED AND FORTY

I had, to put it bluntly, been killing it.

By telling the Larks who I was, especially since they had reacted so positively, I had broken off another huge chunk of fear. The shame that had been dragging like a lead weight behind me shrivelled to dust in the daylight. Not that I should need their approval to make me feel okay about who I was, but when alongside the enormity of my public disgrace, it certainly helped.

I'd spent nearly three weeks now furthering my forays into the big wide daylight world. Jase had dropped the car off, and I'd been back to the farm shop, and made a quick excursion round the supermarket. I had even driven into Nottingham and managed a couple of hours in the shopping centre. It was still exhausting, and stressful, and the stupidest things could trigger my pre-panic-attack warning signs (I handed a toddler back the stuffed monkey that she'd dropped, and her mother said thank you in a way that made me wonder for the rest of the day and most of the night if she'd recognised me, as if it even mattered). But I was getting stronger, and braver, and my resuscitated addiction to winning was driving me on.

On the evenings I could spare the time I watched Joey train. Cee-Cee came along a couple of times, and of course Sean was still here, waving off any questions about how long he was staying and how his company was surviving without him with some vague mumblings about expanding Mansfield Recruitment into the UK. For reasons I didn't think about too hard, sitting with Sean offered a sort of protective back-up, someone to chat to if I felt anxious, or needed to pretend to ignore any unsettling looks or whispers (my burgeoning rational self knew there weren't any of these, but the paranoid section of my brain had been ruling the roost too long and still struggled with her enforced abdication). I had asked – begged – the Larks to keep my secret for now, on the basis that if I got asked not to compete, it might create negative publicity for the campaign. Plus, they wanted me swimming because they now reckoned they actually had a chance of coming first, and it seemed as though I wasn't the only one who could grow fixated with winning.

But as I perched poolside, looking so much more like my younger self (back straight, chin up, hair brushed), I knew it wouldn't take much for someone to realise who Joey Piper's mum was.

Still, I kept going. The worst that could happen was utter humiliation, a panic attack that felt akin to dying and a barrage of nastiness. I had faced all that before and it turned out I survived.

This evening, Joey had asked me to come to Chicken Thursday, and having come up with no decent excuse, here I was.

'Hey, Champ!' Sean greeted us from their 'usual table'. How lovely, and not at all galling, that it was now *usual* for my son to spend time with his previously completely absent father. 'Amy, you look lovely.'

'No need to sound surprised.' I was wearing the dress I'd bought for the wine and cheese evening, a decision which I'm sure had nothing to do with Nathan's politeness with me since the last challenge, and how that contrasted with Sean's eager openness. I probably looked over-dressed, but after slouching around in slobwear for years, I had some catching up to do.

'I'm not surprised you look lovely. I mean, I always think you look lovely. I just haven't seen you in a dress before. It really suits you.'

'Okay.' I couldn't deny the flush of pleasure that swept behind my initial prickle of irritation.

As the evening carried on, Sean continued to be nice and charming and nothing but positive. Occasionally managing to chat about school and my job in between all the swimming talk.

Sean continued to call Joey 'Champ', his whole face lighting up as he

raved about the previous gala and the forthcoming trials, egging Joey on
with improbable scenarios about where the Gladiators might lead him.

'It's probably too late for 2020, but 2024 in Paris? Why not? What an
epic story. They'd probably make a blockbuster film about it one day:
Amelia Piper's son, the swimming lessons with her old coach, then the
trials offer. Amelia relents and overcomes her phobia to watch her son
compete. And even though he's a couple of years behind, boy, does he
have what it takes, he's all his mother's son, and this time, she makes
sure he does it the right way. Boom. Redemption, glory and that circle of
gold. And as a little side plot, the idiot long-lost father shows up, a
changed man, willing to do everything to earn forgiveness. We'll have to
wait and see how that works out.' He winked at me across the table.

I reminded myself that Joey was present, and for that reason and that
reason only, I restrained from smashing my plate of chicken Caesar
salad over his head. It would have made an interesting scene in the film
but probably wasn't worth upsetting Joey over. Besides, I was hungry.

I gritted my teeth throughout the rest of the meal and waited until
Champ had got to training and was in the pool before asking Sean if we
could talk upstairs in the viewing area. From the glow in his cheeks, I
think he was expecting some demonstration of how the long-lost father
subplot was going to conclude. But this wasn't Hollywood. And things
were about to get real.

'What the hell are you playing at?'

'Um, excuse me?'

'To be honest, I've been amazed at how well things have been
working out. How you've been reasonable, and considerate, and nice
without pushing it.'

'That sounds like a good thing, but your tone of voice and angry
expression are suggesting it isn't. I'm confused.'

I leant forwards in my chair. 'I'll spell it out for you, then. Number
one, stop calling Joey "Champ". Number two, stop filling his head with
crazy scenarios about films and gold medals. You're encouraging him to
give up his friends, his freedom, his fun and any chance of a normal
future for some ridiculous fantasy which, in reality, would be nothing
like you make it out to be.'

'I'm encouraging him to go for his dream. Helping him believe in
himself.'

'No. You aren't. You're making it appear as though you will love him more and be more proud of him if he's a successful swimmer. And right now, his biggest dream is to have his father think he's a son worth having. He will do anything to earn your approval, and you're convincing him that's conditional on him fulfilling this preposterous ideal.'

Sean went grey. A bead of sweat dripped down the side of his face.

'And what makes me really angry. What I'm particularly baffled about, is that you saw what the power of parental pressure did to me. You hated the whole culture of competitiveness and expectations and giving up everything just to be able to splash through some water a tenth of a second faster than anyone else.'

'I think we've established that at twenty-one I was a total arse.'

'You hated swimming, Sean. You never once saw me in the pool. Never experienced the thrill and the beauty of watching the human body pushed to the limits of its power, the glory of someone giving their all.'

'I saw you swim. And it was all that and more. Breathtaking. You were magnificent. But you had no one looking out for you. They all saw you as a gold medal, not a person. That will never happen to Joey. With our support, he can do it the right way.'

'You saw me swim?'

'You were so focused, you'd never have spotted me.' He pulled a wry smile. 'I, on the other hand, could not take my eyes off you.'

A vague memory of something Cee-Cee had said at Christmas floated to the surface. 'Did you talk to Cee-Cee?'

He ducked his head, tried to look contrite. 'Yeah. A couple of times. I wanted her to understand how you were struggling. See if I could convince her to back off a bit, or at least talk to you about it. I was young, stupid and smitten enough to think that an Olympic coach would take advice from a business studies student. I didn't want you to have to miss the Olympics. I just didn't think it was worth your soul.'

'Right. For the record, everything I said about Joey still stands. I am still extremely annoyed about it. But, well, thanks for trying. Talking to Cee-Cee is one thing. Going back for seconds is pretty impressive. I retrospectively appreciate you doing that.'

'You're very welcome. Maybe one day I'll show you the scars.'

Oh, damn your charming, oh so soft and caring blue eyes, Sean Mansfield. You are not going to get the better of me this time.

STOP BEING A LOSER PROGRAMME

DAY ONE HUNDRED AND FORTY-THREE

That Sunday, Sean drove Joey and me to a gala in Loughborough. A TV advert family: mum and dad in the front, son in the back, unspoken issues jammed in all over the place. Internally, my anxiety pranced about, twirling all the horrible memories and unresolved emotions like a feather boa. On the outside, I was bringing my A game. My back-from-the-dead, undisputed-superior-parent-on-every-count game.

Walking into the spectator area was like a smack in the face with a flipper. It was like the energy dial of the training sessions cranked up to max, with a flickering montage of memories in time to the buzz.

I clutched at the edge of Sean's jacket, interrupting his move towards the last two empty seats on the front row.

'Not here.'

'It's the best view!' He glanced back at me, briefly, then stopped and took a proper look. 'Right. Up there?'

I nodded, mute, clinging onto the jacket until we'd shuffled along the second to back row into the far corner. It wasn't a warm, strong, comforting hand, but it kept me upright.

'Better?' Sean asked, brow creasing.

'I just need a minute.' Or ten.

I closed my eyes and dropped my head onto my chest. Once my breathing had steadied, I gradually allowed the echo of competitors' voices and the warm-up splashes to sink in, recalibrating to the muggy, chlorine-drenched atmosphere of my native home. I was gearing up to add sight to the sounds and smells, when a whistle blast sent me reeling again.

Come on now, Amy. You can do this. One eye at a time if you have to.

Snapping both of them open, I firmly scanned the panorama, like a hunter sweeping the horizon. Kids in swimming costumes, goggles perched on their heads like bug eyes. Towels, tracksuited coaches, everything shimmering with light bouncing off the water.

I quickly found Joey with the rest of his team, his face fierce with concentration as he passed his water bottle from one hand to the other. I know I'm biased, but he was like a prince among plebs, half a head higher than the others, even sitting down. The breadth of his shoulders and long, taut limbs made it obvious who was the one to beat.

I held on to the surge of pride, mentally pinning it to my jumper as a reminder that this was not about me. It was Joey's time, his story, his future. His choice.

And, oh my goodness, he certainly made the most of it.

'Is it completely different, being a spectator?' Sean asked, after we'd watched Joey take another first place, slicing through the water with stunning power and grace. 'Or are the emotions the same?'

'I was too focused to feel this nervous when it was me. It's definitely different having no control over the outcome. But internal self-criticism was like a playlist on repeat. I never took enough time to enjoy the victories.'

Who cares that I won every race – was it by enough? Was it my best time? Had I got the angle of the turn perfect? Could I have pushed my muscles that one-hundredth of a second harder?

'With Joey, it's all good. Nerve-wracking, but good.'

And being there, being able to witness it first-hand? That was beyond amazing.

Sean leant closer. 'Imagine how nervous you'd be if you were a different kid's parent.'

'Nervous, or resigned to hoping for a silver?'

We grinned at each other, bumping elbows before making a joint embarrassing mum/dad wave to Joey, taking his place with his team. He acknowledged a fist-bump from Ben, ducking his head to speak to a girl before engaging in a brief jokey jostle as he sat down. I thought he hadn't seen us, or at least had decided to ignore our manic gestures, for which I couldn't have blamed him. But then he looked up into the spectator seats, pressed one hand to where his beautiful heart beat behind his still-dripping chest, and nodded, his smile so gentle I could just about find it through my tears.

* * *

I don't remember anyone having a conversation about it, but Sean ended up joining us for dinner, sitting round the table with 'healthy' home-made pizza and salad. Joey replayed the day while we ate, Sean tiptoeing on the edge of encouragement, constantly glancing at me to check whether he'd crossed the line.

The evening felt... okay. Over the past few weeks, I'd been gradually replacing the horrible mix of memories about Sean with the man who was here now. I didn't trust him an inch – he was still the person who'd abandoned me – but he was trying, and Joey loved having him around.

At least, he did until suddenly remembering he had homework to finish, coincidentally the moment he'd made us all a coffee. As if doing homework on a Saturday evening, following a competition, was something he'd EVER done before.

'You might as well stay and finish your drink, though, Dad. Maybe Mum'll show you my baby photos or something.'

He galloped upstairs before either of us had time to cry, 'set-up!'

With no better idea of how to push through the resulting awkwardness, I dug the photo album out. Before we knew it, two hours had gone by. Sean had wanted to know everything, carefully examining each captured moment as if it was a prehistoric butterfly specimen.

'I missed out on so much,' Sean could barely speak. He swiped his face with one jumper cuff, not wanting to drip tears on the pictures.

I nodded, no words of consolation to offer.

'Will I ever be able to make it up to him?' He shook his head. 'Part of me wants to stop feeling so damn guilty all the time, because it'll spoil what we have now, but the other part... how dare I forgive myself for this?'

And without planning it, or meaning to, I let another chunk of anger and bitterness crumble away. For who was I to judge not being there for

Joey, not sharing the parties and the holidays and the competitions with him? At least Sean was an ocean away. I was right here, and I simply hadn't found the guts to face them.

It was an ugly truth, one that had anyone else even hinted at, I'd have thrown them out the window, but if Sean Mansfield and I had one thing in common, it was that we had both abandoned our child.

Would we ever be able to make it up to him?

Only time would tell, I guess.

But I have to confess, when Sean gently and gingerly hugged me goodbye, I wondered for the splittiest of seconds whether one way to make things up to Joey was to consider very carefully whether or not I could live with some more of those hugs.

I know. I don't know what the hell I was thinking, either.

STOP BEING A LOSER PROGRAMME

DAY ONE HUNDRED AND FORTY-SIX

Another email from the delightful Moira Vanderbeek. So charming! Such flattery!! So many exclamation marks needed to describe how *thrilled* she was that I would be at the grand opening!!! She was very much hoping to meet me (!), and to snatch a morsel of my time to ask a couple of questions (!!), snippets the wider community would be *dying* to hear (!!!). Any chance of a teensy interview before then, to boost the PoolPal campaign? A couple of photos with her *enchanting* photographer, Howard, to give the article some pop, draw the right kind of attention?

Ugh.

Or, as Moira would say:

Ugh!!!!!!!!!!!!!!

I thought about the mantra of my mother for the five years she was my self-appointed PR agent: no publicity is bad publicity, but good publicity is where you control the publicity. Not the snappiest of catch-phrases, but I remembered and pondered the wisdom of it all the same.

By the evening, I had made up some interview questions, answered them and pressed send. Moira could cobble together a decent-sized article from Amelia Piper's enthusiastic yet diplomatic responses about making sport accessible for all, including Tate. I sprinkled the interview with some shocking statistics and, after a quick chat with Mel, attached a couple of photos.

I also strongly hinted about a more personal exclusive after the triathlon, as long as I was happy with her 'journalistic integrity' up until then. Once I'd made a speech and swam ten lengths in front of a crowd of gawping strangers, she could ask for my bra size and I'd happily chuck in my knickers, too – pose for the enchanting Howard, if she really wanted, give her the scoop on the truth about Athens, and maybe a short, sanitised version of where I've been since.

There. One *teensy* interview, sorted.

And, I prayed, some peace for now.

STOP BEING A LOSER PROGRAMME

DAY ONE HUNDRED AND FIFTY-FIVE

A few days after Moira Vanderbeek's article appeared in a national trash-paper, Mel and Dani did their usual Saturday morning trick of breaking and entering. Only this time it was a Friday, and they hadn't brought breakfast.

'No way I'm eatin' until after,' Mel said, barrelling into my kitchen as I hastily saved the care home brochure I'd been editing on my laptop. 'Not that I care what people think, it's for me kids, don't want to embarrass them more than usual.'

'Um, I hardly dare ask this, but after what?'

'After the try-on.'

'But the triathlon is weeks away.' I was even more confused than normal at what on earth Mel was talking about.

'The *try-on,* not tri*ath*lon,' Dani added, taking a swig from her travel mug. 'Which may end up nearly as exhaustingly energy-sucking as the race itself, but for very different reasons.'

'What's a try-on?' I know I'd been out of action for a few years, but I remained bamboozled.

'We're getting kitted out for the triathlon.'

'What? But it's still ten weeks away.' Ten weeks, twenty runs, a couple of hundred high-protein, low-carb meals and possible face transplant away.

'Yeah, but Selena wants us all matchin', to present, like, a united brand. And there's a sale in Sporting Warehouse on some trackies and that, in the Lark colours. We need to get in there before it goes.'

'Can't I just order them online?'

'Well, where's the fun in that? Never mind team bondin'. Nathan'd be well grieved if he thought you missed the try-on.'

'Never mind the fact everyone wants to thank you for your noble sacrifice,' Dani said. 'The picture of you by the bus was tragic, but it worked, the JustGiving page has gone nuts.'

As used to being used by gossip journalists as I had once been, as prepared as I was to have my name and associated nonsense in harsh black and white, after seeing my interview answers squeezed in amongst an overblown, sensationalised recap of my 'Olympic shame!' and a whole other page of wild speculations, complete with six old photos of me, looking everything from 'Proud Champion!' to 'National treasure pushed to the brink!' I had dry-heaved up the idea of the breakfast, lunch and dinner I hadn't been able to force down for the rest of the day. But as the JustGiving donations had risen, so my perspective had corrected itself and my stomach settled.

If people wanted to read, and then actually pay attention to, tabloid drivel with zero new information and minimal hard facts, that was up to them. To my astounded relief, when I thought long and hard about it, I concluded that their opinion meant nothing to me, especially not compared to that of my friends, my son and my coach. They were proud of what I had achieved in the past few months, and for the first time in forever, I was proud of myself, too. And that made me even prouder. I had come so far that what should have been a disaster felt like a triumph, and this was the ultimate win.

I decided this made me just about invincible.

I remembered that feeling. It was flippin' awesome.

'Come on then, let's get this over with.'

* * *

Sporting Warehouse was on a new retail park just off the nearest motorway junction. I had hoped that on a Friday morning, the Larks might be the only people there, which turned out to be an underestimation of the draw of cut-price athleisure wear. As we prepared to squeeze our way into the fray, Selena popped out of it like some freakish newborn shopping baby, arms loaded with bags.

'Is it finished?' I managed to squeak, already preparing to make an about-turn and hightail it back to somewhere with an average population of less than three per square metre.

'Hardly. These are personal items, nothing to do with the triathlon. Everyone's manning the swimwear section, far right. You'd best get a move on!'

With Dani tugging my hand in front, and Mel shoving me from behind, we jostled and elbowed our way to where the rest of the Larks formed a human barrier, preventing anyone else from getting near to a rack of sky-blue clothing. Selena had already managed to deposit her bags and slink back through the crowd and currently stood inside the barrier, holding up four fragments of Lycra.

'About time! I'll take this one.' She threw the tiniest scrap over her shoulder. 'Mel. Amy.'

Mel took hold of one proffered swimming costume, for it appeared that's what they were supposed to be. 'Are you chuffin' kiddin' me?' she retorted, attempting to stretch it over her solid midriff. 'You goin' ter tell us where the rest of it's hiding?'

'What do you want, Mel, a wet suit? Victoriana flannel bathers?'

'I want a cossie that covers more than one bum cheek. Life for my seventeen-year-old is 'ard enough without his mates seeing 'is mum's boob pop out mid-front crawl.'

'Are you sure that's the right size?' Dani asked. 'I mean, I'm all for being loud and proud of what God gave you, but that's pushing the legal boundary of indecent exposure.'

'Nah, it's the right size. Just the wrong style,' Mel huffed.

I took mine and checked it. 'This is actually two sizes too big for me.'

'Ouch,' Bronwyn winced on my behalf.

'Well, it's all they had left. At least both bum cheeks will be covered,' Selena snapped.

'Why can't I try that one?' I pointed at the remaining costume in her hand.

'This is Audrey's!'

Bronwyn broke the human barrier to grab the label. 'A size twelve? Are you joking?'

'I'm a size twelve.' By the triathlon I might be, anyway.

'And Audrey is most definitely, a) not here, and b) not anywhere close to a size twelve.'

Bronwyn grabbed hold of one strap and started to pull. Selena dug in, leaning back like a waterskier, both hands gripping the plastic coat hanger.

'Get lost, Bronwyn, you haven't even got the balls to wear a costume, in case your overly controlling, borderline abusive, probable pimp plus drug dealer, scary boyfriend actually figures out how to tell the time and bothers to turn uuuuuuuuuAAAAAAAPPPP!'

'How dare you insinuate he's stupid!' Bronwyn yelled, letting go of the strap so that Selena pinged back into a male mannequin holding a surfboard. The mannequin stiffly toppled over, his surfboard shooting into the end of a long queue of women waiting for the changing room and sending them tumbling. Those nearer the front of the queue, oblivious as to what was causing the crush, began to scream, sending panic rippling like a Mexican wave out across the store. Others began pushing and shoving to get to the entrance, knocking over displays and yanking armfuls of clothes off the racks as they went.

Alarms began to go off as frantic shoppers poured out through the double doors with their unpaid for purchases, unwilling to risk losing a twenty-quid Nike hoodie, even if it cost them their freedom.

Two men, hearing the hullabaloo, came sprinting out of the changing rooms in a pair of speedos and a ski suit respectively. Five seconds later, a woman hopped out after them, both legs jammed into one half of a pair of tracksuit bottoms.

The security guards and staff piled out to apprehend the looters, and within less than two minutes, the Larks were standing in their circle protecting the remaining sky-blue sportswear from an empty shop.

I might have been the only person there relieved to have caused a public stampede.

Bronwyn swore, even as she pulled a wide-eyed Selena to her feet. 'Sorry, Selena. You all right?'

Selena straightened her jacket, shaking her hair off her forehead. 'Are you kidding?' She nodded her chin at the remains of the mannequin behind her. 'He's the most animated man to have his arms around me in ages!'

'Well, ladies,' Marjory lifted up a pair of blue cycling shorts. 'Now we've made a bit of space, shall we get shopping before the police arrive?'

And so, somehow, in the jumble of Larks herding into the deserted changing rooms, I found Dani and Mel stuffing me into a two sizes too big swimming costume.

It was like slipping into my second skin, muscle memory pinging the straps up without me even thinking about it. But at the same time, the memories of another life, another me, reverberated through my head, sending it spinning. I tilted my head away from the mirror and focused on a clump off fluff on the floor while I went through my anti-freak-out exercises: Breathe, count, focus. I kept at it until the past receded, taking the panic with it.

'Once upon a time, top sportswear designers begged me to wear their labels.' I half laughed, half sobbed, as Dani handed me a tissue to blot my tears and blow my nose, while Mel hitched up the sagging straps to preserve my nipples' dignity.

'Well, you have to demonstrate in the flesh, as it were, or Selena won't surrender the other one,' Dani said, ushering me out of the cubicle and into the main changing area. 'Selena! Take a look at this!'

Selena stepped out of her cubicle as if she was used to parading her toned muscles in a tiny patch of fabric trying to impersonate swimwear. 'Ooh. Maybe a spray tan before the big day, Amy? You look like a woman who's not seen the sun in years.'

'Give it a rest, Selena,' Bronwyn groaned. 'Just cos Amy's the star of the day. Like, literally. Try and be less obvious about your rampant jealousy, why don't you?'

'Forget a spray tan, maybe a costume that doesn't resemble a plastic bag?' Mel barked, planted with her feet apart, hands on hips like a compressed Wonder Woman in her correctly fitting, still eye-wateringly tiny, swimsuit. 'Hand over the size twelve, or else our best, most high-profile member of the team will compete in non-branded colours. And how will that affect hashtag GetPiperaPoolPal?'

'Yeah,' Mystery Woman One chimed in. 'If you want Nathan's eyes off Ames and onto you, sticking her in a cossie that gapes so bad it shows her hoohaa isn't the way to go about it.'

I didn't know whether to be more concerned that she thought we'd reached nickname territory, or that a woman whose name I didn't know had seen my hoohaa. Or that she called it a hoohaa. Either way, my hoohaa and I were going straight back into the cubicle.

'Fine!' The smaller costume flew over the top of the cubicle door and draped itself over my face. I wondered if I could keep it there for a few days. 'But, for the record, I don't give a crap if Nathan's or any other eyes are on me. I took a day off work to try to help by finding some decent team outfits that won't break the bank and create a fun, bonding moment for us all and for *pity's sake, how hard can it frigging well be to remember THREE WORDS IN ORDER!*' Despite the increase in volume, Selena's voice began to fade into the distance as she must have stomped away. 'It's HASHTAG POOLCHUFFINGPALFORPIPER!'

'That's five words, then, innit?' someone said.

'Hold these, I'll go after her,' Bronwyn said, leaving the only sound in the changing room a few awkward shuffles and coughs.

'Come on, then, Amy,' Dani tapped on my cubicle door. 'You'd better try it on at least, after all that.'

So, I did. And with everything else going on I barely had space in my head to feel bothered about it the second time. And, aware that resistance was futile, I stepped out and showed them all what it looked like, too. I mean, I was going to be in front of a whole lot more people before long, might as well get back in practice.

'How is it?' Marjory asked, as I gazed at the woman in the mirror, nipples and hoohaa both decently covered. 'Is this the return of Amelia Piper?'

'Amelia Piper plus about three stone of baggage?' I shook my head. 'No. This isn't the old me. I'll never go back to being her again.'

There were a few mumbles of protest from the women behind, all kitted out in their sky-blue running and cycling gear.

'Oh, no, that's fine. I don't want to go back. Amelia Piper was stressed and miserable and confused and... lost. She couldn't stay true to who she was because she didn't have a clue who that was.' I backed up and put my arm around Mel, who'd added a pink swim cap and a pair of orange armbands to her outfit. 'Amelia Piper was lonely. She gave up because she didn't have a squad cheering her on when it really mattered.'

'What about Amy, then? What about now?' Dani asked.

'*Amy* Piper is brave, and beautiful and doesn't give a crap about all this,' I gave a couple of my flabbiest bits a slap, 'because this is the weight of experience, and wisdom, and a splendid amount of yummy breakfasts with her squad. Amy Piper knows what a real champion is made of, and that right now she's looking at one. A crowded shop, in the middle of the day, half-dressed? She's taken on her ultimate foe and kicked its sorry ass. Moira Vanderbeek might write a bitchy article about how Amelia Piper has let herself go, ended up a no one in nowhere doing nothing. Add a load of carefully non-photoshopped photos with arrows pointing at cellulite and stretch marks and saggy bits. Screw her! I'm not ashamed of my battle scars. I earnt them and no one but me knows how hard I fought or what it cost me.'

'Hurrah!' my new, true, sky-blue squad cheered. They cheered even harder as I stuffed my clothes in a bag and strutted out of the changing room still in my swimwear, 'I think I'll just go on and wear this baby all the way home!'

'Um. Excuse me, madam. We'd like to have a word.'

'Oh! Right! Yes! Would it be okay if I put a few more clothes on first, Officer?'

'I think that would be a good idea.'

STOP BEING A LOSER PROGRAMME

DAY ONE HUNDRED AND SIXTY-ONE

It had been a mixed week. Propelled by the victory in Sporting Warehouse, I had done a phone-in interview with BBC Radio Nottingham – all very pleasant and focused on the campaign. On Monday, I had attended a far more significant interview, having driven to a small industrial estate in Nottingham and clicked right on up in my mustard heels to the office of Winlock Tenders. Grant Winlock, who had last seen me in person about three years ago, offered me a seat, a giant hug, a homemade coconut cookie to go along with my coffee and a promotion, effective immediately. I had even invited Cee-Cee for dinner again, and only got so annoyed I wanted to stab her with my fork twice.

On the downside, I had spent the week being haunted.

Haunted by an itsy-bitsy, teeny-weeny, sky-blue... swimsuit.

I had two options when it came to my big comeback:

Plan A was to pretend it wasn't really happening, get as fit as I could from running with the Larks, spend the rest of the time buried in senior bid writing, turn up on the day and dive straight into my first swim in fourteen years.

Plan B was too scary to think about right then.

But that swimsuit kept whispering to me. It chased me through my dreams. It fed me one dread-inducing scenario after another. What if I panicked, belly-flopped, choked, threw up in the pool, ended up having to be rescued by the lifeguard? I could cope with the inevitable national humiliation – after all, I'd faced worse. But could Joey? Should he have to, only a few weeks after the Gladiators trial? And what about the race? The Larks were counting on me. The campaign was counting on me.

Swimming came to me as naturally as breathing. I knew that, even after such a long time, I could manage a respectable time compared to most. But I wasn't most. And with a bit of training I could do the girls proud. Give the crowd something to feel good about, and hopefully take more notice when I gave my little speech about the PoolPal.

And, more to the point, until I knew for a fact that I could get back in the water without having a coronary, that foul beast I called my anxiety would remain in my head, lording it over me while wearing an even more miniature sky-blue swimsuit.

So. Here I was. Bag packed. Heart thumping. Off to the Brooksby Leisure Centre public swim.

With a spontaneous detour to enlist my support network on the way.

Nathan couldn't have looked more surprised when he opened the door and found me standing there. Since New Year's Day we'd seen each other at training, and Joey's events, but while things had been friendly, it was clear I had been firmly placed back in the client-zone. Maybe after an entire day out, Nathan figured I didn't need his help any more. But I still had a major hurdle to overcome, and he was the best man for the job. Which was of course the only reason I was here. It had nothing to do with how much I'd thought about him, wondered if we'd be friends again, missed him...

'Amy. Hi. Had we... planned something?'

'No. I kind of made up my mind and had to go and do it right then. Only halfway there I realised I could really do with some support. Just in case.'

'Right.'

'Are you busy? I mean, I could come back another time. We've weeks to go. I just, well, it's been a momentous few days. I'm on a sort of roll, and the swimsuit keeps taunting me. I've started this massive project for a technology company. It's my first one as a senior writer, and instead of writing a brilliant bid, all I can think about is whether or not I'm going to mess it all up on the day and let everyone down, when I was the one who volunteered to swim and started this whole campaign for little Tate, and they've really got their hopes up, like everyone's counting on me, and it's been a long time, but some weird and not good memories about people all counting on me winning a race have resurrected themselves like memory zombies and while I know it's hardly the same, a local triathlon compared to the Olympics, it seems to matter more, when it means so much to Mel and Tate. And this'll be the first time Joey's seen me swim, so I want him to be proud of me and the least I can do after everything, so many times of not being there and letting him down, is to make him proud. And, well...' I managed to stop and take a juddery breath. 'I think he's going to be disappointed if I don't win.'

Nathan glanced behind him, then back.

'I really need to know if I can win.'

He ran one hand through his hair, brow furrowed.

'I at least have to try.'

'Nate?'

Oh crap. *Crap!*

A woman's voice, from inside the house.

A woman. Inside Nathan's house.

A woman who now slithered into view, caressing a glass of wine, deep red to match her pouting lips. My brain did a lightning quick comparison of her slinky charcoal jumpsuit with plunging neckline, her trendy black bob, ridiculously toned arms, versus my faded jeans and yellow hoodie, hair blown every which way from the winter wind.

I lost.

'Is everything okay?' She smiled then, ruining my automatic categorisation of a beautiful, sophisticated woman with perfect make-up as a snooty bitch.

'Uh. Yes,' Nathan and I both answered at the same time, which made things seem even more awkward.

'Amy's... a client.'

'Yes! Yes, I'm a client. I, um, needed a bit of advice about the next stage of my programme. It's fine, sorry. I shouldn't have come. What are phones for, after all! Anyway, I'm so sorry to have interrupted you. I'll go. Sorry.' I attempted to force my lumbering limbs into an about turn.

'No, wait. One second.' Nathan closed the door partially shut, with me outside it. I couldn't make out his soft murmurings, but his guest had no such qualms.

'What about clients never coming to a trainer's house? The rule about not telling them where you live?'

Ugh. This was hideous.

'She doesn't seem it to me.'

Oh, great. She thought I was some infatuated stalker. Wait – *was I an infatuated stalker?*

'...turning up here, on Valentine's Day? That's a little creepy, don't you think? At the least it's an unacceptable invasion of your privacy.'

VALENTINE'S DAY! Why the Jiminy Cricket hadn't somebody told me?! I'd not been anywhere all week except for the interview, and running with the Larks. I'd been too busy not writing a bid to even watch Joey train...

It was a little creepy! I had unacceptably invaded Nathan's privacy! I was now proceeding to get myself the heck out of there! As soon as some blood left my inflamed cheeks and made its way to my feet so they could work again!

'You need to be very clear about professional boundaries... You're going to do *what*?'

All of a sudden, months of running proved itself extremely useful. My feet finally remembered how to move, and before I could even consider what Nathan was going to do, I was halfway down the street.

Three minutes later, to my utter mortification, he caught up with me.

'You're going the wrong way.'

'How... are you... not... even out... of breath?'

'I train hard and take care of my body. Come on, we can cut through this twitchel.'

I stopped. 'Nathan, what are you talking about? Why are you here? You have a date. It's Valentine's Day. This whole thing is embarrassing enough without you chasing after me.'

'You seriously think I'm going to miss seeing Amelia Piper back in the water, for the first time? And even if it wasn't you, I'm your coach. This is huge. I'm not going to leave you to do it alone.' He smiled. 'Believe it or not, I kind of want the Larks to win that triathlon. I'm banking on you helping us to grind the competition into the brand new, all-weather running track dust.'

'But what about your date?' As much as I wanted Nathan to have wanted to ditch that gorgeous woman for me, I didn't want Nathan to be the kind of man who would dump his date – on *any* day of the year. Let alone this one.

He twitched his shoulders as if shrugging off an unwelcome arm. 'It wasn't a date. Kim's a colleague. It was supposed to be a business meeting.'

I squinted, dubiously, and Nathan straightened his shoulders, assuming the Robo-Coach pose in response to my cynicism.

'I didn't realise it was Valentine's Day. Or that Valentine's Day meant a business meeting would automatically be construed as a date.'

'Right. But given that it was, shouldn't you get back to it?'

'I don't date colleagues.'

'Why on earth not?'

He started heading down the twitchel, leaving me no choice but to join him if I wanted to hear the answer to my question.

'I don't date colleagues who, after acting like they were really keen to help, turn up with a bottle of wine and can't even be bothered to discuss business.'

Who do you date? Do you complete a spreadsheet for potential candidates in advance? I wanted to ask. But didn't. Who Nathan dated was none of my business. But, oh, picturing that woman and her wine glass, sidling up to Nathan as if she belonged there, I was shocked by the onslaught of emotions. On the plus side, the jealousy, indignation and longing all swirling together in an ugly and unwelcome cocktail did help take my mind off where we were headed and what I was about to do.

* * *

By the time we reached the pool, I had forty minutes before the public swim ended. I threw a fiver at the receptionist, raced into the empty changing room and whipped my jeans and hoodie off to reveal the swimsuit underneath, head tipped down the whole time. Stuffing my belongings into a locker, I hurtled towards the doorway leading to the pool. *Come on, Amy, you've got this.*

I hadn't got it. As though hitting an invisible wall, I bounced back into the changing room.

Ten minutes later, Nathan found me hunched on the changing room bench, too dazed and despairing to even cry.

He held out a hand. 'Come on, let's do this.'

I shook my head. 'I can't. All those people.'

'There are six other people in the pool, Amy. Minding their own business, completing their laps.'

One of those people now entered the changing room, stopping in surprise when she saw Nathan crouching in front of me. The woman, probably in her mid-fifties, frowned. 'Excuse me, but these are female changing rooms. I mean, I'm the last person to prejudge, or make an assumption, but you are a man, who identifies as male? Aren't you? *Mr Gallagher?*'

'Yes, sorry. I, well... we'll just...' Nathan, face burning crimson, pulled me up and tugged me into the mother and baby changing cubicle.

'I don't think that's allowed either!' the woman exclaimed. 'My dear, are you in need of assistance? Shall I call the lifeguard?'

'No. I'm fine, thank you,' I squeezed out through my scrunched-up face and clenched teeth.

'Well, really. If you're both in there together of your own volition, then I'll definitely call the lifeguard. Have you no shame? Hanky-panky in the changing rooms is against the Leisure Centre Code of Conduct.'

'There's nothing going on,' Nathan called back, dropping my hand. 'She was having a panic attack and I'm her trainer. Section four, subsection three point seven of the Brooksby Leisure Centre Code of Conduct clearly states that if a female lifeguard is not on duty, a male employee can enter the female changing rooms to attend to a female in need of medical assistance.'

The woman snorted. 'Medical assistance! Is that what they're calling it these days?! Kiss of life, is it? Forget the lifeguard, I'm fetching the manager.'

'You'd better go.' I stood as far back as I could against the cubicle wall, arms crossed against my midriff. Still close enough to see the pulse pounding in his neck, hear his accelerated breathing.

'You've got time if you still want to try. I'll walk you there. Push you in if it helps, screw section two, subsection eight point three.'

'I don't think I can. I made a mistake thinking I could just jump into this. I need to work up to it. Put it in the Programme. Mentally prepare. I'm really sorry for ruining your evening.'

'If you're sure.' He took a step closer, ducking his head so that his gentle eyes met mine, at the same time placing one hand on my shoulder, in a gesture I'd seen him do numerous times to his team.

I bet none of his team instantly imagined him then lowering his head to bridge the vast, breathtakingly short distance between his lips and theirs, letting out a husky gasp of desire as a rush of heat nearly knocked them off their feet.

On second thoughts, I bet nearly all of them did. The difference being none of them were alone with him in a tiny cubicle.

Then, it happened.

Nathan dropped his gaze to the teensy-weensy, perfectly fitting excuse for swimwear. He froze, his fingers perceivably gripping my shoulder where before they had simply been resting. I saw his chest rise with one big inhalation, and yes, it was stupid and inappropriate and probably broke all sorts of sections and subsections of the Leisure Centre Code, but when Nathan looked up again, his pupils were dilated to enormous, bottomless black holes, ringed with silver, and I was sucked right in, leaning forwards until my barely covered, far from itsy-bitsy chest swayed dangerously close to his.

Fortunately, one of us was a normal, functioning member of society with a decent grasp on both the general protocol of public conduct and control of their own senses.

Nathan sprang back. 'I'd better go.'

He wrenched open the door and disappeared.

By the time the manager arrived, I'd gone, too.

STOP BEING A LOSER PROGRAMME

DAY ONE HUNDRED AND SIXTY-TWO

The next morning, Nathan messaged me:

Sincere apologies for yesterday. I hope you understand I meant absolutely nothing by it, beyond helping a friend. If you want to make a formal complaint, I'll make sure the correct procedures are followed.

Of course he would.

It hadn't been quite the message I'd been dreaming about all night. Still, I swallowed my pride and mortification and replied:

No problem! I know you were only trying to help. You weren't acting as my trainer, or coach, so I think no rules were broken?

I waited a few seconds then sent another one:

And it did help. A lot.

Then one more, before I started to look like the creepy kind of woman who turns up at men's houses on Valentine's Day and invites them to watch her swim:

Will be a hilarious story to laugh about one day.

Like, one day when I can finally face going back to the pool without feeling as though my stomach is dissolving in its own acid. Or one day when I can stop thinking about how Nathan looked at me, up close in that swimsuit, as though I was a *woman,* not a loser. Or at least one day when I can think about it without breaking into a flush so hot it melts my bones to mush.

Or, alternatively, one day when we are married.

I guess Nathan didn't see the funny side, as there was no reply.

STOP BEING A LOSER PROGRAMME

DAY ONE HUNDRED AND SIXTY-FOUR

That Sunday, I arrived to find the Larks atwitter, like hens who'd smelled a fox. Feeling awkward and embarrassed, I slipped up to the back of the group, deliberately placing myself behind Mystery Woman One, so that Nathan couldn't see me.

Only, it turned out Nathan wouldn't have seen me wherever I did my stretches, because the person leading the warm-up was his Valentine's Day date, otherwise known as Kommando Kim. I suspected, given the spelling, that the closest she'd got to being an actual commando was having it sequinned across her T-shirt.

'So, where did you say Nathan was?' Selena asked, stretching her quad.

'No questions. Focus! You – watch your shoulders!' the fox barked in reply.

'Can we ask questions now?' Bronwyn asked, once the warm-up was over.

'Five K. I'll be in front, so keep up. If you can ask questions, you aren't working hard enough. I expect nothing less than your utmost at all times. If you train half-arsed, you'll compete half-arsed. In which case you might as well keep your lazy, sorry, fat half an arse in bed and save wasting my time, yours and the other competitors. Every woman needs to be dragging herself back into this car park, on the brink of collapse, unable to take another step.'

'All-arsed,' Dani muttered.

'Um, excuse me?' Mel asked. 'How am I goin' ter walk home and take care of five kids if I'm 'alf dead, and can't take another step?'

'Go!' Kommando Kim clicked her stopwatch and hurtled out of the car park.

After exchanging a few bemused and irritated glances, we followed her, Marjory leading the way.

For the next 5K, we obeyed our coach and ran mainly in silence. It was freezing cold, and stinging rain began the moment we left the relative shelter of the village. Except for Marjory, who continued to push on at her own pace, we mainly huddled together in one sorry, bedraggled clutch.

'Physical strength is pointless if you are mentally weak!' Kim shot up and down the group, circling us like a rabid sheepdog. 'It's wet, so what? It's cold, big deal! You hurt, well that's what it takes!'

'Can we push her off the top of the hill?' Bronwyn wheezed.

'How about we just all start walking?' Dani suggested. 'What's she going to do? Fire us all from Kim's Kommandos?'

'NO TALKING!' Kim screamed. 'If you want to chat, join a book group! If you want to win, get that PoolPal for Piper, then shut up and start running like you mean it!'

'Well, she seems to know what she's talking about.' Selena gave a smirk of approval. 'Learnt the hashtag and everything.'

'What everything?' Bronwyn sneered.

Kim sprinted over to Bronwyn and leant as close to her ear as possible while still running. 'EVERYBODY DOWN!'

'Ow!' Bronwyn yelped.

'TEN BURPEES. GO!'

'This is not in the spirit of the Larks,' Selena muttered, eyeing the muddy ground.

'NOW THAT'S TEN MORE! AND EVERY TIME SOMEONE ELSE INSULTS US BY THINKING THEY CAN SHIRK OFF AND HAVE A NATTER, THEN WE All DO ANOTHER TEN!'

'All except for you,' Dani whispered, quiet enough for no one but those either side of her to hear.

'Crap, don't make me laugh. That'll be fifty press-ups or summat,' Mel puffed.

And so it went on.

By the time we dragged ourselves back into the car park, I think some of us genuinely couldn't have taken another step without the promise of a Cup and Saucer breakfast at the end of it. The only reason we didn't go straight to the café as usual was because we didn't want Kim to know about it and decide to join us, screeching insults about our nutritional choices.

'So, where is Nathan?' Selena asked, once Kim had bullied us through the cool-down.

'Still whining and pining for Coach Comfy?' Kim shook her head in disgust. 'Give me strength.' And with that, she sprinted off.

'I think I hate her,' Mel whimpered as we limped to the square. 'I mean, I know it's not Christian and I'll be sayin' an extra prayer of forgiveness at church today, but bloomin' 'eck.'

'Did Nathan bring her in to get us at maximum fitness for the race?' Dani asked, 'because I don't think that kind of brutal motivational style will work here.'

'I want Nathan back,' Bronwyn wailed. 'The Larks is supposed to be fun, and positive and encouraging. Not make you want to commit Kommandocide. If she's sticking around until the triathlon, I might have to call my fella and see if he can have a sharp word.'

'Nathan must be ill or had a last-minute emergency. He wouldn't just hand us over to an evil tyrant without saying anything,' Selena said. 'As soon as we get to the café, I'm messaging him.'

And she wasn't the only one. For the rest of the day, the Larks WhatsApp group was pinging with complaints and questions, peppered with increasingly lurid descriptions of the run and its after-effects.

I kept quiet, half wondering if this had something to do with my lust-addled moment in the changing room. But Nathan had already met with Kim. And he fended off unwanted attentions from his clients all the time, it was part of the job for him.

With every ping, I snatched up my phone, hoping to read that he'd come down with a bug or had pulled a hamstring.

But Nathan kept quiet.

STOP BEING A LOSER PROGRAMME

DAY ONE HUNDRED AND SIXTY-SEVEN

It was an excruciating wait until Wednesday morning.

Snowed under with work and stewing in my own embarrassment, I'd missed Joey's training, but he'd told me Nathan had been at the evening club training, and had popped into his early morning swims.

I walked to meet the Larks with a stomach full of trepidation, not sure if I was more nervous about Nathan being there or Kommando Kim. But I heard the answer long before I could see it, catching up with Isobel, and Mystery Women One and Two lurking at the entrance to the car park, trying to decide whether they dared face going any further.

I left them to it, the furious rant becoming gradually distinguishable as I approached the others, who, instead of standing around in their usual motley group, were lined up in what I supposed was military formation.

Give me strength...

I was going to need it.

'...Some of you have been WHINING to Coach Comfy about being pushed to do some actual WORK for once! He's all *worried* about you! Wah, wah, wah – did you feel a bit TIREDY WIREDY after running THREE WHOLE MILES – HALF the triathlon distance? Did your poor little legs ache for the rest of the day? Did your shoulders feel a little bit sore after doing twenty whole burpees? My heart BLEEDS! Unlike yours, which are too blocked up with post-run PANCAKES to bleed anything! *"Oh, Coach Comfy, please tell the mean lady to stop shouting at us and make her be nice instead, she keeps making us run fast, so we can't gossip or tell each other how fabulous we all are as we cruise in in LAST PLACE!"* What is wrong with you women? You have no idea about the true cost of victory!'

'Ur, Marjory was in the Olympics, and—'

'I'M NOT FINISHED! If this Marjory was in the Olympics, maybe she can explain that the coach-club relationship is not a democracy. If you get to decide how fast and how far you run, you lose. If I decide, you stand a small chance of not being total failures. And when you cross that line with some even bigger loser behind you, someone who had a nice, friendly coach who thought training should be fun and enjoyable and make you FEEL GOOD, then you'll be thanking me. Until then, SHUT UP and do what I say. And for every whinge, grumble, complaint or moan you make – to me, to each other or to Coach Comfy – it's going to get tougher and more ruthless until you learn that there is only one road to victory, and there ain't a lot of smiles on it. Now. Six K this morning. And I want it done faster than the five you did last time. Weekend's over, time to put some effort in.'

'Nothing worse than a woman with a point to prove,' Selena muttered. So that was ten squats before we'd even left the car park.

* * *

We were a morose bunch at breakfast. No one had heard from Nathan, but my report that he was continuing with his other duties was depressing news.

'Why has he ditched us?' Bronwyn asked. 'It doesn't make sense.'

'I'm going to call him,' Dani said, pulling her phone from her fleece pocket. 'Use my courtroom interrogation skills to get to the bottom of this.'

But interrogation techniques aren't quite as effective in a voicemail compared to a courtroom, even Dani's.

'Maybe we should go round, demand an answer face to face,' Mel suggested.

'Only, he makes a rule of keeping his address private, even for clients he forms a close bond with.' Selena raised one eyebrow. 'I would know.'

'Selena, unless anything actually happened between you and Nathan, like, a kiss or him saying he found you attractive, or anything to suggest the infatuation was not one hundred per cent one-sided, it's probably time you dropped it,' Bronwyn sighed. 'Given that everyone here has seen how he acts around Amy, unless he's also asked to give *you* personal, private extra coaching, which somehow includes wine and cheese and dancing, lunch out and the kind of marathons that include pyjamas and romantic Christmas films, you're only making a fool out of yourself.'

For once, Selena was speechless.

She wasn't the only one.

'Eh, Ames might know where Nathan lives!' Mel looked at me, a forkful of sausage halfway to her mouth.

Ames might, but Ames's intestines shrivelled up like a salty slug at the thought of the Larks trooping round to Nathan's and demanding to know why he'd ditched them, only to hear his no doubt wholly factual and emotion-free report on how he was accosted in the Leisure Centre changing rooms. Not only would Ames be the fool, not Selena, she'd also be the fool who went so far as to force Nathan to leave the Larks, thrusting Kommando Kim on them instead.

'Maybe we should instigate a mutiny,' Bronwyn mused. 'Kick her out and run it ourselves. Who says a democracy won't work better?'

'I say!' Marjory chipped in around a mouthful of oats. 'You lot, bickering and blathering like a herd of menopausal sheep. No thank you!'

'You run the Larks, then,' Dani said. 'You and Amy. Surely you know more between you than Power-Krazed Kim.'

'I know how I can succeed,' Marjory pointed her spoon at us. 'But you might have noticed I'm not a natural team player. And I've no idea how to teach what I know. Not a clue how to get the best out of you, or find the tipping point where a challenging encouragement becomes a discouraging impossibility.'

'Amy?' Dani asked.

'I don't think so...'

'Why not?'

'Because – no offence, Amy...' Selena started.

'Uh oh, prepare to be offended,' Bronwyn cut in, eyes wide over the rim of her coffee.

Selena ploughed on. 'First and foremost, a coach needs the respect and trust of their squad. It's not good enough to be liked. We listen to Nathan because he puts the team first, above the individual. He doesn't let feelings get in the way. Amy's all very nice and lovely, and the campaign is fantastic, she's been brilliant, but when it comes down to it, she's with the Larks for her own sake, not ours.'

'Selena, that is harsh, even by your standards,' Dani scolded.

Selena shrugged. 'If Amy can swear that, no matter what, she'll be there on the day and give it her best, then go ahead, I'll be the first to kick Kim to the kerb.'

I took a deep breath, tried and failed to swallow the lump of self-loathing in my throat. 'Maybe we should trust Nathan enough to give Kim a chance.'

I expected Selena to gloat, crow 'I told you so' or get angry. Seeing her slowly push back her chair and walk out felt even worse.

STOP BEING A LOSER PROGRAMME

DAY ONE HUNDRED AND EIGHTY-FOUR

For the next three weeks, Nathan didn't return. After Kim's second training session, he sent a couple of ambiguous messages to the group saying that he greatly respected Kim as a trainer, that while her methods were different they were effective. He hoped to be back with us soon, but would definitely see us at the triathlon if not before.

I did see him before, at a Saturday swimming meet, but with parents confined to the viewing area, it wasn't hard for him to get away with a polite nod of hello from a distance.

That was okay, I kept telling myself. A lesson learnt for my new out and about life: Don't lean longingly into a friend's personal space unless you want a permanent, jagged splinter in your heart. I had started the Programme on my own, I could finish it that way. That is, if Mel and Dani let me. They had taken it upon themselves to be my chaperones, reintroducing me into local society, and so far this had included a karaoke night (yes, we did indeed rock out to 'Livin' on a Prayer'), spa afternoon and, the previous Tuesday, the biggest, loudest and messiest pancake day celebration ever, at Mel's house. Joey ate seventeen pancakes, ditching his new training diet for the day in order to beat Jordan's sixteen. Sean came, along with Tiff's dad, and Gordon, Tate's relief carer, so with Mel's mum too we were a well-rounded gathering.

But time was ticking.

I was doing well, overall, smashing my Programme targets. Totally on track to accompany Joey at his trials, functioning as a nearly normal human adult. But in six weeks, it would be the triathlon, and while Kommando Kim had certainly improved my fitness through her hideous insult-destroy-and-conquer method, I hadn't even looked at my swimming costume since the changing room incident, or faced returning to the leisure centre, and had no plan for getting myself back into a pool.

I wondered about asking Mel and Dani to come with me, but I didn't want them to see me so vulnerable. This still felt too deep to involve them. I considered Cee-Cee, even Sean, but their presence would probably only make things worse. Plus, I didn't trust them not to tell Joey about it afterwards.

So instead I wittered, and wavered, and hoped and prayed that Nathan would return to the Larks, or bump into me in the street sometime, or message me to ask how things were going and by the way did I fancy going swimming sometime.

Then, on the Saturday of the Gladiators trials, Moira Vanderbeek released her follow-up article on what happened to Amelia Piper. And what happened, according to Moira – and it was in a national newspaper, so it must be true – was that Amelia Piper had reconciled with the man who seduced her as a teenager and persuaded her to throw away both her, her family's and the nations hopes and dreams.

Ooh, she was good. Only a smattering of lies, mostly carefully phrased facts wrapped up in insinuation and speculation. How I had been living as a recluse for the past hundred years, relying on my old coach to look after me and Joey (those quotes from Cee-Cee had better be made up). Overweight, out of work, depressed and alone, unable to get over my broken heart. And then, like a knight in a shiny black car, Sean had swooped in.

How romantic! Like a true-life fairy tale! Sean had sold his company (*sold his company!! For four and a half million dollars!!*) and returned to rescue me from my despair and reunite the family. There were photos of him arriving at our house on Christmas Day, arms laden with gifts, the three of us out for Chicken Thursday, snapped at probably the only instant that Sean and I were looking at each other and laughing. Sat at the gala together. What a saint Sean was, for giving up his business and home to risk it all for the love of an unpredictable, mentally unstable oddball with nothing to offer.

And I clearly was, as demonstrated by the photograph of me, in a swimsuit that is the very definition of skimpy, standing in a shop being spoken to by a police officer. Apparently this 'episode' had caused such a ruckus that Sporting Warehouse required evacuation in the middle of the sale, with the store closed for several hours while the police persuaded me to get dressed.

But would Sean stand by me now, given that the Brooksby Leisure Centre manager could neither confirm nor deny that I had been caught engaging in an explicit sexual act in the public changing room, WITH MY SON'S COACH?

It was also well known in the Brooksby Bridge Club that I had a fetish for spying on couples through their bedroom windows. The quote from Audrey's old fart of a boyfriend was brutal.

And then, to top it off, Moira Vanderbeek finished the article by pondering as to whether Sean could prevent my erratic and illegal behaviour from sabotaging Joey's swimming future, in particular his trials with the Gladiators.

I'd had some low days, but this had to be one of the darkest.

Joey and I spent the morning mostly in stunned silence. He'd read the article and listened to my explanation with a mix of shock, disgust and anger, but had paused on the photograph of me and his dad, and I had caught the glimmer of hope in his eye.

By lunchtime, an hour before he needed to leave, we decided.

'I don't think I should go.'

My heart was breaking. This had been the shining gold medal at the end of all the effort and the pain and the sweat, blood and tears.

Joey nodded, his face pale and grim.

'There'll probably be journalists there. And even the other swimmers, the Gladiators coaches, we don't want their attention to be on me. Let alone poor Nathan. You go, hold your head high, do what you do best and make yourself proud.'

'Don't cry, Mum. I'll be fine with Dad and Nathan. Once I'm in the water, it won't make a difference who's there. If you came, I'd just worry about you panicking.'

'I'm so sorry.' The thought that after everything, Joey still had to worry about me was yet another twist of the knife now lodged in my liver.

'It's not your fault.'

'Maybe not, but that doesn't stop it being totally horrendous for you to have those things said about your family.'

He shrugged, trying to find a smile. 'Hey, at least everyone knows my mum's a world champion swimmer now. It wasn't easy, keeping that to myself. And my friends know the truth. The squad know Nathan wouldn't... do that. So they'll probably know the rest of it is bogus, too.'

'Are you sure you'll be okay going today? We can ask them to postpone, they'd understand, given the circumstances.' All my instinct as a mother was to keep Joey here, with me, safe and protected. To shield him from the media circus that once almost destroyed me. It was only swimming. Surely it wasn't worth all this.

I was about to insist that Joey stayed at home, and then he spoke again:

'If I don't go, that bitch'll've won. And they'll be able to say that you *have* sabotaged my career, after all. It'll be fine. I'm not losing to anyone today. Least of all her.'

And I realised, this wasn't only swimming. It was also months of determination and effort, and saying no to parties and lie-ins and junk food. It was choosing a goal, following a dream, and sticking to it, no matter what. It was the chance to shine at the thing he excelled at, pushing himself to be more than he should be, giving his all. It was one of the best feelings in the whole damn world. And after all the crap he'd dealt with, who was I to deny him that?

So, I did not insist. I ignored my better judgement for the sake of an improbable dream, and I let him go.

And it was not fine. Not even close.

* * *

The trials started at two. Sean called me at three-thirty.

When someone starts a phone call with a breathless, 'Now there's no need to panic but,' there is only one reasonable response to that. Panic. So, I could barely hear his garbled explanation through the thunder roaring in my head. This I had understood by the time he rang off: Joey had hit his head in the pool, the paramedics were with him, they were leaving for the hospital now.

I was in my car and halfway down the street before I noticed that I was still in my chequered pyjama bottoms and Joey's old rugby hoodie.

I was halfway to Nottingham before I realised that I didn't know how to get to the hospital. Frantic, sobbing, muttering like a mad woman, I found myself stuck in the clog of city-centre traffic, lost in the one-way system and nearly out of my mind by the time Sean called me to say they'd arrived. Only holding hysteria at bay with the sheer determination to get to my son, I clicked onto speakerphone and allowed Sean to guide me to the Queen's Medical Centre, his calm voice a lighthouse in my frenzied storm.

I don't even remember parking or finding my way to the accident and emergency department. I only remember running, lungs clamouring, until I stopped in the middle of one corridor and, in a loud voice, told the anxiety dragging at my limbs and exploding in my brain to *stop!*

'Enough! My son needs me, and I will not turn up like this. I will be calm, and rational, and strong. Joey said we're not being beaten today, so you might as well eff off.'

As I took a deep breath and prepared to start running again, a nearby woman put her hands over a little girl's ears.

'What? I said eff! I don't swear in front of children!'

By the look on her face, that didn't seem to help. Maybe she'd read the newspaper that morning. Quite frankly, I didn't have the time to care.

* * *

After patiently informing me, multiple times, that, no, I couldn't see my son right now, a nurse ushered me into the private family room. Sean leapt to his feet and pulled me into his arms. I leant into his solid chest and took a brief, lovely moment to steady myself before drawing away.

'Tell me everything.'

Sean visibly juddered. We sat down on adjoining chairs and gripped each other's hands.

'It was his second swim. He must have misjudged the dive and hit his head on the bottom. I don't know how. He's done that same dive thousands of times before.'

'He was distracted.' I closed my eyes, trying to make the room stop lurching. 'I shouldn't have let him go. The trials were pressure enough, but then that article. I knew he ought to postpone. That something would happen. But I gave in to that same old pressure, winning is everything. It's not everything! Not even close! If this is what it takes to win, then I'm happy being a loser. Oh, Joey, this is all my fault. I'm so sorry, so sorry, so sorry...'

Eventually, when Sean had stroked my back and handed me a tissue and unstuck a clump of hair from the half-dried snot on my face, fetched me a cup of disgusting, lukewarm tea and tucked me up against his chest, the nurse returned and gave us what she called an update.

Joey had undergone a CT scan. They were waiting to move him to a ward for observation. The scan results would tell them how best to proceed.

'I want to see him.'

The nurse briskly looked me up and down, her curled-up lip expressing precisely what she thought about my attire. 'Once he's settled someone will come and fetch you.'

'Why can't I see him now?' I stopped myself from adding, '*I really don't think he'll care about me being in my pyjamas!*'

'He's not conscious, so there really wouldn't be any point.'

I scrabbled upright, arms flailing. 'Are you serious? Were you ever once a child? Did it make a difference to know your mother had sat with you when your life was in mortal danger, refusing to leave your side? Can you say, with one hundred per cent certainty, that he won't hear my voice, or feel my hand holding his? Do you think there might be some point, for me, to know that if my son dies, I was with him?'

'Ms Piper, the chance that Joseph will die is negligible at this stage. Please calm yourself down. It won't help Joseph if we have an... incident. Mr Mansfield, this hospital trust has a zero-tolerance policy regarding physical or verbal abuse towards NHS staff.'

'Excuse me? How was that abusive? How is this an incident? How do you know our names? You've read that article, haven't you? And now you won't let me see Joey because you think I'm a raving madwoman. Oh my goodness, Sean, tell her it's lies. Tell her I'm not some out-of-control, unstable... I've never abused anyone in my whole life.'

'Like I said, someone will fetch you once he's ready.' The nurse left.

'This is a nightmare.' I was aghast, beyond distraught. 'I thought things were bad when I ran off with you, but this is actually worse. Moira Vanderbeek has made things even worse.'

'No, she hasn't.' Sean's voice was gentle, but firm. He tilted me back so that his arm was around me and kissed the top of my head. 'This time, you have good friends, and Joey, to get you through it, not just an arrogant, brainless idiot who flakes at the first sign of trouble.'

I blew out a long sigh.

'You did flake.'

'I did. And you... did the opposite of flaking, whatever that is.'

'Clump?'

'Okay, that could work. You clumped. Or how about you stuck it out. Raised a son, alone, starting with nothing. Provided for him, loved him, gave him a childhood full of extraordinary memories. He told me all about the indoor camping and the circus school. And it's not a fluke that he's incredible. The swimming might be genetic, and I take full credit for that awesome hair, but his humungous heart, his beautiful soul, his uncannily wise head. A huge *clump* of that has got to be down to amazing parenting. If you can do that, you can do anything. You can certainly get through whatever news tonight will bring us. Both of you can.'

'Well, it helps you being here. For what it's worth, I'm glad you're no longer a brainless idiot flake.' I bumped his thigh with my fist.

'It was arrogant brainless idiot flake.'

'I know.'

* * *

When the door opened sometime later, jolting me from a restless doze, I assumed it was Sean, back from hunting down something more robust to eat than the measly offerings of the vending machine.

But, no. Nathan.

'I'm so sorry it took this long for me to get here, some of the club members watching were really upset, and I wanted to make sure they were all okay.'

'I didn't expect you to come.' My voice sounded flat, numb. In reality, I wanted to fling myself into his arms and burrow down in there, but I knew Nathan didn't want that. Even before I'd made a national mockery of him in the so-called news.

'Of course I came.' He screwed up his face in anguish. 'Is it okay if I come in? Is there any news?'

'Not really.' I moved Sean's jacket off the seat next to me, making a space.

'I shouldn't have let him swim.' He came in the room but remained standing, running a hand through his hair in agitation. The space between us felt like torture. All at once, holding that safe, strong hand seemed like the only thing that would get me through this.

'You and me both.'

'I'm his coach,' he replied, voice cracking.

'I'm his *mother*.' *Please come closer.*

'How can I help? What do you need?'

You can pretend to be my friend again, until this is all over. Forget that one, stupid mistake and be my friend again.

'I think you've probably done enough,' Sean replied. He quickly dropped a pack of sandwiches on the battered coffee table and went to stand beside me, one arm on my shoulder. 'This room is family only, buddy. If you don't mind.'

Nathan gave one small, tight nod and left.

If I'd had the strength, I might have asked Sean to call him back. But, in a way, it was easier not having him here, since seeing him felt like a chisel in my heart, splitting it open to reveal the longing, the ache, the pointless, wretched love within.

STOP BEING A LOSER PROGRAMME

DAY ONE HUNDRED AND EIGHTY-FIVE

A few minutes past midnight, the doctor informed us that the scan results were clear. I collapsed into Sean's shoulder, the rush of relief rendering my bones to water. The doctor looked faintly perturbed when I asked when we could see Joey, having assumed we'd seen him hours ago, but I was more concerned about getting to him now than causing a fuss about prejudiced nursing staff, so I simply grabbed my bag and followed him up to the ward.

Joey looked horrific. Pale green with purple shadows under dazed eyes. I ignored the wires and all the monitoring equipment, pushed aside my devastation and leant forwards to stroke his hair off his brow.

'Hey.'

'Hnnn.'

'How are you feeling?'

'Did they say yes?' His words were slow and barely comprehensible. 'I got a PB in the freestyle.'

'They said that they hope you're resting up, not worrying about trials, and focusing on getting better.'

My heart nearly shattered all over again with relief. I knew that brains were funny old organs, that Joey needed to be observed carefully because things could look fine and then suddenly not be, but oh my goodness. He was still Joey. I blotted my tears on his sheet and patted and stroked and kissed and fussed and did everything a thirteen-year-old boy does not want his mother to do, especially on a busy ward, and I didn't stop until the nurse came and shooed us out.

Sean and I stood in the corridor, elated, exhausted, too many other emotions to untangle. And I guessed – I *hoped* – it was for that reason only that after clinging to each other for a long time, laughing and crying and sniffing in a most undignified way, when we pulled back, Sean's face only an inch above mine, he bent down, closed the gap between us and kissed me.

And while I didn't quite kiss him back, I didn't move away, either. Instead, choosing to linger in the memory of a thousand kisses, when Sean's touch was safety and sunshine and freedom and anticipation. The sweet, sharp passion of first love.

I could yield to this. To a man who wanted me. To the family my son longed for. To security, and romance, and someone to have my back and rub my feet at the end of a bad day. Someone who loved Joey almost as much as I did, who could share in the fears and the joys of parenting, and in doing so lighten the load a little. I could laugh with Sean, even learn to cry with him. Maybe to trust him again, with time.

The temptation to take the path of least resistance was a powerful one. It felt so good to be held. So comforting to be with someone who I knew, and understood, and didn't have to second-guess all the time.

But when I pushed the past aside, ignored the tenuous promise of a happy-ever-after future, and forced myself to concentrate on the now, on Sean Mansfield's lips on mine, his hot hands against the small of my back, a strand of his hair tickling my forehead, what I actually felt was:

Not a lot.

So I stood back, far enough away so that Sean's hands eventually broke contact. I coerced my skittering gaze to meet his soft-focus smile and gooey eyes.

'Wow,' he breathed.

I swallowed, decisively, and straightened out my hoodie. 'No. Not wow. That was not okay. Especially now.'

'It wasn't?' Sean had the gall to look confused.

'Don't ever try anything like that again.'

Drained of courage and bravado – and after the day I'd had, who could blame me – I turned and ran, clattering down three flights of stairs rather than wait for a lift. As I hurried into the near-deserted main reception, trying to remember which car park I'd used, someone called my name.

Skidding to a stop, I saw Cee-Cee coming towards me.

'Come on, the car's this way.'

'I brought my own car,' I managed to stammer.

'I'll drop you back in the morning, you can pick it up then.'

'Cee-Cee...'

'There are times to be independent and times to accept help from someone who cares. When you've had a total stinker of a day, that's one of those times.'

She strode off through the automatic doors, and, aware that Sean might appear at any moment, for want of no better option, I followed her.

'Had you been there all evening?' I asked during the ride home, having filled her in on Joey's condition.

'Got here about ten. My contact at the Gladiators called. I thought you might need a lift home, so I waited in the café by the entrance.'

'You could have come up to the ward.' Despite currently only seeing him every couple of weeks or so, Cee-Cee still loved Joey like her own grandson. She must have been worried sick beneath the bluster.

'Family only, they said. And I didn't want to intrude.'

I reached across the car and gripped her hand. It was possibly the only time I'd touched Cee-Cee with affection, save for the odd post-race hug, and she nearly swerved into a bollard.

'You are family.' I choked back yet more tears. 'I'm sorry I forgot that.'

She nodded in response, blinked hard a few times and soldiered on.

A few minutes later, as we left the city boundary for the darkness of country roads, Cee-Cee cleared her throat and spoke again.

'The quotes weren't true. I refused to speak to her.'

'I figured as much. There's no way you'd have churned out all those words in one sentence. And I know you don't talk to the press.'

'But it made me realise. Perhaps you were right. I kept on as your coach, when what you needed was a friend. Not sure I knew how to be any different. I'm sorry for that.'

'Thank you.' I paused to swallow. 'For everything. I've never forgotten what you've done for us. And I shudder to imagine what kind of childhood Joey would've had without all your kindness and your help for all these years.'

'It wasn't kindness. Back then, single women didn't have the option of having children, so my squad became my family. And because it wasn't a real family, I was allowed to have a favourite. And after Athens, well. I cost you your real parents. The least I could do was step in. I know I probably never said sorry for what happened. I'm not good at that type of thing. But I am, and I was only trying to show you that.'

'Oh, Cee-Cee. It wasn't your fault that my parents are terrible! Or that I ran off and got pregnant.'

'Maybe not. But I did push you into a breakdown. So, it is partly my fault you've been unwell ever since. It's only right that I would do everything I could to help.'

'If you were in any way to blame for any of it, I forgive you. We all made a lot of mistakes. I'm sorry for running off instead of talking to you about it, and ruining your career.'

She nodded, and I tried and failed to stop crying the rest of the way home.

'I love you both, very much,' she said, as we pulled up outside my house.

The thing with someone like Cee-Cee, when she says those words, she means them. I would have said them back, but before I could find my voice, Cee-Cee had moved on.

'It's nearly two. Would eight be a good time to pick you up?'

'Great,' I managed to croak. Great that she asked instead of telling me a time, too. 'Joey will be thrilled to see you.'

'It's family only.'

'I know.'

STOP BEING A LOSER PROGRAMME

DAY ONE HUNDRED AND NINETY-TWO (ON HOLD)

Over the next week, I had the triple crown of excuses to put the Programme on hold and stay inside. Joey came home after another day in hospital, but he was still prone to getting woozy and clumsy and suffering from headaches. With strict instructions to keep screen time to a minimum, in between frequent naps, he was bored and irritable. I was grateful for his friends calling in after school, for Cee-Cee who popped in on her days off to play cards (yes, she had a new job, in Sporting Warehouse of all places) and even for Sean, who was hanging around semi-permanently in a state of awkwardness. At the same time, I wanted to sit beside my boy on the sofa, hold his hand and monitor his every movement. It would be easy to take 'make sure he avoids any exertion or physical activity' to extremes (does sitting up and eating count as physical activity? How about a shower?), but I knew all too well about the line between helping and smothering, and while I didn't always agree with Joey's assessment of where that line lay, I did try to meet him somewhere in the middle.

The aftermath of the article was another reason to hole up inside. Just until things blew over, I pretended to myself, while aware that when it came to small villages that would take at least another couple of generations, and there was no blowing over, only facing up to it, tackling it head on and riding it out.

And, thirdly, I did have a Senior Bid Writer's project deadline whizzing towards me. It wasn't easy to focus on virtual reality systems when our reality had been tipped over, the contents kicked about the gutter. Somehow writing about immersive environment simulators seemed a bit less important. But paying my bills and not being evicted was also important, so I moved my office into the living room and knuckled down as best I could, one eye firmly fixed over the top of my laptop on Joey.

59

STOP BEING A LOSER PROGRAMME

Cee-Cee's ex-colleague from the Gladiators called in, conveniently at a time when Cee-Cee was there. He asked how Joey was feeling, expressed his complete understanding at how the combined circumstances of the trial plus his mother's 'spot of bother with the press' could have led to a momentary slip in concentration.

He believed in second chances, was confident Joey would have learnt from what happened, and would be delighted if Joey joined the club. Once he'd made a full recovery, obviously. Bearing in mind that he was turning fourteen soon, and there wasn't much time to spare.

But the invitation, coming at such a late age, was indication of how impressed he and the other Gladiators coaches were. He genuinely thought that, with dedication and the right attitude, Joey stood a chance.

Joey nodded, smiled politely, shook the man's hand and said how much he appreciated it, and that he would be in touch as soon as he was back to full strength.

The instant the front door shut, a victory dance exploded out, in blatant disregard of all instructions concerning physical exertion.

I watched, smiled, let him spin me around the living room and tried very hard to grapple with my anxiety monster until I'd crammed it back inside the cage where it belonged.

Life hurts, sometimes. Following your dreams costs, maybe every-thing we've got. Trying and the risk of failure and disappointment come as a two-for-one offer. Joey might not make it, whatever 'it' was. He might sacrifice his teenagehood pursuing a goal that he'd never reach. He would encounter deeper and longer-lasting pain than a mild concussion if he joined the Gladiators.

But he would know the pain of regret if he didn't.

Who was I to tell him which hurt more?

And any pain I might feel had nothing to do with it.

60

STOP BEING A LOSER PROGRAMME

DAY TWO HUNDRED AND EIGHT (STILL ON HOLD)

Joey had been back at school over a week. He had one more check-up in a few days, where the doctor expected to be giving the all-clear to resume gentle exercise.

I had completed my first project as Senior Bid Writer, and apart from a small piece of editing work, had nothing until a new project started the following Monday.

I had not left the house in nearly three weeks, apart from two quick trips to the supermarket and Joey's medical appointments.

Mel and Dani had called in on me every few days, bringing breakfast each Saturday and turning up at inconvenient moments midweek with flowers, doughnuts or a punnet of fruit. They also brought campaign updates. Now only four thousand pounds shy of the original target, they were looking at potentially ending up with enough to fund an aquachair, or an extra poolside wheelchair as well. And, of course, they also provided training updates. Kommando Kim was doing a competent, if bone-breaking and wrath-inducing, job of clobbering them into shape for the big day. Dani, Isobel and Mystery Woman Two (otherwise known as Miranda, it turned out) had started cycling alongside the runners on Sundays.

They had also persisted with the same conversation, every time they'd called in:

'Oh, and me and Selena are going swimmin' whenever we can. Are you coming? You could give us some tips to improve our technique.'

'When are you going? I might be busy.'

'We're goin' whenever you're not busy. Which seems to be most of the time.'

'Let me know when you're at the pool and I'll see if I'm free.'

They weren't fooled by my attempts at fobbing them off. 'Please don't make me go swimming with Selena without you.'

'I said, I'll try to make it. I do have a job and a recovering son to care for.'

Mel and Dani said nothing more, but I caught their worried glances. The grand opening of the Amelia Piper Swimming Centre was three weeks away. As much as I loved them, I began to dread the knock on the door. Being a recluse was a lot easier without friends to challenge and cajole you, making you feel guilty for soon-to-be broken promises and general life-failures.

And I couldn't be with Mel and Dani without thinking about Nathan, like a big, superfit shadow lurking in the corner, crinkling his eyes at me. Okay, so maybe I sometimes thought about him anyway. I didn't have that much to do now Joey was at school, or many other people to think about. But Mel and Dani talking about the Larks, making me stress about how I was going to let them all down and reminding me that at some point I was supposed to make a speech to a crowd of people who thought I had lost the plot years ago and only deteriorated since: that made me miss him even more.

So, here I was, heading out, into the open air, the actual street, to do something that however cringey, clearly beat the alternative.

I scuttled down Foxglove Lane old-school, pre-Programme style, and up to the huge house. Before I had time to run away, or pass out, I knocked on the door.

Audrey opened it, wearing a short skirt and a crop top that would rival my new swimsuit for lack of coverage. She beetled her newly shaped, pencil-assisted brows and pursed her lips.

'Hi, Audrey, how are you?'

'Fine. What do you want?'

Eugh. She didn't look fine.

'Can I come in for a couple of minutes? I want to talk to you about something.'

She hitched her top a millimetre higher up her exposed chest and scanned the road behind me. 'Five minutes, ten tops.'

'Thank you.'

Stepping aside to let me in, she took one last look outside before slamming the door behind us.

Audrey perched uncomfortably on a minimalist, leather armchair, while I sat on the matching sofa.

Given the time limit, I jumped straight in. 'The triathlon is in three weeks.'

'And?' She shrugged, but it was a little too couldn't-care-less.

'I need you to take my place in the swimming race. Please.'

'What?' She wrinkled her nose in a mixture of surprise and derision.

'I can't do the swim. Your mum reckons you're decent enough in the water. If there's only two competitors for our team in any of the legs, we'll be disqualified.'

'You do it then.'

'I can't.'

'Why not?'

I shifted on the sofa, causing it to make a loud farting sound that couldn't have more aptly summed up how I felt if I'd produced it myself. I could go all in, open myself up to shame and ridicule, and Audrey could smile as she booted me out empty-handed and pick up the phone to pass the juicy information on to her new buddy Moira Vanderbeek. Or, I could let the tatty remains of my pride prevent those gorgeous, fabulous Larks from having any hope of even competing, let alone winning a medal.

Okay. I could do this.

'As you'll be aware, along with the rest of the population, I've not been swimming since my mini-meltdown, fourteen years ago. I've tried to work back up to it, I even went to Brooksby pool and got as far as the changing rooms, but I can't. Not without panicking. And the deep end of a swimming pool isn't a great place for a panic attack.'

Audrey looked unconvinced.

'I know your mum was way out of order at the Christmas party, but please don't let that stop you from helping the rest of the club. Or Tate. Nathan would be devastated.'

Audrey frowned, looking pensive. 'They keep sending me messages, asking how I am and stuff. Bronwyn invited me out for a drink a couple of times. But I couldn't go because Graham doesn't... I was busy. But if *she'll* be there, I won't go. It'd be disrespectful to Graham.'

'Okay, Audrey. I'm going to say this, and given my life story, please don't hate me, just know that I'm trying to be a friend: if you don't want to swim, then I accept your decision. But make sure it is *your* decision. Don't give up a whole bunch of people who love and care about you, who are fun and funny and bloody amazing for the most part, because one person says they want you all for themselves. Trust me, it won't end well. No one has the right to demand all of you. You have too much to give to limit it to just him. And if friends and hobbies and living life to the full make your relationship more difficult, not better and richer and stronger, then it's not a healthy one.'

'My relationship with Mum was hardly healthy.'

'No, it wasn't. But I think, with some tough conversations, and probably a huge amount of therapy, it's not unfixable. In her warped way, she only wants the best for you. Are you sure that's true for Graham?'

'Ten minutes is up. Can you go now?' She glanced at the window, apprehensively.

'I can. But if you're worried about how Graham will react if he finds me here, then you really need to think about what I've said.'

'Okay, I get it. Will you just go?'

I left.

Would my words convince Audrey to save the day? At this point, I was more concerned about whether what I'd said would help save Audrey.

STOP BEING A LOSER PROGRAMME
DAY TWO HUNDRED AND THIRTEEN (STILL ON HOLD)

Sunday morning, Selena turned up at my door. She flung her arms around me, enveloping me in the worst of her post-run perspiration, and squeezed so hard my ribs crunched.

'I don't know what you said to her, but thank you. I've booked us a joint session with my therapist and am cancelling the hitwoman. Although, having had Graham under surveillance for the past few weeks, she's considering going ahead and putting him out of action anyway. There's more than one way to neuter a rabid dog.'

'Is Audrey going to swim?' I managed to gasp, once I'd broken free.

'Yes. But you are, too. Audrey's wonderful in her own way, but she's no Olympian. We aren't in this for the laughs, Amy. You're our secret weapon and quite frankly our only hope. Don't you dare even think about missing it.'

STOP BEING A LOSER PROGRAMME

DAY TWO HUNDRED AND TWENTY-SEVEN – BACK ON!

In flagrant disregard of Selena's order, I bravely dared to think about missing the triathlon for the next fortnight. I thought about it while mindlessly completing a funding application for a local charity who deserved far more care and attention. I thought about it while carefully monitoring Joey's gradual return to training, and readjusting my relationship with Sean to one of co-parents, and polite friends, nothing more for now and for as long as he continued to surreptitiously stare at me whenever he thought I wouldn't notice. I thought about it when Cee-Cee came around for dinner, every Tuesday, as we slowly started to settle into a new balance of friendship. I thought about it whenever I went out, which was just enough to stop Joey worrying and to prevent a total back-slide into hermithood. I thought about it when I stayed under my duvet instead, which was more often than I wanted to admit. I thought about it whenever I thought about Nathan, which was even more often than that.

I grew sick from thinking about it. Pale, and irritable, and beyond knackered.

In my capacity as a professional writer, I had cobbled together a passable speech. It wasn't quite '*I have a dream*', but seeing as most people would be too busy ogling for signs of my mental disintegration rather than actually listening, it would do.

* * *

The day before, Easter Sunday, Mel persuaded me to go along to a sunrise church service at a local farm. It had been a gloriously hot weekend, and even at that hour, the air was rich with the promise of spring sunshine, heady with the scent of blossom from the trees above, and the dewy grass beneath. We sang along with the nesting birds, about life, and hope, and all things new. About power, and courage, and victory won. Words that came back to me like a long-forgotten native language.

I thought about how far I had come, in two-hundred and twenty-seven days. How *much* I had done. My life had become unrecognisable. I'd dared to hope the Programme might bring me greater freedom. I'd never imagined it would give me friends.

So why had I stopped?

Because it got hard? Every damn step had been gut-grindingly hard. Opening the door for eleven point two five seconds had been my personal best, at one point.

Because my coach wasn't there to hold my hand any more? I was supposed to be finally living as an adult, not a victim, no longer expecting other people to sort out my problems for me. Accepting help and support, yes, but taking responsibility for myself. If I couldn't do this without Nathan, there was no point in doing it at all.

Oh, for goodness' sake! Of course I would go to the triathlon. I would smile, shake hands, cut the ribbon with a stupid pair of giant scissors, give my so-so speech and hand out the trophy to my old team, the Larkabouts.

It was time.

63

STOP BEING A LOSER PROGRAMME

DAY TWO HUNDRED AND TWENTY-EIGHT – THE FINAL
CHALLENGE

The morning of the triathlon, with Joey at his dad's, I was woken up by
my usual trespassers letting themselves into the kitchen. Waiting until
the smell of coffee, eggs and nervous excitement wafted into my
bedroom, I pulled on a hoodie and my old leggings and went to face
them.

'Come on, Ames, get yerself a proper competitor's brekkie!' Mel
beamed, beneath blue and white face paint and blue plaits.

'Only I'm not competing.'

'Well, you never know.'

Too frazzled to argue, I ate my brekkie, changed into a smartish new
dress and faffed about with my hair until Dani frogmarched me to
her car.

'Dani, is that my swimsuit in your bag?'

Dani shrugged, the essence of nonchalance. 'In case of emergency.
Selena might have eaten too many Easter eggs and need a bigger size.'

* * *

The swimming centre was abuzz already, a good hour before the race
began. Pop-up food stalls selling healthy snacks and their own versions
of a competitor's breakfast lined one edge of the sports field, with two
more sides full of stands advertising virtually every sports club and

fitness class in the county. Kommando Kim was leading a mass warm-up
in the middle of it all, browbeating members of the public, from toddlers
to pensioners, into joining in, using her delightful combination of intim-
idation and verbal abuse. I'd seen children in tears, and some of the
parents were in an even worse state than their kids.

Not quite holding Mel or Dani's hands, but finding enough comfort
and support in their company all the same, I tried to walk tall and keep
my breathing steady as we made our way through the crowd. We found
the rest of the Larks clucking and preening their blue and white feathers
near the outdoor tennis court. To my enormous relief, Audrey was there.
She offered me a small smile and a nod.

With Nathan nowhere to be seen, Marjory took over as captain and
filled us in. 'There are five teams competing – a men's football team,
men's cycling club, a mixed athletics club and a team from the county
council leisure department, plus us. No swimming club team, so that's
where we're most likely to have the advantage. I suggest we aim to come
out of the first leg with as big a lead as possible.'

'What?' Isobel screwed her face up. 'I think a more realistic aim
would be to not come last. We're the only all-women team, that football
team are all under thirty and have you seen the thighs on the cycling
club?'

'Uh, hello?' Bronwyn retorted. 'Firstly, way to have a winning attitude. Secondly, being an all-women team is not a disadvantage, what we
might lack in brute strength, we make up for with grit, guts and girl
power. Thirdly, Olympic champion, world champion!'

'Uh, I'm not actually competing,' I said, horrified that everyone
didn't already know, despite chickening out of telling them myself.

'Yeah, whatever. My mistake.' Bronwyn winked, most unsubtly, and a
coil of suspicion tightened round my spine.

'Right, any questions?' Marjory asked. 'All hydrated, carb loaded and
warmed up?'

They all were.

'Right, let's head over to the pool.'

'Jealous?' Dani asked me, as we walked towards the main entrance.

'I'm going to love cheering you on.'

Dani raised her eyebrows, in wry acknowledgement that I hadn't
actually answered the question.

Before I could admit that perhaps, just maybe, deep in some forgotten cranny of my brain, I felt a tiny flicker of envy at not being part of the triathlon team, a man bustled up.

'Amelia, oh my days, what a relief, we're ready to officially commence the proceedings and the crowd awaits their star!' He held out one hand to shake mine, while using the other one to begin herding me in the direction I was already going. 'Antonio Galanos. We've spoken on the phone.'

'Yes, hi.'

'For a moment there, I thought you might have done another runner! Ha ha!'

Dani, hurrying along on the other side of me, spurted out the mouthful of water she'd just swigged from her bottle.

'I mean, I know we aren't the Olympics or anything, but, well, round these parts a family fun fit day is almost as special. Right. If I could hand you over to my colleague, Janine, I'll get the scissors.'

A while later, ribbon cut, half a dozen official photos, plus half a million unofficial selfies snapped, I was still hanging on in there. The overwhelmingly positive response of the crowd meant that I almost stopped expecting someone to sneer, or jeer, or ask me about the articles. I was ushered towards the pool, over to a special seat reserved in the spectators' area, beside Tate's wheelchair. The rest of the seats quickly filled up, with more people pressed in along the sides and in the aisles, in what I'm sure must have been a breach of health and safety regulations. Joey and Sean were seated towards the front, in amongst the Larks' friends and families, causing another twinge of regret that I'd been such a big wimp, Joey wouldn't get to see me race.

Ten minutes before the triathlon was due to start, I was asked to announce each team as they arrived – the swimmers still damp from their warm-up. The Larkabouts were the final team to enter.

'Eh! This'll be the only time we come in last today!' Mel hollered, waving and giving a manic thumbs up to her watching family.

I'd been doing reasonably well so far, managing not to garble, remembering to smile, ignoring the odd snicker or whispered comment, maintaining a normal respiration rate, but when Nathan trooped in behind his team, in a blue tracksuit and tight white T-shirt, my heart did a triple backflip. He had his game face on... right until he spotted me.

'No need to look so surprised,' I mouthed as he walked past, trying and failing to frown.

He shook his head, eyes crinkling. 'Pleased. Not surprised. I knew you'd be here.'

Well, if you're so pleased to see me, where were you for the past two months?

How about he didn't make contact because he's pleased, in a strictly professional capacity, to have helped a client succeed in one of her goals?

Yeah. I guess that explained it.

'Right,' the manager of the swimming centre said, having taken the microphone from me, 'can the swimming competitors please take their places. All other entrants must now move to the team viewing area to my left.'

There was a flurry of activity as most of the competitors moved off to the side, while the third who were going to swim took off their tracksuits and did some enthusiastic stretches, nearly knocking the manager and a few of their opponents into the water. Something not quite right was going on with the Larks, though. None of them had moved to the side, and all nine – ten of them, including Nathan, were now stripping off their blue and white tracksuits, revealing nine tiny swimsuits and one pair of appropriately sized shorts.

'What the hell are you doing?' I yelled, most improperly.

'We're the Larks!' Dani called back. 'We stick together no matter what.'

'But you'll lose!' I screeched back. 'Isobel can't even swim!'

'I've got armbands *and* a float! I can manage a couple of lengths. Probably.' She stuck out her chin and put her hands on her hips, no doubt aiming for defiant but slightly missing the mark due to the unicorn armbands.

'We've got Nathan, he'll make up for Isobel,' Bronwyn said, gesturing her head at our coach.

Oh my goodness.

He resembled a Greek statue.

Was someone saying something, maybe about a race or something...? I seemed to have forgotten...

'No Lark left behind!' Marjory's battle cry thankfully interrupted my lust-addled stupor. 'We win together or we lose together. But we stick together when it counts!'

'What, like on every training session when you disappear off into the distance?' Selena snarked.

'No Lark left behind!' Marjory called again, and this time I managed to drag my eyes off Nathan and keep them on her long enough to notice what she was holding out.

'The race is about to start,' I jabbered back.

'You can take the second leg.'

I looked at the swimsuit in her hand. Moved my gaze to take in ten Larks. My friends, my squad, my rescuers. From age twenty-two to seventy-five, from an Olympian to a woman who couldn't even swim. Women who'd made fearless choices, and terrible ones, who'd faced crap that they never would have chosen. Strong, courageous women who'd picked themselves up, dusted themselves down and kept on running. Who had forgiven the past mistakes, especially their own. Who had learnt that life is too damn short, and too darn tough at times, to give a monkey's banana what a random crowd of spectators, or online gossip-scavengers, or trash-paper readers would think of them. Women who knew who they were, and what they wanted to do, and let nothing and nobody stop them from doing it.

Of course I would take the second leg!

'No Lark left behind!' I grabbed the suit, pausing to find Joey in the crowd, already on his feet, fists in the air, face shining with joy. 'GO, MUM!'

I waved at him, grinning, before turning back to Marjory. 'But you can start without me just this once.'

It took an excruciating three minutes to wrestle out of the dress, another hurried two while I tried to adjust the swimsuit to cover as much as possible. Ten seconds to get my head in the game.

It was *time*.

* * *

'Amy – you're up!' Dani poked her head into the changing room.

I hurtled out, across the tiles and, barely taking the second to check whether the lane was clear, took a deep breath and dove straight into the water.

Oh.

Oh.

Oh.

No sound.

No thoughts.

Just water.

My long-lost friend.

Instinct.

Joy.

Power.

Peace.

Oh.

At the millisecond before my lungs would burst, I broke out of the water, relishing the hit of cold air like an addict's first shot of the morning. The sound of the crowd hit me, sparking a tidal wave of adrenaline, and without any conscious thought that, *ah, yes, this is a race, I'd better get a move on,* my arm swung up, legs kicked, and I was shooting through the water like a world champion after fourteen years of imposed confinement on land.

* * *

An hour later, we started the cycling leg of the triathlon smack in the middle of the rankings. I'd completed ten of the thirty lengths of the pool, with Nathan swimming eight, Mel, Audrey and Selena two each, and everyone else a single fifty-metre length. And if Isobel had needed a bit of a hand to complete the final forty-eight metres, well, all's fair in family fun fit triathlons.

I think we managed to maintain third place for, ooh, at least three minutes of the cycling leg. While certain members of the Larks – i.e. the ones who were supposed to be cycling, and had therefore actually done some training on a bike – whizzed off ahead, and others who were naturally pretty fit whatever the sport, followed not too far behind them. Mel and Audrey were soon left puffing away either side of the person who'd not ridden a bike since she'd pulled wheelies up and down her cul-desac on a BMX.

'This is easier than it looks!' Mel grinned, giving her bell a good jingle after freewheeling down the first slope, sky-blue helmet balanced on top of her plaits. 'All that fuss about learnin' to ride a bike, nothing to it! Come on, guys, keep up, we're in a race here!'

To be fair, it may have taken me longer than Mel to get back into the swing of cycling, but I wasn't the one using kids' stabilisers. And poor Audrey, I wasn't sure if it was sweat dripping off her as she lumbered along in the freak Easter heatwave, face scrunched with determination, or whether she was literally melting. Thank goodness that for most of the ten kilometres, the roads were free of spectators, so we could huff and groan and grimace with no one watching. My muscles had regressed back towards flabbiness over the past few weeks, and it was amazing how quickly I became breathless.

Five kilometres in, it felt as though the sun's rays had soldered Dani's spare helmet to my head. My legs were trembling with fatigue, and where my backside met the seat, I expected to find a bloody, pulpy mess if I ever managed to haul myself off.

Exhaustion, agony, pushing myself way beyond any reasonable limits. I was loving it.

Audrey and Mel, who'd soon realised that riding a bike up a hill was a lot harder than zipping down it, not so much.

I tried gasping out a few pep talks and motivational clichés, but it is hard to get motivated when you last saw any of your competitors fifteen minutes ago.

And then, whizzing over the crest of the hill came Dani, Selena right behind her on a tandem.

'Don't tell me you've finished and then come all this way back again,' Mel groaned, coming to a stop. 'I don't want to know.'

'Come on, stop moaning and hop on,' Dani replied.

'Hop on where?'

'Didn't you ever ride on the handlebars when you were a kid?'

Mel looked stricken. 'I'm not a kid any more, Dani. I don't think my bum will fit on there.'

'Don't be an idiot. And hurry up – one of the council guys has fallen off at 7K. His bike's a wreck and the rest of the team don't even know because they've gone off ahead and left him. If we put our backs into it, we can beat him.'

'We might not be last!' Mel shrieked, ditching her bike at the side of the road and scrambling over to Dani's.

Meanwhile, Audrey was plodding on ahead of us, head down, pretending to be oblivious to Selena pedalling alongside, repeatedly entreating her to get on the tandem.

I stretched out my shoulders, gritted my teeth, clenched what remained of my buttocks and caught up with them. 'Come on, Audrey, you haven't trained for the cycling leg, there's no shame in teaming up with someone else.'

'There's plenty of shame in having my mum bail me out.'

'No one in any of the other teams has swam and cycled.'

'All the Larks have,' Audrey wheezed, doggedly still going.

'And Mel is on Dani's handlebars.'

'Why do you keep butting in and trying to help me?' Audrey growled, bike wobbling alarmingly as she twisted her head towards Selena.

'Audrey, you're my daughter! I'd die for you! With a smile on my face! Everybody needs help, why not accept it from someone who takes a gargantuan amount of pleasure in giving it to you? I know you can do this without me. I believe you can do anything you put your mind to. But I know you, I know your strengths and cycling is not one of them. Baking, shoulder massages and figuring out what I've bought you for Christmas, yes, you're fabulous at all of those. You're the best person I know at Pictionary. But most of all, you are smart. So use that giant brain of yours to realise that all I want is to share a fantastic moment with my daughter. Come on, darling, hop on and let's not be last, together.'

Audrey pushed on for a few more paces. I wondered if one of those streaks running through the grime on her face wasn't sweat, but a tear.

'Only if I get to go in front.'

Selena jerked the tandem to a halt. 'Well, what are you waiting for, then?'

'Me, please!' I yelled, throwing my rented bike into a bush beside Audrey's. 'Be waiting for me! I want to not be last together, too. And, more to the point, my backside just can't take any more.'

'Where the hell did you get this tandem anyway?' Audrey grumbled as she clambered on.

'One of the athletics club brought it.'

'How did you persuade them to lend it to you?'

'I'll worry about that when they notice I've taken it.'

So, with me straddling the basket at the back, the last of the Larks pushed on through the remaining few kilometres. We spotted the council casualty a kilometre from the finish line, wheeling his buckled bike along the side of the road with an excruciating limp.

'Eh, walking's a disqualifiable offence!' Mel catcalled as Dani pumped them past.

'I think catching a lift on the handlebars is too!' the man yelled after her.

We finished together, two bikes, five jubilant women, whooping as we crossed the line most definitely not last.

Oh, it felt beyond wonderful to be racing with my team again.

* * *

We had another hour-long break for snacks, more photographs and wincing at Kommando Kim's afternoon Killer Kardio session (non-triathlon competitors only). Selena followed me into the changing room.

'Good to be back?' She pulled out her ponytail and fluffed her hair in the mirror a few times.

'Yes, thanks.' I bent down to splash some water on my face. The heat in here was brutal. The brand new changing room already carried a faint whiff of rancid cheese.

'You'll be back for good? Training as usual?'

'I hope so.' And I meant it, too.

'You'd better be.'

I paused, flicking a strand of hair out of my face. Selena demanding me back at the Larks could have been a compliment. But it sounded more like a threat.

'It's bad enough losing Nathan. If he's left for nothing, you are not going to be popular round here. Might want to rethink the whole recluse thing.'

'Excuse me?' I gripped onto the sink as the blood drained from my body, leaving my head empty and spinning. 'You think Nathan left because of me?'

'Well, duh!'

I'd wondered, but to hear it out loud, from Selena of all people. My battered heart felt as though it splattered onto the shiny new floor.

'Did he tell everyone?'

'Darling, he didn't have to. You know his rule. Professional boundaries.'

Oh, no. This was horrible.

'He was the one who told me where he lived!'

She stopped plucking at her hair and turned to face me, hands on hips. 'Well, that confirms it then, doesn't it? Oh, come off it, don't look so shocked. What else was he supposed to do?'

'He should have asked me to leave. Why didn't he? I would have left, if he felt that uncomfortable. I thought it was nothing really, not a big deal, we'd laugh about it and move on. Nathan can't leave the Larks because of me. I'll talk to him, tell him *I'm* leaving. Then he can come back.' I shook my head, confused. 'Why didn't he ask *me* to leave?'

'What, apart from being head over heels in love with you? I'd guess not wanting to send you back into your house for the next ten years, back to a hopeless, friendless and below-optimum-fitness existence. Hoping you'll bring us a victory today. You being the celebrity face and driving force behind hashtag PoolPalforPiper. Not wanting to cause tension between you with Joey's trials coming up and Joey being so excited about you and his dad getting back together. Is that enough for starters?'

'What? *What?* Selena, stop. What? What are you talking about? Nathan is not in love with me!'

She shrugged. 'Well, probably not. But it takes more than a passing fancy or simple animal attraction to turn Nathan's head and surmount his insanely strict code of conduct. Believe me. And if he thought you were worth giving up the Larks for, what would you call it?'

'But... if he liked me, then where has he been for the past two months?'

More to the point, I thought, but would never say out loud to Selena, ever, *why did he disappear straight after I accidentally leaned in a bit close while barely dressed and in an enclosed space?*

'Ooh, training your son, turning up at A&E to find you all cosied up with your ex, who tells him to jog on? Giving you space to decide who you are and who or what you want? Allowing you to decide if you want Nathan, even when you don't need him? Doing the decent thing and bowing out so you have a chance to get back with the father of your child? Using all this as an excuse because he's massively shy and even more scared after his last girlfriend? You know, the whole him forgetting to meet her for a run, her getting attacked and him not getting over it so she dumped him, and married his oldest friend?'

Before my head had a chance to explode with all this information, let alone start sifting through to decide which, if any of it, was true, Bronwyn burst through the changing room door.

'There you are! Flippin' 'eck, you two, the next leg is about to start. Stop preening and get on out there!' She gave me a concerned second look, before disappearing out the door again.

'Come on, then.' Selena held the door open for me. 'You never know, there might be another miracle which means we end up being not last.'

* * *

But in the end, no miracle was required. Unless you call months of hard work, the best coach in the country (and by that I mean our earlier coach, not last-minute stand-in Koach), the strength of a team who have cheered, encouraged and badgered each other on, and – as Bronwyn predicted – grit, guts and good old-fashioned girl power a miracle.

We ran our great, big, beautiful hearts out.

Even Audrey, who gave so much, she half-collapsed in the impossible heat three-quarters of the way round, then tipped a bucket of water over her head, grabbed her mum's hand and kept on going.

Even Mel, whose knees finally gave out with three-hundred metres to go, crawling until Dani and Bronwyn ran back to brace their arms either side of her, the crowd going wild as they hobbled on.

Even me, who'd done my best to get a grip on the turbulent thoughts running rampage in my brain and reclaim the single-minded focus that had won me the world championships. That is, until I remembered that this was a fun run, a team event, and one I wanted to actually enjoy, so I ditched the focus and just, well, enjoyed it.

By some unspoken decision, passed along via the power of our unbreakable team bond, each Lark paused a hundred metres from the finish line, smack in the middle of the new athletics field and waited for the rest. I found out later that Nathan and Marjory had been first and second out of the whole race, and yet they were the first ones to stand and wait while the athletics team, the cyclists, the footballers and three out of the four members of the council team ran, walked and limped past.

Like a game of very badly played sardines, as each one of us reached the others, we stopped and huddled, arms around each other, adrenaline pumping with passion.

'Who cares if we lose the triathlon?' Isobel yelled, as we watched Audrey and Selena slowly overtake Mel, Dani and Bronwyn, going even slower. 'We've won at what really matters!'

'Well, yes, but let's try not to come last at the triathlon as well. We can have both,' Marjory said, frowning.

'Come on the Larks!' someone shouted from the crowd, and they were swiftly joined by a dozen other voices. 'Come on the Larks!'

The final member of the council team shuffled up behind Mel, amid the hollering crowd. She took a deep breath and shrugged off Dani and Bronwyn's arms from around her waist. 'Thanks, girls. Much appreciated, but I've got this.'

To everyone's amazement, she began jogging, face scrunched up in agony, tears streaming down her face, her howled curses thankfully masked by the noise of the crowd.

'Well, come on then,' Marjory yelled at Dani and Bronwyn, who were stood there with their mouths hanging open, 'let's not be last!'

And as Mel and the others caught up, we linked arms, ten Larks and their trainer, and spread out so far across the track, the council runner couldn't have got past if he'd tried.

There were fifty sweet, short metres to the finish line. We were only going to go and not be last!

'Amelia, how does it feel to be scraping fifth place in your first competition for fourteen years? Are you embarrassed to perform so badly in front of your son and newly reconciled love of your life?'

At the end of the line (in an attempt to stay as far away from Nathan as possible, at least until the race was over and I'd had a chance to weigh up what Selena had told me), I was so near the edge of the track that Moira Vanderbeek's microphone wobbled perilously close to me. As I turned, I could see the freckles on her cheeks, the sharp gleam in her eye.

'Do you blame the weight gain, or your mental breakdown for such a disastrous comeback?'

It was stupid, and weak, and if I'd not been so careless with my focus it wouldn't have happened, but as the words slammed into me like a wrecking ball, all I could see was the greedy faces of the spectators surrounding her, ready to feed like coyotes on carrion.

I must have stopped running and dropped arms with Mystery Woman One next to me (Karen? Or maybe Carol?) because I found myself frozen, stricken silent, Moira Vanderbeek's microphone six inches from my nose.

'Amelia? Don't you have anything to say?'

I had no idea if I had anything to say or not. My anxiety, on the other hand, had plenty. None of it printable in a national newspaper. So did the crowd. As my pulse began to accelerate, I could feel more than hear the ripple of morbid anticipation.

And here it was, like one of those old friends you might not have seen for years, but as soon as you do, it's as if you were never apart. Only this time, an enemy: the reeling head, the convulsing heart, the churning wave of nausea as my lungs wheezed like a pair of rusty bellows.

I bent over, hands braced on my thighs, and closed my eyes. The world kept spinning, forcing me to my knees, hands on the ground to stop from flying off into the ozone layer. I was enveloped by panic. Drowning in fear. Surely I would pass out any second.

Then, as if from the end of a long tunnel, a distorted voice found its way into my consciousness.

'Ames! Get up! For the Larks! Come on! You can do it!'

Then louder, more voices, like a drumbeat: 'You can do it! You can do it! *You can do it!*'

I held on to that chant, I dug down and I remembered to count my breaths, to feel the ground beneath my feet – or, in this case, the grass beneath my palms and knees.

An arm went around my waist, the other lifting me up as fingers gripped my hand. 'I've got you, we can do this,' spoken into my ear.

'No.' I shook my head, clearing some of the fog as I did it. 'No!'

'Yes, Amy. We can do this.'

'No!' I pulled my hand from his, tottered to my feet. '*I* can do it.'

I found Nathan's eyes. Held them for as long as it took me to send the 'GO!' message from my brain to my body and took off towards the finish, past the last man a millisecond before he crossed the line, Nathan two seconds ahead of me.

But I didn't stop there, swerving around the jubilant mob of Larks, I sprinted on a lap of victory, past Joey and Sean, around Moira Vanderbeek, to the small stage put up at the far end of the field, where the winners were going to be presented with their prize.

'You wanted an exclusive interview, Ms Vanderbeek, I believe?' I panted, clambering up onto the stage as a circle of spectators formed in front. 'Well, here it is. And where's Antonio? Antonio? Can this microphone be turned on please? This is my speech. I'm doing it now.'

With skinned knees, hair all over the place, my only make-up smears of mud, sweat and tears, in shorts that put the hips in hippo, it was time.

'Is it on? Hello? One two, one two. Right. So. Yes, I've put on some weight. What of it? I just swam, cycled 10K and ran five. I'm proud of my body and more than satisfied with what it can do. And yes, I had a mental breakdown. I've been battling with anxiety, panic disorder and agoraphobia for many years. And for most of that time it's been beating me hands down. But its primary weapons were shame and isolation. I am not ashamed of being ill any more. The only thing I'm ashamed of is how ashamed I was. One in five young people suffer with some form of mental illness. I could blame it on my circumstances, the ridiculous pressure I was under thanks to journalists like you, having no balance in my life, no time to have fun or relax, my parents publicly disowning me on the back of a devastating mistake – at eighteen years old! But I won't, because that's irrelevant. If none of those things had happened and I had still been ill, that would not be my fault either. And I still wouldn't be ashamed. I am not weak. I am not a coward. I am not pathetic. I am not broken. I am not a shirker. I am no less of a person than you. Or any less amazing.

'Today I'm here, and I'm doing well. But that doesn't mean all those people who aren't here, who are watching this on YouTube later because they couldn't quite get out of bed and face the world today, are any less worthwhile, valuable, precious human beings than I am. They, to me, are champions, because they face what most of you will never have to, they push on through it every single day.

'And – I'm not finished, please wait and clap at the end – if you saw what happened today and consider it disastrous, or anything to be embarrassed about, you're even more stupid than I thought. Not to mention a really quite unpleasant person.

'Oh, and I had good reason to think you're stupid, by the way, so let me correct a few mistakes you made. Sean Mansfield, the father of my child, is not the love of my life, or, as your article so nicely put it, the person who gave me a reason to get dressed in the morning. We are not, have not and will never be resuming any form of romantic relationship. He's here in the UK to spend time with his son. I suggest you work a bit harder to get your facts straight before you lose the last shred of your professional credibility.'

I paused, took a deep breath, scanned the crowd, quickly searching to find Joey. He grinned at me, and gave a double thumbs up, an act so cheesy and uncool for a teenage boy, I knew I was doing okay and he wasn't crushed by the public announcement that Sean and I were not happening. That gave me the rush of courage to say what popped out next:

'If you'd bothered to do your research, you'd have realised that I've actually been spending time with somebody else, lately.'

Oh, crap, I couldn't spot him. Bloody hell, Amelia, if you're going to do this, you might as well do it with him listening.

A sky-blue and white cluster in one corner gave out a long, raucous whoop. And there he was, head and shoulders above the rest of them. Face in robot mode, shoulders braced as if prepared for the worst.

'Someone who showed me that I was just fine as I was, and at the same time inspired and encouraged me to be the best that I could be. Who didn't see a washed-up national disgrace, but a person who had got a bit lost and who needed a friend. As do we all. Even you, Moira. He's one of the kindest, sweetest, loveliest people I know. And also happens to be staggeringly gorgeous. Anyway, Nathan, now seems as good a time as any to say that I don't need you.'

There was a collective gasp of dismay from the onlookers. All of them except Nathan, who remained motionless.

'But I would love to spend more time with you. In a mutual, dating, possible girlfriending type of way. If you would like to maybe go out with me sometime.'

The gasp morphed into an oooh.

I peered at Nathan. Had he even heard me? It appeared to no longer matter, as the Larks were now herding and jostling him through the crowd towards the front of the stage. And it looked very much like he was resisting.

To deepen my jitters, he forcibly removed Bronwyn and Dani's arms and held out his hands like you would if fending off a wild animal, creating a circle of space around him. As everyone watched, and several hundred phones filmed, he completely changed direction, the crowd parting to let him move off to the side as if making for home, a hot shower and a cold beer, to help forget this whole debacle ever happened.

Except, once out of the crush, he didn't head that way at all. Instead, he jogged towards the steps onto the stage. Something the Larks hadn't considered when thrusting him towards the centre.

'Hi,' he said, bounding up to join me.

'Hi.'

I held my breath for what seemed like far too long, waiting for him to say something. Was he waiting for me? I'd just asked him out in front of what would probably be millions of people once the videos went viral. Was he trying to find a way to gently let me down, in which case why not wait and do it later on, in private, except of course those interfering Larks hadn't let him do that, so now he was trying to find a nice way to reject me in front of everyone.

I cursed myself for listening to Selena. This was going to be worse than the article. Worse than the Search for Amelia. Worse than my parents on breakfast television. Worse, because that had been about leaving the past behind, and this was about my future. One that with Nathan might have been lovely. And now I had probably messed up our friendship, too—

Nathan's eyes crinkled.

I couldn't keep the smile from bursting out across my face.

The crowd, sensing something had happened, gave a cheer.

Nathan flashed his eyes in their direction and then stepped forwards, wrapped his gorgeous arms around me and, without anyone having to push him from behind, pressed his lips against mine.

As kisses go, it was delicious. Warm and soft and full of tender promise and sweet longing.

'Well done, Coach,' I gasped, finally breaking away. 'That was probably the most spontaneous thing you've ever done. I think that graduates you from the Stop Being an Emotional Robot Programme.'

He laughed, grabbing onto my hand and pulling me back up against him. 'Are you kidding me? I've thought more about that than anything else for months.'

And then, he kissed me all over again.

Until, remembering suddenly, I pushed him away and leant back towards the microphone.

'Oh! And the winners of the first Amelia Piper Family Fun Fit triathlon are... the Greasby Athletics Club! I think there's a trophy somewhere... Antonio?'

But, of course, there were a whole lot more winners that day. I, for one, was most definitely no longer a loser.

The truth I realised that day, on the most important race of my life? I never had been.

Programme Complete

ACKNOWLEDGMENTS

Many thanks to the consistently fantastic team Boldwood – especially Sarah Ritherdon, for her unfailing encouragement, wise insights and invaluable edits. Thanks also to my wonderful agent, Kiran Kataria, for her input and support throughout. Jade Craddock also added some much needed finishing touches.

A special mention to Shelly Joddrell, for sharing her experiences in the world of competitive swimming – I hope you can overlook the bits I made up.

As always, to everyone who has read my books, taken the time to write a review or got in touch to say they enjoyed it – it really does make it all worthwhile (plus it is a great incentive to keep me from messing about on the internet!).

My incredible mother-in-law, Phyllis Moran, decided to join a running club in her 60s, and went from being exercise-novice to long-distance runner in no time at all. Her story has inspired many people, as well as this book. We are so proud of you, Phyllis!

And for all those I love who face the battle against anxiety with courage and strength that most of us will never see – this book is for you.

For Ciara, Joseph and Dominic – may you always hold on to the truth that being a winner is about who you are, not what you do.

And for George, I couldn't think of anyone I'd rather run alongside in this wild race called life.

MORE FROM BETH MORAN

We hope you enjoyed reading *A Day That Changed Everything*. If you did, please leave a review.

If you'd like to gift a copy, this book is also available as an ebook, digital audio download and audiobook CD.

Sign up to Beth Moran's mailing list for news, competitions and updates on future books.

http://bit.ly/BethMoranNewsletter

Christmas Every Day, a wonderful festive read from Beth Moran, is available to buy now.

ABOUT THE AUTHOR

Beth Moran is the author of four novels, including the bestselling *Christmas Every Day*. She regularly features on BBC Radio Nottingham and is a trustee of the national women's network Free Range Chicks. She lives on the outskirts of Sherwood Forest.

Visit Beth's website: https://bethmoranauthor.com/

Follow Beth on social media:

facebook.com/bethmoranauthor

twitter.com/bethcmoran

bookbub.com/authors/beth-moran

ABOUT BOLDWOOD BOOKS

Boldwood Books is a fiction publishing company seeking out the best stories from around the world.

Find out more at www.boldwoodbooks.com

Sign up to the Book and Tonic newsletter for news, offers and competitions from Boldwood Books!

http://www.bit.ly/bookandtonic

We'd love to hear from you, follow us on social media:

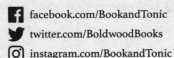

facebook.com/BookandTonic

twitter.com/BoldwoodBooks

instagram.com/BookandTonic